Shemokoman

Shemokoman

The Metaphysical Expedition

RJ Eadler

ISBN: 978-1-7356662-1-1 (hardback)
ISBN: 978-1-7356662-0-4 (paperback)
ISBN: 978-1-7356662-2-8 (ebook)

Design and Typography: E. T. Lowe Pubishing Company

Cover image: Michigan swampland by author

Contents

Part I

*Since the beginning of human existence,
man has been sick. He is infected with a wretched,
filthy disease called morality.*

1

⚜

A Farmer

Vein of Providence

From dawn until dusk, the man in thick gray coveralls worked in a field and dug up potatoes. He was a farmer in Lancaster County; it was his job and everyone knew it. His hands were calloused and scarred, his feet were tough like leather, and the skin on his face resembled the earth that he had been tilling for ages. He never complained about life in the least, as he understood what men who are men may rightly expect and deserve. They fill every day with resolve to improve upon all that is part of existence. And lending a hand to someone in need is also a part of the picture.

Wherever he went the people he met were happy to see him. His neighbors and friends were certain that he was a comrade who could be trusted. And when somebody down in Elizabethtown caught sight of that man in the distance, they casually noted, "Now there is a guy to be proud of. He came to live here from a faraway land with nothing but honest intentions. And since that day, he has proved to be everything good that one can imagine. He takes care of the wife and all of his kids and isn't afraid of the winter."

The last planting season was far from the best. The harvest was not so successful. The sweet corn, potatoes, and wheat he gathered were barely enough to get by on. Even the old apple tree by his house didn't produce enough fruit to make any cider. Thus, he worked hard to ensure that the crop this year would make up for the previous shortfall. He had a cow that was old and set in her ways that often took naps in the pasture. His Red Brahman bull stood fast in the road, where all passersby were amused by the insolent creature. Two oversized hogs in a rickety pen were sloshing around in the mud to round out the livestock.

Now, unfortunately, the farmer had a slight problem. He was terribly sick with fever and chills, and coughing up blood every day. Horrible pain in his chest and the gut foreshadowed impending disaster. He could no longer eat a typical meal, had lost far too much weight, and knew it was just a matter of time until the Reaper came calling. You get to a point where everything's clear, and no one or nothing can save you.

He thought, "Behold, the anonymous martyr! But I will not die for the sins of mankind; I perish because I am human. Even the King of the Jews can do nothing to help me now."

Immigration

The farmer decided to take a short break from his strenuous manual labor. He sat down on a weatherworn hickory stump and thought about some of his choices. He came there to live in the year '35 with thousands of desperate people. And for the past eighteen years, he'd lived in a country where freedom was what he was promised. Well, maybe he had it; but maybe he didn't. It all depended on freedom from what was expected.

"I cannot foresee any point of return to effectively coax and engage me," he thought. "My only direction is forward; it is a path that was meant to absorb me. And challenges wait for responsible men who forsake what is already missing. Of course, those parallel lines must intersect without ever touching. And look to the stars for a cogent riposte about how to embrace contradiction. No, no! The zodiac doesn't confound or ever mislead us. Up there above earth where a twinkle is king, discrepancies fall by the wayside. How can there be any doubt in the end, and is it so hard to believe in? I think not."

A parcel of land was given to him, and he worked like a dog ever since. He did everything just like a man ought to do and went to the chapel on Sundays. He was told to have faith in a merciful God and listen to heavenly sermons. They told him to pray every night for the dead, but he prayed for the living instead. Religion may be a great source of relief; it can also produce disappointment. The outcome depends upon whether or not our souls are devoted to madness. So, what did he manage to accomplish and learn during those years in the

Donegal trenches? Perhaps the hour had endlich arrived for him to consider a tally.

He abandoned the Kingdom of Württemberg, where he was born and raised by his parents. That in itself what he did, he couldn't believe it. And he remembered those days with a delicate heart in the small little dorf called Fellbach. Everyone there was related to him, and his uncles were running the business—making white wine. Nothing but hills and vineyards galore with people whom he could depend on. Even the king and the queen would drop by to see how the masses were doing.

Alas, a random dispute with Johann caused tempers and judgment to get out of hand. The next thing he knew, he was on the *Barque Comet*'s manifest list and sailing away from Amsterdam to America. During the trip, he parleyed with men who were honest, God-fearing, and wasted. They sought to console and convince him: "Everything now will be better, my friend. Just give it some time, you will see." Perhaps he should've stayed put where he was and swallowed the pride that incensed him.

When he thought about it, there were so many people who gave it a whirl to start a new life like he did. The ships were packed full of utopian strays who could no longer stand persecution. For him, there was Nancy—dear, beautiful girl, patiently waiting alone in New York at the end of his seafaring journey. So they pulled into port where he met the fair lady, and soon they were traveling arm in arm to Lancaster County. He had to admit those were glorious days and rarely had he been so happy. With genuine hope, inspiration, and prayer to nourish the soul and sustain him, he never looked back at what might have occurred. Instead, he moved constantly forward.

His mind wandered: "If only the Powers That Be at the time would have called off the war against Indians. How many nights was I forced to report and go slaughter the indigent redskins. It was terrible. The oppressed became the oppressors. I tell you . . . the hour is near when my progeny surges above the exalted manslayers, and there will be stiff retribution. Amen, to that."

And without hesitation he could've gone back, but mentally he couldn't swing it. Wise choice. Had he returned, most likely he would have remained in Fellbach forever. No, he could not risk any sort of mistake that often creates a debacle. That would've destroyed every chance in the book for him to take care of a family. Besides, Nancy would have killed him anyway. So what could he draw in conclusion?

Perhaps one cannot judge what is right or wrong about any single decision, minute or important. We do what we think is correct in a pinch, of course—in line with a Good Life, and get along to another occasion.

Integrity

It was getting near dark when the farmer called it a day and set out for his homestead. Along the way on an overgrown moor, he noticed a man off in the distance who was roaming about in land that was wooded and marshy. So he called out to the fellow, "Hey, you—yes, you. What in the hell are you doing? It is dusky and late, and time to be cozy inside of your house with a family and friends who esteem you. Why are you walking out there all alone? It appears you are looking for something."

The man replied, "Indeed, you are right, my inquisitive friend. It seems that I lost my respect. And wherever I go, whatever I do, the results of my efforts are fruitless. Careless behavior, indulgence, and greed caused me to lose it forever. But I will still search to recover my loss because I'm pathetic and foolish. Plus, and alas, the pain of it all is an agony I cannot live with."

"Well, good luck," the farmer said to the guy, then thought to himself, "He surely will need it."

Inside the House

His wife, Christiana, was waiting for him in the doorway. She had been very distraught of late, for it was plain to see that her husband was ill. When he entered the house, she tendered a hug and gave him the favorite slippers. As Destiny tries to drive people apart, only Fortune will keep them together.

All of the children were snug in bed, tucked under a mountain of blankets. Rose was the oldest, with George next in line, followed by Margaret and Sarah. They were the children that Nancy begat during their eight brief years of being a family. Alas—as the result of a bad medical complication, Nancy died soon after Sarah was born, and losing his wife was emotional trauma the farmer had barely endured. However, a man who must work and has children to raise can't afford to waste time on self-pity. He met Christiana, the daughter of one of his neighbors, and soon they were married inside of a Lutheran chapel. His new wife gave birth to three additional children: Josiah, Leander, and Helen. But Josi contracted a fatal disease and died at the age of one year. Such is the truth about facets of life for a man who came into the New World.

In spite of the fact he had no appetite, the farmer finished a supper meal consisting of pork and potatoes. It did nothing for him, but he knew that it lessened the worry his woman was feeling. He then looked around inside of his house at all the belongings and sundries. A modest collection of staples.

He thought, "So this is the end of my rambling road where nothing can be any different. A big wooden table and chairs made of oak, a clock in a case with a mirror. A wood-burning stove with a pipe for heating and cooking. A kitchen with everything needed—counter and sink, a big iron kettle, pots, pans, dishes, and all the utensils. An old apple mill, a new cider press. Dried peaches, cherries, and meat stored in the corner. A barrel of vinegar, apple butter, lard, crocks and canisters, and baskets. Three beds with bedsteads, a small bassinet, a bureau, a very nice dresser. I made it myself. And for work outside: an ax, knives, splitting and digging tools, saws, shovels, a rake, wheelbarrows, posts, boards, and a ladder. And also a windmill and grindstone. So that is pretty much it. I have everything here to glorify life; but what do I have to forsake it? Donnerwetter!"

For such a long time without even thinking, the man stared at the floor that didn't need sweeping. Then he held up a rag to cover his mouth and coughed to clear out his throat. Alas, a powerful soul may only reside it would seem in a powerless body.

He pondered, "Every morning, I faithfully walked out-of-doors to tackle my business of farming. My whole lifelong, I was a diligent worker. With these two hands I plowed and dug, and sowed and reaped to use the hallowed ground that I was endowed with. And year after year, I gathered the crops that my land so graciously offered. Thus, I fed my family. And I do not recall even one single time when a Maker was plotting against me. No, the gods were always by my side and kept me out of trouble. So, what does it mean to be a farmer? Perhaps—to be as close as one can be to having total freedom. Where nothing that we say or do is used by those against us. We alone control the land and everything upon it. We alone command the earth to keep provisions growing. We alone adore the sun that loves to come up shining. A farmer is a healthy man who doesn't need a crutch or holy savior."

Terrestrial Bodies

By and by, the farmer told his wife that it was bedtime. She glanced at him and tears streamed from her eyes down rosy cheeks onto her nightgown. He took one last check around the house to make sure that all was in order. Yes, everything was perfect; it was just the way he liked it. Then, they both lay down upon the featherbed where many nights of joy and sorrow were remembered.

With her outstretched hand, Christiana cupped the flame of a small lilac-scented candle that stood on a pedestal table and blew it out. Then she turned to him and he looked at her; the moment that transpired was eternal. And the greatest kiss that ever was now came to pass between them. He rolled onto his rugged back and gazed straight upward, far beyond the ceiling. The sky at night above the earth is nothing more than pure imagination. All distant light was fading now, and stars came racing to him. Then, as was her custom, the woman said the words that she knew would bring him comfort: "Good night, Schatzi. Träum süss." But this time, unlike in the past, the farmer didn't answer. The only fling that counts was truly over. And he was at a higher place already, where everything is different. Gottlob Friedrich was gone.

2

The Front Yard

Advent

A bright yellow sun in the east on a misty horizon was on the verge of spreading light to respectable people. Streetlamps were still on as bodies rolled out of bed one by one to greet the new day. All of a sudden, Shemokoman tumbled into the Land of Michigan. He was right on time in a town called Battle Creek in the northern part of a big imperialist nation called America. Permission to stay at the current locale was given to him by someone whom man has yet to encounter. And the benevolent will of the Gracious Almighty ensured that his passage avoided any and all complications.

The more precise destination of his arrival consisted of a small community on the outskirts of town called Waupakisco Park. He was obliged to reside on Jameson Avenue in a big white two-story home that displayed the number 210. It was a place where intelligent life was apparently present. At least, that was what he surmised about the tenants.

Regarding the type of day outside, it was nippy. Nothing unusual. And now a light, cold drizzle began to fall from the clouds to nurture all plant and animal life on the landscape. A coal-burning furnace in every home was blazing away to heat up the dwelling, and white smoke from the chimneys floated up into the sky and vanished. In the distance, one could hear the sound of the old pumphouse churning away full tilt to provide delicious hard water for local consumption. Every back- and front yard was covered with plenty of colorful leaves that would soon be burning. It was autumn and raking was overdue.

The future, the past, and the present comprise ontological coding and data, which supply a means to leverage chance and bring to mind the notion of existence. As for the current state of affairs, Shemokoman sensed a beginning. Residual damage was certain, and yet he knew that his eyes were blinking. Reality on, reality off. And should he have been with so many exceptional neighbors? A question with cryptic panache. Speak of heuristics—too much is left to capricious maneuvers of Fate, an ardent lieutenant. It would have been nice had someone deferred to a wise Potawatomi chieftain down near Nottawa Lake for sensible answers. To know the truth, we have to go to the Keepers of Fire and Knowledge.

Good Lord! The trials and tribulations of a newcomer. They try to behave like everyone else in spite of so many restrictions. Shemokoman looked at all of his digits; nothing was damaged or missing. He stared at cracks in the ceiling above. What else could he do? The curious fellow was thinking. He realized that we all pay a very dear price for knowledge. Responsibility is tendered, chastity fades, and we are coerced to forgo many valuable choices. It can't be helped. The spirit degrades, and the obligation to perish is quite a bit greater. You see, something from nothing is more than a random occurrence.

And what would be his station in life? Afflictions? Predispositions? Some people have all the luck, so how about him? He thought, "The road I perceive up ahead is laden with copious challenge and peril. Thieves are waiting to plunder the bag of sweets I merrily gather. Life is a game with rules and odds that people are pressured to cope with. I wonder how far I can make it?"

Thy Kingdom Come

Hundreds of days and nights flew by so quickly. Then, one early summer morning, a slender young lady of Slavic extraction named Anna, who was the mom in Shemokoman's home, entered a downstairs bedroom where she found him resting and ready to tackle the day. She took the good fellow of lovely descendants outside to the front yard, where he sat down in the shade on a red cotton blanket in dark green clover by the big white house. A black-and-white spaniel with a smooth, shiny coat was sprawled on the ground beside him. Old Stub was there to keep an eye out for any and all funny business.

Shemokoman noticed an opulent world with so many riches to fathom. With pristine intellectual health to shape every neural engagement, he didn't think about yesterday or tomorrow; instead, today was on the agenda. His mechanical speed was incredibly quick to absorb scintillas of knowledge. Yes, that photographic memory, so effective. Reality passed through a critical view where nothing was left unattended. And he didn't waste time to consider if the current impression was part of a much bigger picture. He narrowed the range and focused on valuable detail. The sun was essentially gleaming, the air was clean and sufficient, and he had no desire to muddle his life with strange metaphysical issues.

So now it was time to go for a stroll to pursue and enjoy exploration. Shemokoman stood up on his own two feet—the sign of a free-wheeling man. So far so good; and then, after gaining his balance, he started to move with the aid of reliable vision right in the middle of four intersecting dimensions. The ambulant fellow traipsed far and wide on a portion of land that was modest.

He looked up. A blue sensational sky filled with fresh invisible air was so alluring. He wanted to fly and travel through space, but knew he inherently couldn't. He wondered, "How high does it go? And where does it end? And can there be something mysterious hiding behind it? And maybe a giant is holding it up— But I shouldn't care in the first place. Other, more pressing affairs deserve my attention."

Ever so briefly, he glanced at the sun, then instinctively looked in another direction. It was no conscious decision; rather, everyone knows that this great star high above us—dazzling, godlike, and noble—does not permit just any old mortal to stare at its infinite glory. If so, the delicate sense of sight is promptly devoured. The rules of natural law must always be followed.

And then, Shemokoman looked at formidable trees growing around him. They stood motionless, like titans in a formation guarding the palace. And we understand that a tree will prefer to remain in one place for a lifetime. They have no need to go elsewhere, as their family is planted around them. Alas, from time to time a despicable man deprives a tree of existence. The villain will claim it is valuable wood for building or burning in campfires. Indeed, a capital crime. How would it feel to be felled to the ground and chopped up into thousands of pieces? Certainly, not a good prospect.

Next, he heard the ubiquitous wind that no one can see by look-ing. For some reason, it just doesn't care to be noticed. It is a hidden connection; it can whistle to soothe and enchant us. There is nothing we know of that sounds like the wind. Unique and relaxing, soft and refreshing. Or blowing, biting, howling, and gusting; and bending a tree with the slightest of ease, while caressing the crown of a forest. It is but one of the many beguiling voices in Nature.

The ravens and wrens were flying about with nothing at all to re-strain them. Climbing and gliding and swooping pell-mell in a carefree display of flight with precise navigation. Such ornithological fitness; and, Shemokoman couldn't stop watching. The suave entertainers would hang for a while, so high then low, darting from one of the trees into another. Then, perched on a limb, they started to sing the tune of a song to be proud of. Indeed, a flock of outstanding performers. For they realize that no man alive could ever come close to the musical talent they brandish.

And he thought, "Although, it seems to me that a bird knows noth-ing of math or holistic perspective. Can it be so, that man is a better creation?"

After a while, Shemokoman returned to the red cotton blanket and sat back down. The ground was level, the soil was rich, and human re-mains were undoubtedly much farther under. Man must obey the Law of the Earth; otherwise, a heap of big trouble awaits him. And he, for sure, will be the real loser.

The thick green grass was sodden and cool, and glittered with spar-kly dewdrops. Tiny creatures on top of the ground—many so small that they almost couldn't be seen—were attending to business. Some of them trudged along slowly under a great and heavy burden. Their lot in life was hard labor. Still others scampered about here and there to work on the insect assignments. A few in the crowd with powerful legs could leap a right fair distance. It is never a cinch when you are that small to travel to faraway places.

Furthermore, they all looked up at the giant and thought, "We must take care to avoid getting stepped on, and squished."

From a barren spot in the yard below, Shemokoman scooped up some brown powdery dirt into his hands. Then he let it trickle through his fingers back to the ground, where he noticed a mischievous image. It was his shadow, and what a proficient conniver! Quite the amusing polite silhouette that mimicked his every slight movement. In spite of repeated attempts at deception, he wasn't able to fool it.

Shemokoman looked at the vast panorama around him and thought, "All I behold is a peerless result of design by immaculate Nature. Everything good is included, and nothing at all is excluded."

Constant Exposure

It doesn't take long for trauma we feel to affect a strong constitution. The strength of a man has nothing to do with a powerful soul that is fragile. A mountain of good is often destroyed by trifling lurid behavior. Just think of the man who decidedly changed after he ventured into the room during the brash altercation. In the bat of an eye, he was an ace in the science of aerodynamics. Incontrovertibly, people are breaking, and the result is another disaster.

As accountable souls, we have to adjust to deal with conflicting emotions. Diametrical thoughts are probing the mind, as attitude has to be perfect. That in itself is alarming. And as the interval grows, a dead giveaway is affirmed by a poor disposition. Is there a product of quandary and woe? And how do we cope with affliction? Well—nothing is wrong; it's all in the head, and we don't really know what it means to honestly suffer. Alas, the fatal extreme is never remote but always astir and forthcoming.

Time for a little more walking. So, he got onto his feet with good balance. The property didn't extend very far, but it was enough for the novice. Shemokoman thought, "What a fantastic turn of events. Truly a sweet revelation. It doesn't take long to go from one place to another. I discovered a normal contraction without the intentional parallel bending. All we accomplish day-to-day is due to care and persistence."

While moving along, the explorer pondered a plight he'd been recently sensing. Like how about cause and effect? Oh yes. They loved to invoke that sort of account to preclude any chance of confusion. Hence, no need for a true understanding; and, how are we doing this evening? So much diversification. The bottom line will always consist of a clear combination of factors; and, we cannot contest the immutable law unless a few tablets are broken. Thus, the infidels better think twice about God and treading on sacred religion. And, don't bother with real complications per se; so easy that way, just avoid them. Survival improves so long as we tighten the belt and forget about binging. And when you are dead, you had better be dead if you acted like Satan while living.

Eventually, Shemokoman grew weary and sat down again. He looked at a white picket fence that was built to enclose the entire front yard. It kept things in and kept things out; the rows of tall wooden pales were pointed on top and placed in flawless alignment. One after another, side by side, enforcing devotion to order. His body and mind were now confined to a tangible quantum of soil. And he explicitly knew why the fence was there and remembered who knocked it together. Namely—Duane, the man in charge of his household. With hammer and nails, and paint and a shovel for digging, the divider was erected. Accordingly, Shemokoman quelled the desire to ever oppose or somehow resent it. He was no cheap agitator planning to start the untimely rebellion. He accepted the white picket fence; it was the first in a very long line of essential restrictions.

The parcel of land in front of his home amounted to pure inspiration. It prevailed for beauty itself and served to provoke incentive for heroes. It was a resplendent, peaceful location—everything kosher and well taken care of. A divine flower bed lined the entire inside edge of the fence, and evergreen shrubs were neatly arranged in the corners. And should a weed of some sort so much as appear, it was instantly pulled and disposed of. Everything blended together ideally to form a much broader arrangement. Spiritual power was certainly present. Although . . .

Supernatural

Shemokoman didn't see God in the front yard. Nobody told him about the occult, and he had no use for the likes of a Gracious Almighty. Evil and vice can never exist where everything has to be perfect. Where there is no temptation like sweet fruit of a biblical nature. The undeniable truth, and he had to believe it.

In all he observed wherever he looked, Shemokoman sensed no sacred mind-bending conditions. There were no holy surprises or admonitions to playfully tease him. He couldn't find anything unordinary, abnormal, or too unfamiliar. The physical objects in Nature flat out discouraged insensitive ringers. He was a brave trailblazer deep in the charm of a wild dominion. Wandering, looking, and learning as much as he could for a true understanding. And boredom was never conceded.

To the exclusion of stubborn naysayers, people have got to be ready and willing to praise well-being on earth. As nothing is short of mistaken or credible judgment. Axiomatic, and rightly considered. But is it the duty of man to explore and adjudicate secular matters? And to find every solution involving a manifestation? To think and deduce at the expense of living like natural beings? The question alone reveals a sectarian penchant. It isn't so hard to believe that there is a limit to moxie for people.

Despite the abundance of theistic doctrine to sway him, Shemokoman was able to feel that it couldn't be wrong by rejecting the pious conception. The rest of the world was surely the same and mustn't be terribly different. Nature prevailed, and he was alone without anything bad to concern him. He found the adorable view and never considered the alternate version. For sure, it was all aboveboard, completely objective. And nothing, he thought, could ever come close to altering basic perception. On the other hand, could it be, perhaps, that he was skeptically drifting? The fact in itself—that scrutiny made an appearance—well, he had to consider the impact.

Of course, God may have been there in that special locale; invisible, silent, and pensive. Who knows, perhaps he anointed and maybe protected this one of the transient beings. Tellurians constantly ply to contrive what they need for a suitable answer. The thought of omnipotent power on earth will never be canceled completely.

For all the believers in every religion, a god is the ultimate source of freedom and goodness. He is the very last hope for anything right in a world of evil. But is he eternal perfection? The final result of all we are currently seeking? If only for once somebody could really perceive him, and look at the Infinite Spirit. To see and to touch, and to hear the voice of the One who reigns over existence. That would be swell. And people will always look forward to life in a way that defies comprehension because a god whom they trust is highly adept at performing a host of miracles.

Must there be a reason for God to exist? Or can he endure without purpose? Banish humanity, he would remain to prove he is not what he isn't. And many a sophist and all the apostles for hundreds of years might have you believe otherwise. The very plain truth remains to this day that God is above superstition. Confirmed by a wisp of pure intuition, there is no need to explain or belabor the issue. Call it subjective, whatever. And only a dunce would try to negate the power of simple cognition.

For each generation, a god is defined precisely as needed by culture. His form resembles a river that flows in accordance with settings and backdrops. A lord will appear on the spot where all of the masses require assistance. One day, there may very well be little use for more persecution to slay us. Yet nothing will ever affect the status of God.

Destiny Pays a Visit

Summer was always a season of no disappointment in Michigan. It was a time to get out of the house during warm, humid days and soak up the sunshine. People could store away all of those thick heavy coats and arrange for a trip to go swimming. There was always a crowd at the County Park, where everyone bathed in the river. As a matter of fact, euphoria never was better.

Shemokoman rose to his feet once more to study the physical landscape. He was intent on making the grade and doing a little more research. While attempting to cross the front yard from one side to the other, he was pushed from behind and fell on the concrete sidewalk that ran from the porch to the gate. Both of his knees got all skinned up, and he was writhing in pain and offended. When he finally regained his composure, he noticed a strange, lovely goddess who was floating nearby in the air and cynically smiling. Yes, she was the cause of the vicious assault. She was the one who did it. Then, without further ado, she disappeared into a cloud of sparkling vapor.

Just a little shook up, he sat on the ground and thought about what really happened. He'd heard about her and what she could do, this deity called Destiny. The rumor was that her parents were slain long ago in wars that lauded vainglorious passion. They must have been given to moments of guile to conjure the likes of such a unique demigoddess. And like all of the spirits who roamed above man on summits of high, lofty mountains, Destiny followed eternal disconsonant purpose. She lived to create and then to destroy without pity. To meddle in all metaphysical business; that was her job and so be it.

He knew besides pain, she was also in charge of distributing sensual pleasure. To do her best to ensure that the will of the holy Creator prevailed. She could be helpful and care for somebody who needed the urgent attention, or tear you apart limb from limb and leave you to rot in a crypt at Oak Hill Cemetery. Henceforth, he would have to be careful, or else she might catch him in one of her traps and finish him off forever.

And he mused, "But eventually, the day will arrive when I know she will finally take me. What can I say, as I'm on the side of existence. A fantasy breaks, I wander away and expire without any drama. Oh, faithful Destiny! You keeper of brave fallen warriors. Spare me a moment, a minute, a long, precious lifetime, and you will take joy in knowing that you have made an outstanding decision. Although if your charge is to slaughter my body and soul, then do a good job and be hasty."

Anna soon noticed the fellow was hurt and took him inside of the house. She tended his wounds and gave them a kiss for good healing. It is amazing how remedies work, some of them strange but very effective. Thousands of years attest to the fact that certain medicinal tricks work like magic.

Morning Glories and Lilacs

Day after day, Shemokoman wasted no time and foraged for knowledge. He thought, "Of the discerning five senses I rightly possess, sight is so very important. After all, it permits me to see and examine the worldly objects. I avoid what is bad, enjoy what is good, and learn to adapt and recognize how I can prosper. Nay, I mustn't ever be angry with vision; it is a primary source of awareness. And I want to believe that my eyes will never deceive me. Although should a day ever come when something's amiss and optic delusion besets me, I will be very hard-pressed for adequate land navigation."

"By the same token . . . ," he speculated further, "I must be mindful of undue attention to one of the cardinal stays of perception. We have to please each of the senses, more or less, always in equal proportion. Preference for one of them over the others will only lead to resentment. Careless favoritism of sight, for example, is bound to make somebody jealous. I've heard about fools who just never learn that impunity cannot be sanctioned."

One time, Shemokoman was in the front yard again when he noticed a beautiful sight. For the first time ever, he was face-to-face with a trellis of morning glories. Nobody had told him the name of the plant; he instantly knew what it was. Heavenly clusters of purplish-blue flowers with heart-shaped green leaves in the background. And it all was arranged on long twisted vines that grew up from the ground during springtime.

The blossoms had petals arresting and fine that were pointing straight at the sun. It was a sign that the plant was of noble descent. He stared at the flowers as if in a trance, absorbed in a daze of approval. They made a warm, lasting impression, and the "ideal" was clearly established.

But Shemokoman also was sad and thought, "To live and to die in the span of a day as they will all perish at nightfall. They know what it means to obey the volition of Nature."

After a while, he broke away from the hex that the plant put on him and turned in a different direction. Then he spotted another botanical wonder. On the other side of the white picket fence in the lot beside his home, a thicket of lilac bushes bloomed and exquisitely flaunted their splendor. Fragrant lavender flowers were scattered about in bunches all over the branches. No wonder Syrinx was forced to convert when a god was enamored and chased her. Who can forget the incredible scent that is more than enough to bewitch you? Shemokoman knew that such blessings in Nature were there to embellish existence. He was content with life as is and requested no feverish encore. For now, he was sure to be lucky in life, and evil would not set upon him.

On that particular day just before sunset, Shemokoman sat down for supper at the yellow dining room table in the big white house where he lived. Everyone folded their hands together and looked down per the force of religion. He listened to grace and thought about eloquent words that made up the prayer.

He pondered, "Why do we thank an invisible Lord for food that we grow in the fields and harvest in autumn? After all, he didn't slave away year after year to ensure that the people are fed. Oh no! So what was he doing instead? Well, that would be nice to know. One ought to give credit where credit is due and abolish a holy tradition right before eating. Although if a prayer is needed to placate the soul, then give thanks to diligent farmers like the ones in Lancaster County who worked like mad for two or three lifetimes. They are the ones who earned it, and they are the ones who didn't give up with aching backs to prove it. Does it not seem a little bit funny that we condone profane adulation? Detestable sacrilege."

When he was through with the meal, Shemokoman stepped outside onto the back porch. It was entirely made of cement, and it offered a marvelous viewpoint. He looked up at the sky and thought about truth and deception: "Well, they are completely mistaken because the ancients were right about one thing. Man *is* the center of the universe. I know what I see, and it is no phony illusion."

3

❦

Carnage

Hyperphysical Cogitation

Not to imply that lunatics have any answers, the purpose of anthropological life defies every sane explanation. Forget about theories with logic and proof—that rubbish is very misleading. We cannot throw light on a problem so dark merely by thinking about it. And people who say they know something we don't are most certainly putting us on. The time has arrived to encourage a plunge and abandon the surrogate onslaught. Existence, perhaps, is nothing at all but someone's idea of a fast one. Indeed, people are laughing.

Why am I here? How come they are there? Why is there why? We use interrogative methods. Alas, one cannot rise above any concern to unravel mysterious questions. A clarification of any phenomenal matter—if it were possible—would negate the reason for men to inhabit the earth. Shadows and magical pleasure would yield to a bold and obscure affirmation, and higher levels of life would come forth in forms that we cannot imagine. We would transcend the essence we are, and motion from grace to sacred domains would occur.

Some smart alecks think that enlightenment comes from an act of supreme contemplation. We have only to drift beyond conscious intent to unlock many secrets that faze us. Well, that is fine if the goal is to dance on a cloud where there is no shaman to guide us. Where the circling skies and receding celestial spaces are able to torment the mettle inside us. Where a sensible wish is demolished by grief and emptiness pleads for compassion. Where reason itself is a pie in the sky and cannot be held as sufficient.

Man is at home in a practical world that Nature has freely afforded. To believe otherwise invites a portentous reaction. The tangible side of an aura is not a superfluous delicate matter. And yet, the soul—yes, the soul—the intuitive segment, is a part of man we cannot subject to denial. It "is," for sure, an item devoid of appearance to mortal perception. With this in mind, we put in the time and a notion of life is more than enough for survival. We seek to apply what is right for the *self*, remove what is wrong, and a genuine mood is established.

Volition

Shemokoman tarried inside of his head but never went out of the body. He didn't require a thrill to ignite any sort of ignoble intention. His power to think and remember was coupled with only the best expectations. He was changing each day and becoming remarkably strong and notably wiser. And he desired to travel only to places that presaged rewarding collection. His goal was innate regardless of pressure and shell games.

"If time were to end and oblivion ruled, well, that wouldn't be so terrific," he thought. "Not even a spree for hysterical joy, and it would be hard on the masses."

He wandered and wondered a lot on his block, where everything new was breathtaking. He didn't go far from the big white house because he was told that he shouldn't. And from what he had gleaned about all that he was, Shemokoman had to be thankful. The world was teeming with myriad masses of paupers; but he wasn't part of that crowd. To so many people who saw him right then, he was a special creation. Neither too small nor too large, with shape and a standard proportion. He lived, moved, and roamed everywhere just looking for something of interest. And no one was cynically asking, "What is the reason why he is here?" He simply comprised a healthy addition to neighbors, and, no need for the big explanation. The Almighty Father is justly content when we can accept the world without complication.

On one cold, drizzly day at the start of a winter, when it is hard to be sure which season is really upon us, Shemokoman stood in a sassafras grove not far from the infamous Breaks, just south of Waupakisco Park. The leaves were falling away from the trees and covered the dark loamy ground. It was a pleasing sight to behold.

He pondered, "Eventually, every last one of those leaves will sur-render to fate and go under. They know the end is near and haven't the slightest potential to stop it. A dialectic iota in time is betokening more evolution because each leaf is a leaf and cannot be taken for granted. And all that they are and ever can be is part of the normal arrange-ment, where the elements yield to immutable change consisting of permanent order. Everything new becomes instantly old, portending a glorious future. Nothing is ever created and nothing will perish. Which makes me wonder: How can God exist without me?"

Exodus

The concept of death was unfamiliar to Shemokoman, of little con-cern and pointless. For now, he focused on being alive and how best to advance and enjoy it. Life after death, what did it honestly matter? Life before death was a far better way to approach it. His restless soul soared high to shine each day that a Yahweh had gifted; and, he didn't waste time on deliberation of issues beyond comprehension.

Although on one occasion, he did speculate, "To make any sense out of something like death, you have to be pretty much crazy. You need to be able to summon the will in a way that enhances awareness. It is no easy task, and the trick of it all is how to explore and reverse every logical ending. So, you hunt like a fox when the trail is warm and retrieve what is premium quarry. Of course, the hounds on the ground are there to assist you.

"And do not believe that whatever you bag is a reason to celebrate winning. The knowledge you gain is only as good as delusional row and a pipe dream. You see, death will convert every blithering Joe into dust without an exception. It is a way for people to terminate life and neutralize troublesome feelings. Yes, death is the end of a segment of time for those who desired to take it. And of course, we already know what the cynical skeptics are thinking. The body is frail, frequently ill, and faces continuous struggle. Healthy and strong for punks who are young, but fragile and weak later on. Indeed, there is nothing eternal about it; albeit, the soul may continue to caper.

"We have to comply with a physical law called gravity, pulling us downward. We haven't the strength to oppose a great mighty spirit that doesn't give up. The oldest people alive will tell you that time is the opposite number. Sooner or later, that one terrestrial force is going to get us. 'Oh you in the earth, right under my feet—relentless purveyor of every dead passionate body! Have you no heart, faithful subaltern of Providence?'

"It knows who you are and who you are not, and knows about underground rules of mortified headway. Thus, you freely submit to control of the merciless scoundrel. And every potential reward to live on no longer will justify effort. A tug from below is all we have left, and nothing can finally stop it. You slip out of time and into the ground, and now you are sleeping forever. And just deep enough to be out of sight from vermin with curious mind-sets. So familiar, decidedly puzzling. And not many people are dying these days, but plenty are already dead.

"So now when deprived of appearance and form, the soul may establish a *Oneness*. Oh yes, the preachers were right for a change; although they would never believe it. And there is no need to so foolishly ask: 'Where did he go?' . . . or sprinkle the grave with lavender flowers and teardrops. The permanent *self* will continue to thrive below in the world hereafter. Finally free at the nexus of void and a mythical purpose, that part of a man renounces intent to have any mortal connections. And thus, as anyone may have surmised, humanity passes away in the end just in a manner of speaking."

From the moment Shemokoman first appeared, a catastrophe threatened to break him. It was the plight of forthcoming extinction—the only situation as such, where humans are never unequal. A Reaper is bound by applicable law to stick to a regular schedule. And it matters not who or what anyone is when a graveyard is waiting to have you. Perhaps we are here from beginning to end only to die and be buried. A seemingly rational purpose.

And when at last the Great Beyond is in the cards and looming, there still will be loads of irrelevant questions that haunt us. Like, how do we conjure the point of a start and posit a tangible ending? And how can a thing coexist with nothing at all in the swirling cosmos? Certain dilemmas will never be fully resolved by divinity quartered in heaven. Even our God—the all-knowing, all-seeing, all-everything—even the Gracious Almighty doesn't have all of the answers.

It is not so much that man fears death; rather, the process of dying disturbs him. He ponders the notion with trepidation and tries like the devil to stop it. It seems like the further one gets on in life, the more that he or she is prone to despise it. People get sick and want to get well instead of reserving a plot for themselves in a boneyard. Enamored with hype, they attempt to exist for as long as they still can enjoy it. The inveterate fools should agree to comply and accept what is bound to consume them. For, sooner or later, each and every one of us with little or no recognition will die. And we can make the affair a more splendid event by communing with gods who cajole us.

Try to Exist

An autumn came forth in the one and only Land of Michigan. The days were notably cooler and the nights were getting longer. Colorful flora on trees everywhere dazzled the eyes of a spectator. One might say, a resplendent time of each year. And now, Shemokoman suffered a first major confrontation with an affliction that sought to destroy him. His health was imperiled, and he could do nothing to stop it.

One morning, he woke up at the crack of dawn as was his habit. It was a blustery, inclement day outside, which made him feel happy inside. Heavy gray clouds were low to the ground and rapidly moving aloft. Ducks and geese were high in the sky and migrating south for the winter. Light from the sun came into his room, where shadows of branches from trees in the lot flickered and danced on the walls. All was apparently normal.

However, Shemokoman didn't feel right. He wanted to spring out of bed but couldn't; something was wrong with his body. It was hard to move his hands and legs; they didn't respond as they should have. He had no strength; his anatomical power—sorely depleted. And it wasn't like at night before bed when he was tired from running and jumping all day in the park with friends and comrades. No, this feeling was different and very ill-boding.

Becoming increasingly distraught, he closed his eyes and remained in bed a short while longer. Maybe the problem would just go away. It didn't. Then, he supposed it was only a dream and all would be fine upon waking. Unfortunately, it didn't take long to nix the idea. He wasn't sleeping and knew it.

A host of people are lucky in life, and they can rely on good health, in essence, forever. Regardless of how they repulsively live, nothing they do seems to matter. And then there are those who are not so blessed.

For whatever reason, the unfortunate ones are given to indisposition, ranging from chronic small issues to the very worst that can happen.

"Could it be," he thought, "that *Yours Truly* is part of the group that has to put up with bouts of occasional sickness? Things are not looking so good."

Unbeknownst to Shemokoman, Destiny paid him a visit the previous night. And what was the reason for the nocturnal appearance? Well, it could have been bad; it could have been good; we just never know what she's doing. Certainly, though, polite social calls are not a part of her daily agenda. Destiny is all business.

She is never at odds to complete a command if that lady has come to affect us. Our sentiments don't really matter; oh no, she has the power to change us. Young or old, rich or poor, evil or godlike and righteous. We cannot avoid the volition of special immortals. And orders by gods are followed as long as a god with authority gives them. On this occasion, Destiny was instructed to go to Shemokoman and infect him with the deadly polio disease. The illness would ruin his health and possibly kill him.

On that fateful morning, Shemokoman found himself in a terrible way. So, where was protection from old Saint Christopher—guardian patron? A chain on the neck, are you kidding? For days, which turned into months and years, the fellow was brave and fought like a Spartan with courage. At first, the aggressor went after his legs and tried to completely disable them. He finally collapsed and was forced to crawl on the ground like a paralyzed vagrant. Most people, for sure, would have given up hope, but Shemokoman didn't surrender. He ridiculed pain and battled the tough adversary. A fight for the right to survive was never more daunting. And, even though it appeared that there was no end in sight to the conflict, the protagonist managed to fully prevent a debacle. Physical exercise and a will to supremacy did it. He fully restored the potential to walk and run to his heart's content on two sturdy legs. Mildly put, a tremendous achievement. But there was more on the way.

The adamant goddess subsequently tried to defile his eyes. Of course, we know how Shemokoman felt about optics. Destiny tried to gouge them away, and he fought like the dickens against her. Substantial problems with vision emerged with everything hazy and blurry. Nothing was ever in focus. He was unable to see the particular form of anything real with appearance. But fortunately, on account of sheer determination—"Just follow the pencil from left to right; and don't move your head in the process!"—and even some genuine prayer, Shemokoman overcame the dreaded condition. After many long years of a hard-fought struggle, he was able to see again. It was another great triumph; and, he was the obvious victor. However, the fun and games for him were not over yet.

The spirit, undeterred, once again set out to impair him. Shemokoman lost his power to talk completely. He couldn't make the sounds right, and all that he said was garbled and plain incoherent. Discouragement shadowed deep-seated resolve as the battle raged on and on without any letup. But after another big effort, he was able to speak without problems. What a relief!

He wondered, "Surely there must be an end to it all, my scourge of implacable trouble. How much more can I honestly take until I will throw in the towel?"

In a hundred other ways, the goddess attempted to shatter the fellow. But Shemokoman didn't relent and fearlessly fought her. After each lengthy offensive, he would get back on his feet, take a deep breath of clean, fresh Michigan air, and march to the beat of a resolute drummer. Hayfoot, strawfoot, tell me some more about Jodie. It was a war of attrition, and he wouldn't take a good licking.

Thus, it came to pass that after so much disappointment and feeling the strain of a nasty assignment, Destiny conceded defeat and finally decided: Forget it. Her claim on the soul of a serious man was abandoned. She tried to finish him off but just couldn't do it. So now, he was healthy and strong, and in the mood to encounter more bedlam.

Shemokoman gathered far more than a lesson or two about health during those troublesome years. A desire to live has nothing to do with equivocal words about purpose. Something needs to be present, specifically—courage to conquer misfortune. By the force of a will, a life can be spared and extended. He was put to the test and fought for the right to continue to tread among people. Every soul on the streets in a town he revered was amazed at what he accomplished.

4

Waupakisco Park

Good Lumber

Summer arrived in the Land of Michigan. It couldn't have come any sooner. July was a month especially hot and humid. The temperature soared past a hundred each day with heavy drenching rains that poured just prior to dinner. Shemokoman had now spent eight full years in Waupakisco Park, where he knew the ins and outs of getting by and skirting trouble. Potpourri.

Now it happened that early one morning, he went outside and stood at the edge of the lot next to the big white house that he lived in. And it was there that he thought about villains who think it is fun to intimidate people. Birdbrains. For quite a long while, he was alone. Nobody else was around.

Suddenly, a neighborhood bully called Butchy appeared and started to give him a hassle. He said to Shemokoman, "Give me all of your marbles, including the steelies and green perry shooters. And if you don't, you're gonna be sorry."

The nerve of the kid. Outrageous. After bluffing a bit and buying some time, Shemokoman could see that the thug wasn't kidding. No, that obstinate boy was not in the mood for formal negotiations. Perhaps he got up on the wrong side of bed, or the milk at his breakfast was sour. Who knows?!

And now, Butchy pronounced the ultimate warning: "You'd better give 'em to me, or else."

Shemokoman knew he was moments away from a rumble because he was not about to part with his favorite marbles. Just then,

Butchy took a knife out of one of his pockets and flipped out a long, shiny blade from the dark wooden handle. And while staring at Shemokoman straight in the eyes and grinning from ear to ear, he said, "Okay, now I'm gonna stab you."

Not good. It was time to develop a sensible plan in response to a serious threat. Shemokoman glanced around the area and noticed several potentially useful objects close at hand. What could he use and how would he seek to employ it? Meanwhile, Butchy was slowly advancing and flagrantly brandished the deadly weapon. And as he came closer and closer, Shemokoman backed up against his house until he had nowhere to go and was cornered. Butchy was only inches away and ready to cut him to pieces.

And just when the killer was ready to lunge and perform the nefarious deed, Shemokoman raised an arm and pointed at Butchy's feet.

He said, "Hey look, bud. Your shoe's untied."

The criminal fell for the oldest trick in the book—hook, line, and sinker. He looked down for just a second to check on his sneakers. And when he did, Shemokoman reached behind his back and grabbed the nice two-by-four he spotted a moment beforehand. It was now the equalizer.

In no time flat, with both of his hands he hoisted the lumber high up into the air, and then—with a right mighty powerful stroke, he smashed the board over Butchy's belligerent head.

The assailant fell to the warm sandy ground, where he lay in a mire of shame. Butchy was knocked out, cold as a cucumber. There are moments in life when without a second thought we instantly do what we must to survive. There is no time to consider the lenient angle. A savage opponent must be destroyed by all available means—no hesitation, no pity.

As he stood by the comatose body of one who was riddled with hate, Shemokoman thought, "It just doesn't make any difference. This country is crawling with hoodlums. He started it; I ended it. For sure, he will end up in Jackson. And I will keep my marbles."

Then he left the scene of the crime, and Butchy didn't bother him anymore.

Life on Jameson Avenue

It could have been better; it could have been worse. He never considered divergence. Most of the time, the mood in the home where he lived was pretty much cheerful. The rooms were filled with everything needed to furnish a standard of living. It seemed that nothing required improvement—the way it should be for people the whole world over. He just didn't hear one single complaint about anything someone was doing. "And no, by god! . . . You haven't the right to challenge the word of a grown-up. Get by with what you have and learn to accept it."

The neighbors talked to each other side by side and over the fences. Children were running as fast as they could, chasing swallowtails, mourning cloaks, and viceroys. People inside of their houses opened up all of the windows and doors so that a gentle breeze would be blowing through the rooms to cool things off. The families commingled together as one, and nobody seemed to be worried. Indeed, there was so little talk about psalms in a book that were boding a big Revelation. The status quo was a given, or so they concluded.

If only a dream could somehow manage to change the truth of existence. Unfortunately, humanity knows a case that is radically different. Shemokoman thought to himself, "I know one thing for sure: I'm not going to eat the poison salad."

The people who lived in the big white house were running around and busy with personal projects. The sturdy four walls and roof overhead provided a sanctum of sorts for tenants inside. In a mélange of order and chaos, the main constraint was negative feelings. Certain ideas started to surface that had an effect on behavioral patterns. For example, a credible leader was missing. Someone to really take charge and prudently guide them. Someone who thought about more than a stash and a way to slip in after midnight. Someone who cared about more than a ghost who should have been cleaning and cooking.

As time passed by, Shemokoman started to feel it. Who did they think they were kidding? . . . And, why did they say that somebody had to get with it? Situations appeared that didn't make sense, and there was no clarification. Too many hostile specters, quietly lurking. Say this on your knees and that before bed. Make sure that the hallway door is shut in the evening. Troubles emerged on account of the fact that angels can be hedonistic.

Men

The men in Waupakisco Park were mostly hardworking and very resourceful. Their collars were blue and physical labor was what they preferred to excel at. Nobody banked on making it big; there wasn't a lot of ambition. And it had nothing to do with apathy, or fancy attire and culture. Rather, a way of life evolved for them and that was how they liked it. There was simply no need to rock the proverbial boat and cause any trouble.

A number of men were gainfully employed at the railroad, while others slaved away year after year in the foundry or at a salt mine. A few in the mix were lucky ones who made their way into a cereal factory. All hail, Loco 196! In all likelihood, Shemokoman would join their ranks one day and don the dark green apparel. They only wore a suit and tie to funerals and to the weddings.

As a rule, the men in Waupakisco Park went to work each weekday morning and reported to a bossman. They didn't sit from nine to five behind an office desk pushing paper. No way, not them. And they didn't gripe about aches and pains or go to healers for a pill or tonic. They always did what they could do to make the world rosy for their families and the neighbors. It's hard to say what you will be when you don't have a leg up on the future.

All the men came home from work at six o'clock sharp in the evening, and their families showered loads of blessings on them. So much appreciation for the godforsaken toiler. And then it was dinnertime—a place to let off steam in frank discussion at the table. Their word was law as they avowed what was right and wrong as well as who were big oppressors. Life was no frivolous game for them; it was brief, and it was somber business. Those men were creatures of habit who knew precisely what to expect each day until they joined the ranks of the Faithful Departed.

The men he saw were born and raised right there in Michigan. And sure as hell, it was where they would expire. They worked around the house whenever possible to ensure there were no signs of inattention. Vaulted ceilings got the paint so badly needed, a leaky roof was fixed by putting on a couple of brand-new shingles, and the plumbing was repaired by replacing broken pipes with threaded new ones. And all the while, they liked to tell you stories from long ago when the world was so much better. The past is always such a wistful memory, a place where people like to think that they were really happy.

Some men liked to hunt and fish for useful recreation. So when time was at their disposal, they got together right at sunup for a trip out into the country. For it was there they found the pleasure that they knew would be rewarding. Proud moments occurred when a man came home after a long rugged weekend with a trophy to show for the effort. Like, for example—a 10-point buck. The game they took was bound to wind up on the supper table. Those men were good providers.

Other men whiled away free time in Waupakisco Park with their families. They spent their leisure moments cooking out, for example, or with their children building things, or swinging in a hammock in the backyard catching Z's. Moreover, no substantial row ever came between the men. They did not get riled—no, they did not get cross at one another. And if ever the need arose—and it did—to confront a type of menace, they stuck together like a group of seasoned warriors. Indeed, it was nice to be a man and take the edge off by going out at night and getting snockered.

The men had little use for books or too much education. Classroom work was fine to learn the basics—like the three R's, but that was about it. Because the lot of a man is grueling work and cold servitude until he is totally useless. At which time one retires—with nothing more to do besides deal with callous clowns and more affliction. You see, there's nothing wrong with doom and gloom for rejects and the peasants. So throw away the novels lined up neatly on the shelf, devoid of value. To be sure, the paper pages won't be turning.

There also were the men whose cup of tea was indolence, wasting time and acting rather mellow. Hardship wasn't rectitude, and lethargy could not be seen as evil. Shame for them was minor, and the stigma of a laggard wasn't sinful. What was it like to be lazy? . . . Well, just interrogate one of the slackers. They never even turned a screw or tried to pound a nail in a rafter. They had no use for daily chores and shunned so much as any thought concerning physical labor. They were the obstinate loafers, and they were lamentable jokers. Always another excuse to get out of work.

On the other hand, you never know. Perhaps the passive men were cold inside and simply couldn't function. Or maybe they were ill (e.g., afraid of humanity) and believed they weren't accepted. If only work could have appeal to deadbeat types and cause their minds to honor human values. It would be a godsend, where a slothful man would never slink away from jobs that must be done without procrastination. Alas, those fellows found it hard to find the sense in doing what was kosher. Sorry! . . . There would come a day when the idle lives they led would revert to grimly haunt them.

Regarding the men in Waupakisco Park, Shemokoman thought, "Although, I know that they are full of spite and indignation. Every last one of them. They don't believe that life is fair and hate the drudging muddle they must live in. They will take what they can get and leave the rest for scavengers and outlaws. And that is the truth."

Women

The women who lived in Waupakisco Park were down-to-earth and had sufficient practical knowledge. They never donned a flashy paisley shift or put on tons of makeup. "Too much rouge and paint will make a woman what she ain't." . . . Someone said it. A fancy new hairstyle was always a hit, but store away the pumps and diamonds in a dusty closet in the meantime. And just like women everywhere, they sought to have the basics and essentials. Like a decent home to call their own with twenty screaming children to unnerve them. That uncontrollable maternal instinct was downright overwhelming, and they could not forswear it. For some, a fine quality indeed; but for all the sated others—a ruse for much deception. Then again, all the ladies had a brand of virtue.

Generosity, care, charm, and compassion were part of their great repertoire. Reputation aside, their breaks in life were what they had to count on. Expect the least! . . . So you are sad and also can be happy. And they all shared a keen predilection to remember those troublesome years, when the slightest hint of wild dreams subverted a proper decorum. The truth was key; for sure, they understood it.

The darlings who lived in Waupakisco Park did not work outside the home. To begin with, if such a thing had ever happened, all the men would've gone berserk. The proud male soul in that locale would have never understood it. *He* must bring home the bacon, and *he* must support the family. Although to be perfectly honest, those ladies didn't want to work in a factory or the roundhouse. They were happy dusting wood and glad to bake a pot roast. They liked what they had and had what

they liked, with no reproach or grievance. And it was no astounding secret that their convoluted logic could obtain whatever was needed.

Even though some people said the men controlled their spouses,
everyone was well aware that wedded wives were giving lawful orders.
They were shrewd and scheming with a book of tricks to use whenever called for. So much razzle-dazzle and chicanery—how did they
manage to do it? Most likely, intuition and affinity for flimflam. Those
gentlemen could have their say, but in the end, they knew who was in
charge of family business.

What's more, Shemokoman noticed that, periodically, the women
would fly off the handle. One of them would fight her man and chase
him up the street, rolling pin in hand to knock him senseless. It seemed
they had to yell and scream, to throw and break things, to argue like
crazy and turn life into a living hell for those they loved the mostest.

"It's just the way they are and a stark reminder of their wild nature," he
mused. "And if they do not do it, well, one ought to be suspicious . . . and
ask: What is wrong with that woman? One more puzzle for Zeno."

Grade School

A real long time ago predating the Stone Age, when those cavemen
got to thinking, a wise guy felt it best to set up formal education. In
doing so, every soul would be enlightened, and it would help the human
race to shape a better future. Thus, schools were built throughout the
land for students to attend and learn the ABC's as well as to doze off in.

After only a few short years in the new surroundings, Shemokoman
enrolled in the grade school in Waupakisco Park. Actually, he had no
say in the matter; it was mandatory from September to June every year.
The school was a large redbrick building that stood on a hill high above
the community venue. He went to class each weekday morning, where
pencils, books, and wooden desks and blackboards were the big obsession. Shemokoman sat motionless, listened to the teachers, and completed all assignments. Above all else, he was a good student, never
doing something naughty. Like chewing gum or teasing someone next
to him to cause a big disturbance. Or skipping school and hanging out
with pranksters in the woods. No, he did none of that; he didn't dare to.

So, what went on inside the classroom that provided education? What
was every student doing? To give credit where it's due, Shemokoman

learned quite a bit when he was in the schoolhouse. Most of the basics—
thoroughly mastered. Reading, writing, and numbers were the mainstays
of the program. The same routine without a break, though, made him
suffer somewhat regarding goals and purpose. His mind was frequently
elsewhere when the teacher told him that he had to pay attention. For
example, he may have been at home with old Upanishadic prose; or perhaps he shuffled down a crowded byway near a beach in Old Havana.
He often scaled lofty peaks on mountains that were higher with mellow
hyperboreans where a secret wellspring was the object.

"I have to maintain a low profile," he thought. "My own beliefs can
cause a row and be a major source of sharp contention. Some mentors
whom I know will not accept them. They have never heard of inspiration."

Making friends was easy at the grade school, and the faculty encouraged social contact. When sitting in a classroom where the teacher
was in charge, of course, everyone was quiet. However, during recess
and when school let out to end the day of lessons, he had a chance to
mingle with some strangers. It was during all those months and years
that Shemokoman developed a special relationship with a group of
schoolmates. Alabama, Citizen R., the Doctor, Major LD—son of noble
Albert, and Anastasia came to be his ethical comrades. He was now in
a gang where fidelity ruled, and nothing, he hoped and prayed, would
come between them.

A Sensitive Decade

The months and years went by so fast but seemed to last forever.
Men should not compete with time, as they will find out soon enough
that it is pointless. All of us, day in day out, must deal with brief and
mean, and long duration. The pretense is a solemn fact that limits daily
bottom lines and should never be neglected. Nature's way will claim
respect and we must acquiesce, conceding no advantage.

As a matter of regular practice, Shemokoman hailed the dawn and
dusk each day without impatience. He thought that life was comme il
faut on a planet evidently spinning. And just for fun some evenings,
he shouted at the sun with dour scorn and sharp derision. Then, the
star of stars—provoked—slowly set beyond the multispired churches
far off in the west. Sometimes, it stopped and didn't move at all on a
broad and rouge horizon. It sensed a salty mood and sought to vex the

perpetrator. To retaliate, Shemokoman scolded the brazen god with harsh rebuke and said that he was going to skip tomorrow. It was quite the harmless game between a proselyte and Nature.

The prudence and passion of Shemokoman often clashed with one another. He tried his best to be objective, to avoid deficient judgment. His exploration garnered needed truth from observation, but, regrettably, he discovered that the system often served to work against him and appeared of help to no one. The secret was: we must display credentials to maintain the understanding. Namely, perseverance with honest intent, a will to seek knowledge for moral excellence, and a knack to use good ways and means to complement perception. Shemokoman did not reject compliance.

During one warm August evening, as the darkness lit up the sky, long shadows on the ground did not object to lack of color. Black and white were good enough for them and fading phantoms. However, Shemokoman now thought of something puzzling and familiar. He considered natural order and a set of implications. To begin with, man believed that life and all existence imposed no true arrangement. Rather, a sort of vestal anarchy prevailed everywhere, and everything occurred with no logic or precision. Total chaos for the sullen masses; and yet, commotion with a purpose. Intuitively, a stark contradiction where nothing could be different.

So if there is and isn't order in the angle we depend on, how might we extract the best regarding truth that we should come to hope for? Undeniably, the only means to reach the end is to get experience. It is how we gather and compile what is useful to develop knowledge that can never be disputed. Thought alone and reading books may reinforce the process, but nothing can replace a walk around the block with your senses gleaning detail.

He pondered, "To find the truth and all that it entails is no feat of small proportion. Talismans and amulets are comely pranks, but they can never substitute for pestilential obstacles that drive me. On the other hand, does anyone really know what comes after eight?"

Liberty

A normal man will be upset when freedom is surrendered. "Cool it, bub! . . . Cool it!" No control can only serve to aggravate the soul of human beings. If one is lacking liberty, frustration and disdain give rise to turmoil. And subsequently, very soon, temperaments flare up and there is trouble. The respectable people in Waupakisco Park thrived on independence, and Shemokoman was far from feeling different.

"To think I often wonder precisely why I'm distraught and confounded," he contemplated. "Good grief. They joke and laugh, pontificate, and tell the whippersnapper, 'You are learning.' Anyone with half a mind can see the flaws that permeate the system."

Although through thick and thin he felt repression, Shemokoman accepted a stream of stark draconian measures. Limitations everywhere, and the self-styled leaders in his home imposed more regulation. Moreover—to demonstrate their power, the autocrats did not see fit to justify even one single blasted course of action. Instead, the rules were reinforced with the crack of a hickory switch. For Shemokoman, a tempest now was in the works that soon would wreak pure havoc on the psyche.

Behold! The sanctimonious Caretakers of Right and Wrong. The heels in black who sign and seal, but never get around to staying orders. They hide inside a court of law, dishing out a crooked brand of justice. They are divine benefactors, and they are the holy protectors. Shemokoman stood to gain nothing at all by heeding such a Gospel of the Quipsters. He knew every canon that applied by heart and skirted foolish issues. Forbearance was the byword and employed for his adjustment.

During every season as another one was coming, Shemokoman did not revolt or urge complete destruction. Why be a nonconformist who must instigate and cause more pointless trouble? The leaders told him what to do and faithfully he did it.

Shemokoman was told to wake up and get out of bed. He did it.

He was told to get dressed and then to eat all of his porridge at breakfast. He did it.

He was ordered to sit up straight in the chair. He did it.

He was told to put on his black leather shoes and properly tie up the laces. He did it.

He was told to take out the trash and burn it in the incinerator. He did it.

He was told to listen and keep his mouth shut. He did it.

He was told to feed and water the dog. He did it.

He was told to open the door for the bubblegum man. He did it.

He was told to dry and put away all of the dishes. He did it.

He was told to shovel the snow for a heavyset man who claimed to be one of the healers. He did it.

He was told to go to school, get excellent grades, and finish the year without flunking. He did it.

He was told to do every last bit of the tedious homework. He did it.

He was told to put more water into the furnace. He did it.

He was scolded and ordered to straighten his room. He did it.

He was told to be quiet, no horsing around, and sleep like a log until morning. He did it.

He was never told to think. However, in spite of tyranny—he did it.

In One's Element

As a result of exploration over the years, Shemokoman knew every square inch of turf in Waupakisco Park. The shortcuts and best hiding places, good bike paths, which house was where the witch was, and two or three ways to quickly go to the corner grocery store if there was a need. He always stayed inside his world and never ventured out alone beyond the neighborhood confines. Because if he did, without a doubt, there would be big consequences. Bad people lurked around out there, and he was not about to be a meaningless statistic.

Shemokoman never thought about running away, although he had heard of hooligans who really did it. How does someone just abscond? Where would you go? What about shelter and food? To pull the likes of such a stunt, the imbecile would have to be a moron.

He pondered serendipity in Waupakisco Park: "Shooting marbles in the sandy circles or chaseums to win a new boulder. Watching girls skipping rope, and romping in the lot under mantles made of twilight. Wading through puddles created by rain at two of the main inter-sections. And running through fields in tall green grass as irises and trillium, and daisies swaying to and fro, were growing on account of Nature's impulse. There was no need to stave off melancholy."

New Spectacles

Once again, Shemokoman started having problems with his vision. This time, he couldn't focus on the objects far away. Everything was blurry at a distance. After a series of visits to one of the healers, he was given a brand-new pair of spectacles. The thought of being forced to wear them all the time was not too thrilling. He also saw the world now in a way that *Others* wanted him to see it.

Not long thereafter, he was told to go to a market for food and provisions with a peculiar octogenarian. When the two of them met, the fellow offhandedly mentioned, "Oh, Shemokoman. I see that you have a new pair of glasses."

Shemokoman politely acknowledged with a nod and then replied: "Yes, I most certainly do. A fine observation by you, old man. Your recognition, at least, copacetic. And to tell you the truth, I wish that I didn't have to wear them. Now, all of the bullies will razz me."

The old man asked Shemokoman to remove the new spectacles. Although somewhat puzzled by the request, he acquiesced and did it. And then, for a couple of seconds or so, the fellow looked directly into the eyes of the ethical comrade, evidently probing his optical system.

"Well, I don't see anything wrong with your eyes," the man concluded. "Give me those stupid glasses. I'll throw them away or give them to someone who needs them. And you will no longer have any more trouble with bullies."

Though tempted by the proposal, Shemokoman put the new glasses back on. And then, they were off on the journey. He thought, "He's got to be wrong, but what if he's right? Or maybe he's pulling my leg and getting a kick out of that. I know that quite often people begin to crack up as they get older. Dementia and laughter forever, my friend! . . . Plus, 'ta-ta' to the masses who love me. Maybe not really as bad as we think: assisted living, room and board, and every day without the pain and troubles. The pluses can be a significant boon when someone is going bananas."

The incident left a lasting impression on Shemokoman. He thought about vague chronological points where insanity runs in a family. He was now somewhat confused and wondered if a predisposition to mental disorder might ever beset him.

Fields of Devonshire

Not every man has got what it takes when facing a tough situation. When fear ensues, the easy way out is often the choice of too many. To stand up and fight, and risk losing it all is more than most fellows are game for. The key to it all is potential reward; the challenge has got to be worth it. Alas, for so many people, their courage is just a ruse to fetch an advantage.

A sweltering midsummer night disappeared and the sun came up on a typical Monday morning. After eating a breakfast of biscuits and honey with hot black Georgian tea as the chaser, Anna tossed Shemokoman out of the house. He stood on the porch at the back of his home, looking around and thinking. What should he do? . . . And where should he go? Perhaps it was time to take a walk around the old neighborhood. So he jumped from the porch down to the earth far below, hit the ground squarely without falling over, and made his way into the lot.

The big mighty elm tree, noble-sublime, stood graciously, vaunting no privilege. An outstanding symbol of virtue, it should have been chosen for sainthood. On scorching hot days, it was there with plenty of shade to cool and console you. In the midst of a fierce thunderstorm, it tempered the wind and rain to fully protect you. If you desired to climb as high as the sky, the branches and limbs were sturdy and safe to support you. And its powerful roots went down in the ground to anchor the trunk of it firmly. For the hopeless daydreamer who sought nothing more than to fathom aesthetics in Nature, it stood as a bridge conjoining the earth to the hereafter.

Glancing around at the streets and neighborhood yards, Shemokoman didn't see anyone else outdoors. He kicked up some dirt, threw a couple of stones, and made up his mind to take a nostalgic walk alone in the park. As he shuffled along on the sidewalk next to a quiet Jameson Avenue, he was fascinated by all that he observed. It was as if the flowers were there to enchant him. Black-eyed Susans, daisies, bergamot, asters, and colorful poppies were growing all over the place. Even some wild lettuce was there for anyone who was in pain. He also noticed the milkweed seedlings, a must for persnickety monarchs.

Shemokoman looked at the sun in the sky and thought about tawdry behavior: "Sometimes we are forced to accept and regret an event that we have to remember. I mustn't forget that my woe is a healthy reaction. And time, if you will, is the only true healer of conscience for any young bandit. Well, live and learn."

He walked to the top of the hill in the west and gazed at his town in the distance. It was always a good vantage point for him that provided a marvelous view. No tornadoes yet or even a cloud with the slightest rotation. Maybe some day he would see one, or maybe he wouldn't and that would be better. And off to the right, he looked at some land that was a beautiful park long ago for all the respectable people. It was now the very best spot anywhere to gather up fresh tender shoots of asparagus to put on the table at dinner.

Next, he turned to his left and continued to stroll until he arrived at the Fields of Devonshire—a site where the bloodiest battles that ever took place were fought to the finish. At no other whereabouts under the sun, including the Plains of Troy and Marathon—and at no other time on earth—has humanity ever engaged in such savage and senseless slaughter of its very kind.

"For three consecutive, harrowing years that ended not too long ago," Shemokoman thought, "a terrible war was waged by Outsiders against the inhabitants of Waupakisco Park. And during that brutal campaign, it was myself and the ethical comrades who successfully defended the homeland. We were the warriors and victors, and we were the proud and persistent. And who, you may ask, was the cruel adversary? Well, it was a powerful army of truculent goons who came from the south and tried to smash through the defensive positions. Those villains wanted to kill all the men, torch every home, and take the women and children back to their hovels. Typical barbarous demons; there is no shortage of absolute evil. So much iniquitous death, only to countenance primitive life."

The battlefield lay on a wide-open plain with mountains that bordered the edges. There were scores of deep trenches near the front lines and fortifications in rear echelons. In the center of the combat area, a great round sunken hollow in the earth served as ground zero for every ferocious engagement. And it was always the place of the very last stand for every concluding encounter. Tens of thousands of good and bad men were viciously slain at that spot. Cut down in the prime of their lives by horrible weapons.

During the months and years of continuous fighting, the struggle per se was nothing but hostile warfare. Soldiers suffered from hunger, disease, fatigue, and depression—and typhus especially thinned out the ranks of the troopers. There was no end to anguish; and oh, yes—they fought like the devil.

Shemokoman pondered the essence of being in battle. What could be better than life-or-death for men in perpetual hellfire? It is a type of narcotic; not so good at first, but then you cannot get going without it. Cadavers, more cadavers; it is a bloodbath. You get to a point where the wife, a child, mothers and dads, brothers and prodigal sisters, a home on the lake, and devotion to Almighty God are inconsequential. The only concern is survival and how to ensure it. And it doesn't take long to figure it out in the midst of a gory fiasco: greed is the cause of every great struggle where soldiers have gallantly perished.

Time and again in the Year of the Goat, the enemy broke through a flank in the month of September. With superior ground forces, they were intent on a rout and complete devastation. Unfortunately for them, they never considered the bitter cold Michigan winters and how they could paralyze armies. Thus, when it started to snow and the sleet turned to ice, the weather stopped the advancing units dead in their tracks.

At that point, the soldiers of Waupakisco Park went on the offensive. They counterattacked the dirty rotten invaders. The enemy, now in complete disarray, had to retreat and leave the inferno they entered. The vile campaign had come to a close and the ridiculous fighting was over. The scourge of war, for the moment at least, no longer presented a threat to peace-loving people.

Afterward, a reception was held at the estate of Major LD to mark the outstanding victory. He was the senior commander-in-chief who planned the war and directed all of the action. The celebrants danced to the Emperor Waltz and sipped on rum that came to them straight from the Indies. They listened to stories of hardship and shocking accounts of incredible exploits. All the brave men who had taken up arms, looked death in the eye without flinching, and fought for a cause that was righteous and just were honored that day by the people. It was safe, once again, to live in the park with friendly, respectable neighbors.

In reality, there are only two kinds of men: those who have been in war and those who have not. And that is the truth.

Abingdon Strait

Following sentimental reminiscence about his days in khaki fatigues, Shemokoman hit the road again and went to Abingdon Strait. That part of Waupakisco Park was always sedate and well-maintained by all of the tenants. Sugar maple and paper birch trees lined the immaculate roadways. And wherever one looked while sauntering through, you didn't see very much stirring because that puzzling breed was more than content to stay in their homes in seclusion. They only came out if there was a suitable reason. Heaven only knows what they did for days on end in those family dwellings—all cooped up and avoiding socialization.

And now, he pondered, "So tell me, you people of Abingdon Strait. What goes on in your houses? Do you converse with anyone real and talk about anything normal? How do you move and what do you think; and do you go to the sink to wash your hands just before dinner? I would have to presume that malaise must fill up your hours."

Shemokoman continued to think, "So tell me, you people of Abingdon Strait. How do I get your attention? For god's sake, leave those malodorous dark catacombs and return to life, as it is the sensible choice. Breathe the fresh air and touch the soft ground, and harken unto youthful voices bereft of auld lang syne. Your passion is the only force that drives true wherewithal and can sharpen languid senses. The time is now to say to me as much as you are able about your life and how it was before you gave it up for stale trappings. Pour the wine and sing a tune, and laugh and cry with me for just a moment. You still fit in atop an august summit with a pantheon of gods who want to slay us."

Although it was true that on some days, the folks of Abingdon Strait left their homes and plunged straightaway into the serious yard work. With tools of every shape and size—like shovels, rakes, and hoes and spades, they cut the grass and trimmed the shrubs and hedges. They pulled the weeds and clipped the vines and flowers, and in the front they swept the dirty sidewalk. They also realigned the brick and stone to beautify the landscape. Indeed, those people always had attractive lawns and gardens.

And if it so happened that you were in Abingdon Strait and someone there caught sight of you in passing, they just might cast a smile in your direction and say something like, "Well, good morning, Shemokoman. And how are we doing today? Why don't you come over here for a while and join us in a round of French croquet. We have brand-new hoops and mallets."

The intent of such a proposal would likely be sincere and a game with them soon followed. But that was usually it, and nothing more transpired.

Whenever they finished up outside doing their seasonal maintenance chores, the folks of Abingdon Strait went back into their houses for yet another round of boredom. Of course, your average Joes in Waupakisco Park could never be their equal. Despite the fact there were no tracks for social separation, the people in that venue were a cut above their proletarian neighbors.

Notwithstanding all the aforementioned, Shemokoman was fond of spending time in Abingdon Strait. Especially after winter when the snow and ice were melting on account of warmer weather. There always was a massive flood of water in the springtime rushing down along the streets from the Fields of Devonshire to the bayberry thickets near the pumphouse. When that happened, he put on his high black rubber galoshes, buckled them up, and went outside to traipse around in the icy slush with his comrades.

Shaggy Monster

After leaving Abingdon Strait, Shemokoman went to a place that could not have been less unfamiliar. He stood at the edge of a big field that completely surrounded the grade school. There was a playground next to the redbrick building with swings and slides and teeter-totters, and iron monkey bars for agile primates. During daylight hours when the school was not in session, this was where the youngsters got together.

As he stood and gazed at the surroundings, a rustling sound off to the right and the noise of a chain dragging on the ground made him feel uneasy. He knew without even looking that it was Boots, a savage monster.

Boots was a big brown dog who had terrorized the neighbors for as long as anybody could remember. And that mangy mutt did the same thing every time when he saw you were coming. First off, he growled a bit to let one know that dogs can be a nuisance. Then, after circling round and round beside his doghouse, he would stop and face the him or her whom he was zeroing in on. Next, he scratched the ground a couple of times and charged straight at the victim, all the while fiercely barking. And just before he reached the end of his chain—and he always knew how far it was—he leaped up high into the air with all his might, hoping to break loose. If he were free without restraint, he could maul you ruthlessly and have a tasty dinner.

Alas for him, he never managed to do it. The chain held every time; he couldn't bust it. When Boots ran out to get Shemokoman and the psycho dog was airborne, he hit the limit of detention and—as if a freight train smashed into him head-on—fell down onto the ground in the dirt whining and yapping. This time, nothing was different. He failed again.

While looking at the scruffy, woeful mongrel, a couple of thoughts crossed Shemokoman's mind. First, how was it that day after day Boots did the very same thing, and yet he didn't wreck his body? In particular, how in god's name did he keep from breaking his neck? Very strange. And second, he felt sorry for Boots. Always tied up to his old nasty doghouse, never off the leash, and no one to give him a pet. Most likely, the guy was a basket case with grave psychological problems. Frustration that turned into anger and stress causing people to conclude that he had issues. Boots needed a pal, a good friend he could depend on.

Anastasia and Teachers

Shemokoman started to enter the schoolyard grounds, then promptly dismissed the idea. He noticed that Kay Kay and sister Sandy were playing next to the swing set. And he wanted no part of that little coven. Ever since that chilly winter day when he foolishly laughed after Kay Kay broke through ice in the ditch by the road in front of the school, well—he stayed away from her. The memory of his callous re-action to that poor girl—panicked and flailing about in freezing cold water, soaked through and through—was way too much to handle.

"I'll get you, Shemokoman!" she screamed for all the world to hear. "One of these days . . . if it's the last thing I ever do, I'll get you!"

Oh, how he always regretted his response to that situation. He should have quickly helped her out of the dilemma. So why did he do what he did? It was bizarre and very confusing. But he knew that she would never forgive him, not in a million years. Such is the nature of female ire; they can hold a bitter grudge forever. And she was a big girl at that.

"No," he concluded, "better for now to stay away from the playground until those two ladies leave and are clean out of sight."

After a while, the girls finally departed. Shemokoman walked to the front of the school and stood near the main building entrance. He thought about what he was doing standing alone in the middle of somewhere. Then he sat down on a big rock and considered the role of affection.

He mused, "It sure would be nice if the notion of love was more than a trifling gimmick. Used and abused by people the whole world over since time immemorial. Four letters together for only one horrible purpose: to deprive man of liberty. Unequivocally, love is the highest form of folly. Now as for hate: it is no value of sorts that I can believe in."

Not long afterward, Anastasia showed up at the playground. She was an ethical comrade, and she wanted to talk and listen. While gazing at him with a curious flair and thinking of chocolate ice cream, she inquired, "You know, Shemokoman . . . you and I, and the rest of the gang, have been going to school in this building for quite a long time now. And classes will soon be starting again; I can hear that tardy bell ringing in all of the hallways. So tell me, please, what do you think? Do we honestly get the instruction needed from teachers who try to be funny and like to impress us?"

Then Shemokoman said to the beautiful princess, "Unfortunately, Anastasia, my answer would have to be . . . no. We just don't get the right information. And I will tell you this much in addition. There is more to a fine education than reading a book and multiplication. The system has failed, and students are sinking in foolishness up to their necks. By way of instruction approved for a dork, the destruction of learning is certain. We are the losers and life is overtly degrading. Yes, the notorious cookie is crumbling. Although the teachers are not to blame. It's not their fault; I'm pointing no fingers. They do such a marvelous job of keeping the students in line and spreading the old propaganda."

Anastasia was quiet, said nothing at all for a while. And then, she just had to inquire, "So if the system is critically flawed, my lord, what can we do to correct it? Is there a way to improve or maybe reform it?"

Shemokoman replied, "Well, in fact, it is all very simple. You see, the key to success in education has always been mildly slighted. The means and the end are reversed by design as teachers are cutting the corners. Much better intent and appropriate plans are missing inside of the classroom. And if you ask any brilliant instructor what they hope to achieve by way of a ludicrous lecture, they say, 'We seek to enhance the body and mind to reap the greatest potential. Fundamental transformation, for all the illiterate kiddos. And yes, by god, there will be an explicit improvement!' When, in fact, we know that the system is broken. It is time to burn down to the ground the old infrastructure and rebuild it anew for the next generation of wizards."

He went on, "We have to reject the very idea of rote repetitious instruction. It isn't conducive to learning, and it will sabotage adequate training. The hour's arrived to create a new way to explain the essential conceptions. Although, we mustn't invert every thing that is old and hope for astonishing breakthroughs. We haven't the need to renovate all of the classes; rather, we ought to repair and refine what is wrong to produce a sensational system.

"'Better,' they constantly tell us emphatically. 'Everything has to be better.' Why? What is the ultimate purpose? And better than what, may I ask? For some convoluted reason, people believe that better must always be best. Not so. We need to abolish the myth of comparative grammar once and for all; superlative words are alone metaphorically useful. And here, Anastasia, let me suggest a splendid replacement for students who want education. Henceforth, we will teach them the basic Art of Survival. Just forget about books and sitting in class, and hearing the wearisome drivel. Instead, go out to the beckoning forest and fields, and lie on the bank of a river. For it is there you will learn about meaningful judgment and wisdom, and how to be one happy camper.

"A practical man should go to the land and do what he can to exist without help from anyone else. Apply those God-given senses, and don't be afraid to listen to lyrics in Nature. Forage for food, take care of your health, and sleep on your back in a meadow under the starlight. After all, enlightenment has nothing to do with how many books you read in a year—lest ye aspire to certain betrayal. Instead, you must devote all of your time to discover a valuable lifestyle. People can learn to get by on their own to garner long-lasting contentment."

Anastasia piped up, "Shemokoman, the words you pronounce are laden with karma and foresight. And I understand that honest people have got to play murder the leader. They will extol it. The die is cast to break and forsake our gyves of deplorable bondage. Too many people mistakenly reckon that suffering has to be normal."

So now, the call of a parent was heard in the distance. Anastasia had to go home. A mother and sister, cats and a dog were waiting for her by the oak tree. Tight wraps were always the case right then for all the adorable maidens. Shemokoman bid farewell to the girl, and she went skipping away.

After thinking some more about educational shortcomings, the ethical comrade rose to his feet to stretch and also to scope out the local scene. The playground was totally empty, and nobody else was in sight. For now it was getting near lunchtime, and everyone had to be hungry. Including him. Thus, he started for home.

Shemokoman cut through the large corner field that led up to Jameson Avenue. His trousers got covered with sticktights, but it was only a small inconvenience. He passed the mysterious redbrick house where the ugly witch had been living. She rode on a broom in the cover of night and didn't go out during daytime. And then, as he walked slowly along on the sidewalk, plenty of neighbors proceeded to heartily greet him: "Hello— Shemokoman! Nice to see you. What's going on?"

He always acknowledged and answered politely. There was no detectable angst in his voice; he spoke to respectable people. Shemokoman crossed over Hoxworth Mews and slid through a couple of backyards where he passed a young woman hanging out laundry to dry. He stopped for a moment to lend her a hand; a clothesline pole was needed to hold up the washing. A few seconds more, he was on his back porch, and Old Stub got a couple of pets. The screen door flew open, he hastened inside and devoured a favorite meal. Hot tomato soup, a thick bologna sandwich with cheese, and a big glass of creamy white milk straight from the icebox.

Rainbows

At any moment in the Land of Michigan, puffy gray clouds could move in above and the sky became dark and foreboding. The wind picked up speed and suddenly a terrific rainstorm commenced. The best part of it all—there was never a clue about when the next downpour was coming. Spontaneity has the advantage, my friend, to occasion a pleasant surprise. How can we ever reproach it? And why should anyone want to spoil it? Subsequently, pure soft water fell from the sky to the earth below and nourished all living creation. The neighborhood ladies set pails outside to capture a portion of rain to wash their hair in the evening.

During an exquisite rainstorm, Shemokoman always rushed outside to be part of the great celebration. He randomly ran most often alone, and jumped and danced, and sang a song to praise the excitement of Nature. The weather could not disappoint him. And all of a sudden a bolt of white light would flash through the billowy heavens.

Just give it a second or two and then, the peal of formidable thunder. Rolling and rumbling far overhead, God's tractor was plowing Elysian fields again.

He thought, "And to think there are people afraid of the rain. You'd have to be bloody psychotic."

It was divine entertainment without any altars, beseeching, or icons. Candles are nice for a prayer to Christ, but people require alluvial spirits to worship. And when at last a storm was finally over, Shemokoman went back in his house—soaked to the bone, dried off with a towel, and thought about worldly pleasure. Manna from heaven is more than a windfall. We needn't have much to be happy.

Every so often a rainbow emerged after a storm. It was a sign for all humankind to venerate and to admire. It appeared to the mortals high up in the sky to harbinger reticent purpose. Rainbows came out whenever it seemed that there was a reason to have one. And without any doubt, a rainbow is not accidental . . . no. They were conceived by design; somebody made them.

If Shemokoman noticed a rainbow, everything else went into the background. He sat and stared in awe of the mind-bending wonder, and he was grateful for having good eyesight. A rainbow displayed every virtue in man who occasionally happens to rise above loathsome behavior. They exist to amaze, inspire, and taunt every person who's lucky and sees one.

"When it comes to a genre of beauty," he thought, "is there anything we may observe anywhere that remotely compares to a rainbow? I think not. It is a stunning result of reality breaking; so, we cherish the magic and wonder about apperception. There in the sky, with so many bright, genuine colors, you may also discover a portion of truth and link it to premises, missing. No tricks, no fancy deception, only a ticket to perfect expression. Orange and green have nothing on purple with monochromatic gradation. And man is the prince in a cryptic domain as well as the source of all we assign to conception."

Then it came to pass that Shemokoman challenged the masses, "And now for all of you zealots out there, the day that was promised is here. Come out of the dark and into the light, and greet the magnificent Savior who is high overhead over yonder. He is your archetype spirit, and he is the Infinite Father, and he is surrounded by clouds floating above an auspicious horizon. Your god is supreme, and he is inviting the indigent soul to a banquet. 'So glad you can be in attendance, sir; and I know you are going to like it.' "

On one occasion during the evening, Shemokoman was on his back porch staring at a rainbow when Citizen R. dropped by.

"So why is it there, Shemokoman?" he candidly inquired. "Is there something to it? Could there be a hidden meaning? I sure would like to know what you are thinking."

The comrade thought about what he was asked and then replied, "You know, Citizen R., for that colorful curve to appear in the sky and occasionally gleam so ideally, all of the right preconditions must exist at the proper location. Otherwise, the essence of choice regarding the thing we observe will never develop. Red is permitted to be on the edge and not between yellow and blue. Yes, all of the colors, purple included, according to plan without any deification. At which time, they display our dazzling rainbow. It is a subtle creation with ancient celestial purpose, transcending the previous classification of separate colors in Nature. And it is no sorcerous ruse preconceived to carry a goddess. Rather, a rainbow permits the soul of man to opt out of dispassionate dreaming."

Content with the answer, Citizen R. responded, "Right on, Shemokoman. Another sagacious perspective. It's not enough to stand and stare without an explanation. Furthermore, I should mention that the Outsiders have threatened to attack our peace-loving neighbors again. Right now, we are facing another colossal invasion. Fortunately, a day shall arrive, of which I am certain, when the Fields of Devonshire will be serene and quiet forever. But until then, we fight."

Shemokoman agreed. Then the two men wished each other Godspeed and Citizen R. took off.

Cold Season

The Land of Michigan was called the Winter Wonderland. Now, to get a name like that you must deserve it. And no one knew more about seasonal charm than the men and women who lived there. When the cold weather hit, the snow and ice did not affect the mood of resolute people. They managed to have a fabulous time whatever they aimed to be doing. The days were short and nights were long; so what? . . . It just didn't matter. And there were lots of holidays and festivals, along with outdoor fun like Tip-Up Town at Houghton Lake and curling with the Yoopers.

Despite the honest feelings that prevailed in the park, most people complained all winter long about the climate. It seemed as if they had to even if they didn't want to. They couldn't like the sidewalks, where to slip and fall was pretty much for certain. The drifting snow in yards and roads made it hard to go to needed places. A sharp, brutal wind that could slice a man in two made a neighbor out of sorts and somewhat punchy. Just to get the mail sometimes was quite a hefty challenge. But it was only excess racket because no one who was sound of mind could hate it. And although they didn't admit it, the people who were counting time were satisfied and thankful. The smiles on their faces clearly revealed it.

If the temperature dipped to as cold as it gets, no one stayed put in their dwelling. They got all bundled up and went outside where they shoveled snow, unloaded coal, chopped up firewood, and helped the other neighbors who might need it. The women went to grocery stores to get more tea and sugar for a meeting at the schoolhouse. And, of course, everyone prepared for all the parties during the bacchanal season. "Schools are closed and work is canceled due to inclement weather"—well, for sure, you didn't hear it.

After waking up late one morning in early February, Shemokoman looked outside through a frost-covered window. The sun was shining brightly and there wasn't a single cloud anywhere in the clear blue sky. Icicles were hanging on branches of trees and under the eaves on houses. And all of the clutter and rummage in every yard had disappeared. For now, the entire landscape was covered with a blanket of new-fallen snow from the previous nighttime. Waupakisco Park had been transformed into a magical kingdom.

Whenever it snowed in the wintertime, Shemokoman got all dressed up in thick warm clothing and went outside to revel by himself or with the others. He couldn't wait to live it up and romp around in the fluffy white stuff. And on that particular day, the snow conditions for outdoor recreation could not have been any better. Thus, he went to the sled-riding hill alongside Jameson Avenue. And for the rest of the day, like everyone else—and into that very same evening—he got in line and waited for his turn to do the run. And when at last the time arrived, he grabbed tightly ahold of his Flexible Flyer, got a fast running start, and then, right at the edge on top of the hill, he leapt onto his sled and bolted away on a fabulous trip to the bottom.

While steering as best as he could on the way down to stay on a trail, Shemokoman thought, "Should I go to the right where it is clear or veer to the left for a spin in the yellow birch thicket? Each path is full of adventure, and it seems I never know which way to go until the very last instant. And then, I make a decision. Hmm . . . But how? . . . And why? . . . And based on what? Another enigma."

His feet and hands could be frozen solid and ears the very same way. But it didn't matter; he was addicted. So much joy and carefree play that had to pass too quickly. And inevitably, the fun always came to an end when the shout of a mother called somebody home for dinner. Ten minutes later, the place was completely deserted.

And when at last Shemokoman was home, and could finally feel his toes and fingers, he sprawled out on a couch and thought about life and what he had accomplished. He mused, "Men have needs to do their thing and spin the wheel of fortune. Life is what we live for and all else is not important. We must enjoy whatever conjures happiness, is innocent, and ends up hurting no one. Purpose—no, but it is what we're meant for."

Thus, winter didn't dampen any spirits in the souls who were around him. When Shemokoman looked into their eyes, he could feel it. Antipathy did not replace content for active people. Each and every one of the bitter cold days was plain unforgettable. And moments that glowed were split seconds of time that the gods would have deemed are blessings. Of course, someone somehow had to be there to make it all actually happen.

The Woods

East of Waupakisco Park, there were the woods. Specifically, that area was a vast biological preserve formed by glaciers twenty-five thousand years ago during the Ice Age. Shemokoman often went there to relax in the middle of Nature. Sometimes he was alone, and other times he went with friends. He truly loved the forest, and the forest thought the world of him as well.

A maze of pathways crisscrossed through the woods to take the avid hiker over hills and into valleys. The timber consisted of oak, hickory, and dogwood trees in the sandy uplands, along with birch, ash, and maple in the lowland regions. Yes, birch for the Slavic oppressor! There were three good-sized freshwater lakes in the woods, each surrounded by tamarack swamp with prairie fen and pitcher plants, plus every type of orchid known to man. All in all, it was not a shabby home for the entities that lived there.

The route he took to go to the woods was simple and direct. Shemokoman left his home and walked eastward along Jameson Avenue to the end. Then he went down the long steep hill on that wide sandy road, which turned into a narrow footpath at the bottom. At that point, he was in the lavish wilderness, where solitude and peace of mind obscured all human issues. He moved along and didn't say a word but listened to the sounds of merrymakers.

If Shemokoman plunged into that domain at any time of day or night to take a walk and also do whatever, it paid to pay attention and be cognizant of temporal reminders. He rarely lost his way, although he might lose track of time. And that could be a major sort of problem.

Divine Rejection

On one hot summer day when Shemokoman was in the woods alone, philosophical thoughts weighed heavily on his mind. In particular, he thought about the practice of religion. For several years and up till then, he was forced to participate in bizarre ceremonies inside of Christian churches. And why was that? To eat the flesh and drink the blood from a chalice cup to have communion? It seemed grotesque, like something that a savage just might want to dabble in.

He thought, "For the sake of the *word* of a crucified man, people are dying to perish. Just listen to how they mechanically pray and you will catch on to the swindle. The promise of going to heaven to live appeals to the suffering masses. Just be a good man, do what you're told, and when you are dead you'll love it. The Scripture as written provides a good way to believe in a god who is awesome. A liberal god who administers law according to suitable doctrine. And he is a god with righteous intent who decries every wrong like a zealot. A justification for war on this earth was never conceived so superbly. Time for another crusade."

He continued to ponder, "For a host of devoted believers out there, sin as much as you please, then atone and all is forgiven. Sounds like a pretty good deal to me; the people should never resist it. A compassionate god is terrific, and the implausible god is a cohort. And throw in the part about 'life everlasting'—honestly . . . what could be better? At last, a religion with answers to questions that I understand are convincing. No longer need anyone think for themselves, as a god has been doing it for them. Forget about conscience and Nature, as well; just follow the holy commandments. And do not dare to impugn or confront our God, or you will be headed for hell."

Shemokoman knew that he couldn't perceive or talk with a spirit called Yahweh, and yet he was ordered to pray on his knees every night to that god and ask for his mercy. So what did he honestly do that was bad to require devout supplication? Alas, it was a way to enslave the soul of a man to ensure he conforms to the system. Contentious ideas that appeal to the weak and are designed to empower the strong men. Well, what do you know, that lord is the hideous Führer.

Having dwelt on the issue for quite a long time, Shemokoman drew a conclusion. Namely, that he should not ever appeal to that God, the one he was taught to believe in. He could no longer rely on a lord who said to Obey! without question. A fake, the impostor, a chiseler. A god with the form of a man who they say is in charge of eternal dominion. A king in a glorious realm full of immortal self-righteous cadavers. It sounded a little bit fishy.

He mused, "Life is a tale of woe from beginning to end for plenty of people. And hope is caprice we apply every day to protect our souls from dejection. We live and eat, and drink and sleep, but never enjoy consolation. And as of today, for most of the people, they are in need of a great panacea. So what if they're mad and incorrigibly bad, and merely see nothing but joy in living for death in municipal grottoes. Let them forget about earthly concerns, as long as they get on with evil. Indeed, their God is no reason for genuine faith or a symbol of credible power. As for me, the ancients in Canaan created that God, so I must come forth to destroy him. He isn't dead, yet."

What's more, why should *that* God tell him about life? What did he know about living? A mountain of books could attest to the lore written for docile preachers. He thought, "The time is long gone for that God to prevail and be the albatross with which we're laden. Humanity doesn't have need for the likes of noble deception and penance. I cannot condone the value of man as measured by how much he suffers.

And why must I bear the misfortune of guilt on account of my very existence?"

The unqualified truth was so simple to see without complicating the issue. He knew of a splendid religion for people with souls that went into the hopper. It was called Nature. There could only be one Holy King everywhere when, in fact, it might be there were many. Dependable gods who were jealous of man and euphoric in spite of no heaven. Nature could never require a good crucifixion and resurrection to dazzle the eyes of a sinner; and he should confide in a secular god to overcome notional hurdles. Thus, his cosmological world was true and precluded potential for folly. Humanity had to prevail in time to afford a judicious solution.

Bass Lake

The path through the woods was a pretty good trek but doable and always worth it. Now Shemokoman came to a large bog swamp where millions of frogs in clear shallow water were having an absolute blast. Some of them jumped and cavorted around, while others were swimming and splashing. A few of the green slippery guys were sitting on lily pads and passed the time away with cacophonous croaking. They were not afraid of a man in the woods because of the Rules of Engagement. No, they didn't expect any trouble. Lucky for them.

He needed to cross the soggy morass and get to the other side. It was no problem in winter when the ground was frozen solid and hard, and the water had turned into ice. But during the rest of the year, it wasn't so easy, and draining the place was never a feasible option. And there was more.

The swamp was full of the dreaded sinkholes. Soft black muddy patches of ground where you instantly disappeared into the earth forever if you stepped into one of those places. Heaven only knows how far you'd go down into the endless abyss. And you would move on to a new episode without ever saying good-bye to respectable people. The idea of it all was terrifying.

"I've got to be careful," Shemokoman thought, "and avoid the imminent danger that every sinkhole will be posing. It is a matter of life and death, and I cannot risk going under."

Without further ado, he started to walk around the edge of the swamp. Slowly, inch by inch, he tried to get past it. However, he just couldn't swing it. There was far too much thick underbrush, and the footing below was unsteady. So he decided to do something different, Plan B if you will. He carefully jumped right into the swamp next to a tree where there was ample support. Then he went on to a similar spot, repeating the same maneuver. So far, so good. He continued to move right along in that way until he was finally through it.

After hiking up and over a long, winding esker, Shemokoman followed another footpath, which led to a big rocky hill. He went up to the top, turned to the right, and then he slid down a steep, narrow slope, taking him all the way to the bottom. And now, he stood up and stared at a glassy mirage. It was Bass Lake, more lovely than ever. Someone forgot to include it as one of the world's incredible wonders. Sometimes, other people were back at the lake—fishing or swimming, or bathing in warm golden sunshine. But most of the time, the place was deserted like it was today.

"Just me, myself, and I," he aptly concluded.

A glance to the left and then to the right. The shoreline was one solid cluster of narrow-leaf cattails. And big lily pads with pure white flowers were floating on top of the water around the entire edge of the lake. Large dragonflies were hovering and darting about in search of mosquitos; it was now lunchtime. Their colors of orange and yellow with purple were meant to scare ravenous reptiles.

"I have to believe there is artist in me," he mused. "My feelings are nothing to scoff at. One day I shall paint a fine picture of all I behold with my eyes at this place. And no one will ever forget it, and your disciples will not understand it."

Shemokoman stepped onto the strong wooden dock that extended out over Bass Lake. He walked to the end and sat down with his feet dangling over the edge in the water. He made a few splashes and gazed below into a world of bustling marine life. Silvery minnows were swimming in schools, and crabs on the bottom were crawling along and stirring up clouds of black muck. He rolled up a sleeve and plunged his right arm into the water to test it. As usual, it was ice-cold. Spring-fed lakes are like that. They do not ever warm up very much; not so inviting to take a quick dip. So now, it was time to lie down on the dock and relax for a spell without any type of disturbance.

While he reposed and was drifting along on a floe of amends and remission, again he mulled over the role of independence in his life.

"No doubt there are times when I really enjoy a taste of legitimate freedom. Like now, here at Bass Lake in the woods where I am beholden to no one. It is a world apart from those forces that want to control me, and the best part of it all—I am smack-dab in the middle of Nature. Far from the crowd and killing some time in the daylight just waiting for tokens. Oh, this wonderful place, so fine. Who could ever reproach it? Unfettering and consoling me; indeed, I shall always be grateful."

He continued to stay on the dock for a spell where unusual thoughts set upon him. They rushed in and out of his continent mind as he pondered the plight of misfortune. At least he was not curled up all alone someplace in a flat during the siege of a city where you had to avoid the hysterical freak who was trolling for something to munch on. Yes, Sawney knew all about that. They say if you do it one time— look out! For sure, you will never recover. Then he prayed for the souls who perished when bridges were open at night in the darkness. When a town that had wept on account of a war was in chaos and frightfully plundered. And but of course: so much to complain about deep in the nether terrain of Waupakisco Park.

Now, there was credible rumor about a few ill-fated people rubbed out in the woods. Sometimes when he happened to be at the lake, he had to take notice and wonder: "So how many lives both flaming and dear were doomed to be taken forever here without pity? Oh yes, the gruesome stories are more than abundant. The notion of death and rotting of flesh can make me feel very despondent. For heaven's sake—I am thinking about the neighbors I knew who were laughing and suddenly vanished. So much inhumanity everywhere, and why does it have to transpire? Perhaps for the sake of unthinkable pride, or to sate the yen of a primitive conscience."

As he sat on the dock that day at Bass Lake and lingered beside the still waters, Shemokoman had no soul for a god to restoreth. He was at peace in a tangible world without any tricks to annoy him. There was no malaise to cause him the blues, no sign of undue trepidation. And in spite of the crime that assuredly happened right there in the woods he was fond of, his fear was a simple emotion that he would now brush aside and abstain from. Otherwise, there never could be the redoubtable warrior.

Finally, the comrade decided to call it quits. He left the utopian mise-en-scène and went straight back to his home. There was always plenty of work to do around the house.

Imagination

The cognitive realm of Shemokoman had two complementary parts. On the one hand, there was the empirical side, which detected the nature of what he sensed by way of his perception. He watched the world flow by like a stream and recorded the meaningful details. The other half of his mental design was devoted to only one basic endeavor: imagination. To a greater or lesser extent, every person has to have it.

On one occasion, he contemplated, "Day after day, I am destined to live in an orderly way and improve what is called understanding. I am told by men that a tree is a tree according to form and particulars. But how is it some thoughts that are present in me comprise a distinct contradiction? Maybe I need to investigate trees to remove the effect of chimeras. There is simply no sense so much of the time in what I presume, or is there? Perhaps it is best for me to believe in the transposition of knowledge. I have to adjust to a previous way that served me too well in the past. Oh yes, I nearly forgot! It is time to upset the diaphanous cart and acknowledge the obvious fiction. Here, I defer to imagination."

"Seeing was never believing," Shemokoman thought. "Who on this earth could rightly conclude it?! I mustn't fall into a trap, as fate could never forget and forgive me. When I reflect about the truth, there is only one idea that serves to manage my sensory turmoil. Specifically, I have to observe and imagine a yarn to render a shape with appearance. Amen to that.

"And what is reality? What is it that fills the Euclidean space both rising and falling around us? Well . . . it is a dream that we had wide awake as pagans at midnight were sleeping so soundly. It is a wish to recuse and lay waste to the vouchsafing Infinite Spirit in heaven. It is a claim to neglect the caliginous light that glows around a sterile magnificent bonfire. It is the song of a diva who didn't give up or a hoot about life until she had music to grieve for. Godforsaken reasoning, and the best of every trick inciting a frenzy.

"Whenever an object in somebody's mind falls short of a good expectation, they can toss it away and conjure up two or three others. That is, should one desire to exalt the *self* on account of a sweet delusion, it is possible. By way of imagination. Or, should we covet mirth and felicity when even cheerfulness deigns to elude us, it is possible.

By way of imagination. And if the soul of a man should care to obliterate men who enjoy persecution, it is possible. By way of imagination. Indeed, the magical ivory towers with nothing inside or a stable appearance do not require aesthetic perception for insight. Furthermore, there is no need to bend or warp, or to distort the length and breadth of anything held nonexistent, as we can always learn about trees and the earth, the sound of a nice variation, the mountain lakes and purling streams that remain to provoke a sensation. And do not forget that without imagination, there can be a significant downside.".

How many times did he hear people say, "Use your imagination!" Well, a purpose must exist to justify the words that we banter on occasion. Thus, how and why, and when and where? There has to be a channel and a context, no recession. Nothing burdens man quite like resolve when he is told to find a resolution. Can we spot a distant star behind the cloudy heavens after nightfall? It is shining. Do you hear the mellow melody of a nightingale even though she hasn't started singing? Music, the universal language. And can we see a gray sirocco that is deep inside the mind and so enticing? Shooting upward! Let us hope that we can do it all without the aid of supernatural powers.

Shemokoman decided, "Maybe we should learn to question everything that fosters a conception. The cavalcade, a rhapsody, the song and dance of olden days with tambourines and bongo drums, and cypress harpsicords produced in Venice. It is time to get the story straight and study information where the standard rule may be a deviation."

As an afterthought, he observed, "Of course, we must be vigilant. A person with too much imagination may find it difficult to launch a real crusade should the effort be required."

Vince

One chilly autumn morning, Shemokoman was walking in Waupakisco Park when he noticed and greeted a man called Vince. The guy was a regular pacer who could be cordial as well as eccentric. Back and forth, back and forth, all day long on a short stretch of sidewalk in front of the house where he was a boarder. Most likely, guarding a barrel of secrets. Vince was tall and thin, and he always wore a light gray pinstriped suit. And he was a veteran soldier; so, of course, he knew how to fieldstrip those cigarettes. Clean as you go, my friend.

Whenever those two fellows talked, the conversation was philosophical, and today would be no different. Shemokoman said, "This much I can tell you with certainty, Vince. The conscience of man is never a vague proposition. It comes in only two flavors, and you have it or you don't. There is no in-between, no mean, for any intractable swindler."

"Now, as for people with that type of a conscience," he continued, "their behavior is purely atrocious. They live to exist with a decadent twist and befriend every affable stranger. So convincing, so disgusting. While sitting in odious taverns at length in rags they will tell you are clothing, the debauchers ridicule you and me and everything else on the planet. Yes, they have a good laugh deriding the hardworking masses and pay no attention to anything that concerns a moral convention. Rather, the spice of life and a treacherous fling is what they prefer to engage in. Their conscience never bothers them; they never feel repentant, sad, or guilty. And how and when and where they strike is not a hard decision. Just take a look at the crowded horizon to see the ranks of willing volunteers.

"So what do we have? Well, here is a hint. Marauders who don't care for clues and think that someone else is not affected. And who's to blame for what occurs? Indeed, there will be no confession. Not on your life! Oh, how they love to tease and appease us, the sleazy offenders.

"And in the end, when morning arrives with air that is clean and refreshing, a body is shoveled onto the back of a lorry. It is the meaning of victimization; nowhere to go and tired of hiding in stairwells. Meanwhile, the arrogant bums go into asylums where life is sweet and the brew they get makes coping with incarceration easy as pie. Lord have mercy! No wonder they are cracking up, as you and I can make the rounds and meditate on rabble-rousing shysters. So how about that, my illustrious friend? What are you pondering now?"

Vince continued pacing and replied, "Well, I was just thinking. I need new gloves for my old hands because they're chapped and aching. My fingers and my thumbs should have protection. Oh, how I do wish that Mother were here to help me make the big decision. Alas, she met a man who told her he could not provide contentment. And without exception, we know how that goes. So, I haven't heard from Mother since and nor has anyone else. You see, the woman was the type of broad without a touch of conscience. If only I could hate her;

really, that would be a pleasure. The tramp deserved some punishment in prison at hard labor. Indeed, it was neglect, and only out of weakness can there ever be forgiveness."

Shemokoman knew that Vince was horribly rattled. Something happened long ago that made him lose the common sense that commoners are born with. A good enough guy, but the logic in his head wasn't right and much distorted. He could not escape from "la-la land," where demons provoked and reviled him.

The two of them spoke for a brief while longer, and then Shemokoman went on his way. He mused, "Some people are fated to live out their days in a quaint sort of way and accept it. Somewhere somehow he blew his mind, and then he couldn't function. Tough luck."

Mr. J.

Later on that very same day, Shemokoman went to the corner grocery store on the High Road. He had to get some sweets to slake an insatiable craving for candy. He was a sugar addict and couldn't control it. Along the way, he stumbled upon a feeble old man who was staggering roughly in circles. He knew the cagey reprobate; it was Mr. J.

"Got to be careful with him," Shemokoman thought.

Mr. J. was tall, thin, and haggard; and also should we say a little musty. He apparently ate no wholesome food, so malnutrition took his feeble body. A painter by trade, he was usually dressed in white with big splotches of color splashed all over his working attire. But today he donned a shabby black trilby hat, and wore some dingy tweed duds. Houndstooth, no less. For sure, his appearance was not attractive. Unshaven, unkempt, unfortunate; and, most of the time, perpendicularly unstable. But who knows? There may have been a day when he looked more like a gentleman. Anything is possible.

Now it just so happened that Mr. J. had an unusual problem. For many years, a bottle for spirits was glued to the palm of his right hand. How very strange, indeed. And no matter how hard he tried each day, he couldn't resolve the dilemma. He wanted a final solution; however, where on god's earth could he get it?

Aside from the obvious hardship on account of the odd little issue, a benefit did exist. At any time and anyplace, Mr. J. could guzzle a nice little hooker. Convenient, we have to admit; and, it made him feel lucky and happy. Moreover, in spite of intent and what he professed with respect to a principled lifestyle, the man displayed a weakness for thirst that could only be quenched by throwing more hooch in the gullet. It was no big secret; everyone knew it. Mr. J. was hopelessly given to the bane of a wicked compulsion. The heavy cross was flat on his back as he preached and prayed for those who wrongly condemned him.

When the two men met, they greeted each other and started to chat about trifles. As usual, Mr. J. did all of the talking. He gave pointers on how to proceed in life and spoke about gainful employment. Shemokoman listened with interest, in spite of the fact that he had heard it all a hundred times before. And then, in the course of his lecture, Mr. J. said something at issue—an assertion that "by nature, man is good, and—"

Shemokoman interrupted the fellow, requesting a pardon for cutting him short, and said, "You know, Mr. J.—many great thinkers in history believed in the presence of totally *All* or simply of *Nothing*. It was a grand universal prescription meant to explain what is true and uncertain. Life is entirely this; or perhaps, it is conclusively that. However, in reality, it happens to be somewhat different. As a matter of fact, we live in a world where nothing can be without having a parallel converse. Where every appearance of fact or fancy is linked to a plain contradiction."

"Now, unfortunately," he continued, "the wide-open spaces on this Mother Earth are teeming with men who are filthy. We have to accept what is actually true and not be of a mind to dispute it. As such, we seem to get by with a mixture of bitter polemics and countless agreements, as well as a blend of the cardinal sin with heretics posing as chiselers. So please, my friend, you have to be prudent and trust me."

The fellow agreed with the comrade, and then went on with his dubious speech. And after another two hours of yielding to bunk with terminal value, Shemokoman thanked the man for his time and insight, and said that he had to be going. Thus, they parted company.

As Mr. J. moseyed away, he took a drink from the infamous bottle glued to his hand. An air of high spirits and renewed confidence slipped into his languid comportment. He was momentarily pleased by the soothing effect of consumption.

Then—all of a sudden, he went stark-raving mad and shook his right hand to once and for all be rid of the bloody affliction. Unfortunately, the man just couldn't do it. For several minutes, he sat on an old wooden bench and cried like a baby. Emotions run high when the soul is deprived of its honor. And now his eyes became stricken with fear as a twisted smile came over his purplish face. He placed the hand with the bottle under his left jacket lapel and stood up, using excellent balance. "Nice," he had to be thinking. He looked to the left and glanced to his right and stole away quickly and cheerful. He was beaming with joy like a burning new star in the cosmos. And finally, Mr. J. went into the shack that served as a home already for more than a decade. For one more day in a pitiful life, the derelict man suffered and struggled.

For a brief spell of time, Shemokoman reflected about the poor fellow. Wretched, for sure, but with a heart and soul full of old-fangled compassion. He would give you the shirt right off of his back if need should occasion the gesture. Too bad he was so mixed up, even though he was a trustworthy devil. No family or friends, completely alone in a world of zealots and fakers. Every day of the week he cared for nothing besides that dreadful next droplet of booze in the stomach. He was astray and benumbed by sorrow and guilt with dozens of demons locked up inside of his closets.

"At some point in life," Shemokoman thought, "Mr. J. was horribly damaged. Perhaps by a father, the wicked stepmother, or lecherous teachers inside of the sanctified classroom. Heaven only knows. And he no longer remembers the source of his pain that he managed to fully sequester. Thus, the plight he confronts has no real objective as he wanders about in a liquored-up limbo. Of course, his dignity—totally vanquished; and he is without a trace of obvious virtue. Mr. J. will never convert to a healthy or normal lifestyle, preferring instead to protect a wonderful illness. His lamentable days will always be empty and awful."

Everyone knew that Mr. J. had hurt many innocent people. And regrettably, he would continue his decadent style into the foreseeable future. Whenever he turned to insidious ways, the deed was completely forgotten the following morning. How convenient. And believe it or not, there were idiots living who knew him, and idolized the man because, lo and behold, they followed the very same pattern. They couldn't revert or evolve in the least; they loved what they were, and that was a fact and a puzzle. They flat out rejected the very idea of shady behavior. "Naughty, delightful, and give me a tryst; it is a favored position. Fun for a while, but don't tell a living soul about the liaison. After all, it is so nice to have an assortment of secrets."

For ten long years thereafter, and well beyond the demise of that neighborhood culprit, Shemokoman appealed to the Gracious Almighty to help Mr. J. get rid of the bottle. Every night just prior to bedtime, he prayed on his knees for a man he knew to be rotten. He asked his God to save a drunk who had the terrible problem. However, it just didn't happen. The goddess Destiny was up to her old tricks again, and she was one adamant vixen.

Truth About Values

When considering goodness in people, Shemokoman couldn't help being suspicious. Of course, there were many fine souls out there, and he could not dispute it. On the other hand, every day of the week seemed full of outrageous surprises. Waupakisco Park was loaded with stories that one should not have to get used to. Alas, he knew it would always be rough for some of the neighbors, as they seemed to be a part of a plot that only defiled them. And although everyone meant well, situations emerged that had no conclusive solution. The evil do-gooders were such a despicable gaggle who did not understand about infamous ways and the shame of contemptible habits. Verily, they were but slaves to Lucifer.

"It doesn't take much for someone to get into trouble," Shemokoman thought. "Contention appears and people are prone to take action. This place is loaded with too many hot-blooded tempers, and the foolish clowns insist on flirting with danger. Spoilers! . . . Nothing but spoilers. Reasons for vile behavior abound, and we need a plan to eradicate moral delinquents. And what is the source of so much despair? What are they honestly thinking? The neighbors I notice have everything needed for comfort, which leads to the only conceivable cause of bad behavior. Avarice! That's right, avarice. The cretins around me are greedy, and righteous intent has given way to lust and amorphous perversion. All they do is take, take, and take, and, never enough to be happy. Has anyone heard about giving?

"The virtue of man is part of a plan for those who are willing and worthy. A fine reputation, compunction, forbearance, and sweet moderation are vital for one to be peaceful. To obtain any *thing* that is pleasing in life, you have to work hard and deserve it. And for sure, you will never be sorry; and for sure, every scoundrel in town will be dying of envy. The world has plenty of vice as well for all of the wayward fanatics. Sloth, betrayal, promiscuity, vanity, and hate are just a few of the patent examples.

"So here in my pastoral neck of the woods, what is it I frequently notice? Well, to begin with . . . nothing's for show or considered a fraud where people encounter awareness. It is the only definitive case that will lead to a fine understanding, for high-minded citizens falling. And given the right set of direful straits, even a god who is peachy as hell recurrently errs and will stumble. That being said, I shall live every day in a provident way, and it will imply intuitive care and discretion. 'Oh, hear me, you Reticent Prophets afar! . . . And confirm all my valuable choices. The one who is simple and chaste can only do right by the others around him. The one who is simple and chaste must bleed until heathens are calm and collected. Come now! . . . Why do you laugh and accommodate serious matters? Perhaps we need better rapport to relate, as no one is hitting the jackpot.' "

Shemokoman stood on the hill beside Jameson Avenue and gazed at the High Road below. It was clear that he wanted to take it. Then he looked at Waupakisco Park, a charming place to all of the naive believers. And off to the west, the sky was a shade of magenta as the sun was about to go under. To the east, there were pearly layers of dark thunderheads stacked up one on top of the other across the horizon. A right mighty storm was coming his way, and no one or nothing could stop it.

5

⚜

Shoot the Breeze

Saint Johns Wood

Another year passed and another one too. Now it was early in autumn again. During that marvelous season, the panorama of colors in the Land of Michigan caused a great stir in Shemokoman. He was in awe at the beauty around him where moments that slid from the present to past created a lasting impression.

He realized, "Every thing that I see in the tangible world is stable and couldn't be better. It is the work of an artful master with staggering talent. What a shame. It would be nice to believe in a Yahweh with a forté for divine intervention. So much for a big fabrication."

It happened one day that Shemokoman and most of his ethical comrades decided to explore the north side of Waupakisco Park, an area called Saint Johns Wood. It was named for a chap whose mother could dance a mean tango. The excursion was planned in detail, and soon they were off to the races.

After walking a spell in a roundabout way to get where they needed to go, the Doctor said, "Hey, why don't we take the path over there. It's a shortcut. We'll save time."

The recommendation was promptly approved. It was a worthy suggestion. And shortly thereafter while moving along, somebody shouted a warning, "Hey you guys. Look out for the sumac! Don't wanna catch that stuff. For men like us, there is no time to be laid up, and any philosopher knows it."

It wasn't too long and soon they arrived at Saint Johns Wood. They went down the embankment by Coventry Road, passed the old junkyard, and wound up at "the pits." It was a desolate hilly terrain with limestone quarries, bicycle paths, and mountains of pebbly gravel. The inquisitive fellows inspected the uncharted territory for two or maybe three hours. And then it was time for a break.

So, the ethical comrades sat down around an old abandoned campfire. They could tell the place had been recently used by hoboes. Bindles were scattered about on the ground, and the smell of mulligan stew was still in the air. Rarely seen, yet they for sure were out there, the hapless souls who roamed from town to town without any permanent shelter.

The days of soup kitchens and hard pink glass were not that far behind. A nomadic way of life was wrought for vagrants who were good enough at hopping onto a freight train. And to somehow return to the fold of a normal existence wasn't an option. Those men and women could never adjust anymore to a common lifestyle. So they moved about and posed no threat to the likes of a general public. The wealthiest nation on earth could have done more for impoverished drifters, but the men in charge just blew it off, didn't budge an inch, and went to dinner at the ritzy yacht club.

Circle of Time

A short while later, Shemokoman thought of the Doctor's useful suggestion during their travels. And thus, he asked the aspiring professional, "So, Doctor . . . Do you remember that you said we could 'save time' by taking the shortcut? I was wondering. What did you mean by that?"

The Doctor tilted his head to the right, thought for a moment, and answered, "Well, Shemokoman, I guess I meant that we could get here quicker that way."

"Precisely," he replied. "And yet, there really is no way to save some time for later on, and pull it out of storage when it's needed. That's a given."

Now the comrades were puzzled. Where was he going with this line of thought, and what was the point of discussion? After a period of silence, Alabama spoke up: "So, Shemokoman. Please, indulge us. What do you know about time?"

He pondered the question for only a moment. And, what could he say that was useful? Then he stood up and grabbed a big stick that was lying nearby on the ground, and inscribed a large round circle in the dirt.

Thereupon, he spoke, "My dear comrades. To begin with, I should note the following. Unfortunately—information we get, more so every day, is nothing but jive and a viewpoint. And all that we know about time as of now is a product of science created by men inside of their ivory towers. They look down upon us and believe that we are inferior. Oh yes, the Exalted Ones, the enlightened jabbering apes, so much grander. Now, in light of the fact that man can never be perfect, it follows that science must be flawed as well. So it—science—mustn't have the final word that pertains to truth of natural matters. Sometimes I am amazed when I think about reason and theories, and how people have abused them. Therefore, considering what I've said about man and dispensing with copious nonsense, permit me to tell you the very plain truth about time we ought to consider. I will do my best to state the facts without inessential rendition.

"To start with, there was no beginning. No end is in sight. Intuition a priori produces a standard. And even though people imagine a line, time is no linear product. It bends and careens and shrinks and expands to serve any schema you favor. And if you happen to be at rest, then time is, of course, nonexistent. By Jove, we love to invoke it. The patrons of more information try to resect every mystical issue; thus, reality has to be based on stable conclusions. They seek to elude any need to explore for anything short of acceptance. There is the door— the finger is pointing . . . so use it! It is a sad philosophical weakness, truly without any marginal value.

"First and foremost, the clocks on a wall and watches we carry betoken a temporal standard: 'It is a quarter to four and late; you'd better get going.' Our limited time is ticking away, in spite of the fact it's eternal. Time is a gift from the Gracious Almighty, and it is a sin to waste or somehow misuse it. So, be careful, my ethical comrades."

He paused for a moment to wait for questions or comments that may have developed. Hearing nothing, he went on: "Our time on the earth resembles the image I drew on the ground here before us. It is a circular natural shape, and nothing we do can affect it. A geometrical form—and, just look at the logical center; you cannot see it. Amen! Think about that for a minute, and you will be woozy. For time to elapse in a meaningful way, it flows like a torrent of feelings; and, you have to be able to tell it. What good would it be if time were ignored? ... I guess we would basically lose it. Freely revolving and spinning around, Beseech! ... The anonymous Juggler. In spite of what people will say about time, it is no scandalous villain plotting to waste you. No, indeed. It is the wary Performer, and it is the innocent Dancer. And it is the honest Composer. Balancing out the dos and the don'ts, time was never intended for passing amusement. Verily, strange paranormal forces are silently working.

"So, we have to respect our tentative time for as long as we're vertically stationed. It comes and goes like a breath of fresh air, and we couldn't be breathing without it. And time will serve us well, without doubt, to measure a span of duration. In that, I can see nothing touchy or quaint, but a great metaphysical purpose. So when we are forced to surrender sweet life, time is not greatly afflicted. Unequivocally, you cannot destroy or somehow adjust or invent it. Time is forevermore moving along as a thoroughly vital convenience."

At this point, the Doctor requested an explanation. "Okay. You say that time is eternal; however, I'm sensing a slight contradiction. Can it be true that everything here is delusion?"

Shemokoman knew what the Doctor was thinking, as the expected reaction prevailed. He replied directly, "Right you are, wise Hippocratical scion, to request a clarification. The Banshees of Otsego could never have been more judicious. Let me explain. Leaving the fold of time as we know it, there is only one other realm to share coexistence. It is—Eternity. Every object we sense, the emotions we know are a part of the nominal pattern. It is almost beyond comprehension, and yet, it is more like a single perception. Eternity—yes; Infinity—no, and that is the way to describe it. A boundless domain where nothing can be without subsequent nullification. And no, you cannot escape it; but yes, we need to expressly enjoy it. Time didn't grace the immaculate rose; we just never honestly had it.

"And therein, my ethical comrades, lies the plain truth of your 'slight contradiction.' Of course, it is hard to produce any true resolution; although I will give you tout de suite the only conclusion. Namely, regarding time and Eternity, they completely negate one another. You can only have one excluding the other to satisfy justification. The obvious choice: Eternity rules, forever and ever; no limits. And time is a gift to us all— here and now—that evades every prudent description. The Impostors will tell you they know otherwise, but do not believe their baloney. They seek to deceive any soft, easy touch with folly that borders on evil. And all we perceive that the universe owns is nothing remotely fictitious. It is pure representation, of course, confirmed by human sensation. Furthermore, the vast cosmos isn't as large as a reasonable man might suspect; a dimensional system—notwithstanding. Indeed, it is quite a bit bigger. And your mathematical laws are used in a pinch to explain away paramount issues. Viz., our lives are a part of the cold perennial mix that thinking men have never been able to fathom."

Now, Shemokoman stood up and gazed at the sun overhead that shined upon mystified faces, and said, "You know, I would like to ask that my ethical comrades indulge me a few minutes longer, as there is something more I wish to explain. We must go further above and below into the phenomenal regions, and sift through smoldering ashes where the truth is akin to venom of poisonous dart frogs. For it is there that a man who repudiates fear may derive a conclusion or two regarding the system."

Fundamental Theory

"Metaphysics," he said. "A term that may greatly perplex you. But what in tarnation is it? Well, gentlemen, I will tell you. It is a fancy word created by Greeks who were plenty confused and anxious to learn about being. It is the branch of Western philosophy that studies existence and knowledge. So let us investigate this for a while to see if there's anything to it; and, we shall talk about human cognition. Most importantly, I need to describe three fundamental propositions. And triads, as we all know, are entirely perfect.

"To begin with, there is the First Proposition. It is as follows: 'The laws and operations of this one irrefutable pure paradigm—in and of themselves, overall and unconditionally—are sufficient to preclude the possibility of any other conceivable set of propositions to contradict the current conception. We affirm the supreme universal; it is what is, was, and ever shall be.' Simple and very straightforward. I give you a tenor concerning the truth—to the exclusion of anything else. It just couldn't be any plainer.

"And next, my ethical comrades, we have the Second Proposition. I will say it verbatim: 'Matter and mind, and whatever is else must always be one and the same. Nothing but equal existence, and there is no imperative difference; and the will can provide the space and time for what everything has to abide in.' Hence, the mind is a part of the body and the body conjoins with the mind. And here, the human condition conforms to a very bewildering presence. Again, this law is concise, no shocking surprises.

"So let us move on, at once, to the Third Proposition, which is the heart of a rational doctrine. It declares the following: 'It is always possible to successively divide a portion of any one separate thing into smaller and smaller components, the measure of which may or may not be equal to what was partitioned. Evolution proceeds in a negative way, ad infinitum, forever. And it is always possible to combine discrete portions of any two separate things to form a new and different creation, the measure of which may or may not be equal to the sum of the separate components. Evolution moves in a positive way, ad infinitum, forever. Ultimately, all vectors of change will undoubtedly merge outside of coordinate systems to cancel the other ones out. Necessity has to demand it, and our zero-sum game is authentic. Hence, a premise is only required to show and destroy any notional object.

"Now, when these two contradictory yet compatible postulates of the Third Proposition are applied to dynamic existence of anything real or imagined—and, no part of a genuine object need remain on a permanent basis—then the gist of explanation resolves into the Fundamental Theory of Disintegration and Combination. Or, as I will just call it—the Fundamental Theory. It is the only true law about space and time, and the causality hanging around us. Eternity hasn't one single constraint—no size, no edges, no nothing. No extreme in one direction and no end that delimits the other. And, of course, there is only a semblance of representation save for a need of the orientation."

Shemokoman pressed on, "Thus, the Fundamental Theory completely defines the unusual world we live in. It cannot be wrong or mistaken, and surely there are no omissions. So, what are the main connotations, and what can we draw in conclusion? Well, with the occasion of combination, we have to rule out the chance circumstance of anything deemed as the biggest. Something can always be greater than anything due to the fact of enlargement, *sine fine*. Thus, your behemoth is doomed and must be expelled from all causes, bases, and reasons. It is a pseudo conception that is made use of to hoodwink and dupe us.

And in the case of disintegration, we have to exclude the possibility of that which is held to be smallest. The result of division is always the same, regardless of ramifications. And, if substance or mind, or anything else may be reduced—*sine fine*, it follows that disintegration has to proceed to a logical vanishing point. Where all that is left is whatever should be and what you can aim to believe in. Yes, there is a place where nothing at all is subliminal sane economics. A place where the blink of an eye may obliterate carnival rides or restore them. A place where falling asleep in your bed is a ploy to make certainty purple. A place where all of creation itself depends on immortal observers. Reduction implies the denial of transfiguration and also affirms it.

"So here we are now at a mythical point on a curve south of Hickory Corners. Furthermore, it is clear that the case for prevalence of a fundamental particle must be abandoned completely. For we are not able to have an idea tantamount to a wily phantom; it would be madness. The Fundamental Theory precludes the potential for such a defective convention. Show me the minuscule tangible whit, and a monster will smash it to pieces. Nevertheless, take note, my ethical comrades, that we may still retain faith in perception. We all have a consciousness anchored in flux to handle the role of cognition."

He finished up, "Clearly the truth is not stranger than fiction; rather, the former and latter are equal. The real bottom line that we cannot reject is a quantum of Om and nirvana. Yet who among men on a gyrating earth would desire that it could be different? Humanity learns to adapt to anomalous milieus. Gentlemen! . . . Heed my words, and allow me to duly inform you. We have discovered Universal Transcendental Negation, and the lack of a credible nexus where deception pervades every entity wrought in a mind we may ever consider. And life shall remain in the shadow of death in accordance with how it was plighted. So, let us call the epistemological tide copacetic as well as a carousal laced with explicable tidings."

God

"Bravo, bravo!" shouted the Doctor. "You make good sense of all that I thought was nonsense. But tell me this also, my ethical comrade. Should I believe in the Infinite Spirit? What about God and religion? Perhaps we can talk about that."

For a moment or two, Shemokoman stared at the Circle of Time inscribed on the ground as a symbol. Then he spoke up: "So, you want me to talk about God for a spell—about the Gracious Almighty, omnipotent Being. Well, let me say this for the record. To begin with . . . God is above, below, and beside us, everywhere all at one time. He has to be slick to exist in so many places. How does he manage to do it? Honestly, I—don't—know. And we are not privileged to see him on earth; instead, you have to be dead and make it to heaven to view him in person. Quite the reward for living in pain for so many years with a sinner. And God may reside in the soul of a man, as he has to keep tabs on what we are physically doing, for the Great Reconciliation. Now, if you go to the orthodox classes at church, then you can learn all about God. The instructors are there to fully ensure that your brain has been thoroughly washed and hung out to dry. Moreover, it was written in that great masterpiece, long ago, that 'the Lord God formed man from dust on the ground, and breathed into him the glitter of life; and man became a living soul.' In light of rhetorically elegant prose, I need to tell you the rest of a fabulous story.

"You see, God is no glorious holy Creator, and man is no sacred creation. We simply *are*—and that is that—without a divine explanation. You needn't be sharp as a tack to really perceive it. Just look at the souls who walk on a street; they are so proud to be human and clearly believe it. The truth about how we have come to exist has nothing to do with a Yahweh. Although the legions of Righteous Impostors insist on exploiting the pious tradition. They tell us impossible magical deeds are proof of a god who is living. And I'm telling you that without any doubt, they are officially crazy. My dear comrades . . . it is time to renounce your most treasured, time-honored persuasion, and you must do it without hesitation. It furnishes solace that puts us to sleep in a world where eyes must be open. I implore you to live for the truth and discover a credo with no preconditions. You needn't be part of the Great Beyond to behold what is truly immortal."

Ever so briefly, the men glanced at each other. And then Alabama piped up with a grin: "So, to zero right in on the question. Please, Shemokoman, tell us some more about God. What is he like and what does he do in the meantime?"

As he aimlessly paced to and fro on the ground and thought about spiritual concepts, Shemokoman shut everything out of his mind to improve concentration. Eventually, he looked up and said, "Okay, Alabama. Now let us deal with this God for a short while longer. And allow me to say what I ought to reveal to divulge a compelling admission. Namely, that God is the sovereign of men on the earth, and he has the absolute power. Although he does not give any orders; instead, humanity rambles along on its road where it makes indiscriminate choices. It is a fact that mystifies man every day on the way to extinction. Alas, the holy apostles just had to believe that a dour Creator contrived us. Rubbish!

"The eloquent darlings, for too many years, ensured that our God was in exile. We need to eliminate guile and fraud to remove the prestige of tradition. In order to make out the nature of God, let us find out what he isn't. For starters: God is no lawgiver; he issues no lasting commandments. Period. And he may or may not be merciful; it is hard to tell about that. God is no judge—without any real jurisdiction; black robes and habeas corpus are not his dominion. And he says nothing at all about sin, as that is for us to resolve and determine. God is no shallow predictor; he offers no stark affirmation to man, no concept of ultimate purpose. And God does not chastise or punish mankind; he is no magistrate, ruling. Rather, it seems to me that *we* punish *him*; I've heard from the gossip, he often gets fed up with people. You see, even though man has come a long way from pagans and primitive practice, it is foolish to ever believe that we have the knowledge to know what he's thinking. Although if you must and cannot resist, and you want to perceive the Gracious Almighty, then I would suggest a diet of steady devotion. Like repeating the Act of Contrition until you are blue in the face and choking. Who knows? They say there is no harm in trying.

"Moreover, you will not find God in the velvet terrain by using the hidden advantage. Most of the time, he is working like hell because heaven's a lot to look after. And the Almighty prefers to be close beside anyone seeking out spiritual blessings. It shows him that they are aware of his grace and value as more than a sidekick. God oversees the great course of events and maintains the glass temples we live in. People are given their limited days and most certainly know how to waste them. Some go by fast, others are slow; there is no regular cadence. Fortunately, the God that I know can regulate temporal forces in lasting succession. All moments we have must collide into One at the start of a tortuous journey."

"So, Alabama," Shemokoman said, "we have a final conclusion. How is it we come by a portion of time? The answer is God, a sire we have to believe in. He is in charge of the exquisite Circle; and, he is the source of all unexplained apparition. Pure inextricable linkage, and we are constantly bending and turning. The holy Creator distributes the days and nights from season to season according to schedule. Yes, it is he who will set the agenda; and, it is he who is rigging the system. For every begrudging naysayer, time is the only significant ax to grind on a permanent basis."

Citizen R., who had been quiet for most of the outing, now made a few relevant comments: "You know, everyone, the Lord sure made a hot one today. And just like the wicked witch in the west, we should have already melted. Of course, nobody doused us with water. Ha-ha! And you are right, Shemokoman. Our God is no wild pretender. Like it or not, like an eagle aloft, he will be scoping us out and watching the sandbox."

Shemokoman nodded and added, "I think that everyone here would agree that life is a phase for romantics. We pray for good health, adventurous days, and avoidance of major affliction. And although it is common to constantly seek to extend our stay among people, we cannot rely on a great deal of time in the future. You see, gravitational waves are taking their toll; they never give in and do not let up for an instant. All of us—helplessly stuck on the ground; no bodies are randomly floating. And there is a mighty good reason for that, as the day will arrive and the earth will declare—'That's it, the party is over.' The sun will depart for the very last time as they lower you into a gravesite. And there I can promise you this, my ethical comrades: Nothing will trouble your spirit or soul because you will be dead as a doornail. And isn't it strange, for as much as we certainly die in the end, I hear tell that we go right on living. Wow."

With that, the men discontinued their talk about God and thereupon left the campsite. After wandering around some more in Saint Johns Wood, everyone went to Shemokoman's home and fooled around in the lot. They climbed way up high in the big elm tree where nobody thought about falling. They skipped some nice flat stones in a puddle of rainwater. They played some ball and scored a few runs, and didn't break anyone's window. "Cool it, bub . . . Cool it!" They built a big castle of gravel and sand, complete with a drawbridge and moat. Discussion about philosophical matters no longer were part of the program. It started to sprinkle, and then it turned into a downpour. The party broke up, and that morning was over forever.

6

Thou Shalt

Southeastern

It came to pass that Shemokoman was now leaving home each weekday morning to go to a different school for education. It was another massive brick building called Southeastern Junior High, on top of a hill in a part of town called Postumville. He was told to learn as much as he could and make it through class without flunking. So be it. He prepared for three long years of more intriguing scholarly labor.

The new institution resembled the old, and the function was really the same. The three-story school had plenty of spacious classrooms, big windows, and all the essentials for learning. A green metal locker was assigned to each of the students to store away books, coats, and other personal items. The hallways were packed with impetuous knaves and teachers who sought to control them. One day as he walked on his way to the gym where Raymond was letting them have it, a hooligan shouted, "Capped that chip-tooth beggar down and good."

Except for his ethical comrades, Shemokoman didn't know one single soul in the new academic surroundings. He had to attend every lesson without any personal choice in the matter. And all of the students were forced to change their classroom right at the sound of a bell every hour; plus, instead of one teacher to have all day long, they now had to put up with many. Behavioral theories were stylish and rapidly spreading.

He managed to feel pretty good at the joint; his spirits were never too dampened. Participation in sporting events, especially, provided a splendid diversion. But was it a way to compete and stay fit or was it a form of suppression? For now, he recurrently tackled as well a tsunami of mental confusion. Where was he going in life and why? No one had suitable answers. Many a day, he left the new schoolhouse perplexed and walked along the railroad tracks beside Porter Street to go home. It was a problem that plagued him, and he had trouble when trying to shake it.

One time, after watching a freight train go by, he thought about mounting frustration, "Hmm . . . five hundred and sixty-one railroad cars. That was a hell of a long one. And look at that nice red caboose at the end; I wouldn't mind being the brakeman. Alas, a horde of towns-people are mad as can be, stuck over there at the crossing."

The Environment

Shemokoman frequently questioned the source of dissonance at his new school. He desired to fully consider some thoughts that often affect the emotions. In particular, he wondered a lot why his circle of friends didn't grow at the place of confinement. It was a fortress with many brave knights and precocious disorganized maidens. What was it that seemed to inhibit a greater expansion of closer acquaintance? And why were companions important for him to begin with? Perhaps his expectations were out of alignment.

He pondered, "But maybe their feelings are similar to mine, with pain and commotion exceeding my personal torment. Perhaps it is they who are really the suffering victims. On the other hand, I am the lad who's been busting my tail, and maybe subconsciously I am the one who rejects any true integration. No more to it than that. Or perhaps they believe they are better than I am and quietly mock and betray me. A mob of presumptuous odious brats, above and beyond the true master."

Concerning the faculty members, their motives were good and lessons were fair, although they were somewhat stilted and prone to be bossy. There was no shortage of vanity in them to mollify ample pretension. Not like the ones in Waupakisco Park, the schoolmarms, who were so full of deceit as well as compassion. All students could see that they had to accept a new wave of instructional dogma.

The teachers provided the wisdom to pass and scolded all talented stragglers. They flaunted assorted scholastic degrees and never missed out on a chance to sit in the lounge and puff on a Camel. Little did they realize that the *Inquisition* was coming with big changes—on the horizon. And each of the know-it-all pedagogical staff was silently thinking, "Once again, I will preach my gospel to this cabal of naive neophytes. We say the Pledge of Allegiance and then pursue intellectual business. And some of the stiffs who hear me today will be better and brighter tomorrow. I'll give them plenty of homework right at the end of another great hour. That'll make 'em happy. And when the workday is finally over, I'm going straight home to be all alone and make myself one hell of a favorite cocktail."

In any event, the teachers did their job and toed the line, and made sure that every lesson had the best indoctrination. It was group instruction at its finest. Consequently, as Shemokoman wandered through the hallways day after day, he noticed that espirit de corps, by and large, was missing. Enthusiasm was deficient, and the students were not fired up.

He thought, "So easy to see why some of the gang will snap and go off of the deep end."

Erasers and Blackboards

When Shemokoman entered a classroom, he knew precisely what was in store. He had to remain in his seat and be silent for most of the hour-long period. He raised his hand to talk out loud or ask permission for the right to take a break if he didn't feel well. The simple procedure was meant to prevent the spontaneous outbreak of chaos.

Looking at all of the brazen insurgents, he concluded: "Oh yes, I believe that civil unrest is quietly seething around me. The forces of evil are plotting to seize control of the fortified building. Most of these boys and girls strike me as the incorrigible violent types. If I were the teacher—just to keep them in line, I'd give them all from time to time a sensational thrashing."

In reality, most of the students at Southeastern were obedient with fairly good manners. Regarding their mood: they could be jolly or sad, quiet and gloomy, disturbed, dynamic, incensed, or very reclusive. Who in the world can tell you the truth about the fickle mental condition of people? While sitting and facing the front of the room, most of them cared about only one thing in the future. Namely, the ring of a bell to signal the end of the very last period of classes.

Learning was more than a trying affair for most of a trim student body. Just throw the young monsters into a room and tell them to "sit still" for the better part of an hour. My goodness, you have to be kidding; bundles of energy must have an outlet. There once was a Greek who was right on the mark—physical action and play for more than a decade. Indeed, a revision was very much needed, at least; something to hold their attention.

Therefore, Shemokoman proposed some ideas to produce a learning enhancement. The works of Plato, Aquinas, and Sartre, for example, were not anywhere in the program. But imperious teachers ignored and dismissed all of the useful suggestions. So there was more reading and writing, and all of the numbers were notably bigger. A bright, rosy future was promised to those who earnestly studied and finished up all of the homework. Unfortunately, Shemokoman knew that some of his peers would never be able to make it. One day, he'd arrive at eight on the dot in his homeroom, only to sadly discover that a trusty new friend wasn't "Present" when the teacher was taking attendance. "Yeah, bring back; ah, bring back; oh, bring back my Bonnie to me, to me."

Caissons and Drums

It was the month of November, and Shemokoman was sitting in Current Events class. Outside, it was cold and snowy with blizzard conditions—the kind of weather that made him want to go hunting for ducks in a cornfield. The old radiators along the wall were pumping out heat full blast, so it was warm and cozy inside of the schoolroom. The instructor, a one Mr. H., was giving a valuable lesson about the American federal system. So perfect—checks and balances; totally useless.

And then it happened. An elderly lady, one of the administrators, burst into the scholarly venue. Her face was stricken and red, and covered in teardrops. She went to the teacher, said something to him in a barely audible whisper, and convulsed even more with sobs and frantic emotion. Then she quickly departed.

At that point, Mr. H. lost his composure. He turned pale and faced completely away from the students. For a minute or so, he stood by a window and stared at the masses in Postumville. The crowd that he saw was milling about, unaware of the latest news that was about to affect them. Then he swirled around and walked to the front of the room, where he said the following words with a very great effort: "I was just informed that our Grand High Exalted First Citizen of America has been slain. Taken from us in the prime of his life. A vile assassin killed him."

Upon hearing the stunning announcement, all of the girls broke down and wept like crazy. The boys were in shock, stared at each other, and said nothing at all of any importance. The moment right then was frozen in time, and everything stopped for everyone there in the classroom. Like it or not, we always remember historic events, and what we were doing exactly when they surprised us.

As a matter of fact, Shemokoman wasn't too startled. It is usually for no ambiguous reason that a head of state falls prey to a cold terminator. People have motives, of course; and desperadoes will settle the score. In the not so distant past, there were a good many nasty rumors about the dead crooked leader. Too many infamous scandals and a penchant for strong medication. Careless behavior so often will lead to a current regime being toppled. The hit was the work of a gang of professional mobsters; or maybe the deed of a single delirious kook— but very unlikely.

During the days and nights that followed the bloodshed, Shemokoman felt no depression or undue sorrow. He was indifferent to uninterrupted public and private bereavement and, in a strange sort of way, greatly relieved to be out from under the sway of such an impertinent fellow. Sometimes we have to purge the ranks when circumstances dictate and reconnect to blaze a trail for the welfare of the people. It's all about the right of having power, and how it's used to dominate a country. As for now, it was time to mend the fences, recalibrate, and learn a vital lesson from the outrage.

A Particular Morning

The holiday season with Christmas and New Year's came and went so quickly. And now, it was late in January—the middle of winter and freezing. The snow was coming down in sheets and drifting everywhere, and most of the roadways were one solid glassy sheet of ice. Uptown, downtown, in town, around town—people were on the go and making a living. Customers were in and out of the grocery stores, pulling carts and toting sacks with food and other staples. A decent crowd was at the

Bijou Theater, where matinees were good for any person with the va-
pors. The lagoon in Irving Park was open for ice-skating each day until
way late into the evening—weather permitting. A reason to complain
in Battle Creek was never so remote or ill-considered. Prosperity flourished for all the respectable people. Lucky dogs . . . didn't know how
good they obviously had it.

Shemokoman rolled out of bed and stood up, stretched out, and
slowly got dressed. He slipped into the old faded blue jeans with
patches on both of the knees. He put on his favorite red flannel shirt
and buttoned it up in the front. He snapped on a pair of matching sus-
penders—not really needed, but they were in style. Then, as he was
going downstairs for breakfast, the memory of a dream the previous
night came to mind and gave him the creeps.

He was sleeping in bed tucked under a mountain of blankets in the
pitch-black wee small hours, when suddenly, a horrible winged green
ugly ogre tried to get into his room. The creature attempted to enter by
way of a window over his dresser. Good grief! . . . Shemokoman thought
he was going to be killed and was scared completely out of his wits.
Again and again, the brute pounded his fist against the glass; he wanted
to smash it to pieces and clamber inside. However, to no avail. Try as
he might, the savage fiend just couldn't do it. And finally, the frustrated
ogre gave it up and flew away into the darkness, brooding.

Somebody couldn't stop thinking about it. It seemed so real, he almost believed it. But it was only a dream, or was it? Perhaps some kind
of an omen or, maybe, occultish manifestation. God only knows. And
how many nightmares do we have in the course of a lifetime? Too many
to count and remember, that's for certain. But, for some unusual reason, there are always a few that we never forget. They stay in our minds,
so striking and clear, and continue to eerily haunt us.

After he finished the morning meal, Shemokoman put on a heavy
corduroy coat, donned his hat with the earflaps, and wrapped a plaid
cotton scarf around his neck. He slipped on the pair of black rubber
boots, buckled them up, and left the big white house on Jameson Avenue. He walked to a street corner two blocks away, where the Doctor
and Anastasia were already waiting. No one had too much to say because they were all just a little bit groggy.

It didn't take long and a yellow trolley was tooling around a corner
in Saint Johns Wood. Their ride was coming to pick up the comrades

and whisk them away for one more day in the schoolhouse. A few minutes later, the trio was settled into their seats, bouncing and moving along on the way to receive more education.

Fire Alarm

They rode through the rest of Waupakisco Park and made the rounds in Fairfax Heights. Every so often the vehicle stopped to pick up additional students. After the very last passengers boarded the trolley on a street that was called Electric, they turned to the left and merged out onto the High Road. They went up and over the old small bridge where people kept losing their stomachs. Then they turned to the right and cruised through Bradford Commons. It was a nondescript, strange sort of place with dozens of small, square one-story dwellings. Shemokoman never did know a single person who happened to live there.

Eventually, they arrived at the junior high school. All riders got off of the trolley and marched up a long concrete stairway that led to the building's south entrance. Now fully awake, it was time to pay homage to textbooks and teachers again.

No one can give you the lowdown about an event that will happen tomorrow. A round crystal ball of clairvoyants and prognostication have nothing in common. While the students were busy arranging their lockers, talking with friends, and rushing to get to a homeroom, something occurred that made everyone stop and take notice. The fire alarm went off. It blasted away and echoed through all of the hallways and into the classrooms. Good lord, what a clamorous racket.

Everyone quickly left the building and gathered in groups outside. A head count was taken and no, nobody was missing. And as a matter of fact, there really was a fire blazing away in the school cafeteria. It was no random drill for people to practice. The red fire engines were soon on the spot with firemen and their equipment. Ladders and hoses all over the place as torrents of water gushed from street corner hydrants. Eventually, the principal called off school for the rest of the day, and said that a normal schedule would promptly resume the following morning.

So what were the students thinking as they departed? Well, only one thing: lucky break. There are times in life when nobody honestly cares about policy riders. And now, Shemokoman made a proposal to his comrades from the park: "You know, we are in a classroom for umpteen tedious hours each and every day. The teachers give their sermons, put on airs, and tell us we have to do better. You work like a dog to get a C+, and they say to us it's nothing to be proud of. At times, I believe we are being prepared for slave labor in socialist gulags. So tell me, where is the justice in that? . . . And when do we get a siesta? Indeed, you have got to be kidding. Now as for today, we have a good chance to get out and do something different. Perhaps it is time to go roam and explore the streets of a booming industrial town. Supposing to start with, we go down to Postumville to walk, observe, and mix with factory workers. What do you think about that?"

They all agreed with Shemokoman; and presto, planning—decided. They left the school and slowly walked away, as the cold lake-effect Michigan wind was blowing straight into their faces. It was nice to be free and on the loose if only for a while.

Just then, the ethical comrades heard the unmistakable sound of the famous North American Keebird coming from somewhere. It was: "Kee . . . kee . . . kee . . . Kee . . . -rice-st, it is cold up here."

Stomping Ground

As they walked on the sidewalk next to Southeastern headed for Postumville, Shemokoman glanced across the street at a place with a reputation. It was none other than Smoky Corners. As a rule, this was where the slightly rebellious young men hung out every morning just before going to school. They arrived with a pack of cigarettes neatly tucked under the sleeve of a T-shirt and proceeded to burn up tobacco. Most of the time, those rascals sat on the high stone retaining wall, puffing away, and said nothing at all. It was a way to be thoroughly cool and take the edge off.

Shemokoman thought about all of those nicotine fiends. "Some pretty good guys, I've got to admit. No hoods in the crowd I'm aware of. They just need to finish a couple of smokes before facing imperial teachers. Nothing wrong with that; they have to unwind. One day, I will give it a whirl myself when women are driving me crazy."

Five minutes later, the group of friends arrived at the Main Boulevard. They turned to the left, continued to walk, and thought about finding a place where they could warm up at. They passed the very best root beer stand in the world, but now, it was closed for the season. Reason—freezin'. And there were several small taverns scattered about with plenty of clients inside them. It was fun to drink as much as they could while trying to prove they were sober. So how many people who labored in town watched half of their lives go by in those dark, dingy places? For sure, too many to even consider. "Hey bartender, give me another cold one." The sound of those words had a mighty nice ring to a drinker.

It didn't take long until they wound up at the center of Postumville. Quite the impressive location deep in the heart of a two-party country. People were standing all over the place and stared at the means of production. Ladies and gentlemen followed the rhythm mechanically marching to work. All of the factories were going full tilt as everyone praised the Industrial Revolution. Everything seemed to be right for lunch-bucket tricksters.

Postumville

Battle Creek was a town that was famous for mainly one principal reason: cereal. The mills were running day and night to make those crunchy flakes with wholesome nutrition. It was a tasty comestible product made from corn or oats, or wheat or rice, that everyone ate with milk at breakfast time. Indeed, it was the sort of food that made people feel better and stronger quite a bit longer. They would have less indigestion and truly be glad upon smiling at neighbors. Moreover, whenever a tourist arrived in his town and passed by the cereal buildings, they immediately smelled the pleasant aroma of fresh-cooked grain that was in the air.

So what could be said about breadwinners who were employed in the cereal plants? Well, that was a pretty big deal. They were proud of their jobs and life couldn't get any better. They had social respect, extravagant toys, very nice homes with fine cuisine, and all the other perks of an upscale lifestyle. And if you didn't know better, you might suspect that they were a little conceited. Indeed, they were mostly aloof as if something had spoiled them rotten.

When the factory workers at Postumville came home for dinner each day, they sat at their dining room tables and talked about issues. They spoke about every conceivable thing, including the trivial matters.

You almost could not get a word in edgewise, as everyone had so much to say. The existence of God and virtue of man were rarely if ever considered. And, as time continued to slip away and the evening came to a close, the discussions inevitably circled back to one overwhelmingly favorite topic: cereal. They extolled their trade and took it for granted that nothing could ever affect it. A slight mistake.

First shift, second shift, third shift. Put on a happy face; and, they couldn't stop making the cereal. It was a lucrative business for sure, and Marx would have been disappointed. Who could have ever imagined that the exploitation of workers was finally over. The managers cared about more than a clock as free enterprise prospered exactly as was intended.

The great whistle at the main plant was a symbol of strength and dominion. It always went off at eleven o'clock in the evening to mark the shift change. The masses could hear it for miles around, and it was the sign of a thriving town at its zenith. Regardless of where they were standing or sitting or what they were personally doing, everyone stopped and fell in at attention, and listened with solemn approval. And when it was over, the rank and file were satisfied because the question—What is the meaning of life?—no longer required an answer.

The ethical comrades had to get out of the cold, so they slipped into a warm hideaway that was run by a guy named Hoagy. The smoke in the joint was as thick as could be, but no one had courage to cut it. The Age of Reason was clearly adrift, and common sense was never so distant and needed. After grabbing a booth, they ordered hot drinks and the better part of a morning disappeared at the popular diner. Ronnie the Card was in charge of the grill and cooking like mad for the patrons. "One Early Bird special, comin' up!"

The place was packed with factory workers and men employed at the railroad. Everyone there knew everyone else and strangers were eyed with suspicion. Voices were loud with greetings and lawful directives, advice, directions, friendly satire, and worship. It was still early and people were getting their bearings.

"So, do you like this place?" Anastasia asked the Doctor.

Without any kind of a sweetener, the healer sipped slowly on steaming black coffee. And he looked up and replied, "Yeah, it's all right. But please tell me this, Anastasia. What will we do for the rest of the day? Like Shemokoman was saying, it's time that we ought not just fritter away, so we have to do something constructive. We need a good recommendation."

"Yes, we could use a suggestion," Anastasia agreed. "And I have to admit that it's hard to compare satisfaction like this to feelings I have in a classroom. I understand we must study and learn; however, it's good to be rid of the teachers every so often. There is a limit to persecution in school, and we must take care to not reach it. Thus, we are free for the day to do as we please with a host of practical choices. Perhaps we should go to the Kingman Museum to take in some natural history. Or maybe visit Gull Lake, chop a hole in the ice, and see if the bluegills are biting. What do you think, guys?"

"Well, we have to come up with something," Shemokoman said. "We can't sit here for the rest of the day, just lounging around, or can we? For certain, the god's honest truth is . . . 'Yes, we *can*'; but everyone knows that we shouldn't. And thus, I'll go off on a tangent . . .

"Lately, I notice that too many people are brimming with spite and derision. It seems they are all incredibly bitter and gloomy. Nothing is right; everything's wrong. And of course, they never come up with anything slick on how to improve things. They love to excoriate failings and faults of 'we the convictable people.' What is it on earth ever made them believe that they are superior judges? That they have the right to condemn us? And, that they have the power to slight us? And the saddest part of the whole escapade is that your average man on the street couldn't care less about cynics and grouches. He does not give a hoot about someone with genuine spleen. Like—'It's none of my business.'

"Therefore, in a teetering world that totters too much, it is we who have got to restrain them. Yes, it is we who must boldly confront them. Otherwise, a dreaded Fifth Column of freakish con men will attempt to win over the masses. We have to accept the true nature of man and defeat what is bound to wreak havoc on us."

Decisions, Decisions

A tempest of splendid polemics ensued, the likes of which has never been seen on the planet. Then the Doctor picked up the tab and the group left the diner.

"So, where are we going to now?" Anastasia inquired.

Always Johnny-on-the-spot with a brilliant idea, Alabama made a proposal: "Well, what do you say we go thataway and tour the main cereal plant. It would be nice to see how they make our breakfast. And we have plenty of time to do it today."

It is far too often the case that simple, obvious choices tend to slip by us. Anastasia exclaimed, "Comrade Alabama! You did it again. A man with a knack for the game plan. Your suggestion is perfect."

The Doctor said, "And I will second the motion. We live in a town that is renowned as the preeminent maker of cereal; and yet, we've never set foot in the factory buildings. Yes, it is high time for a visit."

"And we can learn something of value today by observing production in action," Citizen R. added. "I'm sure as can be that there is a way to cut back on the high cost of labor. And the very best part of it all for us is no teachers. Hip hip hooray! For now, we are briefly free of the ornery bastards. There will always be hope for the lot of us all when you, Alabama, are thinking."

The very same man whom everyone called Alabama was embarrassed and casually smiled. There is a time in life when all of us need to hear it from somebody else, no-nonsense approval. But over and over again, far too many people see fit to ignore it.

The Main Plant

So, off they went to visit the main cereal plant. And when they arrived, the usual large crowd of people was at the Visitor's Reception area, waiting to catch the next tour. In spite of the frigid cold weather outside, the place was jam-packed with day-trippers. They came from far and wide in the Land of Michigan and elsewhere just for a chance to observe firsthand the production and management process.

After standing in line for about an hour, the show finally got on the road. Everyone put on their white paper hats just like the factory rats. Nothing like good sanitation; it is the way to control a big nation. A set of instructions was briefly announced, and then the big adventure was underway.

To begin with, they plunged into Building 16, where everyone followed the guide—a middle-aged lady and no spring chicken at that. While very well-spoken, her anxious demeanor revealed that she just couldn't wait until the workday was over. Having delivered the very same spiel hundreds of times in the past, she knew the words by heart and pretentiously smiled at interested people. But when she turned away, her face betrayed something different. For reasons unknown, the woman was given to copious guilt and frustration.

Shemokoman thought, "There are some things you just can't hide."

The tour group started to make its way through all of the shops and departments. The visitors oohed and aahed; it was a truly amazing experience. The lady in charge began her presentation, "It is here at this big loading dock that we receive the shipments of grain. Either corn or rice; or perhaps golden wheat that is harvested out in the Farm Belt. And then we take the grain to the rooms over there, where it remains in storage for a couple of weeks at least. After that, it is put into one of these big cedar vats, where secret ways and means are used for mashing. Indeed, can you believe it? Right now, the grain is cooking away and soon it will be in your favorite grocery store. Wow!"

She went on, "Next, we add malt, hops, and yeast to the grain to continue the wonderful cycle. Perhaps you're getting the drift; it is a riot. Then we wait and wait, and wait until the boss man says it's ready. At which time, to wrap things up and finish the patented process, we dry and press the grain into crispy flakes of cereal. Big machines with conveyor belts move the product into cardboard boxes. And that's the end result of how we hope to turn a profit. It is really just fantastic, like a blessing from Jehovah."

The woman led the group into a special room and continued, "So now, why don't we perform a little taste test. Something that the palate can relate to. Please, come over here with me to try a sample of the cereal. I'm sure that you will find that it's delicious; so good and so nutritious. There now . . . I'll bet you never had a treat as good as that one. Nothing can compare to the cereal that we make here in the factory. And so . . . thank you very much for your attention, and I hope that you enjoyed the tour. You were such a pleasant group. Please, come again to visit us whenever. Good-bye for now, and have a nice day."

The experience was very enlightening. Creative types know what the public wants and will provide it. They sense our every need by probing human passion we are born with and then invent the one and only item we get hooked on. And regarding that particular industry—namely, food production—it didn't take long to change the way that people nourish their bodies. It started with some healers at the San who were not about to let their patients suffer. They simply devised a much better way for people to eat right at mealtime. Shemokoman couldn't dispute it.

The ethical comrades left the main cereal plant and walked back to Waupakisco Park. They passed the Country Market, which was always full of fresh local produce in the summer. Like lettuce, cantaloupe, green onions, potatoes, watermelon, tomatoes, carrots, and corn. Anastasia complained of a headache despite the fact that she felt better than ever. They played some jokes and laughed a lot, and spoke about a big winter storm that had yet to come and paralyze the town. How and what we know is such an esoteric matter, best left to lords a-leaping in the palace.

Shemokoman remarked, "There must be time, from time to time, to clear the mind of all the foolish nonsense. Otherwise, the folly that will plague us is soon bound to overwhelm us. Every so often, we must digress and think about the sort of junk where nothing has an impact. Inconsequentialities, and then some. Yes, be done with all the somber incantations and fly away to shadow stricken empires. And I promise you this, my ethical comrades. You will sleep much sounder afterward because you rose above the wrong behavior. Please listen to me, everyone: I seek to implore you. As philistines insult the very essence of the almsman and infidels are predisposed to preaching, the clerics at the banquet want to hypnotize and vaporize the people. Don't let them do it!"

Along the way, the Doctor chimed in with a few of his comical stories. He joked about red-blooded men and how they are bound to be frugal and seedy. It didn't take long and all of the friends were ecstatically rolling in stitches. They did not even notice that *time*—the great Benefactor—was slowly but surely counting down consecutive hours and minutes.

Proprium of Man

Some problems in life would suggest that they are a charge for the total duration. We cross the bridge and, like it or not, we can't go back to the beginning. It can make one think that all we are and ever will be is the result of a foregone conclusion. We must accept a fate that cannot brook or bar a distinction. That being said . . .

Occasional bouts of despair and malaise were bound to disturb Shemokoman. A common solution for frequent encounters, he felt, was to simply ignore them. But that never worked for most of the time in the long run. The demons returned with more of the same to afflict him. The cause of it all apparently seemed to be trying conditions around him. He had many doubts about knowledge itself and didn't want to bet on the luck of a draw.

Advice from healers was always the same. They told him the problem was nothing to fret, and it would be gone in the morning: "Get plenty of rest, take vitamin pills, and pray to every god that people believe in. That way—you're covered." Whatever happened to helping the patient and providing the right diagnosis? The old status quo didn't have many suitable answers. And medicine men would have to do more than practice their chosen profession.

A quest to repair the damage in him required the personal touch because Shemokoman knew he couldn't depend on a qualified expert for treatment. Their pockets were deep, and honest concern was precluded most of the time. In spite of a trend that was sweeping the land to rely on physicians and shamans, he didn't cave in and allow the play-actors to cheat him. Nobody, save for the Infinite Spirit, was ever aware of what he confronted.

To top it all off, Shemokoman ran into people galore who failed to even perceive him. He knew that invisible men are hard to get noticed. In spite of a wish to be one of the crowd and subject to frequent detection, he had to get used to some kind of a curse that made him, in essence, transparent. Another incurable illness? Maybe. So where is the justice in that?! . . . Although and perhaps, it was only a passing phase due to expire. In any event, the syndrome prevailed upon him, and he had to submit and accept it. Another lovely vignette of his time that he was compelled to contend with.

Central

Even though his time at the junior high seemed to have no end in sight, it didn't last long, and Shemokoman passed every test to finish the program. Then he moved on to an even bigger place of deluxe education called Central. It was a public high school located smack in the center of town. Of course, another massive brick building that was on top of a prominent hill. You had to ascend, go up very high, to get there.

The new institution, as one would expect, provided outstanding instruction. More reading, writing, and numbers; and those numbers were bigger than ever. And just like before, he was ordered to go without having a say in the matter. C'est la vie . . . And, he proudly belonged to the French Club.

Shemokoman rode on the same yellow trolley that took him to school at Southeastern. The driver was also the same; however, the pickup and drop-off times were a little bit different. And there was plenty of talk during most of the trip with all of the neighborhood gang. Albeit, casual conversation. Chitchat, nothing serious. Like . . . "What is a true a priori design?" and "Does God ever take a vacation?"

Upon their arrival at Central, the students from Waupakisco Park had to split up and everyone went their own separate way. The hallways were full of dispassionate men who touted the status of courage. My god, they tried so hard to make the impression. The girls he noticed were wearing a mask, as they were afraid of their beauty. Yes, everyone all decked out according to what was considered in fashion. And a cacophonous tune that students preferred could not have been much more revolting. Nothing but thunderous clatter that was intended to drive someone crazy. As for his preference, Shemokoman remained partial to that old Slavonic chant. It was the sound he adored from his days at a Byzantine altar. Gospodi Pomiluj! Perhaps a monastic lifestyle for him would have been more apropos.

The high school alone could never do justice to learning and being successful. One cannot acquire the critical skills from someone with merely a sheepskin. He needed to visit the rest of the world and glean what he could for improvement. The only dependable teacher with qualifications, talent, and wisdom is *experience*. Moreover, a long time ago the educational system was wrecked by implacable villains. They reckoned that it would be best to manage oblivious minions instead of controlling intelligent shysters.

The high-and-mighty Powers That Be at Central were deep in collusion. One day, they put a spell on Shemokoman; and, they sought to remotely control him. Without his consent, decisions were made while he was avoiding the rage of a plump student body. But it just didn't work as they so dearly expected. He soon figured out how the setup was rigged by a system designed to support him. Notwithstanding the forces arrayed up against him, Shemokoman avoided suspense and skirted the wretched injustice.

"I've seen you lie, cheat, steal, and try murder. You've done everything but begging. Now, get down on your knees and beg" (quote by a guy who meant business).

The Beaten Path

It doesn't take much for someone with smarts to size up your great education. Shemokoman's take on his new school: it resembled most other asylums. From teachers who should have been rocking in chairs to the curriculum meant for a numbskull. Where nothing important he needed was learned, and trivial junk was remembered. Indeed, tautological phrases. It was a venue on earth where he was scheduled to make just another appearance. And he did.

Man, it was so hard at Central to keep and maintain any good concentration. Without exception, there were too many distractions. Like the ungodly slamming of metal wall lockers by students who had a bad temper, and the shouts and screams of hysterical types who came from dysfunctional households, and the endless noise of those haughty whip-crackers who never did stop on account of the dastardly pleasure. Discipline needed improvement. Doesn't it always?

Shemokoman had to take test after test to prove he could guess the right answer. And if that didn't work, the sole of the shoe of a classmate was also an option. He had to be ranked and compared to the rest, and high marks were how he was measured. It was a glaring shortcoming, and he knew it to be a disaster.

He thought, "So if I fail my test in mathematics today, perhaps it is what I intended. To skew up the curve and help out a friend with a physical learning disorder. And yes, I will stay after school in the cold study hall to put in the punishment hours. I know they are trying so hard to forget, but I want to try to remember."

And what was the point of it all during those years of attendance in classes? Preparation for life considered by some as well-rounded as well as essential? No way, it just didn't happen. No one could teach them the rules of the street in a country that favored corruption. And no one provided the lesson that would've helped to get rid of religion. Nobody told them the truth about man who is nothing but sham animation. Verily, too many partisan interests that were competing for partisan profit. Maybe some day he would trade it all in for bread to nourish the children. A righteous approach, regardless of stories in Paris.

It wasn't too wise to contradict irreproachable teachers at Central. They were the ruling elite and everyone knew it. The fact that a student had scant self-esteem and believed all the wrong information granted the teachers remarkable leeway and leverage. They had the absolute power, indeed; and, they were prepared to exploit it. "Insubordination! No, I'm afraid we will have none of that." It was a major mistake to challenge His or Her Highness even on seemingly insignificant issues. Nothing was minor to them; no, everything—major and crucial. So please, "Straighten up . . . Don't get out of line . . . No snide remarks . . . you underling flunky from nowhere." To wind up in trouble meant taking a trip to the principal's office, and a chance to sit down for a chat. Of course, *chat* in French means "cat." The next thing you know you are kicked out of school, onto the street on a permanent basis. A miserable life with nothing to show for it would be the regrettable outcome. "I give you the flexible dummy, and I will give you the serious dropout who can do manual labor in ditches. He doesn't need to be smart or even clean-shaven."

In spite of the rules and stiff penalties regarding illegal behavior, the school was a place with appeal to belligerent scoundrels. Especially those from Northeastern who had a chip on their shoulder as big as an Idaho boulder. The violent thugs were always uptight and causing another disturbance. Maybe they hung around bulletin boards and tore up the latest announcements, or perhaps they demolished a glass trophy case that was crammed full of athletic mementos. Some of them came to Central with dangerous weapons, and they knew how to effectively use them. Civil disobedience was gaining more ground, and many riots erupted to prove it. Shemokoman often sensed a potential for scandal when too many cards appeared on the gambling table. The next thing you know, all hell would break loose, and an otherwise peaceful day was ruined by tragic misfortune.

Notwithstanding some challenging days with rigmarole that vexed him and after three full years of perfect attendance, Shemokoman completed all graduation requirements. Indeed, no one performed any better; he was the best in his class and provided the finest example.

Psych! But now, he was silently thinking that could it be he would possibly miss it? Admittedly, a trove of fond memories remained from it all during his years in the trenches.

It came to pass on a hot June day that Shemokoman went to a big ceremony along with most of his classmates. Some of them just couldn't make it . . . splitting headaches along with the blahs. The solemn event marked the end of the line for choice academics for students who wanted diplomas. And of course, it was called the *Commencement*— right on the button. The graduates were told by a speaker who was dressed up in the latest regalia to "go forth in life, use that God-given talent, and, you will be wealthy and prosper." Alas, Shemokoman knew it was just an elaborate case of hype and deception. There was still so much to do, and he understood it was serious business.

"It is finally time for me to dispense with all theory and generalizations," he thought. "I have to proceed out into the world, and find a niche where no one is doing me favors. Above all else, I should remember: 'Know thyself' . . . backward and forward."

The Bend

Shemokoman slashed his way through critical stages. He tried to do his best in light of what his conscience told him and often faced a crucifixion for the honest effort. If the truth be known— Good god, it's amazing he made it. A couple ten years on the swirling earth for man can be tough and exhausting. The body and soul can undergo every change that one may conceive of. It can happen on old country roads to the north, or on the wood of gymnasium flooring, and also deep inside of the mind to cause a mechanical breakdown. Why must Destiny relentlessly seek to affect and so often degrade us? Of course, a master gives the orders and a servant must fulfill them. While everyone else was having their fun, Shemokoman did what he had to do to get through it.

How does it occur that we as we are, are what we are in the first place? For sure, it requires a wise understanding of dark supernatural forces. And many more senses are needed for comprehension with better perception. Too bad, we have only five. Let us excuse it.

The implications of cause and effect kept Shemokoman up in the evening. Maybe heuristic models in use were impaired but nobody knew it. And why did the autocrats conjure the bloody distortion to only confuse him? What in the world could certain people be thinking? Didn't they have enough on the plate from everyday living to deal with? Yes, they the praetorian heroes; and they, the mockers of virtue; yes, they the insensitive haters of regular people. It was a pagan con artist who claimed to be chaste and insisted, "Your spurious doubt and sacrilege will cause you great sorrow hereafter. Count on it, Shemokoman."

He thought, "The essence of outright fraud by a devious mongrel. Everyone drenched today in deceit, and no one looks back on tomorrow. Lamebrains, most of them."

A massive body of water called Lake Gitchegumee bordered Michigan to the north. It looked more like a sea where people relaxed in sleepy coastal towns and strolled on the beaches. The lake was green and blue, and deep; and the shoreline running every which way stretched out as far as one could possibly see. There never was a single soul who said they didn't love it, and that's the truth.

Shemokoman decided to take a vacation to that very lake. Twelve years in public schooling can take its toll on anyone and leave them somewhat weary. Thus, he packed a bag with all of his gear—like tanning cream and extra clothes—and didn't tell a soul where he was going. It doesn't hurt to wander off and be alone when the body needs rejuvenation.

As twilight fell from the sky to the earth in silence and settled around him, Shemokoman was wading in water on the magnificent coastline. He thought about the challenges that faced him. And he started talking to himself, the sort of chat you need to have when purpose is awry but not forsaken.

He said, "So how can I improve myself, and what should be accomplished? There must be consolation; and what good can I succeed in? Truth for the sake of truth is not the answer, as there should be a useful application. Furthermore, as time does right by those who brook and thus will then embrace it, I must concede that life can never be what was expected. For the most part, all that I was told—Believe!—was total fabrication, made up by the faint-of-heart afraid of truth, despite the fact that it was all around them. As for now, I need to clean my scruffy boots and set my sights above the broken line of demarcation."

7

Mass of a Common Man

Too Many Choices

Men are encouraged to climb big mountains and go as high as they can to reach the top. On that account alone, they are exalted. Although, which mountain should they choose at first, and where is the beginning? It was far easier long ago when all was set in stone at birth for most of the average people. A Smith would be a smith, case closed, and no one dared refute it. Family tradition directed the glorious effort of labor and other important arrangements. However, as for today, most men start out with pockets that are begging for attention, and to find a place beyond the sun requires luck and patience. To be a true success, we must go out and firmly take it. And if you do not make the grade, then you're a good-for-nothing stupid loser.

Moreover, what if you live on the sweeping Great Plains where mountains don't prevail? Must one look for lofty summits where they're simply nonexistent? Give chase to utter madness? Or perhaps you roam in the grassy lowlands of the beautiful Midwest. Again, what should be the right approach? Will you search in vain to find a peak where they never towered in the heavens to begin with? Certainly not. In cases such as these, the answer is fairly straightforward. One must try another way and opt to reconsider. There is always choice for any man who is bold and willing. By the way, you really needn't quench a thirst by stopping at the taphouse, as it's a waste of time and will delay you.

Shemokoman did not ease up in pursuing the cool premonitions. He never encountered a difficult snag that made him resign, buckle under. But now, the distinction between all virtue and vice began to fade and annoy him. Painstaking efforts to resolve baffling issues seemed pointless and wide of the margin. Questions of any importance defied a clear and evident answer. How do we put up with such incontinent straits and knavish conundrums? With so many years of investigation now under his old leather belt, he couldn't afford to go for broke and risk what little insight had been gathered.

Optional Knowledge

It came to pass that Shemokoman enrolled in an institution of higher learning in Battle Creek called the Community College. Nobody forced him to go; rather, he felt that it would be prudent. It was another brick building on top of a hill, staffed by the finest teachers that gold and silver could lure. He took a bunch of courses to learn about the fine and liberal arts as well as anything else that could prove to be beneficial.

When he desired to mingle a bit, Shemokoman was apt to call on strangers. Those benign, effusive types were often playing euchre in the student union instead of at a lesson in the classroom. And so, his circle of friends was constantly changing. Each day some new ones made the scene, while loyal cronies from the past proved to be two-faced as hell if there should be a reason. And every soul knew what it was, and no one had to spell it out for lightweights.

One day when it was early in the morning as students guzzled coffee to revive their senses, congestion on the campus of the college reached an apex. People felt the pressure as the place was overcrowded, and frustration peaked when bodies blocked the one and only exit. There has to be an egress to relieve the concentration of compression. Indeed, more and more so much of the time, the undergrads put up with outright bedlam. They had to stomach nonsense till another dean could intercede to end it. Perhaps a novel synthesis from Grecian dialectics isn't what they really had expected.

"No wonder so many bambinos today are wretched and down in the doldrums," Shemokoman thought. "A plot was hatched, they sprang the trap, and ancient souls were sent away repining to Gehenna. They say that wisdom comes with age. But sometimes—people just get old and that is it."

A Happening at Goguac Lake

Late in the month of October, Shemokoman was with some friends in a home on the north side of town. It was your typical Michigan weather outside during that time of year, cool and drizzly. They kicked around some rough ideas about their many choices for excitement. Finally, it was decided to go to Goguac Lake and have a sailing party. Yes, to frolic and dance in a magical land with all of those glistening raindrops.

Everything was in the boat: provisions, oars and anchor, and carousers. They put the craft into the water and floated away from the shoreline. With ample wind behind them now, they drifted on that picturesque lake through eerie mist in silence and seclusion.

After a while, Shemokoman noted, "Well, well, my friends. In light of our location and potential for a rainstorm as well as water depth right here below us . . . I think that—all things considered—we should rule out fishing for today. Besides, we don't have any poles, no bait or tackle box equipment. And I am sure as I can be that the fish are spooked by now by the noise we have been making. Therefore, I'd like to suggest something different. Why don't we take a swim and splash around in such refreshing water, and rejoice as if we bite the dust tomorrow. How about that?"

By a clear consensus, the proposal was accepted. The group of friends prepared to take a dip to stimulate and cheer them up, and please the alter ego with some horseplay. Indeed, it would get their blood a-flowing. Then, one by one, each person dove into the lake, where they treaded water and exclaimed, "It is freezing." Everyone was laughing . . . playing games, and dunking other chipper heads around them. And finally—after taking a deep breath along with a hefty jump to propel him—Shemokoman leapt from the side of the craft, pierced the surface of the lake headfirst, and plummeted to the cryptic nether regions. Little did he realize that . . .

On that particular day, for reasons unknown to anyone human, the God of the Lake was in a bad way and fuming. Angry as all get out. Maybe he argued with some other god; or perhaps a much bigger spirit badly maligned him. Who knows?! In any event—as Shemokoman descended, the indignant immortal spotted and then viciously attacked him. *Someone* was in the wrong place at the wrong time, and for sure there was going to be trouble.

With green lightning bolts shooting out of both eyes and raging like Jove was on fire, the god seized the man with a powerful grip, shook him senseless, twisted him into knots and threw him ferociously downward. Shemokoman crashed into the bottom of the lake with an excruciating jolt. His head hit first and caused the neck to suffer heavy trauma. He tossed and turned, and thrashed about inside a cloud of muck and silt among the weeds that filled the space around him. For sure, it wasn't pretty.

And as if that weren't enough, the angry spirit grabbed hold of a long shiny trident, which he ran straight through the victim's neck. He wrenched the spear to right and left to try to slay the fellow. It seemed as if Shemokoman was on the verge of giving up the ghost.

Thus, with almost nothing left in him to mount a decent struggle, Shemokoman did what he could to carry on the battle. Tough job—fighting a god on his own turf. For several more hours, the confrontation persisted; until finally, a passion for life and the will to survive helped to save the warrior. The God of the Lake lost his hold on the man, who swam to safety up through murky water. And with a final ounce of energy that remained inside his body, Shemokoman pulled himself up and over the side of the boat and into the bow of the craft.

The injured man lay flat on his back, degraded and barely conscious. He stared up at the sky in pain for such a long time. The rain continued to fall from the clouds in a slow, steady drizzle. It struck his face and aching limbs; it felt so good, he fought capitulation. He thought about his comrades and the friends he had in Waupakisco Park. Then he remembered that great Slavic prince who fought at Borodino long ago on a cold battlefield. The sensation he was feeling was the same. And he considered the fate of ancestral kindred and how he could never be different. A parade of men through yesteryear who could not contain the searing passion. Ergo, an event like today was sure to occur for each generation that followed.

So now it was he who endured the great tribulation. His turn in the ranks at the front line to take on a bloodthirsty rival. And how did he really get by in detestable combat? . . . And was there a sensible plan of martial engagement? With dozens of hazy directions to take, a reduction of woe wasn't likely. Anarchy is always the greatest in hostile matters of fray and contention; but that didn't honestly matter. For Shemokoman, there was no need to avoid a disastrous outcome. He knew all of the answers long beforehand and set up a mental formation. Thus, the fighting was basically over even before it was time to get started. His blurry eyes that were tired and sore appeared to be gradually closing.

Shemokoman had to save his life all by himself and pronto. The sheer devastation sustained in the row could easily prove to be fatal. All of the others were gone from the lake; of course, they couldn't be trusted. They were the genuine rascals; and, they were not who he could count on. A long time passed by as Shemokoman didn't have strength to move in the least. But eventually, he stood up on his own two feet—the sign of a freewheeling man, made his way onto dry land, and searched for the care of a healer. Within a few hours, he'd managed to locate the medical help required.

Regarding the terrible wound to the neck that he bore in the heat of the battle, Shemokoman knew he would suffer with that for the rest of a natural lifetime. So what did he do to be worthy of such an endowment? And why was he forced to put up with a truculent monster? Alas, it was one of the frequent ill-fated events that we wish could've just never happened. But they do.

Ecstasy

Battle Creek had its own brand of charisma. And thousands of mighty good men and women managed to fully enjoy it. Most of them were born, grew up, and passed away inside of, or near, the municipal limits. Like serfs on a sugar plantation, they rarely traveled far away; there simply was never a reason.

It was a booming town with industrial strength and other diversified business. Above all else, there was production; workers made things. Free enterprise flourished according to how competition and markets directed. And at the end of a day, laden with toil and effort, the proletariat sat in big easy chairs at home, contented with what was accomplished. Arbeit macht nicht frei; although it's a pretty good bet for gratification.

To a great extent, Shemokoman felt like most of the other townspeople. He had no desire to leave Battle Creek; no justification existed. He liked it there, and notions of disappointment were seldom considered. But as for the scoundrels who left on a permanent basis, well, they were the ultimate traitors. What could be worse than deserting your family, friends, and a wonderful homeland. Indeed, a capital crime.

There were open-air markets, amphitheaters with concerts, dime and department stores, auditoriums to stage a performance, haberdasheries, outdoor cafés and restaurants, a big opera house, plenty of schools, churches of every denomination, bars and nightclubs, millinery shops, bookstores and apothecaries, a couple of hospitals and the "San," an amusement park, the Youth Building, a public library, delicatessens with epicurean treats, and a booming financial sector. You couldn't go wrong in a town at its best; it was a special location.

A slim dapper gent was frequently spotted wearing tuxedo and top hat. To have a nice treat, the Ritzee was there for a malt and your steak plate dinner. Trolleys and trains were running on time to take the passengers to locations near and far. Public transportation was always the best, in spite of swinish men who would decisively destroy it. An army of soldiers from nearby Camp Custer flooded the streets to flirt with the prettiest girls in all of the world. No, you just wouldn't lose if you were a part of the ethnic diverse population. At least, for most of the people.

Adding one final touch to the rest of it all, a wide, lazy river flowed right through the center of town. Its water was clear, and pure and clean, far from being polluted. The left and right banks were teeming with men and women in trendy apparel. They jostled for space and attention, and they were looking for incoming signals. Reciprocal signs will brighten the day for any lone downtrodden soul. Of course, nobody was able to fake it.

Shemokoman mused, "I'd have to believe that the status quo at this place has never been better. There simply are no major problems that are producing commotion and trouble. Everything going their way and no one ashamed of Cain they are raising. Some day they will surely be taken to task—no doubt, the indulgence and pomp will truly be done for. And that is the truth."

Confusion at the Dance

A Friday arrived; it was cold as the dickens outside in January. A strong wind was blowing and gusting with sleet that was crashing right into their bodies. The ground was covered in two feet of snow with drifts that were up to the waistline. Shemokoman finished up work for the day at the college and walked out of his very last classroom.

While strolling along in a hallway, he bumped into a female friend whose name was Persephone Quick. He learned from her that there was a dance scheduled for that very evening in the Main Concert Hall on the campus.

"Perfect," Shemokoman thought to himself, "as I have nothing to do for the rest of the day. I will go to the dance with a few of my comrades and see what the hip generation is up to."

He thanked the woman for the information, said he'd see her later on, and then went home to get ready.

The tuna fish wrap was a pretty good meal; no time for a typical supper. And then, Shemokoman prepared for the social occasion. While playing some tunes on the old phonograph and sipping on hot black Georgian tea, he donned a gray woolen suit and selected his high button shoes to serve as the footwear. Such sartorial savoir faire! After using a mirror to check out the stylish raiment, he slipped into a full-length black suede coat and promptly went out for the evening.

A short while later, a trio of men from Waupakisco Park showed up at the Main Concert Hall at the community college. The Doctor and Major LD decided to go as well. After getting a stamp on the back of their hands and going inside the building, they shuffled around in a pretty big room that was dark and crowded with people. A profusion of light was flashing and flaring all over the stage with musicians. The sparkling colors and special effects caused you to feel like you'd entered a new constellation. It created a certain mind-blowing effect for all of the youthful stargazers.

For quite a long time, the place was a drag. No conversation except for occasional greetings. You know—the simple mandatory sweet pleasantries with someone who must be acknowledged. While everyone focused on everyone else with hope of equivalent action, Shemokoman and his comrades leaned up against an empty wall to passively watch all of the current proceedings. Indeed, they did nothing at all but observe without even moving or blinking. Impassive behaviors don't go out of fashion.

The band was in tune, practicing scales, and soon they were playing the music. Not the best sound in the world; however, everyone knew they were trying. Shemokoman sought to conceive an idea but was unable to hear himself think.

He watched the performance and pondered, "Ah, yes—the tasteful musicians. So please, tell me, sir . . . Has there ever been any courtly ménage that even remotely compared to these fellows? I think not. And where could they have possibly come from? . . . And, where will they go when they're finished? With lutes and a drum, and horns and a dream, there must be a plausible angle. And who do the prodigal minstrels want to inspire? Well, a god only knows about that. They play the hysterical song to stagger the senses while the masses get all whipped up into a frenzy. No wonder the commoners love it, like a narcotic for squelching awareness. A flash of finesse and surely, my sensitive cohort, the heavy excitement is too much to honestly handle. But now, I am restless and need to think over some ponderous personal issues. I wish that just for once, I could come to a place like this and truly enjoy it. But I don't. Hmm . . . There must be a good explanation."

As the crowd was swarming and spinning around on the hard tile floor of the Main Concert Hall, Shemokoman said to the Doctor, "So please tell me, sir. Is that—" And he pointed at dark silhouettes close by that were twisting and doing the boogie. "Is that what you really call dancing? Or did I lose my bag of marbles with new perry shooters? Something is funny; I feel like my judgment is haywire."

The Doctor replied, "Don't know, Shemokoman. Maybe it is, or maybe it's not. Everything's different these days according to Hoyle. In any event, I can tell you this much. If they continue to gyrate like that, I will have plenty of business in just about eight or ten years because they will all be in need of a healer with potions and tonics. Their joints and bones will plainly require a good realignment and treatment."

Shemokoman knew that the Doctor was right and flipped him a ducat for insight. Then he continued to look at the revelers tear up the bustling dance floor. He thought, "Isn't the purpose of people who dance to engage in the elegant movement? . . . And to follow some sort of a pattern? Of course. And what do I see with my very own eyes? Nothing but certified chaos. And that is the truth. I simply can't even describe it. A disorderly mob of show-offs who think there is value in faking dementia. It is a sign of the times that we are confronted with tripe and preposterous carriage."

By and by, Shemokoman decided to take a walk. He told his ethical comrades that he would soon be back and departed. And while strolling along in the dark surroundings, a peculiar dull sensation came over his body. He couldn't make it out at first, and wondered if his feelings were an artifice intended to mislead him. Could it be that he was out of touch, and what he felt was just another mind-set? Whatever.

Suddenly, a Voice from Afar deep inside of his head commenced with a delicate whisper: "Well, well. Shemokoman. Here we are once again inside of a dance hall. Have you nothing better to do on a Friday night than to destroy it with aimless charade in this noisy grotto? You should be home and reading a book, watching a play at the theater, or with a woman you love baking bread in a galley-type kitchen. You're losing more ground every day and surely you know it. So where are you going to this time, my friend? . . . Some place where you sense excitement? Still counting on revelling in pleasure? Give it a break and try to relax, be realistic and thoughtful. By the way, what is the deal with so many more classes and teachers? The men in Waupakisco Park who are old and wise have told you before that your only business is labor. Get a job, damn it! And where will you be in, let's say, twenty years? My goodness, let's pray that everything falls into place. But don't get your hopes up. You're part of a scheme that will never break big and the curtain is already falling. And of course, it goes without saying that you need to remember the Golden Rule; for sure, it will help in the future. Aahh . . . Shemokoman. Your effort is righteous, sublime, and befitting; and you will never be bothered by conscience. But please, just make the adjustment, or there could be woe in the end for one of my better-respected disciples. Think about it. Will you?"

What in the world was that? Shemokoman felt just a little bewildered. A message from somewhere inside of his mind that a rational spirit delivered. Yes, he was really affected by the effect of a clear admonition. In a rush every day, hobnobbing with friends and hearing the riveting lecture; indeed, there was plenty to gain, but something was missing.

When the dance was over, like everyone else the men from Waupakisco Park left the campus. They made their way to a favorite coffee shop in the oldest part of town called Verona. It was a quaint little joint alongside the road with traces of gangster nostalgia. And no, it wasn't that long ago when men who were downright God-tearing dabbled in crime they were proud of committing. A still in the basement was still being used to make a few barrels of booze, for special occasions. And yes, three X's were marked on each of the jugs to account for the taste of the product.

A hostess seated the men, and they ordered hot drinks that were served. They talked about everything under the moon for two or three slow-moving hours. Verily, those were the nights that seemingly lasted forever, when no one expected a sun to come up in the morning.

"It is nice to spend time at a hangout like this where we can relax with a parley," Shemokoman noted. "Tasty food, strong drink, a sociable ambience, and nobody causing trouble. Alas, of late nowadays, there is too much crime in this town that is constantly edgy. It would be best to impose martial law and sanction a very strict curfew. After all, freedom's but one of the sordid ploys that people are taking for granted."

Unlikely Interlocution

For some strange reason while he was at the college, Shemokoman experienced a transformation of body and mind. It is hard to say what really occurred to cause a change in the fellow. However, this much was apparent. The entire episode was notably painful and puzzling. He went through a stretch of irregular time in a daze and highly unstable, and nobody knew about his defective condition. Shemokoman just couldn't focus. And there were times when he thought the whole nine yards would ignite and blow up in his face; but, it didn't.

During the hours of daylight, he managed to put up a fabulous front. It was a challenge for him to get up out of bed and stick to a standard routine. Although he did it. He was busy with chores, appointments, gymnastics at the Great Recreation Hall, and shopping for food at the grocery market. His performance in school was nothing too swift; he showed up each day in the classroom, took a few notes, and completed the homework assignments. Superior marks and any cum laude for the time being had so little meaning.

But after the sun went down in the evening, the story concerning behavior was radically different. Shemokoman was a drifter. He followed a road that zigged and zagged and led to unusual havens. Making the rounds at apartments in town was much of the usual pattern. It wasn't a ride that didn't include a lot of outlandish adventure. His life resembled a merry-go-round, constantly moving and spinning; there was no way to avoid getting flustered and dizzy. Some bodies got on while others got off, and those who wanted to give it a go bewailed the trouble it caused them. You couldn't stand up to remain in one place, as every Newtonian force in the world was working directly against you. Thus, wherever he went, Shemokoman found a good seat on the floor and didn't say much about nothing. He hung around friends who joked and cajoled about devils who tried to enthuse them.

And behold! One night when he was alone at a dive where sailors quite often were drinking their liquor and cursing, the walls in the room started talking. "Greetings, lonely wayfarer! Old friend of the seadogs and lubbers. Yes, we are speaking to you—Shemokoman. Glad you dropped by for better or worse; you'll know on the morrow which is it, of course. What have you been up to lately? Most likely, searching for truth in mysterious quarters. How commendable! . . . The trades are behind you as always. And we are aware of your struggle concerning a stable somatic condition. What—a—mess; but, please, do not ever worry. Like it or not, you're about to get well in two or three months after Easter. Destiny says that you are a trump with fortune ahead in the future. As for now, you should drink up a tankard of luscious dark rum that was made in Jamaica for pirates. It is holy and good for the spirit, and also the harrowing pang of the horrors. Here, let us pour you the likes of a nice little hooker. Healers prescribe and consume it themselves and say that libations are good for the ailing patient. Like you, right now, with your illness. And let us remind you, Shemokoman. This place is an isle with no expectation of cutting you loose until daybreak. So kick back and relax, and enjoy it. You are marooned for a while with us in the midst of a buccaneer coil."

With justifiable apprehension, Shemokoman listened to words and advice from walls that had always been silent. But after hundreds of millions of years since the dawn of creation, he was the one they finally wanted to talk to. He pondered, "What do I perceive? These walls shouldn't talk. Perhaps it is I who is plastered. Although I can always rely on my God-given senses."

As he continued to roam in community places, Shemokoman noticed that too many people were yakking. He tried very hard to decipher the words; quite often, he bailed on listening. And he had to be somewhat indifferent, or else the torment could soon overtake him.

Composed and cool as a cucumber amid the din of a loud conversation, he stood passively by and nothing at all was remembered. No great loss.

In spite of the fact it was hard to recurrently function, Shemokoman looked at the sky and the earth, and concluded that he was between them. That in itself accounted for something astounding. He didn't muse about parapsychology, or the occult, or constraints of equivocal meaning. He was no clever savant, walking on ground that was holy and higher. Broken behavior is always a hoot, but it will not go on forever. Thus, his resolute faith was never extremely affected; it was all a part of the much bigger picture. And oh, what a joy it was for a while to see a world where nothing is basically normal. Where others continued to dally and stray to eke out a type of existence. But eventually, he would come to a point where the fantasy fades and illusion is only remaining. Many are they who will try to elude what unavoidably has to affect and reform them.

Ideality

Although you can even be feeble and frail, many people live to a ripe old age. They have a shortage of physical troubles along with appropriate medical care. As a rule, they do not purloin or lift any secret advantage; they are just lucky . . . that's all. And then we consider the rest of the gang—those who are destined to cope with problems without any slight intermission. Every day they're alive is another colossal dilemma. Constantly searching for ways to get better; there must be a magical power. Enough is never enough when looking for cures to honestly help them. So much pain. One thing is for sure: those people must live to accept and enjoy many quiet and sad celebrations. It is the truth.

After a couple more years went by him in sequence, Shemokoman managed to quell his gloomy Dark Ages. He felt better with each passing day, and he maintained a standard routine that changed very little. It was a good thing for him. He continued to go to the Great Recreation Hall on the north side of town, where he now engaged in the chivalrous sport of fencing. "En garde!" There is nothing like pivots and parries with flexible foils to fully suppress the plague of a bothersome quandary.

On one particular day during the springtime, he completed some business at school and left the community college right after lunchtime.

He walked slowly along on empty old lanes on his way to go home as usual. And as he approached the lagoon that was inside of the plush Irving Park, he noticed a woman sitting on grass, silently staring out over the dark placid water.

Shemokoman gazed directly at her and she smiled at him, consequently. So now, it was time to commence with some casual chitchat tête-à-tête. He approached the woman and said, "Good afternoon, ma'am. Don't believe I ever noticed you here before. Could it be you just moved into town?"

The woman had long dark hair that fell to her shoulders. A face with high cheekbones, exotic green eyes, and a smooth satiny-white pure complexion. She wore a pink-and-blue dress made of fine cotton lace; she had to be righteous and modest. The shoes were off and beside her.

She glanced down for a moment, then quickly back up, and while looking at him she responded, "No, as a matter of fact, I have lived in this town for a good many years . . . like, all of my natural lifetime. Just never came here before—somehow overlooked it."

"Hmm," he reacted politely, and then inquired, "May I introduce myself?"

She provided a good affirmation and so he stated, "My name is Shemokoman. Nothing more, nothing less. It is what everyone calls me, save for the sharks with a case of amnesia. And you are?"

"My name is Catherine . . . Catherine Hesse," she answered. "But most of my friends just call me Katya. How do you do, Shemokoman. It is a pleasure to meet you."

"Same here," he responded sincerely. "And it has got to be nice to have such a beautiful name that is clearly enchanting. May I join you?"

"Please do," she replied.

So, Shemokoman sat down beside the brand-new acquaintance. They talked for a while—her style was chaste, unassuming, and one or two hours were idled away in the meantime.

Among other things, he told her, "You know, Katya, there was a day not that long ago when a starry-eyed boy came to this place during winter with his ethical comrades. He and the gang on a cold afternoon, with snow flurries swirling about in the air, walked straight through a town that was brimming with action to get here. And for most of the day and into the night when the streetlamps glowed with sparkling halos around them, they blissfully skated on smooth, shiny ice reflecting the wooded surroundings by this lagoon. Oh, how I wish that I could go back there to join them, for only a moment or two to admire and see them, and to tell them how I am the one who was fated to miss them. There never was any time or a place where humanity had it much better, when that boy was alive and turning the tables on fortune. It was the best—and that is the truth. Life in the trenches was perfect for Battle Creek people."

She smiled at him. "It must be nice to be the last romantic. To live inside the dome without a need to tantalize or rearrange things. And watch the years go by but not go with them. Where spirits never vex mankind and every single trace we apprehend is dwelling with them. The opposite of what we sense inside the misty realm of our existence. Shemokoman: you must keep it up, I want to listen."

He did.

Finally, Catherine said that she had an appointment at a styling salon in town. So they finished up the small talk, agreed to meet in a couple of days, and parted.

It didn't take long to figure her out. He looked into the eyes and found a story. Judging by the brief encounter, Shemokoman knew that the woman was no stray cat who was looking for someone to lean on. Catherine had sophistication, sagacity, and wherewithal about the things in life that truly matter. Her gentle mood and mild disposition exposed the essence of culture. She clearly rose above a threshold and would serve to be a paragon of gender.

Shemokoman met with Catherine again the following Monday. They had lunch at a Greek café and burned up many hours talking through the afternoon. Indeed, there was so much in common. Like art appreciation and an appetite for fine cuisine, the awe of metaphysics, and a yen to study history of the world.

"What is it that makes somebody we meet on a random occasion so special?" he wondered. "Perhaps, nothing more than a gleam in the eye and the ineffable sway of emotion."

Sin

It was just after lunch and Shemokoman was at the public library, drafting a speech that he had to give the following day to some cord-wainers. The business of making fine shoes requires considerable specialized knowledge. The consummate shape and a durable heel are signs of a highly skilled master. Just ask any woman, and she will tell you.

Catherine happened to be there as well and spotted the studious comrade. She crossed the room and went straight to his table.

"Buenos días, Shemokoman," she said. "And how are we doing today?"

"Very good, Katya," he replied. "Just going over my text of a lecture that needs to be done by tomorrow. I have to inspire those fellows who want to design and make stylish footwear. They need to believe that what they do is important to so many people. They've chosen to work in a difficult trade; female ire quite often can be unforgiving."

"And anything new besides that?" she asked.

"Not really," he said.

The lady sat down beside him to work on her own very personal business. She was partial to the liberal arts and focused on rhetoric, grammar, and logic. It seemed like the right thing for her to study, as too many people forget that they belong to a much greater genus. It is called humanity. And thus, for three to four hours they sat together, not saying a word to each other. Finally, both of them finished their work for the day and developed a plan for dinner.

That evening, Shemokoman and his acquaintance arrived at a small Ukrainian pub overlooking the river that flowed through town. A hostess seated them at a round wicker table in a portico next to a large bay window. They ordered a bottle of sweet white wine and Slavic hors d'oeuvres to snack on. Stuffed mushrooms and red caviar on Black Sea bread were the luscious delectable treats. Shemokoman looked outside. Scores of people were rushing about in the maze of sidewalks below.

He noted, "Yes, they unequivocally are just little people. Friedrich was right about that. Although I have so little doubt that every last one of them knows what it means to be bigger."

Catherine was quiet, looking around and pondering spiritual issues. Then she said, "You know, Shemokoman, I was just thinking. And thus, there is danger aplenty. Now, aside from that, please, can you tell me the truth about something perplexing? Namely, do you believe in sin?"

Shemokoman stared out the window at a man below who was preaching the End of the World. Repentance! . . . For vile offenders . . . Or, at least, an Act of Contrition. And who really knows if a biblical

Armageddon might truly be coming? Do not rule it out; we never can tell about scriptural writing and presage. Then he turned to her and replied, "Yes, Katya. I do believe in sin. Although it is not what a pontiff will teach you."

The woman was piqued by the answer. "So what do you mean? I don't understand. Please, tell me the point you are making."

As always, in dealing with issues like that he answered in definite detail: "Well, sin, so they say, is humanity's way to violate holy commandments. It is the act of a man who, in defiance of God, does what he wants according to feelings. And for sin to be sin, it has to be sin the commission of which is intended. Some people are driven by instinct, you know; such is the luck of a madman. The commandments were given to us by men who claimed to have mystical knowledge. Men who believed that they parleyed with God and knew what he wanted for humans. And so, they gave us the law that they insisted was straight from the Gracious Almighty. Hence, we have to obey their commandments that are stored up inside of the Ark because if we don't, it is sinful."

He went on, "You see, for Christians who live in a storybook world, their God is the infinite goodness. He is the one who says to reject the deliberate doing of evil. And he is the one who says to avoid the allure of a devil's temptation. Their God is the one who says to follow his word to the letter and then some. For he is the one who will send you to hell if you are obscene and deserve it. He has legitimate power; their God is a generous master; and he is the source of existence. Just do as you're told, don't step out of line, and everything soon will be rosy. It sounds too much like a cult to me, and that is a little bit scary.

"So, Katya, how do we actually sin to break the commandments that seek to control us? Well, the answer is not so confusing. We simply react in a natural way when somebody plots to assault or critically harm us. Or, we do what we must on account of the fact that to do otherwise is abnormal. And turning the other cheek—so good!—a way to get hurt but stay in his personal favor. Compassion is nice and forgiveness a must when villains are plotting to slay us. When you think about it, could anything ever be much more bizarre than the gist of *his* sermons and teachings? I think not. And that is the truth."

After pausing to take a small sip of his wine, Shemokoman continued, "Now, unfortunately, something is wrong and they are not right—the sages and prophets who gave us the holy commandments.

Liars! . . . Liars! . . . Pants on fire; all of them, terrible swindlers. They're out for themselves with fingers that itch and want to enslave you and I. And when it is time, they cut and run like bats from unbearable hellfire. Katya, nothing we know of can ever be due if it goes against the grain of legitimate reason. Thus, I must remind the souls around us that the commandments in the Good Book are a scheme that lowly charlatans concocted.

"Now, we need to believe that a god is no sacred announcer of great proclamations. Jurisprudence has nothing to do with anything tethered to spiritual systems. Therefore, you may ask and expect to find out: What is this thing called sin? Well, it is the wanton contempt of a natural law where man is devout and supreme. And what type of law is that? you respond. To which, I would say with assurance: It is a secular, moral, terrestrial law for us that requires compliance. It is a purely intuitive, righteous array that is given to man by the conscience. Yes, the conscience delivers advice and guidance for people to steadily follow. And, such knowledge belongs on tablets of worldly canons.

"The venial sins are minor of course, and as such of little importance. The big mortal sins reveal the appearance of evil on earth by offenders. You have to be mad to commit them; they are high crimes of the very worst order. And there is no such thing as original sin, and Eden was not the beginning. Although many zealots in Michigan here still cling to a myth and believe it. Good fiction can be analgesic; and, it is getting so easy to come by. And sin has nothing to do with a man on a cross because of his preachings. It was one hell of a prank for people who trembled with fear to honestly fall for. So easy to pray on the way to the big coliseum. Furthermore, for all the believers among us—yes, there is a hell for the sinner.

"So what do I mean, and what shall we draw in conclusion? Well, Katya. There will always be men who cannot control their lust for outrageous behavior. They are the fools, devoid of remorse, a scourge of perennial sinners. Everywhere walking, planning, and stalking another ingenuous victim. They eat and sleep, and steal the fresh air and take what is yours and mine because they are evil. Some of the finest homes in this town even belong to those culprits. And they often appear at the bench with counsel to have a good laugh on the masses. The shrewd insidious men in black robes ensure that the villains never receive even a minor conviction. Although in the end when the hour is near, you can find this contemptible breed—the heretics—in filthy crimson rooms with painted harlots. They lie in the beds that reek of their terrible vices, writhing and wailing thanks to poetical justice. And for these nefarious men—the lowest of wretches for sure, it is during those very last moments of life that they are taken to task and tremendously suffer. The seconds that turn into infinite time with torture and permanent anguish. 'Are we having fun yet?' the holy Creator will taunt them. 'Ten Hail Marys will do you no good. Your chance to do penance has vanished.' And so they are punished and burn forever in flames that cannot be extinguished. Oh my, Katya—the sinful men are just horrible monsters."

Catherine pondered the speech, and finally said, "And have you noticed that sinners will often reach up as they die out of sheer desperation, hoping that angels will pull them away and spirit them off into heaven. Idiots."

"Je suis d'accord," he replied.

Lamentation

One evening, Shemokoman was at Catherine's home on the south side of town near Beadle Lake. It was raining cats and dogs outside, with jagged flashes of lightning and peals of thunder. They drank cup after cup of hot green tea—from a pot with a needlepoint cozy—and played backgammon for several hours. After she won about ten or twelve games straight, he told her that women are wicked, conniving, and lucky.

Catherine decided to get some fresh air, so she went out the front door, walked down the steps, and stood on a wet empty sidewalk. The storm had passed, the sun had set, and a full moon was on the eastern horizon. She looked up at the evening sky and gazed at a pair of big gray clouds that were rushing across the heavens. A shooting star streaked for a second or two, and she made a big wish that would always be her little secret.

Shortly thereafter, Shemokoman took a break from what he was doing. He went to a window and looked outside; he couldn't make out very much because of the darkness. He pondered the Circle of Time and how it related to chance and a sure thing. Albeit, he couldn't attribute a wonderful turn of events exclusively to simple aberration. He noticed Catherine standing alone and concluded, "Indeed, she is quite the lady who knows too much about playing your classical board games."

A few more minutes slipped by, and then Catherine started back. She paused for a while to stand on the porch, then opened up the creaky screen door and went inside. Shemokoman was now on a red satin sofa with his feet propped up on a matching hassock.

She sat down beside him and said, "You know, Shemokoman . . . despite the fact I didn't check to see if you were looking, I know that you were watching me when I was just out front. And how can that be so? Hmm? Hmm? . . . You may wonder. Well, you see, it's because us women—we know everything. It is a blessing and also a burden. Although, and of course, my goodness! Who do I think I'm kidding? Women. What have we ever accomplished? And what have we done that is noble? And . . . what have we made that is awesome? Without further ado, I will simply tell you. Nothing. Not one single thing."

Then she paused and went on, "The tale of man is a story of men. It is they who have shaped the world. It is they who are truly superior; and, it is they who have all of the talent. And it is they who are clever and mighty. All famous leaders, inventors, writers, composers, pioneers, scientists, philosophers, builders, painters, warriors, and tyrants . . . yes, even the tyrants, they were all men. Not one blasted woman to speak of anywhere among them. And why are we so frail, weak, and helpless? Indeed, why have we not managed to achieve a lick of greatness? I'll tell you why. Because all we do both day and night, without an interruption, is to think about the men that we have spoiled. How we should tease and support them, and how we must constantly serve them. We simply cannot get you out of our minds; my word, what a deadly obsession. Our only job is to propagate, to coddle, and care for the species. And that's about it, short and sweet. The way it's been and the way it will be forever and ever for certain. Such is the fortune of women today, as nobody sees the impossible effort we're making. So, do you agree, Shemokoman?"

Catherine now looked down; she was dejected. Perhaps the gist of what she said was way too much to handle. Shemokoman tried to comfort her and spoke up to the woman, "You know, sometimes you think too much. And then you get into trouble."

She smiled at him to acknowledge a mirthful effort, and said, "Shemokoman, you are my friend. More so than the rest, and you know there is only illusion. We live in a world of perilous myth with nothing but shadows to chase us. Reality serves to honor the truth because we are part of the past as well as the future, if only for vanishing moments. You taught me these things soon after we met, but now I should say something different. I've come to a point where I need to express a feeling that mustn't be silenced.

"You see, it is you who opened my eyes that I may see the ephemeral grandeur. And it was you who inspired my soul to get me thinking about a persona. You were the one with a splendid solution to show me the righteous advantage of notional pleasure. And you were a breeze that encouraged my faith on a warm autumn eve before nightfall. Now, I know you were thinking of *us* as well, so what are you planning on doing? I wish I could be at your side in the light of a golden horizon forever. Then, with a small portemonnaie, I would surely be happy."

The lady paused and quietly added, "Shemokoman, I'm sorry. I should have said nothing at all."

And now, she was weeping. Once again, he tried to console her. "Poor, sad girl. There will always be days when people have got to admit what is precious inside them. Alone in the world like everyone else except for a sprinkle of stardust. My goodness, how you are so plainspoken and honest. If purpose proffers a righteous reward, then regret will always be the least of your worries. Without a doubt, the best way to live and be happy."

Stability

Shemokoman thought about life in his town and prospects regarding survival. In spite of more scholarly labor in school, nothing seemed to be clicking. In fact, the chances of finding a means to the end where he was had surely diminished. Indeed, there was nothing but disinformation and hype to make a man suppose that he was something. The hour was swiftly approaching when the momentum would force a departure. Clairvoyance was saying that all was ordained and emerging. He also believed that a day would arrive after years of wandering elsewhere when he would return to Waupakisco Park to be with neighbors and comrades. So many intuitive thoughts of a man with a sense of impending estrangement.

On the very first day of a Michigan summer, Shemokoman rolled out of bed at the crack of dawn. After eating a bowl of porridge with milk and fresh blueberries, he tackled some household chores assigned by Anna. Like dusting the tables and chairs with lemony polish, replacing a few knitted tidies, and scrubbing the floors in all of the rooms and sweeping the sidewalk outdoors.

Having completed his daily assignments about halfway through morning, he went out the back door and stood on the porch to look at the marvelous venue. The air was still and crisp and clear; the sun was already high in a sky that couldn't have been any bluer. And nothing was changed or vanished away during the previous nighttime. The woodshed next to the vegetable garden, all homes of respectable neighbors, the big elm tree and lilac bushes, and everything else was there in perfect order.

"Verily," he thought, "who really knows what transpires during mysterious nocturnal hours when man is in bed and asleep? When the light of our star has trickled away and a mantle falls over the landscape. At that time, Nature finagles whatever she wants to transform the native surroundings. And what does she manage to do in the end? Well, you have to get up the following day and go outside to find out. As for this morning, all is the same. Not a shred of appreciable difference. Indeed, someone up there pervading the sky didn't see fit to make any changes. Praise Eternity!"

And now, Shemokoman opted to go for a stroll. He went down from the porch and followed a path that led to the front of the house. As he stood by the road, he looked back at a fence that was recently placed alongside of his home.

He recalled, "Too bad that Duane got into a fight with the neighbor over that dog. The crazy mutt—Schenok!—wouldn't shut up for even a minute. Barking, constantly barking. Then the surveyors came out to review the estate, and what do you know about that. The fence went up and land that we used for years no longer existed. Unfortunately, it was a part of the neighboring parcel. Fee simple absolute. So what a horrific surprise. And what about adverse possession? As for Duane, he had to concede because he could do nothing about it. Glad that's over."

The Oracle of Waupakisco Park

The ethical comrade slowly shuffled along, heading east on the sidewalk. He didn't step on one single crack because of a funny belief in a childish jingle. As he approached the first set of crossroads, he ran into a lady who was famous throughout the land. It was the Oracle of Waupakisco Park. While chanting an old Grecian mantra, she sat in the grass on a magic carpet, surrounded by curious objects and in deep meditation as always. She was divine and reserved with emerald eyes and lavender hair that bewitched the people who saw her. A white woolen tunic that flowed to the ground and followed the curves of the body was her attire.

"Good morning, Your Highness," he said. "And how are we doing today?"

After revealing an affable smile designed to welcome a scrupulous devil, the Oracle said in a barely audible whisper: "Ah . . . Good morning, Shemokoman. Nice to see you. My frame of mind couldn't be better. I have been taking up space and doing a bit of rethinking."

"Anything in particular?" he inquired.

The Oracle said: "Well, I was wondering. Do people on earth look forward to life or simply try hard at existence? It has to be one or the other, you know. I'm afraid there is much of the latter. And what is the point of a seedling in field where nothing can grow to be gathered? I dare say, that stagnation will soon overcome us. But for now, let us get down to business regarding you, Shemokoman. If you should know, and I feel that you must, I need to address some matters regarding your life that are basic and heavy."

Shemokoman remarked, "Yes, my lady. I am aware of the issues. And I know a few things that you apperceive about my foreseeable future. Shall I explain?"

She nodded in the affirmative.

He went on. "All right . . . Your advice for me concerns a way to deal with troubling matters. Specifically, where I should and shouldn't go to seek the truth. Like it or not, the time has come for me to go away from here, into the outside world. I need to travel high and low and far and wide to other distant places on my own. Only experience—nothing else—will prove to be the means to find contentment. Thus, I must depart and soon, perhaps tomorrow. Am I correct?"

The Oracle gazed at a man whom she had known for many years. He was no indolent straggler. No. He was an ethical comrade. She had no wish to see him go but knew predestination overruled it.

"Roger that, Shemokoman," she answered. "You are right. The time has come to say 'Farewell' to all the respectable people. You need to go, cannot stay here; otherwise, you will soon be blue and brokenhearted. It is the conscientious thing to do. And remember, you'll come back to Waupakisco Park when the odyssey is over. But for now, you have to leave and be the bold explorer."

She continued, "And when you go away from here, great pain will strike the soul and guts inside you. The incident at Goguac Lake was hard as hell, but wait and see what Destiny is contemplating this time. Shemokoman, yes, the people suffer. Although I know for sure that you'll survive and conquer rage without the kindly aid of any savior. The faith you gained throughout the years will help you fight and decisively get through it."

"One more thing," she added. "When the Pretenders of Righteousness say—partake, and participate in corruption, tell them: 'No. I cannot do it because it is not my nature. And yes, I must obey my inner conscience.' Stand your ground, Shemokoman. Enough said. Basta per oggi."

He spoke with her about an hour more, although no longer. It was always a devil-may-care dialogue with flashes of jocular pretense. They talked about the sign of the cross, the fate of gods, confession, and both of the Testaments in Christian literature. And after they finished up, he continued to walk on the streets and avenues that soon would be a memory with major lasting value.

Thoughts in Script

That evening, Shemokoman prepared for his departure. After packing up all personal belongings, he sat in a chair at the foot of his wooden bedstead. A million random, vivid thoughts were passing through his open mind and causing apprehension. But as for now, he had to write a letter to his ethical comrades. They deserved an explanation. So with pen in hand and paper on the table, he started to compose the correspondence.

> My Esteemed Ethical Comrades,
> Greetings to you, immaculate friends. I'm afraid I've somber tidings. Alas, I am leaving Battle Creek, but never really wanted to desert it. Oh my! What a comforting heartache. And, oh my! . . . for the oxymoronic. The hour is near for me to pick up my bags and start the journey.

I wish that I could stay; however, a Power that is greater than the lot of us is telling me I shouldn't. Nature makes the rules that we must follow; or else, the scorn of Mighty Yahweh soon will be upon us. Yes, conformity is honored.

Of course, you are aware that I never had a choice in this decision. The stars were in alignment, and everything that I could see pointed to a tragedy for someone. My soul was that of hopeless men who cannot find the sanity to justify their freedom. Perhaps I should reject it; or maybe I'll accept it. The truth is that I must confess that truth was a critical factor. I just wish that certain people would have had sufficient courage to be different. Regrettably, so be it.

And after I have wandered far away, many years will pass us by, and your feelings I believe shall find another shore to set their sights on. Praise Eternity for common sense and fidelity that we can place our trust in. Adios, amigos.

Shemokoman

He placed the message in an envelope and tucked it away deep in one of his pockets. Shemokoman would drop it off at Major LD's home when he was leaving town. And then he grabbed his only bag of worldly possessions and, with the greatest of reluctance, without delay departed.

Good-Bye with a Promise

All the respectable people were sound asleep inside their houses, exactly how he found them many moons ago upon arrival. Shemokoman was going west, briskly walking next to Jameson Avenue. For him, the world now had turned into a dismal shade of gray, and all that he observed was circumstantial and bizarre. He knew a stint in Waupakisco Park was finally over; it was an ending.

The night was dark and still amid a heavy, muggy quiet. Yes, someone who was inside out could've heard a pin drop. Shemokoman thought about endless running and jumping, and more hide-and-seek after dinner, climbing trees and kicking cans, feeding gray squirrels, and eating tomatoes straight from a vine in the garden. Yes, he could always remember—so melodramatic, although what good would it do in the long run? We must go on and buckle down, forget the past, and act as if the happy days and nights don't really matter.

And when at last he reached the hill that led down to the High Road, he stopped and turned around to take one last look at his neighborhood. Suddenly, everything that up to now was hazy came into perfect focus. This was home—where he belonged and nothing under God's green earth could ever change it. But now he was to venture far away, and for what? . . . *Free will*—despicable villain. The time was nigh to seek and probe, and deal with all the trouble that had vexed him. His conscience told a pious soul that every single twisted thought in life cannot be normal.

Having had his fill of introspection, Shemokoman turned back around and went down the hill to start the expedition. It was a path he had to follow so he took it. Suddenly, a terrible illness grabbed hold of his entire body. It beat the man, and tore him up, and ripped his mortal flesh and bone into many pieces. The Oracle was right without a doubt: he had to suffer. Indeed, it was a dreadful beating, and he figured out the song and dance behind it. He had to give up a part of the *self* that would always belong to his home ground. He left it there to be a stake in wistful olden days because the places where we tarry need a dole for their existence. All is the endless mosaic of life as well as a quantum of nothing.

The fellow barely remained on his feet and gradually recovered. While licking his wounds, he thought, "In spite of what people would like to believe, sometimes there is only one side to the god-awful story. And that is the truth."

Part II

Why should I want to know what they think?
The lewd purveyors of bigotry, ire, and greed.
If possible, I need to know what think I.

8

Ke-kalamazoo

In Exile

The hard part was over. No need to fret over details. The boulder was pushed away from the cave and Shemokoman walked away on the road to Damascus. Regarding events where he lived up till then, now it was all in the past. Memory lane was a furious storm that lasted a couple of decades. After he dropped the letter off at Major LD's place, he traveled all night long going west. As daybreak appeared, he was fatigued, hungry, and thirsty. He gazed at the star in the sky to the east and paid homage for fortunate passage. Apollo was pleased and showered the man with a spate of fresh golden sunshine.

"What an enormous advantage," he thought. "Right now, I am strong and resilient. A day will arrive when that which is born of the flesh is ailing and done for. I need to make a pot of chicory."

Shemokoman came to a town that was called Ke-kalamazoo. And it didn't take long to figure out that most of the culture and everything else was different. With cheerful intent, he pondered the stolid behavior of people around him. Unlike the complaisant mood back home, the climate there tended to be a bit chilly. At least that was the way he perceived it. It was pragmatically bleak with traces of any compassion apparently missing. The leitmotif on every street corner was business; nothing else honestly mattered to the collection of libertine hawkers. He couldn't condone what he saw and didn't request any public reception.

"So, what have we here?" he thought to himself. "A town full of born-again heathens? Like it or not, that's what they are, gasping for air and courting the stifling squalor. From what I have gathered thus far on the street, these primates have no idea what it means to be chaste and appreciate virtue. It is akin to being crucified, dead, and buried to prove that you have been living by somebody's book. That would explain the conversion, and I'm beginning to get the big picture. Their world is only defined by one aspiration: indulgence. And there is no end to what they pretentiously worship. All of them here, so proper and modestly righteous."

In spite of the current conditions, he didn't have time to investigate crank demographics. Shemokoman had his own set of issues to work on. He soon found a house on the south side of town on West Vine Street to reside in. It was a very urbane neighborhood with plenty of snakes and arrogant scoundrels. And fortunately for him, some ethical comrades and people he knew decided to pull up stakes in the Cereal City and moved to Ke-kalamazoo as well. For sure, it was some consolation; living alone can require sedation.

At home in a chair next to a front porch window, Shemokoman studied the trending inertia and thought, "How in the world did I end up here . . . in a town where morons are cringing? From what I can fathom thus far about life, everything coming before has got to be after. And here, there is nothing anew and nothing to do, as every player I see is constantly flinching. I need to get out of this place somehow and move to a different location. But in the meantime, I will try to enjoy what little I can and carouse with the local storekeepers."

The Old Enemy

Thomas and Jude the Artist were Shemokoman's friends in the town of Ke-kalamazoo. They lived on a street called Harmonia Lane with neighbors who favored contention. He often went to their homes for social occasions, where he was silent most of the time and said nothing at all. And as he reclined wherever he was, the people were milling around and voicing opinions. He listened to them while learning the ropes, not missing a single word that someone had spoken.

Late one night, a group of debaters gathered together at Jude's place. The topic of conversation acquired a clear philosophical flavor. Thomas was talking with someone about the shape of the world tomorrow. After a while, he turned to Shemokoman and said, "So, my good fellow. What do you think? We are discussing the pros and cons of science and possible fiction. Got any inside information?"

There was no way to avoid it. The need to reply was important. He looked at his friend who was biding the time and responded, "Yes, Thomas. Indeed, I most certainly do. Ladies and gentlemen . . ."

A brief pause followed, after which he started the heavy oration: "Life is a solemn affair we confront with challenges ever so pressing. You need to believe what I'm telling you now, as there is no reason for me to engage in deception. At this point in time, the lot of us all is facing a sinister villain. And soon, every minute you tread upon earth will be filled with unthinkable danger. And no, I'm not making it up; rather, I give you the god's honest truth. This foe every day is becoming much larger and stronger. And struggle we will with the infamous brute who seeks to negate our very survival."

"And yet, the irony is," he went on, "if you ask your average man on the street about the developing monster, they tell you the beast is a blessing. Even a godsend. They say the invader is such a good friend and life will be wretched without it. And I'm telling you they are crazy! With every new day we are flooded with misinformation, and crafty indoctrination that is designed for a peachy brainwashing. Even the local gazette is in league with the likes of the hideous culprit. The editors promise so many good things on account of their horrible 'hero.' But I am here to assure you that nothing could be more immoral; and, nothing could be more disturbing. A devil is coming to get us, and then sure enough to firmly enslave us. It seeks to demolish, once and for all, the essence of civilization. Moreover, the intruder is taking the shortest approach to hasten the treacherous effort.

"And who, you may ask, is the enemy that I refer to? Well, my friends, I will tell you. It is—progress. Make no mistake about it; the dude is a purely iniquitous demon. Feigning to be the innocuous friend, it seeks to attack and prevail. Progress would like to destroy us."

He continued, "For hundreds of years, we had the occasion to deal with the good-hearted fellow. It wasn't a threat and under control, and never some type of a menace. Man obeyed unwritten natural law and progress was always subordinate. It was a darn good arrangement, but then a very surprising thing happened. Opportunity flared when humanity's guard should not have been yawning and napping, and the fiend slipped out of a tower meant to contain it. So now, without doubt, the tables are turned and we have a case to consider. Who could've known or ventured a guess regarding the size that progress might ever grow into? No one. And thus, with the aid of outrageous proportions of late, its power has greatly abounded. We have to abolish the thing in its tracks before it is able to zap us instead.

"Oh yes, a battle is coming. Thus, we need to be marshaling assets for the greatest campaign that man might ever conceive of. And when at last the armies we raise are engaged in a fight to the finish, the outcome may be disappointing. We could be roundly defeated. In fact, a massacre. So allow me to keenly advise you. The villain will never be satisfied until every last soul on this lonely planet is slaughtered. Until we are dead and gone into vile perdition; and, until it alone is the master. Progress desires a glorious day when humanity suffers extinction.

"And where, you may ask, is progress right now? Well, don't be alarmed when I tell you. It is roaming the streets and inside of your homes, deep in the forest as well as in every school—tempting the children. It is controlling the market and slowly replacing the physical labor you furnish. Progress is everywhere. Almost like God, you cannot escape it. The future is only a moment away, and progress is waiting to take it. Yes, the scientist-kings are a-coming."

The crowd in the house was taken aback as everyone carefully listened to the speech of a reticent newcomer. And then Jude spoke up: "So please indulge us, Shemokoman. What should we do to avert a disaster? How should we deal with the villain?"

Shemokoman replied, "You know, it is not as clear-cut as one might imagine. To confront such a brute requires both wisdom and courage. Most people today are dealing with life that they are obliged to obsess with, and, they don't see a need to co-opt the urgent solution. So even more troubles emerge and expand where attention is sorely deficient. Thus, I will provide the following guidance, my friends.

"To begin with, we must apply as never before the power of common sense to fight the invader. Learn to say 'no' and forget about 'yes,' and try to renounce whatever should not be supported. To tether control at moments that test resolve will serve to repress it.

"Reason and purpose unfettered are yours, and progress deplores the role of a critical thinker. It loathes any real opposition and tries to curtail it. And if you decide to take any pains to ensure that the will can be leveraged, you should be on the right track and ahead in the game.

One must divine and perceive, and also refrain in keeping with good natural order. Tear down the temples that progress creates and replace them with hope and redemption. Yes, my friends, you will tamper with promising ventures; and yes, my friends, it is time to go bravely and do it; and no, my friends, there cannot be hemming and hawing. And never consider the faith of a trick by people who worship contraptions. Burn the machines and fight every urge to consort with all venomous angels. Take hold of the reins and pull very hard to impede the advancement of breakthroughs. A little progress is fine, you know, but too much progress for us will surely be final."

Jude was pacing back and forth, and thinking real hard about progress. He was consuming a green libation made from a spirit with water and sugar. Then he chimed in, "Well, Shemokoman. I have to admit that I'm always amazed at the tizzy you manage to conjure. Any final comments?"

"My friends, I will tell you this much," Shemokoman said. "There's no other choice; we need to protect and preserve the eventual future. We cannot allow a detestable beast to threaten the next generation. The children today must be happy and fit, and bound to encounter tomorrow. And please do not try to improve upon innocent Nature, for it will always be perfect as is. Instead, learn to live as you are and be what you can and do as you must without failing. Forget about life that leads you astray, no matter how much you enjoy it."

He concluded, "Thus, we must aspire to regulate progress; we cannot allow it to rule us. Remaining alive is a touchy affair when living is called into question. And what is the point of existence at all when life has been thoroughly ruined? Perhaps some day the masses will change and learn to regard what affects them. But for now, intransigent minds have got to prevail. Above all else, we need to avoid the appeal of degrading behavior. The Spirits of Guile will beckon us on with allure that is only temptation. Indeed, what is the use of a Yahweh for man, if progress is running the show?"

Plight

The nut was a hard one to crack. Some people were even indignant. They considered his language an outrage—even sacrilege, and not worthy of proper attention. We haven't the right to adjudicate how we develop or slowly evolve. And things will always work out in the end, and progress will surely enhance us. Unconditional credence, for those who are lazy and foolish. Man is truly resourceful and, if need be—somehow in the end—well, we will get by regardless of Judgment and doomsday.

Shemokoman thought to himself, ". . . the unwitting multitudes."

A few in the crowd, though, had praise for the powerful message. They agreed with the speaker and thanked him for answers and insight. As for Shemokoman, the response to what he had said was what he expected. Mostly loud and preposterous talk from shallow partakers who gathered nothing at all from a significant warning.

The gathering finally broke up not long after midnight. A good many people had something important to do on the following day—like go to a job. Some were merchants who worked in the Victuals Market, where they haggled with thrifty townspeople. Others were builders who made their mark by excelling in housing construction. And about twenty-five ladies and gentlemen worked at a local factory making rods, reels, and tackle boxes for people who liked to go fishing. Unfortunately, almost half of the crowd had no job at all, a typical bad situation. The absence of access to suitable work was far too commonplace during those years in the Land of Michigan. It was a terrible state of affairs, especially bleak and very pervasive. A man could pound the streets in any one town for months on end in search of a decent position and still wind up with nothing to show for the effort. Talk about mortification; you better make sure that your ducks are in order.

After saying a bunch of good-byes to his friends and the people that he got to know there, Shemokoman stepped outside of the home to surveil the affluent quarter. He saw numerous wide empty cobblestone streets and large Victorian homes with big dark windows. And it was obvious to him that the town council spared no expense to ensure that appearance was top-notch in all the right places. Well-maintained sidewalks and roadways, nice public parks with precision landscaping, and new municipal buildings for government deadbeats. Alas, it was all a case of brazen deceit forced upon those who endured a pauper's existence.

He often told strangers who moved to Ke-kalamazoo, "Go north . . . forget about west—I tell you, go north. And you will discover the truth about who is in clover. Oh yes, the Great Society, with plenty of trash and broken glass to embellish the old neighborhood. Prosperity thrives for a hustling knave and those who dance without a Circassian frock coat. Go look for yourself and see what it means to be happy."

Alone

As he rambled along in the darkness and leisurely made his way home to West Vine Street, Shemokoman passed a few slumbery men who walked a great deal before bedtime. Oh yes, the demons have got to be clobbered. He took a deep breath of the cool summer air, which made him feel quietly grateful. There were still a few things that escaped the pernicious talons of progress, advancing. Thank god for small favors.

His head tilted back and now he looked up at the sky of the night high above. And he observed the twinkling stars as if by way of astonishing eyesight. It seemed as though he could reach overhead and touch every heavenly body. All of the glittering dots of light—so close—and he was enamored. Perhaps imagination again, or could it have been the result of a holy sensation. And he admonished degenerate men on the earth who offer too many solutions. In particular, he thought, "Acceptance—alone, and leave it at that. We've nothing to gain by providing too much explanation. Alas, we frequently find what should never be found and disturb a fine balance in Nature."

It was easy to think of the past and identify reasons for copious trouble. In no small part, it was due to the pranks of certain respectable people. The ones who had all of the pull and demanded that everyone follow the leader. Those incurable saints who could not resist yet decried all devotional pleasure. Shemokoman searched for the truth in spite of no end to the chronic obstruction. Maybe, who knows, he would find it someday by visiting too many places. At any rate, Ke-kalamazoo would never suffice and he knew it. Acute apprehension disabled resolve, and there was no way to forestall it.

A small white cabbage butterfly was darting around near some bushes. My word, what a delicate creature, and Shemokoman watched for a minute. From whence did he come and to where would he go so gracefully flitting and gliding? Indeed, such a fine navigator; he was no pest, but a skilled aviator. Then he landed on a yellow rose and started to search for a source of ambrosial nectar. Those beautiful guys need always beware, as they are so low on the food chain.

At long last, Shemokoman reached that point where all esoteric reflection and his whole train of thought devolved into mediocrity. Everything got completely mixed up, and the whole philosophical row in his mind resembled a swirl of madness. One thing for sure, he needed a break. He had to relax, forget about problems, and find a more leisurely pastime. He wondered, "So who in the world was Jimmy Crack Corn? I don't even know but I really do care. Perhaps it is time for some research."

Tapestry

Shemokoman lived on his fine shady lane not far from the center of town. He frequently talked with his neighbor Roscoe Green, who spoke about steady employment and his profession. Namely, the man was a tapestry weaver by trade, and he recently covered the wagon.

The fellow once told Shemokoman, "First of all, you go to a client to measure the wall, the couch, or whatever desired. Then you must figure out the decorative need and what is required to fill it. After that, you return to the garret inside of your house to make up all of the product as it was ordered. Next, you let the customer know that everything is ready. Finally, you go back to their place where you fit and adjust, and cut and sew, to finish a job to perfection. It is a craft that calls for talent, including a knack for beautiful handwork. And for the rest of your life, you think about all of the people whom you had occasion to service. What could be better than that for pride and contentment? Indeed, I would have to say nothing."

With shuttles and yarn, a loom and a bench, that guy is the ultimate master. He did his best every day of the week to beautify life in the ghetto. He tried so hard to set the stage, and slug the hooch and make a basic pattern more than striking. Indeed, it takes so little to distract a working stiff—a speck in the swirling cosmos—to make him clean forget about the fact he isn't something.

Routine Correspondence

By way of the post, Catherine stayed in touch with Shemokoman. They would send mail to each other at least once every two or three weeks. The language they used was never laced with hyperbole, motive, or falsehood.

In one of his letters, he wrote,

> *To the Esteemed Lady Hesse,*
>
> *Greetings! I hope that my words find you right now in good health and high spirits as well. I am slowly adjusting to life at this place, in the uncommon Ke-kalamazoo. Very strange nomenclature, do you not think so? I'm sure there will be an occasion in life when I mention the name of this town, and I am certain no one will believe me. And yes, there really are girls who happen to come from Ke-kalamazoo.*
>
> *I now have practical knowledge to use to establish my better credentials. It is a major improvement for me and, indeed, so very revealing. Things are a little less foggy these days and not what they seemed without distance. And none of the people I notice right here resemble the folks in our town. For starters, the embattled deceivers who want to be strong are constantly shouting from rooftops. And righteous play-actors suppose they are weak unless they believe in a Maker. Nobody here has ever went out on a limb to look for a better approach or different connection. It is a shame.*
>
> *Last night, I attended a church service with a flock of devout Holy Rollers. It was a big-time revival meeting, and their Jesus showed up to deliver one hell of a sermon. Really, the Son is a pretty good speaker, although he needs to brush up on the grammar. Anyway, yelling and dancing, screaming by people who truly were madder than hatters. I sat on a bench in the back of the place along with fanatical fruitcakes. We listened to hate from the mouth of a saint who told us that Satan is coming. I cried out, "No, he isn't . . . You're crazy as hell!" . . . and turned and smiled at faces of startled parishioners. And then, when I tried to get up and leave the joint, I was told by three big men to "sit down and stay for a spell."*

The fellows were wearing black armbands with Aryan symbols and spoke about radical leanings. They carried big knives and shields and swords, and billy clubs down by the waistline. They noted that I was in need of some reeducation. Hmm . . .

So now, I was watching a very outlandish type of uncanny performance. A man with a saber was prancing around up in front of the whole congregation. The edge of the blade was as sharp as a razor and gleaming in flickering candlelight. Then he put a watermelon on the belly of another fellow who lay on a bench and told everyone there that miracles seemingly happen. He wanted to show that mind over matter was truthful. And, he wanted to prove that freaks with sabers are loco. And all of a sudden, with one mighty swing of the weapon, he sliced the fruit without touching the man into two individual pieces. To say the least, I wasn't impressed; it was a stunt with equivocal value. Thus, I rose to my feet and bolted right out of the chapel through a horde of imperious guards and vacuous zealots. The show was enough for me for the night and really way more than expected. It is amazing what glorified zombies have to get used to. And all for the sake of an outspoken preacher.

Sometimes, it is best to let old superstition live on and on—no revision. And after a while, when doubt is erased, the people will call it religion. We ought to adhere to the pagan ideals, as there is simply no need to forsake them. For they are more righteous and close to the truth than much of the current conviction. I know without doubt in a day long ago that people were savage and happy. And maybe they didn't have all that we do, but modernization and progress just didn't matter. For what is the sense in a world we share if we can't even learn to be civil? Not much.

Shemokoman

Catherine enjoyed reading letters from Shemokoman, whose life resembled a bold, incredible saga. He never sat on a couch with nothing to do—oh no. He could be rather aggressive, and he was a gallant explorer; and, he had a passion for learning. Sometimes, there was a nice chunk of dark chocolate included along with the mail he sent her. It is a treat in the main relatively addicting. Hopefully, there would be chocolate in heaven.

Seneca Queen

It was a Saturday afternoon and early in autumn. Shemokoman strolled on the main boulevard where leaves that were falling away from trees covered the soft soggy ground. He was just coming back from the Victuals Market with plenty of fruit and vegetables. Apples and pears, bananas and berries, and melons. Plus—carrots, potatoes, turnips and beets, cabbage and red-ripe tomatoes. The only thing missing was bread; yes, he needed to find a good loaf or a couple baguettes.

He went down the big hill and passed the old coliseum, a spot where he frequently jousted. The black cinder track that circled the field was in terrible shape and in need of a major improvement. As he moved slowly along on his way, he was smoking a fresh cigarette. He had fancied the habit of late; and really . . . How could something like that ever be harmful? Give me a break.

Soon thereafter, he was joined by a lady whose name was Seneca Queen. She was a countess of old Scandinavian peerage who recently came into town to upgrade scholastic involvement. She attended the big university that was on top of the hill behind them. So day after day, she sat in her classes and listened to funky professors. Plenty of reading and writing, and also, she counted the very big numbers.

It didn't take long for them to procure both leavened and unleavened bread at a favorite bakery. Then they slowly made their way back to Shemokoman's place. After leaving the food, they went over to Seneca's flat, where it was planned to meet and dine with two other people—George and Martha. They were students as well of political science and had no idea about who was in line for the rip-off.

The guests arrived at 7:00 p.m. on the dot for the social occasion. A combo of scrumptious hors d'oeuvres were put out to ease the refined appetites. George opened a bottle of Riesling wine—a marvelous vintage from Fellbach—and placed it on a table next to four crystal glasses. And when everyone had had their fill of pâté with caviar, crackers, and olives, they went into the dining room and took their places for dinner.

Seneca Queen served wild turkey as the main entrée, and provided all the fixings such as mashed potatoes, dressing, and mixed vegetables along with condiments. What could anyone say, it was delicious. They praised the hostess, who had prepared a truly great meal for her friends. As a show of appreciation, she curtsied to them. The royal persona was right at home with pots and pans in a galley-type kitchen.

At one point during the dinner, Shemokoman noticed a clown on the balcony ledge of the neighboring flat. The fellow was practicing tricks and juggling pins, and getting his act together. The ethical comrade chose to say nothing at all about it to anyone there at the table. Clowns can be terribly scary; there was no reason to spoil the party.

The sun disappeared and stars reemerged once again to bespeckle the heavens. As the evening rolled on, those people conversed about Ouija boards, business, and pizza. Shemokoman mainly just listened; too many people cannot seem to do it. Regarding Seneca, she was no stranger to doing a number on traits of particular victims. It wasn't a common forté for her to temper a primitive weakness. She especially liked to belittle the stature of others, ad nauseam. What a terrible way to spend most of one's life—on a mission to criticize people. The trouble was that on occasion, she appeared to make awful good sense.

Every so often, Shemokoman thought, "Why should I allocate time to a slanderous viper? Ms. Queen can be out-and-out evil. The way that she talks about everyone else—we haven't the right to mock or ridicule others. Indeed, there is no way to forgive her."

And then, quite out of the blue, George said, "So here we are once again in a room that is under a roof made of shingles. Could it be it is time to talk about something that ought to receive the attention. Like our duly elected officials. That is, the politicians."

He then turned to Shemokoman. "And as for you, my respectable friend, do you have any special opinion? Maybe a word or two to the wise to unmuddle the difficult issue."

Shemokoman had no intention to talk, but for the sake of chat and edification, he replied with a flurry of comments: "Well, to begin with,

I think that the obvious must be stated. Namely, that there is no such thing as an honest politician. Never was or ever will be. They are beget unto man, grow up to be creeps, and die in the sewer like rats. Indeed, the exemplary people; and for sure, the impertinent scions; and in deed, the opprobrious jackals. Regarding the horrible creatures, I must tell you with patent assurance: duplicitous—yes; inculpable—no . . . a gang of contemptible mongrels. They're out for themselves and nobody else, all lackeys of prosperous gangsters who insist they were fairly elected. And despite a knack to insinuate care, any concern is not of their druthers. My word! . . . They love to exploit us; speak of theatrics, they are the masters. Stale, detached, and set in their ways, they just can't figure it out why many constituents hate and avoid them. Of course they are fools, and yet they profess to be mentors and prominent leaders. What's more, they always propose the affordable deal, a way to extract as much as they can from people who think politicians are God-given rulers. What a deplorable joke that isn't so funny. For me, they serve as a grim reminder that the Gracious Almighty did not create man. He would have wailed away till Eternity passed in light of a terrible blunder."

Everyone at the table had that blasé look on their face, and they mechanically gestured agreement. You cannot dispute the essence of visceral musing. Especially, that all politicians are swindlers. The topic of conversation now changed to something less controversial. Namely, discussion concerning dark matter. And as the evening wore on, for the most part, they all had a smashing good time. The occasion ended on a high note with Seneca Queen playing her grand piano and charming the group with creative renditions of music by Chopin. Martha wept bitterly when the hostess played No. 4 in E minor, from Préludes Op. 28. Timeless.

Around Town

While he lived in Ke-kalamazoo, Shemokoman frequently met with Seneca, Thomas, and Jude on the east side of town at a tavern called the Office. It was an old gray three-story mansion that was converted into a beer joint. At that place, they talked and joked, played whist every night, and even got into some fistfights. "Cool it, bub . . . Cool it!" Dark shiners were good for a laugh about violent tempers. And it was many a night they conjured a plan to embark upon cool entertainment, whereupon they left the tavern to engage in spirited mischief. Perhaps on the banks of a murky millpond or out in the boondocks at Gilkey. Or in the back of a paper mill factory where it was crazy to fish in the river.

One time, Jude and Shemokoman found themselves at the crack of dawn wandering through cool white mist in tall, dewy grass next to a body of water called Crooked Lake. They tried to determine why they were there in the first place. Maybe somebody lost something of value and they were there trying to find it. Or perhaps, they intended to visit someone but went the wrong way at the fork in the road. Unfortunately, the reticent glades, dells, and forest refused to whisper so much as the hint of an answer. Both of the men were a little discouraged and anxious.

Jude cogitated, "Woe is me! Yes, woe unto me! It feels like I've been through the wringer. And, so much for bodacious semantics."

Traces of solid contentment for Shemokoman were hard to come by in Ke-kalamazoo. You pretend it's all right and people think you are one of the gang, a survivor. However, in fact, you are mostly alone and slated to be on the outside. Good god, he was tired of sitting and staring outside at the street through a window. It frequently seemed as if he were fighting a battle of epic proportion against a legion of spooks straight from the past. And little by little, resounding defeat for him could not be averted. So what should we do in the face of a rout when nothing we fathom is clicking? Listen to me. I will tell you.

You have to get up onto both of your feet and go to a job to be working. And—with a shovel you trust, for example: dig the straightest, widest, and deepest ditch that anyone sane can imagine. Then you will be happy and proud, as it is a red-letter day in your lifetime. And you cannot care to reflect anymore about matters that ruffle your feathers.

The Fair Sex

It came to pass one day that Thomas was sitting with Shemokoman on a bench near the center of town across from the courthouse. The former had recently entered into a new amorous liaison and asked for advice.

Shemokoman was tossing bread crumbs to doves looking for handouts. There were no hawks, no eagles with claws, no peregrine falcons with blinders. And then he answered, "You know, Thomas, when a relationship starts to get serious, then it is usually time for you to make tracks and fast. Although if you're already into it over your head, then listen to what I can tell you. I often observe that most women behave in precisely the very same manner. Sooner or later, they tell you something like . . . 'Darling, I do not care about riches you have. Wealth doesn't matter to me. I simply want you to be you as you are and that is my only desire. Of course, I need love and attention each day, and, hmm . . . by the way, I should tell you. I want you to get me a pair of new shoes, a matching dress, and a silk parasol for my wardrobe. And you can forget about watching the game with the boys because here is a list of your housework and errands.' What do you say to that, Thomas?"

The suitor was thinking of scattered cathedrals without any bodies to worship. Shemokoman went on, "Thomas, my friend, you mustn't be fooled by the total distortion of reason. If a lady insists that she doesn't need wealth to be happy, I tell you— Beware! Look out for the devious vixen. For she will try clever deception; and believe me, she surely will use it. The ladies are good at concocting a scheme to manipulate passionate men. Every day of the year, every thing that she wants will cost you so dearly, my friend. Your treasure will soon disappear, and then—you will become a man of the street who chooses a barrel of fire. Therefore, as soon as the subtle suggestions appear, it is time to clamp down with a vengeance. You have to be firm and unyielding."

After a pause for a moment or two, Shemokoman continued, "Thomas, I swear that the women are swarming around us like so many hornets. And, they would like nothing more than to buzz for a while and sting us. You need to be mindful all of the time to avoid the effeminate guile. Consequently, never commit to a pledge that you cannot relinquish. To proceed otherwise is a grievous mistake and invites quintessential misfortune. Now . . . in light of my words, I will tell you besides with no reservation to boot: women can never play fair; alas, their dream is to see us men bitten. So, you need to ensure that all of your shots and immunizations are current."

Thomas replied, "Good advice, Shemokoman. I will follow it to a tee. Thank you."

"Before you go—just one more thing, Thomas," the ethical comrade added. "Regarding ambitious female types—they are all exactly the same. Women who deprecate sanity, and the women who vilify people. They are never in sync with a normal routine and desire a ride to scandalous ritzy adventures. So watch out for them as well. Nothing but fun with a thrill here and there, and then they will flat out destroy you."

"More outstanding advice, my friend," Thomas declared with insistence. "Now I feel better than ever. Oh no! I nearly forgot—the birthday party. I'm going to be late and my honey is going to kill me. I need to go somewhere, and fast—where I can get flowers for her—or I'm in the doghouse again."

Thomas took off without further ado, hurdling hedges and fences. Shemokoman couldn't believe it. He continued to feed the doves and thought, "I talk and talk, and continue to talk, but rarely does anyone hear me. People will always be set in their ways, believe what they must, and nothing can ever affect it. And men will behave as expected, driven by gender and coy histrionics."

Coup de Grâce

As time wore on while he was in town, Shemokoman kicked up his heels even more with Thomas and Jude. They caroused every night without bending the law until daybreak. As for Seneca Queen, her balanced behavior began to erode and then she went bonkers completely. Gracious sakes alive, it happened so quickly.

She would stay out real late almost every night with a gaggle of self-styled misfits. They were frequently spotted at gloomy municipal graveyards, taking part in a pagan tradition. Bottles of water with Mr. Chumak, and rattles and beads were a few of the ritual objects. All the while, she listened to music of feeble old men with long white hair who were over the hill and disgusting. With their lutes and fiddles, and harps and a drum, they pretended to entertain people. It was quite the ordeal for a brunch connoisseur with bohemian kindred and leanings.

Seneca said it was absence of pity to justify harsh indignation. Somehow, in some way, she had to give in because phantoms were plaguing her conscience. Shorn of her poise on account of the pride, the towers were notably cracking as the voices of martyrs fell silent to pennants and banners that waved in a zephyr. Indeed, the lions were hungry; and what is more, the coyotes were thirsty. And nothing appeared to be level on earth except for a field without players.

Life! . . . What is life? The amusing affair for too many cynical oddballs. Seneca couldn't do anything right for people who callously wronged her. So she prayed to spirits who wouldn't respond, and no one else bothered to help her. Finally, she threatened to kill every last man, woman, and child in town and in all of the local surroundings. Wow! . . . That got her the special attention. And thus, a concerned constable who was taking the strong medication threw her into the back of a medical cart and hauled her away to the nuthouse.

The asylum was crawling with deviant staff, and not so remarkably, she understood them. After all, the woman's demise was not a result of any real mental disorder. Rather, due to the presence of unabashed disciplinarians, Seneca Queen deferred to a nice little breakdown. And who can find fault with the option for sure—a viably practical choice. Everyone knows somebody someplace who is a certified crackpot.

Regarding the straits of his Seneca friend, Shemokoman noted, "It's easy to castigate everyone else and have a good laugh on the others. Although, take an honest look at yourself sometime and tell me if you do not see a familiar reflection. Like maybe a face that is vile with shame and a body you think is repulsive. Judgmental design and disparaging talk are not bound to be inconsequential."

Swan Song

Shemokoman stayed in his Michigan land until he felt pressured to leave it. Many lessons were gleaned in the school of hard knocks, and he had the bruises to prove it. So now, he was fixing to shove off again all alone to a different location. He knew it would be one more time in his life when fate would contrive to provoke him. And thus, the Gracious Almighty cut him the orders.

Along with the final touching farewells exchanged with the people who knew him, everyone waved good-bye as if they had meant it. A major portion of life was finally over. He stepped out on his porch, and while looking far off in the distance, Shemokoman mused about merit and righteous intention.

"So, what do I have to show for myself? How do we measure the value of honor in living? Well, I am able to sleep every night of the week without being bothered by demons. And I am a man who can honestly smile and look at myself without choking. Not bad. And thus, it is time for me to go forth onto the trails that cover this planet. Who knows, perhaps I will strike a bonanza."

9

Separation

Move Along

As twilight enshrouded the guise of a town with too many secrets to fathom, Shemokoman packed up all of his modest belongings. Very little, indeed. He strapped on the watch with a wide leather band and took out his magnetic compass. Then he grabbed hold of his things and started to walk. He followed the Old Territorial Road, a Native American treasure. It took him away deep into the night and in a southwestern direction. The moment of truth had arrived. Now it was time to go for a while beyond every Michigan border.

The ethical comrade crossed over land that was level and rich, heard crickets and katydids calling their mates in the evening, passed hundreds of rickety Mail Pouch barns, and listened to owls hooting away on the silos. He traveled on old country roads in counties with names like Cass and Van Buren, making his way through town after town where nobody bothered to lock up their doors in the nighttime. But eventually, there was nothing to see anywhere except for the miles of midwestern cornfields. Civilization had pretty much vanished. And he never looked back, oh no; for the time being, he couldn't do it. And he still didn't have any clear-cut idea about where he was certainly going.

Nevertheless—for mollification and looking at things on the bright side, his Michigan life all those years garnered plenty of tricks for survival. Like starting a fire and witching for water by using a couple of sticks.

It is tough when a man is compelled to conform and chuck everything with reluctance. Especially regarding a place to call home where he can relax in the parlor. No matter how strong are the body and soul, the spirit undoubtedly suffers. And now as before, Shemokoman felt additional harrowing torment. It happened right after he started to walk and lasted for more than an hour. He was cold with the chills and his body was aching all over. But in spite of the physical troubles, he charted a course, leaving nothing behind except for a fresh set of footprints.

He thought, "You just never know, the luck of the draw. But I am not stewing or moping. A man's gotta do what a man has to do even though it seems pointless and painful. I have to go on without any regret to wherever a Yahweh may take me. Hopefully, a day will arrive at long last when I can look back and be proud of the things I accomplished. Furthermore, I need to redeem and to save a few souls that I will directly run into. It just couldn't hurt to help out a few of those devils. Albeit, I must bear in mind that there is no such thing as a good deed that goes unpunished."

Shameless

During the first night of travel, Shemokoman noticed Iniquity walking beside him. She looked very fine all decked out in white, with jewelry all over the body and lilies arranged in her hair. She must have been bored to be out of her den and on the prowl for a stranger to charm. Yes, he knew she was there for a reason; he would find out in a matter of minutes.

Sure enough, it didn't take long and a brash altercation developed. Shemokoman struggled by all mortal means to prevail and roundly defeat her. He was having no luck for quite a long time; she wanted to take him so badly. The slow hours passed and he fought on and on like so many warriors before him. And finally, with one incredible show of strength, he managed to push her away into a portal of nebulous mire where ladies like her no longer can cause a disaster.

"Yes, my wayfaring friends," he thought, "it is my job to inform you. One must take care when traveling on desolate roads in the middle of nowhere. Especially if it is dark and you are alone, it can be risky. Around the next bend or up at the junction there may be perilous pitfalls, and there can be evil awaiting. A temptress appears who wants to engage . . . procure, assay, and corrupt you. Man. They think you are weak, an easy touch, a desperate skate who cannot control the immoral desire for feasting. Thus, if you want to stay healthy and upright, I would suggest discretion and greater awareness until your own journey is over."

A Party of Men

On the second day of his travels and while strolling along in the evening, Shemokoman came upon a clankety ox-drawn wagon. When the driver noticed him, he pulled hard on the reins and the buckboard came to a standstill. The two men made their acquaintance and casually talked for a while. In the back of the rig, there were six other men who were laughing, joking, and having a merry ol' time.

Shemokoman just couldn't help but inquire, "So please, tell me, sir. I'd sure like to know. Where are you taking these fellows? . . . What is the story? It appears a bit strange that you should be hauling a group of such men around so late in the day. Like here, on this old country road."

"Well," the fellow replied, "if you must know, and I'm at a loss to believe that it ought to be different, I'm taking them now for a quaint rendezvous inside of a church cemetery. Per holy decree, the time has arrived and they must be straightaway buried, six feet under. You see, I am the undertaker."

Puzzled, Shemokoman said, "But I don't understand. Are you sure that interment was ordered? All of these men still appear to be living and healthy."

The undertaker took a deep breath and explained, "And that is what the townspeople thought as well. However, let me tell you about *these* men, Shemokoman. In spite of what reason would seem to imply regarding a human condition, all of them died a very long time ago. The lives that they led were full of deceit; their vices were many and virtue was basically zero. Destiny told me that it was my charge to take them away to God's acre tonight, where they will be placed in a tomb underground to preclude further mortal involvement. Yes,

Shemokoman . . . I need to remove these filthy scoundrels from the ranks of the masses beside us. Their nefarious deeds caused untold numbers of innocent people to suffer."

He continued, "If they are inspected more closely, you notice their power of vision is missing. The ocular sockets are barren; and, they cannot see anymore. For too many days and too many nights, they couldn't stop gazing at evil. They had a big eyeful of looking at blasphemous things that humanity shouldn't. Their skin is all wrinkled and cold and gray, as malice defiled their bodies. And none of them have any heartbeat as well; they traded their courage and goodness on earth for everything vile and wicked. If you talk to them, they cannot hear you. That particular faculty also was given up ages ago, after refusing to shut up their traps and listen to somebody speaking. They squandered the office of sweet respiration likewise because they didn't have time in the middle of play to be breathing. The fact they retain any image at all, well, we both know the truth about physical life and illusion. Yes, my friend—your theory is constantly working. And you of all people, Shemokoman, you understand how men are adept at kicking their very own buckets."

Upon closer examination, Shemokoman saw that the undertaker was right. The men in the wagon were truly devoid of existence. He grabbed a small handful of pebbles from the ground and tossed them one by one at the motley collection of fellows. Each of the stones passed through the visible specters and landed on the other side of the road. Indeed, there was nothing alive that he could account for.

Finally, both of the men bade a hearty farewell to the other and traveled in different directions. The sinister sounds of frolic and fun of cadavers who sat in the buckboard could be heard for miles around. Very spooky.

Shemokoman mused, "Verily, I say unto thee, the graveyard is really a place for those who are living."

He stuck to the road and stuck to a plan that was not of his very own making. You've got to move on with so little remorse to prevent psychological damage. Any and all passing thoughts regarding the Land of Michigan were now far, far behind him. His only concern was deeply entrenched in a future he could not imagine. It was time to turn over another new leaf, only how would he happen to spot it? And what would there be underneath it? Shemokoman walked on a quake in the earth of a route that was constantly shifting. Where was he likely to finally end up, and what would he possibly do there?

It came to pass one evening that he stopped alongside the road, sat down at an old picnic table, and had a bite to eat. The ethical comrade devoured a fresh baguette topped with creamy butter, drank a full glass of hot spicy glühwein, polished off a slice of Gruyère cheese straight from the Alps, and ate some wild huckleberries. Last, he smoked a fresh cigarette—a Cameo no less—by the light of a silvery moon. He hadn't a wish to be anywhere else despite the demanding conditions.

He gazed upward and thought, "Night after night I see the original gypsy, way high in the velvety kingdom. As always, afar and alone with no one beside her. She shines to bestir and affect melodies that Nature so lavishly offers. And casting a spell called enchantment namely is what she is powerfully good at."

Missoura

A man, the road, and nothing to spare except solace and seasonal mind games. Shemokoman never got lost, although sometimes it occurred that he couldn't determine location. And in spite of a knack for having the best recognition, nothing he saw was familiar. He was on real foreign soil now, and he had to keep looking and thinking. The rocky land, the dogwood trees and eastern pine, the lakes and mountain streams, as well as the countrified people—well, every proverbial thing was totally different. He was in the Province of Amber and Stone deep in the heart of the Land of Missoura.

Before long, Shemokoman came upon a small hamlet nestled in the foothills of a snow-covered mountain range. A wide, choppy river with rippling whitecaps flowed through the picturesque region. The trace that he traveled looked like the road up to Ritchie that was deep in Canadian reaches, where long ago he quite often went with Duane for hunting and fishing.

The sleepy old sun was peeking above the dim edge of an eastern horizon. Apollo prepared for his daily routine to blaze across the deep-blue shimmering heavens. Shemokoman was in a good mood: the four main fluids were in the appropriate order. Interestingly, he had a brief dream the previous night where, in no uncertain terms, a sage told him that "tomorrow will always be better."

As he approached what really amounted to only a couple of buildings, somebody swinging an ax far away in the forest shouted: "Tiiimberrr." Shemokoman decided that it would be best to stop someplace for a breakfast. And at the very first corner in town, he noticed a shingle hanging above the entrance of a local roadhouse that read "Dry-Gulch Grill."

He thought, "Well, there is no doubt I've been traveling west for quite a long time now and then some. I've heard about joints with names like this that are strange to a midwestern fellow."

Shemokoman went inside the place and glanced around for a moment. Then he sat down on a lunch counter stool that was red and round, and made a few leisurely circles. It was a clean, hospitable dive with down-to-earth charm that was one-of-a-kind.

In due time, a waitress appeared and said, "You wanna menu?"

He replied, "Yes, madam, that would be splendid." And then she gave one to him.

After perusing the list of cuisine and early-bird specials, it didn't take long for the man to place an order. Bacon and ricochet poached eggs, porridge, and toast with a big slab of butter. He also requested a glass of the very best brandy that was straight from Armenian barrels to aid in digestion.

The waitress scribbled the order down on her notepad. "By the way," she said, smiling, "my name is Bathsheba. And, I do hope you're reading the Bible. You are new in these parts, never seen you before. Just passing through, I'd suppose."

"Well, right you are, my perceptible Fräulein," Shemokoman replied. "Your powers of observation are nothing to scoff at. And I would have to surmise you are seldom bamboozled by scammers or cagey deceivers."

The lady was duly impressed and he went on, "My name is Shemokoman. And I hail from the one and only Land of Michigan. I have been traveling for several days and nights and covered the better part of a very long journey. I'm hoping to go to a promising place that offers me something of value. I really would like to discover a town where people still venerate heroes. Not too much of that lately. And, I seek to resolve many questions in life that occasion dejection and sorrow. I am bedeviled by too much confusion as well as a lack of legitimate truth. Thus, new faces and customs, and everything else will be helpful to me in the effort. So, my little chickadee—what are you thinking about at this very moment?"

Bathsheba stared at Shemokoman in a peculiar way and said, "Oh, nothin' much. Only 'bout my lavender nail polish." Then she turned and walked away into the kitchen.

About ten minutes later, his breakfast was served. He dug in and promptly consumed it. And when he was through, a discussion commenced with Bathsheba concerning how best to harvest a crop of persimmon. Actually, she did all of the talking, and her customer had to be listening. Nonetheless, it was a pleasant encounter because nothing we ever confront is deficient in value. It all counts. Finally, Shemokoman told the woman that it was time for him to leave.

Then she politely inquired, "So, big boy. Like . . . do you think you'll ever be back here again for an encore?"

"Well," he said, "regarding a revisitation, who knows? Nothing in life submits to easy prediction. Maybe yes, or maybe no; and that's about the size of it, Bathsheba."

With those words, Shemokoman grabbed his belongings and made his way to the exit where he stopped and turned around to ask the lady a final question: "By the way . . . what is the name of your wonderful town? It has to be something befitting."

She smiled and answered, "Eden, Shemokoman, you are in Eden. The fetching locale of Original Sin. Where temptation, I believe, is basically legal and the apples that we like to eat are somewhat sweeter. Get my drift? At least, that is what I hear regarding the vice that we have to deal with. But I must admit it's not so bad to stake a claim and be here. You simply need to be alert and careful. That's all. So please, come back sometime when you are free to see me. I need to know some more about the truth and other circumstances that bore me half to death when I am living. Just remember—we all need each other, and you are no exception. Take care, honey."

Shemokoman nodded and lowered his head, impressed by words of the woman. Then he turned around and left the joint. Her parting advice in every way was right; of course, he knew it. That feminine mind; what can you say? They have the intuitive presence. At any rate, he felt improved by dropping in and meeting with and talking to Bathsheba. It was a sanity check.

Babylon

By and by, the traveler sensed that the end of his trip was coming. He had to be much closer to wherever he was going. Along the way, he met countless numbers of people who said they were having a "very good day." More blatant misrepresentation! . . . They couldn't all be feeling so dandy. And he was still in the Land of Missoura—day ten—when a signpost up ahead declared in large gothic letters: Babylon—the Pride of Akkadian Justice. It was, for sure, his destination; and it was reputed to be the most beautiful place in all of the civilized world. For certain, he'd finally made it.

After the long and strenuous journey, Shemokoman could rest the rest of the evening. He got a room at a local hotel called the Palace of Mesopotamian Knaves right in the center of the town. And despite the fact that he was very sleepy, he was also starved and had to find some dinner. So he ate a square meal at a Persian restaurant that was adjacent to the lobby in the building, where the dialogue was booming all around him from men who were dishing out opinions.

The voices that he heard in there were loud and so unruly, and they only spoke of course about two things: war and women. So much for thoughtful minds that should prevail, and so much for indigestion and a seltzer. Shemokoman eventually called it a day and dragged himself up to his room on the seventh floor. He hit the sack and said a prayer in which there was no plea to any god for holy mercy.

The following morning, he was up and at 'em long before the break of day. He sat in a hard wooden chair next to a pedestal table and sipped on hot black Georgian tea while eating a blueberry tart. After a while, a red rooster crowed and people flooded into the streets of Babylon. Everyone was bartering and bargaining to get the goods and lowdown from the frugal wealthy merchants. The time drew nigh for him to get a move on.

Shortly thereafter, Shemokoman left the hotel and merged into the scrambling public. His first day on the job, so to speak, was replete with everything but monkey business. He was here and there, and everywhere to organize and iron out the necessary details for a visit. And for the most part, people were friendly and helpful with a pace of life that was even slower than the other places where he had resided. No one seemed to be in any hurry; people chewed the fat and took it easy—or any way that they could get it in Missoura.

By the end of the day, he was able to find a suitable home to live in. It was on the edge of town near Sowa Lake, and right beside a charming boggy swamp. For sure, the place was just the way he liked it. After that, it took a few days, but then he was finally all settled in.

Take It Easy, Man

Shemokoman made several friends in Babylon. Darla and Daniel were two of the crew, a couple that he ran around with. In spite of the fact that some of their views appeared to be radically different from his, they tempered the tone of contestable thought with sensible balanced perspectives. Some people don't know how to do it, which only leads to monotonous sermons—that is, if someone has patience to listen.

One evening when it was a Friday, Shemokoman made plans to go into town and visit some places with entertainment. Daniel and Darla were free for the night and decided that they would go with him. So just before dusk, the excursion commenced in search of adventure and action. Babylon was noted for nightlife and a profusion of reckless abandon. The town was also close to old Lost-in-the-Woods, where soldiers milled around and waited for orders. For god's sake . . . guard those man-eating horses.

They strolled along on the quiet streets and passed an endless array of fortified storefronts. Pawnshops, cheap and expensive restaurants, ateliers, furniture stores, and, of course, the bars and cabarets. Finally, they went into a nightclub called the Cradle that was smothered to the hilt in glittery neon. After finding their seats and ordering Jax to brighten the hue of surroundings, they listened to half-witted boisterous talk that filled up the smoky location. The sounds of a banjo and mandolin echoed throughout the rowdy place with bluegrass music. It was time to unwind, take a load off the mind, and find out what the scene was really like in a junkwater town.

Now, it seems that a gal named Delilah started to rant and rave about the need for people to give up their weapons. She said that everyone had to disarm to stop the spread of more violence. She talked about peace, and love and goodwill, as if they had really existed. For her, the time was then and there to implement many big changes.

In particular, the woman noted, "Our friends and neighbors, they suffer and die because of the terrible weapons. Young mothers lose their babies and for what? Because some stupid leader someplace thinks that it is best to have Amendments. Is there no mercy? I'm telling you—we need to go forth and travel the land and confiscate all of the weapons, or else we will be taking a bloodbath. We have to eliminate all of the arms before they destroy us instead. For Pete's sake, I'm just so sick and tired of it all."

Some folks in the crowd who agreed with Delilah provoked an obstreperous uproar. And now, they talked about the way to handle villains. A fellow called Tubby insisted, "Most bandits are merely good people gone bad who require some reeducation. Positive reinforcement—yes, give the hardened gangsters homemade candy. And let them kill whomever they please; after all, it's you and I who really are guilty. Unfortunate, but true. And then—by the grace of God—there will be a day somehow someway when they are compliant, law-abiding, and gentle. It all depends on how we deal with crime and its offenders."

Darla and Daniel thought the spiel was asinine, lacking prudence. The judgmental pitch was so naive and amounted to absolute nonsense. As for Shemokoman, he thought, "People think inspirational dreams are like divine solutions. They believe that foolish heed is real and has a bona fide purpose. Alas, the truth for sleeping souls defies acceptance as the hope they had is lost upon their waking. They need to roll out of the mythical haunt or vanish along with a Maker. Of course, one and the same. Egocentric Pollyannas!"

Shemokoman remained quiet. He heard more talk that missed the point and tacitly chided a brash conversation. The clientele was crude and rude, had little tact, was on a tear, and thought that they were fit to kill dismissive country cousins. You just never know what the loaded sots will mumble. One pompous fellow thrived on interruption, while his prissy wife tried to prove that she could be profound as well as witty. And then at last, the surge of foolish rhetoric about the spread of lawlessness subsided. Silence reigned over the Cradle.

Brass Tacks

Tick-tock, tick-tock, tick-tock. The sound of a pendulum clock on the wall, and time was passing by them. Finally, Shemokoman looked at Delilah and said politely, "Excuse me, madam. But would you care for a different perspective? Believe it or not, when reality cracks, you must consider flukes and know the flip side."

Delilah was quite the impassioned contessa, and obviously not accustomed to effrontery. With a look of disdain in cold, sullen eyes, she glanced at Shemokoman and snapped back, "So, you think you can embellish the commotion we are brewing? Huh, mystery man? What do you know about crime? And what do you know about weapons? Please tell me, I'm dying to hear it. We could use a fairly good laugh right about now."

He replied, "Delilah, your contentious words just minutes ago resounded and virtually shook us. And, I have no claim to expertise, but there is one thing I gather for certain. You have a convoluted awareness of the culture we currently live in. So if you do not mind, it is time for a plunge and allow me to voice a position. Believe me, I have no desire to hurt you, and there is no hidden agenda. I promise you that."

The woman was caught unawares, although no way that she would have confessed it. Shemokoman paused and continued, "I heard you say just minutes ago that you are raising a daughter . . . a girl named Toleration. Now the question is this: When you are home in your condo tonight and after the child's in bed, what makes you think that you and your sweet Toleration will have the good fortune to see a new sunrise tomorrow? Why do you believe that the future will be devoid of all great tribulation? The world is such a precarious place with danger around us, impending. Degenerate felons and prophets abound who thrive on corruption to temper the hate they are feeling."

With everyone notably silent now, he glanced at a clock and went on, "You see, Delilah . . . when nightfall has passed and the stars come out after darkness veils the land, a slayer of men who despises mankind breaks into your home to pay you a nocturnal visit. For him, the hour has finally arrived to conduct a fine execution. To do it and then to remember.

"Delilah, I tell you, it happens something like this: He slips in through a door that should have been locked and enters your upscale home. You just fell asleep and started a dream but open your eyes to the sound of a hinge that is creaking. It is no nightmare. No, rather, a dreadful ordeal with incredible fear that happens to all other people. And slowly, ever so slowly, he moves to your elegant bedroom. The maniac knows you are in there. The presence of random destruction is wearily looming; and god, how they thoroughly love it.

"So you in a panic decide to go hide in a closet with white louvered doors, holding your sweet Toleration. It is the classic reaction, and it was a bad decision. So now he is near, just moments away, and you see through a slit in the door that he is walking, searching and savoring genuine slaughter. Your body is numb; the heart is aflutter, and, the curtain is rapidly falling. Alas, you make a small sound and your cover is blown; he slowly turns around now and stares in your direction. The devil is taking his time, as there is no hurry. For this is the part that he wants to prolong and enjoy, the riveting final best moments.

"All of a sudden, he flings the door open and you and the child are face-to-face with a killer. It would have been nice to have had a little protection. Do you not think so? Like maybe a mace with a spiked metal head, or perhaps a shield along with a double-edged saber. Too late, my darling—all of your weapons were taken away because of a ludicrous frenzy. Your home is engulfed in harrowing screams and anguish beyond comprehension. Inch by inch, the filthy smiling bum is euphorically moving toward you. A lovely ambition has come to fruition; with joy, he revels in evil.

"And now when you see any hope is no more and death is a certain conclusion, you cannot help but wonder: 'Where is goodwill and peace on the earth? . . . Or perhaps my worldly view was a miscalculation. How could it happen to me? . . . My god, I was so caring and righteous.'

"Thus, you give in to fate that you don't comprehend without a good justification. You're dead on the floor in a bloody morass along with your sweet Toleration. It is the deed of a villain who feels no remorse or trace of the slightest compassion. And all on account of a silly belief regarding the merit of weapons. Cased closed."

The story was cogent and chilling. Delilah was sulking and silent. Some people are given to fanciful taste about everyday life and injustice. In spite of a wish to progenerate change, they have very little to offer.

For the rest of the night, the entire group spoke about matters we deem superficial. It was a memorable time with everyone laughing and drinking. Shemokoman relaxed. He didn't think about ethical comrades or the effect of the pain he was feeling. He was able to shut it all out for a while as girls were dancing on tables. And shortly thereafter, Delilah surprised him. You see, she was burdened with sundry misgivings; and so, she thanked him for such an opinion. It was a welcome concession and quite unexpected.

After having had his fill of excitement that evening, Shemokoman left the Cradle with both of his friends. They talked about the adventure in town and mused about people encountered. It doesn't take much to enjoy a night out if expectations are realistic and tempered. Life—a conga line of sentient bodies.

Now, after only a very short while the threesome got weary as they trudged along up a strawberry hill going homeward. The hike to get back was just too much, and there was no public conveyance for them to get onto. So they looked for a place that was cozy and safe to stop and relax for a breather. Finally, a decision was made to rest in a tree with squirrels and birds right next to an Anglican chapel. By golly, they really did do it, and that is some more of the absolute truth.

Land of California

In spite of the fact he was smitten with love for the rugged country around him, the stay in Missoura proved to be fleeting as ever. A sign from the moon and stars up above betokened a new relocation. Astrology had to be honored per a devout Potawatomi chieftain. Thus, Shemokoman had no say in the matter; immortals were pulling the drawstrings, and a big change of pace was impending. Babylon was one more place like so many others where he knew he could easily live on a permanent basis. But, tough luck.

So, he packed up all of his bags and soon departed. But where should he go and what would he do? There had to be a purpose and intention. Thus, he made up his mind to follow the wayward wind to wherever it took him. All right . . . from east to west; the direction was clear, and Shemokoman spent many days and nights traveling far away through dusty plains and over a big mountain range called the Rockies. At last he arrived in a place renowned for adventure, lettuce, and romance. He was at Monterey Bay in the Land of California right on the Ocean.

As he stood on the top of Presidio Hill, the view was a feast for the eyes. Towering pine trees covered the land, shedding their cones and needles to carpet the ground. The fog rolled in and then rolled out, just like every storybook tells us. He saw shiny white snow on high mountain peaks away to the east farther inland. The air was light, and fresh and sweet without any trace of pollution.

At daybreak every morning in that fascinating place, the bark of sea lions who lived in the bay could be heard for miles around. With great finesse, they hammed it up for anyone who came to see those rascals at the coastline. They clapped their flippers, chased a ball, and pranced up high on cresting waves to show off for the public that was watching. Such simple entertainment in that day and age was getting hard to come by.

Shemokoman felt a sigh of relief to be where he was by the Ocean. Although, at times, he did confess to have some apprehension. He thought, "So why am I here at another cool place, where nothing could be any better? I am no prodigal transient man or restive impractical dreamer. Oh well, as long as there's no other choice, I will hit the beach and walk in the sand, and swim in the wavy salt water. And I shall watch the monarch butterflies that come here every year to the eucalyptus groves and remain throughout the winter."

Every so often, Shemokoman went to the wharf on the bay where he spoke with men who worked in fish canning factories. The old-timers told him unusual stories about life and death when men were men and women were only the chattel. They frequently spoke of a gang in town who rejected all modern conventions, like how to trick an unsuspecting green frog in the swampland. Shemokoman always listened with great interest while gazing at the trees and birds in Big Sur through a buccaneer spyglass. He spotted a solitaire thrush one time and was commended by hip flower children. As the big waves crashed in on the jagged shoreline at Monastery Beach near Carmel, sweet fruit was on the trees and vines a stone's throw away in Salinas.

One time as he sat on a bench by himself near the congested marina, he thought about earning one's keep: "Life is so short, a flash in the pan; and only a fool surrenders to passive behavior. People must carefully balance the hours of labor with practical leisure. The Circle of Time was never designed to put up with trifling slackers. In order to meld on a temporal plane, you have to be part of the system.

"Therefore, regarding the nature of people, one ought to respect a good set of standards. 'If you don't work, you don't eat' is something we need to believe in. I remember Duane often said it as well, along with the qualification: 'Socialism isn't all bad.' Consequently, indolent dregs should be starving to death, but instead they are putting on weight. Hmm . . . They're eating like pigs without any restraint, and should be confined in a sty."

Enter the Maze

While living in California, Shemokoman met a woman called Magdalena. She was polite and self-centered, forward, and prone to be sassy. Quite the reluctant patrician, truly a fine decoration for any successful collector. They started to talk and the more he continued to listen to her, a puzzling story developed. It was a cold, regrettable tale, and her mind was especially moonstruck.

"I would have to believe that this woman," he thought, "has suffered too much on account of her forebears. A substantial part of her generous heart is greatly afflicted and broken. Magdalena's accustomed to living with grief; therefore, I will cheer her up with a round of amusement. Something to make her forget about time and the whim of a decadent preacher. Although one must be careful. Fraternization with women like her may entail significant danger."

Shemokoman continued to talk at length with his new acquaintance. And after a while, they went for a walk on Asilomar Beach in the moonlight. As they passed many obsolete maritime fortifications, the sound of the surf was crashing to shore to soothe an estranged visionary. It is a not so ambiguous way that Nature may use to restrain and enthrall us.

Eventually, they made their way back to where shadows were longer than ever—on top of Presidio Hill. She complained of the cold and sprinkles of rain, so he gave her a brown woolen blanket to keep off the chill.

"You know, madam," he explained to her, "nothing can ever be different. We live in a land where everyone has their own expectations and feelings, yet the multitudes share identical hopes and dreams. Accordingly, we mustn't ever discountenance manna from god or falling from grace if required. But as for now, it is time to stop in at Compagno's store and get a nice treat from the deli."

By choice or perhaps a lack thereof, the fate of a night we extol is rarely considered. We play on the earth with all it contains while time slips away disregarded. A pathway in life has nothing to do with a practical conscious decision. And the volition of will imposes no special conditions. Thus, to resolve any serious issue almost requires a competent shaman. Meanwhile, parapsychology needs to obtain recognition. Forlorn on the ship at a faraway sea with waves that are smashing against us, we stand at the helm and steer as best we can to avoid any trouble. Although the vessel will constantly sail according to schedule, no matter how much we want to believe that a miracle ought to prevent it.

A Noble Profession

One morning when Shemokoman was having brunch with Magdalena, he said to her, "My dear, if you have no objection, I would sure like to talk about something we haven't discussed up until now. Namely, your current profession. What is it you do for a living, or is it a secret?"

Glancing at him in a skeptical way, Magdalena was ruffled and then looked away in the distance. The sky was full of ravens and swallows; it was that time of the year for them to be swarming. Then she said with a haughty inflection, "I am a latter-day chick and dance for a living. It is all that I ever wanted to be and all I shall do in the future. Ever since I was young and lacking in fine social graces, I dreamed about being a starlet. Without tangos and waltzes and sambas for me, I surely would up and expire."

She paused and then quietly added, "So what do you think about that, Shemokoman? You have to admit, it's exciting. Resist, I say to myself, conformity's glamour."

"Well, I suppose it's all right for a couple of years," he replied, "but not very good in the long run. As a rule, it takes quite a bit—like forswearing respect and a whole lot of luck—to be a success. Only exceedingly talented people can make it. Most of the wannabes can't pull it off, fall flat on their faces, and haven't the strength to recover. And that is the truth. So, have you ever considered a new line of work? The world is loaded with options. Perhaps it is time for you to explore the potential in other vocations. I would suggest that you ought to try out for the opera."

"Not on your life," she responded. "Are you kidding? I will not! And let me tell you a little secret, my friend. When I'm on the floor and dancing away, then everything's perfect for me. The lights are gleaming and music is tastefully playing; emotion is high and people are streaming around me. When I am dancing, my troubles are gone and nothing remains to affect me. There's no one to critically judge me, and no one to say that I'm sinful. The men that I know are caught in a spell that I cast to completely subdue them. I mesmerize every last one of the boys who dream about having my kisses. And the other girls—of course, they are engulfed in a torrent of envy. They wish they could dance exactly like me, and be such a ravishing siren. Furthermore, although they can never admit it, the people who watch at a distance in awe have nothing but lust and passion inside of their bodies. When I'm on the floor, it is total control; I'm free and my worries have vanished. When I am dancing, all is so very straightforward, you see; humanity gives me approval."

Shemokoman listened with growing dismay to a very delusional woman. He inquired, "Well, if you don't mind my asking . . . Have you made a great fortune in silver and gold by plying the trade that you favor?"

Magdalena smiled. "Silly guy. As a matter of fact, let me enlighten you, fella. When you are the artist like I am and move with the poise of an angel, then you don't have to think about riches. Never. I am no dilettante, no way. I am the royal tsarina. My soul is a delicate spirit, and the world is at my behest. I may have whatever I want and need, and every last fool who's mad for me is willing to give it. My only ambition wherever I go is to take and take; material wealth is truly my one predilection. Hand-outs, you know—just a little blasé. At least I work for a living. My slightest desire enamors a king to provide anything that I covet. Like servants, they offer the basics I need without any shame of contrition. It is surely the best way to live for me, and I cannot ever forsake it. No, no . . . I will never stop dancing."

She flaunted the colors that graced her mystique and finished a vinaigrette salad. Shemokoman sensed the urge to confront a lady with mental derangement. He said, "Well, it all sounds fine and dandy for now, as you seem to have figured it out. Although what happens to you when the future arrives and the immaculate legs are scrawny, and wobbly and tired? What happens to you when your talent to dance commences to drift right out of your second-floor window? And what will you do when the hustle you played is chided by those you thought could be trusted forever? And perhaps you will cry even more when you learn that your dancing is no longer legal. The authorities think it is hurting the youth and causing a horrible uproar. Do not be surprised if the craft you enjoy is forgotten and buried with honors. What then, Magdalena? Please tell me; I'm dying to hear it. How will you cope with such a chaotic debacle? Or maybe you just never bother to think about unhappy endings."

On Desire

Her reply, predictably so, was somewhat confusing, lacking coherence and rational thinking. She sought to avoid any serious tone to shelter a sensitive conscience. She was so clever! . . . And really believed it. And while talking about a profession she loved, Magdalena referred to the God of Excessive Indulgence.

She asked, "So is it that wrong for people like me to give in and comport with desire? Or must I always refrain from something to make me feel better? It doesn't seem right."

Shemokoman stood up and stretched for a bit, returned to his seat, and said, "You know, Magdalena. Desire, the virtue or vice, is very elusive. It teases with sweet moderation at first, and then it is tough as can be to firmly control it. My word, what a pitiful shyster; and my word, what a lecherous bandit. We must be careful to give it its due and also avoid the occasion of sheer ruination. It is never so easy to manage the likes of a demon."

"You see," he continued, "for year after year you are down in the dumps and chase a mysterious notion. A foolish, relentless obsession, something to prove you are better than nothing. A passion is thoroughly lodged in your head and desire is driving you crazy. And even though forces of evil are clearly advancing, you couldn't care less because now you're pursuing ambition.

"Of course, you are puzzled and given to bouts of compulsion, and frequently worried and driven to chronic neurosis. An illness perhaps and only a passing condition. So you decide it is time to give it a break, but you are not able to cease-and-desist for a minute. The struggle is bold and continues. Although it is best to bail, and fast, you simply can never commit and finally end it."

And he went on, "Thus, a sinister fetish continues to haunt you. The work you enjoy is cause for concern and may be potentially lethal. You fathom your soul and try to divine if what you are doing is prudent. Are you adrift on a treacherous course that may result in a bit of misfortune? The important thing here is to clearly distinguish the difference in need and desire. Strictly speaking: the people on earth have a manifest right to receive every thing they require. No one can ever deny it; they are the needs that we cannot dispense with. On the other hand, desire itself can be nothing but greed, totally wrong and inherently vile by nature. Indeed, we should often avoid it; or else we surely destroy a delicate balance required for sensible living, and we invite unacceptable hardship. People who tender their souls for a dream soon know of travail it causes."

"But who knows?" he said. "At long last, the chance is at hand to have something you want, and certainly quite unexpected. Of course, it will frequently happen. You are told *it* is yours, you have it; the journey is over. But now, for some reason, you find that you really don't care about what you desired. Rejection ensues as if it were cursed; it is not what you thought it would be. And you have to admit that deep in your heart, the goal of your dream was never the actual purpose. Rather, desire itself with no other frills was always the poignant objective. Oh, how it can play on seduction to gain your most worthy, affectionate favor! It is the artful companion; and, it is the creep that longs for excessive attention. You were dragooned to engage in a horrible mischief."

He finished up, "People must deal with the ponderous void to halt the irrational pretext. We faithfully try to stay just above ground, discounting impending disaster. And yes, a fiasco may be the crowning result in the final engagement. You just never know. Thus, you see, Magdalena, regarding this dancing of yours: Do not be surprised when your life is awry and shattered because of a samba. And, the passion you had is a thing of the past, along with the style your vanity came to admire. Perhaps it is time to move in a different direction and to look for a new line of work."

Shortly thereafter when he was alone by the Ocean, Shemokoman thought to himself, "Maybe she'll change. But I know that she won't. I heard that she comes from a very long line of overachievers and air-heads. And I am sure that explains a few things."

Nice Revelations

Two full years flew by for Shemokoman in California. During that time, he was no rebel intent on producing a melee. Rather, he was a patient freethinker, and good information to glean and use was simply the purpose he fancied. It just couldn't be otherwise. He felt better with each passing day and learned to reject many troublesome issues. Furthermore, he never let go of a passionate love for Nature wherever he wandered.

Many were those he met in the West who thought about striking it rich. A few of them did, but most of them didn't so much as discover a nugget when panning in rivers. Wealth is a god for those who are seemingly ready. For sure, a miner has got to be awfully lucky. Most of that crowd wound up in a mess, broken and poor, and begging for alms on a corner. Alas, there is little regret in the soul of a man who is needy and fit to be tied.

Once in a very great while, an image appears that has no conceivable equal. "Dusk at San Simeon!" It is a view that can haunt you forever.

After the sun would go under the earth at the end of a typical day, Shemokoman closed his eyes and fell into slumber. He rarely bothered to dream when asleep; there was plenty of that in the daytime. And he was never alone wherever he was, in spite of the fact that nobody circled around him. The point of it all was mistaken belief that man is entangled with people. Just gather more light and pretend it is real; by Jove, what more could we hope for?

It happened one day that Shemokoman met a slender soubrette who offered a token of friendship. Oh yes, she was quite the role-player who said she was steadily probing as always. She thought it was better to stray on the coast and nestle with terrible pirates. So much better that way, when the world knows nothing about you. Just do as you please and blow twenty years, and then you may have a good family. Amen to that! Couldn't she see it was all an appalling diversion? Was she devoid of her senses? There never occurred any true revolution of values. Instead, it was only deception and myth for all of the credulous people. Certain convictions will always apply to the letter; and, they will forgo preposterous odds of replacement.

The longer he lived at Monterey Bay, the more he detested the thought of having to leave it. And why, once again, did he feel it was time to go elsewhere? Well, there were too many special attractions there by the Ocean, such as a magnificent coastline, and beaches with sand where emotional people could languish. Boutiques full of art that conquered the soul and provided incomparable magic. There were ethnic festivals all year round and international musical shows of every conceivable genre. The reflection of moonbeams out on the bay was more than a fellow could handle. Big Sur was another example that offered contentment for hikers and camping. For sure if he stayed, he might soon pass away because living in bliss is a perilous gig for a comrade.

"It is such an adorable venue," he thought, "yet I must prepare for departure. Is that all there is to my journey . . . only a tale of heartache and drifting? Perhaps the effort in finding the truth is really much more than I banked on."

On the Lam

Intuition alone was enough to suffice as a reason to get out of Dodge. He knew that he had to pull out and simply get rolling. Shemokoman felt that it would be best to go far away from the Land of California. The thought of it all was driving him nuts; he needed another perspective. As a result, he decided to move to an old königreich called Deutschland that was located over the Ocean. It was a country with people who knew about glory, misfortune, and courage.

All of a sudden, straight out of the blue, he was facing a serious crisis. So what was the problem this time? Well, he was tipped off by a woman named Abigail Lane that an army of local constables was getting ready to nab him. She said they intended to capture and charge him with fraudulent trumped-up corruption.

Thus, he lamented and pondered, "How can it be true? What have I done?! My life at the coast by Monterey Bay was a fine celebration of virtue. Oh well, I cannot stay here to allow any man or a party machine to oppress me. It is high time to skedaddle."

Shemokoman packed up his modest belongings and thereupon pronto departed. As he was leaving, he noticed a poster that hung in the old town square. It read:

LAND OF CALIFORNIA
The People's Implacable Court of Criminal Justice
Plenipotentiary Directive
Public Writ of Urgent Intervention / et al., Chop-Chop
Apprehend and Neutralize: Shemokoman !!!

———————

For crimes of a Lunatic Nature.
He is guilty of:
    intent to abscond with a portion of national pleasure;
    corrupting the youth with truth;
    condoning forbearance for people who have no willpower; and . . .
    defending the right of man to think for himself.
He was also observed deriding abuse and liberal torture in public.

———————

REWARD:
A dinner for two at your local cantina with Crazy Invaders

Forever another dilemma. Of course, Shemokoman wasn't surprised. It was important those days for the public at large to have a good villain to hunt for. It took most of the night, but soon there was hope as he came to a natural border. And even though the ethical comrade was tired of walking for hours on end, he went up and over the big mountain range and crossed a great desolate plain. Now he had pretty much made it; it was a clean getaway from the lynch mob. Yet still he was somewhat bewildered. Must he remain a fugitive from injustice for the rest of his natural lifetime? Or what could he do to address it?

Just then, he stumbled upon a sight for sore eyes. The Statue of Limitations was standing before him. And right on the spot, he was informed by the lawgiver that there was no need to worry whatsoever. His case was truly a "cause célèbre," and he could look forward to great accolades and exoneration in the near future. It was all the result of an ethical life where equity has to prevail. He knew what he was and always would be in spite of a stab to negate it.

Thor and Brünhilde

It came to pass one day that as Shemokoman was leaving Califor-nia, Magdalena was out for a stroll by the bay when she happened upon two vagabonds. A man and a woman were sitting alone in tatters and very dejected. When asked about where they belonged, they said they were down on their luck and banished. The latter-day dancer decided to take them in for the day, providing board and shelter. Such a heart.

The man said that his name was Thor, a mighty god who reigned over all of Nature. The woman was Brünhilde, a Valkyrie and queen who seldom ventured from Valhalla. And they both knew that light was day and darkness was the night, and they breathed as much fresh air as either wanted. It's hard to tell where deities and regal, sultry ladies will end up at, when all's for naught because the royal fireworks were over long ago.

Upon learning of the kindly deed, Shemokoman mused, "To rescue them without a second thought, so very touching. Alas, compassion comes and goes in those who haven't anyone to truly care for. The real question is: How much evil in her is lurking there as well?"

Time to Sail

A couple more weeks went by in perfect succession. Nothing re-mained for Shemokoman other than relocating in Deutschland. All preparations were made with meticulous detail. And now, the dancer said that she wanted to come along on the trip with him. He didn't ob-ject, although perhaps he should have. Decisions occur like fortuitous pranks with no rhyme or reason about them. It is the way that life really is: desultory.

As he stood on the smooth white sand of a beach that was close to the Port of Departure and viewed the formidable Ocean, Shemokoman summoned the Lord of the Deep, Mr. Poseidon. In particular, he said, "Tomorrow, I sail across your domain to a hallowed imperial kingdom. I implore you, my friend, to grant safe passage to me and to her with whom I will travel. Our fate is a perilous journey in time that rends the Eternal Divider. And you are the one to guide us to ruin or freedom."

10

⌒∞⌒

Deutschland

New Continent

It was your typical wintry day in December on the coast of the frigid North Sea. A strong wind was blowing with heavy snowfall and drifting. A big gray ship loaded with passengers pulled into the Port of Arrival. The name of the place was Bremerhaven, a small town in the province of Lower Saxony in Deutschland. The curious eyes of people who disembarked from the seafaring vessel were suddenly blinded by whiteness. Some of them thought about sailing back, afraid of what they might be in for.

Shemokoman was tired, yet alert and exceedingly careful. Fatigue is a reason for too many big mistakes and measly slipups. He was in a new land with unusual people and remarkable medieval buildings. There would be much to enjoy and do during the trip overseas.

Everyone who got off the ship needed several days for rest and recuperation. It was a long, arduous trip; they had to recover. And it didn't take long for Shemokoman to realize that he had to deal with the language. Wherever he went in that nice little Stadt, the story was always the same. He did not understand one single word that anybody was saying. So he started to listen and learn, and soon, he mastered a new kind of speaking. Modal auxiliaries, past participles, four cases, articles—der, die das, and the rest of the Aryan lingo. Now he was able to fluently talk with people he met in Deutschland. Guten Tag!

Each morning thereafter, the ethical comrade rose out of bed bright and early to greet the new day. He walked to the old part of town where he sat on the cold wooden benches by the rough hyperborean waters. It was the very best way to fit in and converse with indigenous people. He watched as Beamters swept the streets and all of the scurrying Teutons rushed into and out of the stores. Mainly bäckereien, metzgereien, and konditoreien. Shopping was more than a simple routine; it was their style of living. And down at the piers, they were loading and unloading all of the maritime cargo. Enormous white seagulls with fair yellow heads were soaring on high and thinking about a return to the Harlingen sanctum.

Eugen, Bernhard and Wolfgang, Karl and Heinz—they were Shemokoman's friends in town, and they were the jovial gang. He thought to himself, "These men whom I know are surely no different than I am. We are all from a mold that is one and the same, maybe totemic connections. However, and unfortunately, they had to put up with events for thousands of years that were wretched and savage. I read a few books concerning their fate, and some of the opas recounted the horrible stories. Of course, they are bothered by negative mood, accounting for rigid behavior. But I will tell you one thing for sure: they are proud, strong, and happy."

Superior Folk

The people in Deutschland had always been very particular and fully obsessed with "die Ordnung" (i.e., "the Order"). Everything had its time and place, and tradition had to be followed. Citizens walked, and stopped and talked, in precisely the orthodox manner. Die Ordnung. All neighborhood streets in each city and dorf were spick-and-span; no rubbish to badly pollute them. Die Ordnung. At night, they lit up the streetlamps and put them out each morning according to schedule. Die Ordnung. They delivered the bier to the front of a house at 9:00 a.m. sharp without fail. Die Ordnung. Trains and trolleys that crisscrossed the land were always on time, no exceptions. Die Ordnung. You had to show up wherever employed and work like the devil and then some. Die Ordnung. It all amounted to stark depolarization. A national *will*, if you will. A cogent reminder for telling the world that "we on this soil— in Deutschland—we are the best. We're second to none. Die Ordnung precludes any and all deviation."

As he took note of terrain in the land to get a good orientation, Shemokoman saw large black patches of earth that stretched for miles across the countryside. He thought to himself, "Hmm . . . I am looking at scars that come from the past when there was much war and destruction. No wonder that most of the people appear to be somber, bound and determined. It is a marred federal state with serious Menschen."

The Deutsche nation was always so downright creative. The people excelled especially in every branch of the arts, to include literature, theater and opera, music and poetry, and dance. You name it, they certainly did it. The celebrated immortals—from Wagner and Goethe to Nietzsche and Bach—during the days of old gone by provided the world for years to come with a treasure trove of their talent. And although they had to put up with many obstructions, the scope of aesthetic production continued to thrive far beyond what anyone might have expected.

Above all else, it was apparent to any foreigner that these people were committed to knowing the truth. They didn't beat around the bush and liked to tell it as it is, never lied, and had to be straightforward. Fidelity was valued, and if anyone so much as even thought of fabrication, it would prove to be their utter downfall.

One evening, Shemokoman was sitting at a table outside on a patio under an umbrella by the seacoast. He was drinking a maß of bier and eating a gypsy schnitzel with fried potatoes. One of his favorite meals. He looked up and saw the colorful hues of an unusual orange horizon. A single big white fluffy cloud was giving chase to reverie intently in a northerly direction. The setting sun, as he could tell, had a yen to shine much more without the daily grind of going under. But even celestial bodies have to obey die Ordnung.

Progenitor

His first few weeks in Deutschland could not have flown by any faster. For people with busy agendas, time is insufficient and often chaotic. In any event, Shemokoman made the adjustment. And now he had to leave Lower Saxony and go south to the city of München. He needed to find a place somewhere to serve as a suitable homestead. Thus, he made plans with the dancer, who would then join him not far in the future, packed all of his belongings, and departed.

He decided that it would be best to travel by rail, on die Bahn. The trains were always neat and clean and ran on schedule. It would take the better part of two or three days to reach the new destination. So, after going to the Bremerhaven Station and making his way to the platform, he boarded a shiny new steel passenger coach in the early hours of the morning. Mind the gap! He entered Compartment No. 38, and there was one other fellow inside it.

Having tossed his luggage into the overhead rack, Shemokoman sat in a seat next to the window. The other traveler was a young man, obviously deutscher, who was reading the latest issue of the *Fellbacher Zeitung*. Shortly thereafter, the fellow introduced himself; his name was Gottlob Friedrich. Shemokoman responded in kind; and to be sure, a peculiar discussion developed.

"Well, it appears to me that you are a stranger in Deutschland," Gottlob said. "You came to see the sights and also learn about our customs. You want to meet and get to know the people who abide here. For example, sitting with some locals at a Stammtisch on a Sunday would be perfect relaxation in a Rathaus. But most importantly, I think you have a goal—philosophy; and the truth is your objective. What you see and what you don't are sources of confusion that perplex you. So how am I doing thus far, my friend? Am I correct about your intentions?"

"Yes, you most certainly are," he replied. "Somehow, categorically, you are aware of my program. And how can that be so? . . . I mean, of course I'm somewhat puzzled. But I must digress to now explain some other significant matters. Namely, everything that I see appears to be vaguely familiar. The narrow roads in rustic towns, people walking down the lanes, and rivers flowing from mountaintops to peaceful valleys below. And here, for example, I notice we're passing the Saalburg, so imposing. High up on the Taunus ridge and deep in the province of Hesse, it looks to be that I was there when Romans fought barbarians to keep them out of the empire."

"Indeed, I get the feeling," he went on, "that I was here in person in the not-so-distant past. The crowded double Straßenbahn, the old Romantic Road that runs through Augsburg, the sour grapes that growers have to harvest in a vineyard. Even he who made the shoes—the poet-cobbler—who jumped right off the Perlachturm and didn't go too far, but killed a brood of chickens. It is all like déjà vu, and it is all so overwhelming. I can't explain impressions that I get recurrently just looking at the faces here beside me. But as for you, Gottlob Friedrich, please indulge me. To what rosy destination do you travel? And whence comest thou? You strike me as the sort of chap who has a stirring story."

To say the least, Gottlob Friedrich was blown away by what his fellow traveler had to say. And with a smile, he said, "Well, if I must confess—and something in my mind is telling me, 'You'd better do it' . . . notwithstanding the grandeur and prestige of the great Reich where I was born and lived for twenty years, I made up my mind to cast my lot in the land of another great nation. It's a risky plan, for sure; especially in the light of noble kinship I am leaving. We spent many years together working hard and drinking bier, mending broken fences, and building the Waiblingen bridges. And for what? God only knows. Alas, I will forsake the golden wheat fields and the vintage on my hillsides that will soon be turned to wine. You see, Shemokoman, I'm going to your country, to America, where I shall be a farmer in Lancaster County. In just a few days, I will sail across the Ocean on the handsome *Barque Comet*, which will take me far away with my belongings to my fiancée, the dear Nancy. Then, we will go by post chaise to Pennsylvania, where I will live with her and she with me until they bury us together in the graveyard by a church in Donegal Township. Not a single progenitor did it; verily, what a ménage to be proud of."

He continued, "But first, I need to spend some time in the city of München to wrap up personal business. Then it's off to the sea for me. To the cold, windy north, to board a great ship and sail on the bounding main and journey to my freedom. I leave this land forever; it is time that wasn't wasted. Two people that I know who could never let it go, of course, betrayed me. They told me lies and veiled truths, which only led to total alienation. They were the righteous mountebanks, my Autocratic Duo. And when I'm gone, they probably will not know that someone's missing. Or perhaps—they will weep and wonder for a while and tell every soul about the facts that didn't even happen. Colossal fraud is what the team was good at. Moreover, the next generation in Württemberg will surely never know that I was ever born and once existed. Enough said. Basta per oggi."

It was obvious that Gottlob Friedrich was having a pretty rough day. He was vexed by strong emotion and the likes of deep compunction. And even though he was young and resilient, and very decisive at that, the trip for him was not about to be a simple cakewalk. Of course, it would be a big challenge. As anyone knows, you think it's a breeze, and suddenly everything's haywire. And the woman to whom he alluded—his Nancy, hopefully she would be worth it. A precarious move, a leap of faith; it could end up costing him dearly.

Then, after a period of silence, Gottlob added, "So now it's your turn, Shemokoman. Tell me something, tell me anything; although I must give you a warning. I will not be bored with stories about young love or emotional drama. It is a waste of time. And I cannot stand the pointless junk that passes for adventure. Enough of that already in a lifetime. Furthermore, I do not like the legends of those foolish small men who thought that they were giants. All I ask of you is this: please, just tell me the truth."

Veracity

Sometimes, we encounter a situation that's out of sync with existence. No doubt the work of strange invisible forces. Shemokoman paused for a minute or so and then gave voice to what he felt he had to: "First off, Gottlob Friedrich, I would say . . . The world that I know and see is full of loathsome evil. And down through the ages, many good men tried to do something about it. But they all failed miserably. You see, the impostors will look at you straight in the eye and savor the taste of corruption. It must be a national pastime, as they go out of their way to enjoy it. And as I travel about to explore the faraway reaches, I am saddened by so much affliction. Alas, there will always be plenty of vice on earth for old vigilantes with torches. And that is the god's honest truth."

Shemokoman sipped on a cup of hot black Georgian tea that he'd obtained in the restaurant wagon. Then he went on, "I don't know how and don't know why, but it seems to me that our meeting here today is more than a random occurrence. Indeed, somehow I know you. Though, by golly, I am baffled. Perhaps we met some other place where pale phantoms plagiarize the daydreams. And I know about Nancy as well, a wonderful woman."

God, praise! The man who was bound for America truly adored the anomalous spiel. The vernacular was something he could wrap his mind around and then get used to. Direct and right to the point, pulling no punches. He needed to hear and confirm it from someone who honestly couldn't deceive him. The words of Shemokoman bandied about in a portion of time that wavered. He spoke the truth, and Gottlob Friedrich expressed his approval.

As the train with all of the passenger coaches continued to roll through Deutschland, the occupants of Compartment No. 38 managed to hit it off pretty well. So much so that they failed to notice congenital auras between them. The present, the past, and future converged into one paranormal partition. It is hard to describe every thing they discussed, mostly talk of a sensitive nature. Albeit, obscure information that in effect only had serious meaning. While munching on bayerische crackers and cheese, they spoke about whether or not the Saturday beatings—intended for good measure only—were apt and effective. "You dare ask me what for! . . . If I knew what for, then I'd really let you have it!" And women were given a spot in the light where notable features were lauded. Both men acquiesced to a mystical fold for the brief interlude while traveling, enchanted by fate and the spell of a sorcerous wellspring.

In due time, when much of the dialogue pretty much ended, the ethical comrade thought about Catherine. He took out a pen and paper, having decided to write her a letter. In it, he spoke of a tale regarding two men who traveled in different directions. And yet, the Circle of Time ensured that they were bound to run into each other. It was a paradox born of devotion; it was a paradigm boding no mayhem. So what is a true destination? And where do we honestly think we are going? Well, perhaps to a realm where we tarried about although we've not actually been there. Indeed, stranger things have happened.

Moreover, a happenstance wasn't the point of it all for men with a favored perception. And guile—as it were—was purely forbidden. They traveled along on reliable tracks for a lengthy spell to catch up on meaningful details. And now, Shemokoman wondered, "We only live once on the opulent earth, but how many times do we perish?"

Toward the end of the second day, the train entered Bavaria and soon arrived at the city of München. Gottlob Friedrich and Shemokoman exchanged contact information and promised to stay in touch for more than a lifetime. Then they parted. Every so often, we bump into someone along the way—it can be on a desolate stretch of the road or wherever—and we instinctively know that a part of the *self* has connected. It is the exception and highly unlikely but really can happen. Such was the case with these two men. They shared a few brief moments in life that, as it turned out, were eternal.

Giesing

Shemokoman found a place to live in a small city suburb called Giesing. It was nothing like what he expected, but then again, what did he expect? He thought, "Did I have any sort of an expectation for housing here in Deutschland? Hmm . . . of course, now I remember. No, I did not. I was too busy with personal chores to give it exclusive attention. With so much to do and to plan the trip, I couldn't afford to think about incidental extraneous matters. Maybe next time. So now, at least I've managed to fully resolve the troubling issue. Hooray! Thank god for small favors. Yippee!"

The new residence was in a so-called Low Teutonic home, or Fach-hallenhaus. It used to be a government building, recently converted to housing for farmers and working-class people. The exterior was made of dark half-timbered construction, and white louvered shutters enhanced the large rectangular windows. It was spacious inside with several big rooms; the ceilings were high and vaulted. A little austere, perhaps in a way; there were no frills to speak of. But all in all, it was a splendid abode for a party of two to reside in.

During his first few weeks at the new location, Shemokoman spent most of his time preparing the house for occupation. He was aware that wandering souls require a temple to play in. For what it was worth, he couldn't refrain from doing the bidding of angels. Thus, he made ready an excellent home for himself and the latter-day dancer to stay in. He also determined the way to the Victuals Market, where it was best to catch a tram if he wanted to go to a Bad, and how to get to the Post.

The neighbors he met who lived on the block were cordial and basically helpful. Especially the young ones, who didn't know much about plunder, warfare, and evil. They advised him on the ins and outs of life and tradition in Deutschland. In particular, they noted: "More than anything else, do not be afraid. Get out of the house and mix with Bavarian people. It will be very rewarding, and it is the way to make a good friend for a day or even forever."

So that is what he did. And thus, Shemokoman met up with loads of people. Come rain or shine, he was out and about, consorting with Aryan natives. The aborigines at the Hofbräuhaus were uncommonly keen on discussion. They often talked for days on end about the current events. Like why should they have to put up with a king who couldn't stop building the castles. And who should enforce the Purity Law, das Reinheitsgebot, to make sure that all of the bier was fit for consumption. Everyone asking questions and wanting answers.

Together

After about a month of getting adjusted, Shemokoman was joined by Magdalena. He met her at the railroad station in München upon her late arrival just like always. Then they got onto a crowded trolley and went straight home to relax in the new surroundings. The sun, the earth, and moon that day were all in proper alignment. Thus, the signs he noted coming from the cosmos appeared to indicate that life was normal.

Location Fascination

While living abroad, Shemokoman visited scores of charming places. Besides the pleasure he derived from seeing all the sights, it was like a higher education. He went to old historic cathedrals and toured plush palatial castles. He took slow walks beside the Isar River during every season of the year. He rode in boats that chugged along on Starnberger Lake and frolicked on a sandy beach in Italia farther south. Above all else, he enjoyed well-spent time in the fabulous Deutsche culture.

Meanwhile, the dancer didn't take a break from cha-chas and a mambo. How could she not dig the place, almost everywhere another nightspot. Alas, she didn't see that much was wrong and little right as her shaky art began to suffer. People left the club in droves, inexplicably, just as she was turning up the heat. For sure, the pain was in her soul; but she would not admit it. And laughter for the dancer, yes—that mirthful disposition we call laughter, was how she slipped away and went to pieces. The moments of spinning to music with empty stone faces were starting to haunt her. The latter-day girl who always had all of the answers was out of sorts and lonely now.

Stadt Zoological Garden

A cold, snowy winter and drizzly spring passed by in Bavarian country. Summer arrived just in time for all of the diligent people. The föhn wind blew in for a couple of weeks, so everyone had to be crazy. It was the perfect excuse to strangle a spouse and say, "Temporarily, I was insane."

At that time of the year, Deutschland offered a wealth of things to do for anyone who liked to be outdoors. People often left the dorfs and cities to go to the country and Volksmarch. Up and down the hills, across the fields, and through the forest on the walking trails. Nothing could compare to that; it was recreation at its finest. And a hiker sure was proud of every medal, patch, or plate that was earned after knocking out those grueling twenty klicks.

On one particular morning in July, Shemokoman as usual got up at the crack of dawn. And after having breakfast, he went to the Stadt Zoological Garden. It was a large menagerie with wild animals, birds and snakes, big and little fish and pesty insects, and other living entities from countries all over the world. Life evolves in astonishing ways, and all too often there is no appreciation.

When he arrived at the zoo, it was already packed to the hilt. People came early to have ample time to see the captured creatures. As usual, he entered by way of the south portal and passed the medieval stonework. Then he walked down the steep set of stairs and went to the first exhibit: the flamingo lagoon.

My word, what an elegant species. Unbelievable bright orange plumage. The sight never managed to cause something other than incontrovertible wonder. A portion of tangible proof on earth that God is enamored with beauty. The flock consisted of hundreds of motionless slender wading birds located in still, shallow water. It almost appeared as if they were sleeping.

While he looked at the birds, Shemokoman thought, "These creatures are perfect in every respect and nothing is offbeat or missing. With two thin legs for symmetrical poise, they use only one while standing. Of course, good balance is always a critical need, and they do it with ease for a lifetime. The species to which I belong nowadays could learn a great deal by observing these marvelous guys. They have what it takes for survival.

"It appears that flamingos have scant little need to soar high aloft in the sky. Albeit, the instinct to fly is a latent desire that occasionally hedges inside them. But most of the time they remain on the ground; it is their home and they like it. Nature provides what they need every day, and the rest is reserved for tomorrow. With no thought about malice, envy, or greed, these birds comport with their fine feathered friends while foes are sequestered in exile. There is no apparent corruption, and hardship is never an issue."

Shemokoman now moved on to another exhibit.

"And what have we here?" he thought to himself. "Who do I see that is roaming the bounded savannah? Why of course, the lanky giraffes. So noble and proud, mellow and also genteel . . . Good heavens, they almost appear to be friendly. But make no mistake about how they react when danger imperils the tower, as a giraffe has ample protection when it believes that a threat is impending. With only one kick from their powerful legs, a hostile brute can be instantly out of commission. And just get a load of their kids: oh yes; they are so cute, and they are so big. For any giraffe, the sky is no usual limit. Although it has got to be tough when they get a sore throat and whenever the weather is stormy with thunder and lightning."

After a while of watching the big spotted mammals, Shemokoman noticed and went to another display of animal neighbors. It was a band of merry elephants. He thought, "Who can refuse to adore those punk renegades who are the scions of a long and happy existence? With nothing to dread on account of their size, so slowly they move without a desire to cross any shouting insurgent. And just take a look at those long, swinging trunks. How much can they hold? Well, enough for a trip through the jungle. And the white ivory tusks are wanted for gain by every contemptible poacher. Oh, such a remarkable cohort, and such an adorable rascal. Furthermore, what do I see over there by that fence? Holy cow! A Byzantine home built especially for them right here in the center of München. Talk about luxury."

"Indeed," he mused, "who are the masters and who are the lowly bondservants? And who is in heavy confinement in the enclosure? Sometimes I wonder."

Continuing on and traversing through rough territory, the Michigan man spotted a dazzle of zebras. He paused to observe and admire them; how playful and purely sublime. They were cavorting and beaming, and trotting around and eating the long green grass, a favorite dinner. The black-and-white stripes are always unique; you cannot mistake any one in the zeal for another. Yes, the zeal. They have to accept it.

As Shemokoman gazed at the zebras, he sensed a trace of distinct apprehension. Yes, for sure, he detected some panic. And why? A glance over yonder beyond many fences led to a gripping discovery. Three panthers were perched up high in a tree, lying on branches and spying a bloody fine luncheon. For sure, we know what those fellows were thinking. The carnivorous cats will constantly search for a chase, the kill, and consumption; it is their nature. And although the chances of such an event taking place in the zoo were slim to none, the zebras would always be leery.

The morning soon ended and now it was lunchtime. Shemokoman was in the mood for sampling Deutsche cuisine. So, he decided to eat at a small Schnell Imbiss, where curry- and brat- and weißwurst, plus several desserts, were promptly requested. The traditional meal was served outside on wrought-iron patio tables under a canopy. Some fat honeybees were buzzing around and trying their best to get at his fresh apple strudel. In spite of a try to prevent it, the quick little thieves managed to swipe a few morsels. When he had finished the tasty food, he got up and stretched, and then resumed the excursion.

Next off, he entered a frosty locale called the Polar World. Good grief, it was cold over there, like a hundred below. The main attraction was taking a swim and fooling around for the youngsters. It was the polar bear, your typical show-off. He always put on the impressive performance for all of the people in need of amusement. Just one immense provocative guy; a shaggy spontaneous comic who was endowed with inherited talent.

Shemokoman stared at the regal white beast and pondered, "Nice fellow, as long as he stays over there and I'm on this side of the wall. And what does he think while staring at me? For sure, he couldn't care less about gandering people. Most likely, his thoughts are focused on home and drifting on fragmented ice floes, and catching his balance while running through cold empty spaces, and diving and hunting for seals in clear frigid water. For sure, he remembers a day—not that long ago—when everything sparkled to herald another new sunrise. I cannot imagine how much he dearly must miss it. It is a shame that he cannot go back for even one visit. Moreover, he just doesn't care about illness or weather conditions, or anything else that affects superior prowess. No, not him. The great polar bear is fully aware that dependence is never at issue because he can do fine by himself. And his home is wherever he vies to exist, with stunning auroras that dance in the boreal heavens."

Moving along, the comrade thought, "So what is next on the schedule? What sort of wonders await to intrigue me? Wow! . . . It is a waddle of emperor penguins. And each of them wearing a perfectly tailored tuxedo. With stately black heads and those puffy white bodies and streaks of bright yellow for accent, they endure an inconceivably difficult lifestyle. They breed and reside and consort with their kind where justice is never considered, no way. And they never suspect or decry whatever might happen. Waving their flippers and cracking a joke, they revel like fat little men on the edge of a glacier. Who cares about wind and rain or a deadly tsunami? They can do nothing about it. So dashing and plain charismatic, they pay no attention to welter in life or courage for death in a blizzard."

Thus, the enchanting safari continued. Antelope, lions, and bears soon appeared with papas and mamas and children. He mused, "What is it in people that serves to neglect and desecrate principled values? A rather disgusting occurrence, I would say."

And finally, a large group of patrons was gathered en masse at the site of an awesome exhibit, with everyone quiet and staring. It was the savage Siberian tiger. They admired the cat as he walked to and fro on a high stone wall directly in front of the crowd. With the aid of immaculate senses—and who knows how many he wielded—he was the absolute sovereign; and, he was the ultimate creature. He knew about stalking and hunting, and he would never think twice about killing. So where do you find the formidable fellow? Well, he is often afoot and lurking about inside of a mangrove swamp, or perched in a tree to surveil and have the advantage.

For Shemokoman, there was always one particular quality of the Siberian tiger of special interest. Namely, it tends to be highly reclusive. It doesn't develop affection or trust in animals who belong to the very same species.

"On account of a penchant to be all alone with a nature that disavows friendship," he thought, "the tiger is forced to live by itself without any faithful companions. Day in and day out, he moves to exist, to feed and to sleep in the boondocks. And with only some minor exceptions, the tiger is really at ease in total seclusion."

The big cat continued to pace back and forth while sightseers eagerly watched him. And just for a sudden brief second or two, his cold amber eyes locked onto the gaze of Shemokoman. That pair of particular animate fellows decisively noticed each other, not even blinking. The moment defined a detachment in time as feelings and knowledge were clearly exchanged between them. The tiger then nodded and mused about man, and remained by himself inside of the lair that keepers saw fit to establish.

The visit wrapped up with a walk through a part of the zoo that featured exhibits from America. A herd of bison was roving the plain, and prairie dogs scurried about in their underground tunnels. And last but not least, there were humans. They were some vile, deplorable specimens, and a gift to the city of München from the God of Divine Retribution. The caged miscreants were tawdry and mean, and dirty, with hideous faces. They all were obtained without putting up any resistance on Easy Street in their slovenly shanties.

Shemokoman thought, "I hope that they are the last men."

It came to pass that one more visit was over to the Stadt Zoological Garden. Shemokoman left the place contented and grateful. Then he stopped in for dinner at a Balkan restaurant called the Fasanenpark Gasthaus and feasted on mountains of cordon bleu and drank a few maß of bier. And he just didn't bother to trouble his mind by thinking about any dancer.

The Expatriate

Once upon a time, there was a fellow named Mr. Madorney who lived in Deutschland. Shemokoman often would visit the guy because they were on the same wavelength. And usually, those two men would sit up for hours until it was late in the evening discussing a wide range of topics. And nothing was ever off-limits. It's nice to have someone to talk to who's not afraid of colloquial hang-ups.

On one occasion, Shemokoman spoke with his friend about personal matters: "So, Vova, please tell me. You say that you worked as a lumberjack deep in the forest of old Belarus. You felled many trees of aspen and spruce from morning till late in the evening. And one by one, you chopped them up for people to heat up their khatas. You say that you lived there for thirty-plus years, but then a disaster occurred. You received a call to arms, and a great patriotic war forced you to come to this country where you fought like a socialist devil against many Aryan fathers and sons. Of course, you have the medals and scars to prove it. And there was finally a truce, now there is peace, and your family is still at home right where you left them. So why don't you return to the great Motherland to be with the wife and your children?"

Mr. Madorney answered, "Because if I did, they would kill me."

The scourge of war and its grave consequences create inconceivable sorrow. The vestal masses can never imagine what it is like to be thrown into battle. The corpses and blood, and pieces of bone as scavengers feed on the cold, rotting flesh of the fallen. Ares, of course—a slimy, despicable monster. And victims who manage to live through it all are forgotten, as no one remembers. Thus, we are not able to fathom the plight of unfortunate souls beside us . . . namely, the expatriates. Mendacity towers to veil the truth, and casualties probe as much as they can in the search of a shred of their honor.

There ought to be proof that redeeming essentials are coming. Meanwhile, the world is stuck in a syndrome of war that started when humans were monkeys. Mr. Madorney was tricked by a man in a desperate land that always was brutal and ruthless. He was impressed to aggression, captured, and forced to admit it. And thus he was branded: Enemy of the State. "So please, it is best that you do not return. Indeed, you may come to regret it." There is your choice, and there is the rotten solution.

Visit of an Ethical Comrade

In August of that very year, Citizen R. went to Deutschland. He crossed the great Ocean and then took a train that carried him straight to München. After finding his way to Shemokoman's place, he knocked on the door . . . a *rap, rap, rap*. And— "Holy smokes! What a fantastic surprise."

The guest was invited inside the home and treated to snacks and libations. The two fellows talked for the better part of a gray afternoon about their significant issues. Citizen R. said life in the park was about the same, and nothing much changed save for a few of the neighbors.

Shemokoman said that life where he lived was never the same, every-thing changed, and people made fun of His Highness. Later on, they boarded a trolley that went to the city and found a gasthaus on the Marienplatz at which to relax.

No one was giving a fiery speech at the Bürgerbräukeller intended to start a rebellion. The nation was leery of passionate men who couldn't deliver as promised. The public was tired of fighting for lead-ers who talked about cleansing and vengeance. Too many slogans can lead one astray and into a frenzy with sheer ruination. While Citizen R. and Shemokoman consumed a few maß of bier, they tried to sur-mise if political slobs are essentially pleasing to Jesus. Probably not, and what a theistic conundrum.

After they finished hobnobbing at length with a few of the blond desperadoes, they left the city and visited part of the country. As they stood on the banks of the beautiful Tegern Lake and gazed at the rip-pling water, Shemokoman noted, "We ought be on a schooner right now with the 'Roger' hoisted above us. With sea dogs, sabers, and bar-rels of rum, and laughing at lads who never knew mother or father. High on the bounding main to plunder the galleons passing beside us. Indeed, we really should be with the sirens right now who would sing a sweet song to enchant us: 'Young man, it is time to descend straightaway into the dark nether regions—and discover the pleasure that you and the shark bait are missing. You have to go down to as far as you can if you want to be living it up. Please, oh please, come sail to me, to the coast of a rapturous isle. Where people can stay for as long as they play without ire or thought of a Yahweh.'"

Citizen R. was rather impressed by all he discovered in Deutsch-land, where a visiting man with a curious mind could go on exploring forever. The buildings and fountains, landmarks on every street corner, municipal parks, museums, and everything else was there for a public beholden. It was worth every bit of the effort he made to go on the trip overseas. The indigenous folks went out of their way to present a mag-nificent country. Furthermore, he went to the Great Oktoberfest with Shemokoman and partied in each of the bier tents. Eleven of them, to be exact. Man, what a big celebration; perhaps, the greatest in all of the world. Plenty of music, chicken and wurst, and lots of rides outside for fanatical thrill-seekers.

On the last day of his visit, Citizen R. and Shemokoman traveled north to the beguiling Fields of Glonn. It was a bright sunshiny Sunday—the perfect day for an outing—and they picked a whole bushel of strawberries. And although a small man was prancing around in a green adjustable Miesbacher hat, no one or nothing spoiled the pleasant excursion. When they got home, the reward for what they accomplished was plenty of shortcake.

The hour drew near for Citizen R. to be going. It was time for him to return to his home and assign those fun story problems to kids in the classroom. The triangles, limits, exponents, and theorems were waiting. Thus, the two ethical comrades bid each other a hearty farewell and retired to separate places. Furthermore, the traveling man also managed to leave with more than he ever expected.

Catherine in Bavaria

Exactly one month after Citizen R.'s departure, Catherine paid a visit to Shemokoman as well. It was another surprise; he had no idea that the lady was coming. She traveled alone for the very first time to Deutschland and stayed for exactly five days.

Her lodging was booked at a rustic auberge less than a klick from the city. The accommodations were modest and clean; a receptionist got her checked in. She had convenient access to all the amenities: a big shopping center, excellent restaurants, ground transportation, delicatessens, and everything else required. Oh, look . . . look . . . look! Look at the trolley!

The lady went straight to Shemokoman's place on the very first evening she got there. Their meeting was such a delightful affair; it couldn't have gone any better. They spoke about Michigan current events, the lagoon in Irving Park, work, play, and travel abroad, where everything old was new and so very exciting. Meanwhile, the dancer said little and left in a hurry for prior and pressing engagements.

Talking with Catherine was easy to do, and uplifting. She knew what to say and what not to say without trying to make an impression. Very few people can do it; speech is a way to inflate alter egos. In particular, tonight she critiqued Shemokoman's quest to find the truth and clear up a mass of confusion. When should he stop and give up, and when is enough enough? You have to be mighty perceptive, given to liberal wisdom and courage.

In the days that followed, they took long, leisurely walks down in the city and shopped in novelty stores for what was unique. They went to the Neuschwanstein Castle high on a mountain, ate plenty of native cuisine, and polished off stein after stein of Hacker-Pschorr bier. All the while, a clock inside of Shemokoman's head was ticking. He wanted to feel it pause for a spell, but time is a torrent, unyielding. No, we cannot ever restrain it. Everything everywhere was moving and rolling along at a pace going forward. Shemokoman knew that he was no conjuring wizard who was able to toy with dark supernatural forces.

Catherine Hesse was such an exemplary woman. She dressed in the finest of finery wear and shunned maquillage for the most part. She never stared at a soul anywhere impolitely and didn't waste time on trying to prove that she was a cut above others. The lady was undefiled, self-effacing, and never harsh but mostly very gentle. She had a particular frame of mind that didn't louse anything up or let anyone down. And Catherine adored children, the bottom line for any decent female who claims to be a credit to the species.

Finally, a day arrived that could not be avoided. It was time for his guest to leave. So first thing in the morning, Shemokoman went to the main train station to see the lady off. Inside of that cavernous building, he said to her, "Katya, you know that reality waxes and wanes to lessen emotional impact. It is a product of the *Juggler*, who is always dealing with a rosy converse. So, I will see you once again when the Martyrs of Injustice plead for us to be together. Cheerio and tschüss."

As the huge locomotive was chugging away with all of the cars behind it, Shemokoman thought, "It isn't fair that I am here and she is there. But I can do nothing about it. So many words and afterthoughts with so little applicable value. Oh well, I have to persist—notwithstanding progenitorial subversion."

Hit the Slopes

The Alps were a vast mountain range south of the city of München. On a clear day in town, Shemokoman could easily see the snow-covered peaks off in the distance. Always so very inviting, he frequently went there to ski at his favorite places.

On one chilly day in early December, he arrived at Partenkirchen in the foothills of the Alps first thing in the morning. He collected equipment that he would need to spend the day on the slopes. Then he went up to the top of a challenging run called the Zugspitze. After reaching the summit and looking around with Salzburg off in the distance, the view resembled a scene from a fairy tale.

As he stood on top of that mountain above the clouds and civilization, Shemokoman thought, "So, now it is time to start my descent to see what I'm honestly made of. The beginning is here; the ending is there and awaits me. And who's to know about the perils that I will confront in the course of such a journey. There will be times when the trip will be smooth sailing—no problems, when I may relax and enjoy it. And there will also be times when danger is present, and I need to be on the ball. Maybe soft patches of snow where I can sink into ambrosial spaces, or narrow pathways that call for perseverance to avoid the big collision, or the edge of a jagged cliff where one mistake and I plummet to worlds of anguish. I need to have fun as well as be awfully careful."

It didn't take long and all of a sudden, Shemokoman lunged from the top of the peak into a magical kingdom. He sailed along at a very high speed and euphoria swept through his body. And now it was hard for him to divide the heaven above from earth below; all that he could see was one solid sheet of blinding whiteness. As instinct was a lodestar, intuition held sway to guide the skier.

After hitting the tree line, Shemokoman found himself in evergreen forest. He was exceedingly careful; one single mistake could ruin the day and be costly. Then he crossed over into an open space with nothing but powdery snow. It was fun to zig and zag, and race and jump, and carve a turn while bolting through the fluffy, smooth terrain. Next he skied into a narrow chute, where the snow was packed down completely, like ice. He had to be alert and safe; to fall would be a disaster. After that, Shemokoman came to a wide, silky plain with no end in sight that went on and on forever. And without a simple somber thought to plague him, he took his time and glided through the transcendental region. It was more exhilaration. And just to set the record straight, he was never by himself—not even for a second. No, the seraphs and Khione were beside him. It helps to have the paranormal with us.

About halfway down that great mountainside, a group of entrepreneurs who managed recreation saw fit to build a gasthaus. Nothing wrong with that. The physical challenge of tackling slopes was more than enough to work up a healthy appetite. So it was time to stop and take a break, and have a bite to eat.

Shemokoman arrived at the place and came to a screeching halt. He stepped out of his skis, propped them up in a rack, and went inside the restaurant. After finding an empty seat, he ordered lunch: pfannkuchen with vanilla syrup did the job on that specific day. And when the meal was finished, he stayed and talked with other diners sitting at his table. They were from Austria, performers at the opera in Vienna. Said they needed talent, mainly singers and musicians. So now, he longed to go to Kärntner Straße to lounge around and patronize the Schweinerhof café . . . what a joint! Finally, he thanked the friendly people for a round of conversation and stepped outside the gasthaus to resume the big adventure.

He snapped on his skis, grabbed hold of the poles, and continued his run on the Zugspitze. Shemokoman barreled along, going down multiple treacherous trails. He jumped over felled trees without any real trepidation and plunged straightaway into the nippy surroundings. It was the essence of pleasure, and there was nothing for him to get torqued at. And it came as no surprise that not a single living soul was there in sight or close beside him. Sometimes, we need to be alone to figure out how much we care for others. It can be enlightening. Then at last, he reached the end of the line and one doozy of a trip was finally over.

After two additional runs on triple black diamonds, Shemokoman finished up the excursion. He turned in his gear and boarded a passenger train going north to the city of München. En route, he glanced back at the mountains and thought, "What a marvelous day, and I wasn't about to waste it. Almost as good as the sled-riding hill; it would've been nice had a comrade or two been with me. But no—no dice. For man, there is no better place to be than out in the province of Nature. Alas, some people do not ever get it; they are content to completely avoid it. Inside of their musty grottoes with friends, they don't even care about sunshine. 'Picture men dwelling in a sort of subterranean cavern with a long entrance open to the light' . . . Gospodi Pomiluj."

Litany of Why

Time and again, Shemokoman took long walks in the city and gazed at towering steeples high up around him. The point on a map where he presently was could not have been much more alluring. It was so pleasant to aimlessly stroll in the labyrinth of cobblestone streets and secluded byways. During those moments, he frequently thought of the past and reflected on personal matters.

One night as he shuffled along on a road not far from the Englischer Garten, he pondered the days of his life in the Land of Michigan.

"I attempted to find and unravel the truth with everything stacked up against me. The challenge I faced was quite a big job and replete with untold complications. So why did I do it?

"I saw a bambino abused in his youth because of the three wicked sisters. And *they* could have put an end to it all, but no, they just didn't bother. How come?

"I remember my friends who said that they were friends, but when it came time to support me, without saying a word they turned their backs and fled, and I was betrayed. Why did the bums do that?

"I recall the young boy who wasn't too bright. He lived in the house on the corner. A knave and nonconformist, a defective hell-raiser who couldn't control a wish to incite more commotion. And what was the reason for that?

"I had to mark time in the secular schools for many legitimate hours, where my one reward was vitriol from teachers who meted out torture. Why did the parroting pedagogues double-cross us?

"I put up with vice from a God-fearing vamp who shattered a sanctified promise. Why did she need to do that?

"I was blessed with a bias for pain and malaise that seems to beset me forever. It is often intense and protracted; moreover, it can be pleasantly charming. Why do I brook the indulgence?

"Oh yes, the fine art of dancing. A lass that I know cannot let it go and is rife with unseemly behavior. I must defer to the fabled Almighty, sadly, as children are bawling and bleeding. How can she do it?

"The word of a god that was written by man who had the interior angle. The right and wrong, and who is to blame? . . . And what does it mean to be evil? Another anecdote. Suspicion must never submit to reproach by marginal men as abnormal. Why must pigheaded disciples cling to a pretense?"

◆ ◆ ◆

If there is a chance to inspire mankind concerning the moral convention, those who need it the most will surely reject it. Just give it a try, and soon you will be nothing more than a cheap agitator. Most people prefer to maintain and preserve the shackles that bind them together. They adore being one of the gang and anything else is never considered. They do what they're told and say what they did and mingle with elegant swingers. Thus, why seek to assist the indigent One with propitious scintillas of knowledge? It is a waste of time; we need to forget it.

The masses are part of a profligate race that favors the kilter of sleeping. No! . . . I'm telling you, no, by god; they do not care to be hearing it. And thus, they avoid any valuable talk concerning the truth and whatever else makes them feel queasy. Instead, they repeat the words of a naughty stepmother who couldn't equate the sign of the cross to anything having approval. Pass it on, my friend. Just pass it on. Because you know that they really do like it.

At one point, Shemokoman thought, "A responsible man is a damnable man who knows what is good for the game. I have to move on while avoiding the ropes and purging a surfeit of hogwash. It is time to recalculate primitive needs and isolate promising trade-offs. Something is choking my mind; I think it is knowledge."

Personification

It came to pass that Shemokoman was going home one day after shopping for tiddlywinks and cotton pajamas. He passed the Königsplatz and strolled along through the busiest part of town. It was already dusk when he crossed the Isar River and walked up that long, gentle slope that led to Giesing. Soon thereafter, he started to get very hungry.

So he stopped at a popular restaurant in a section of town called Harlaching. Shemokoman was greeted and seated at one of the clean wooden tables. He ordered a meal—Schweinhaxen mit gemischte salat; the entrée was another big favorite. The place was nearly deserted except for a couple of other patrons, including one middle-aged man who was sitting alone in a corner.

Shemokoman decided to talk to the fellow: "Grüß Gott, mein Herr. So tell me, how is the meal you are having? Schmeckt es gut?"

The man, who was hovering over his plate and eating a portion of blutwurst, immediately straightened up and looked at the speaker. He paused for a moment, gathered composure, and patted his lips with a clean Serviette. Then he cracked a strangely familiar smile and said, "It is good, very good. You know, we have very strict laws here in Deutschland regarding the meatpacking business. Especially, how we must slaughter the swine."

"Well, if that is the case," Shemokoman said, "then the next time I'm here I will order the very same supper. It goes without saying we need to eat right for energy, tone, and resistance."

The fellow said his name was Castillo, from the Province of Holy Toledo. And in spite of a surname that sounded Catalan, his appearance was clearly Teutonic. He confessed to as much, admitting to a long line of Aryan ancestry.

Initially, the two men conferred about only the trivial matters. Food, the weather, and canine behavior in public. But it wasn't too long until the conversation turned in another direction. As is always the case where Teutons are fully engaged, they started to talk about controversial issues. Mr. Castillo was very upset and complained about a distressing political climate.

He said, "I honestly cannot believe it. There is far too much trouble in Deutschland. People are greatly afflicted and we need to do something about it. Yes, we have to get moving and help them. My friend, it is time to develop and launch a great transformational movement. Every soul that I see is crestfallen and blue, and burdened with meaningless freedom."

The spiel was sound and disturbing, and Shemokoman listened with interest. There are so many people in love with the earth and it seems that they want to improve it. But how can we ever advance in the light of so many significant hurdles? Man will never be different; he is a purely barbaric creation who is hell-bent on atrocious behavior.

State of Implosion

"Yes, mein Freund," Castillo continued. "This country of mine is beyond recognition. The apocalyptical crash is rapidly coming, and the nation is bracing for havoc. You see, we have traitors who tell us they know how to lead as people are hitting the ceiling. Our living conditions have never been worse and production has come to a standstill. It is a sad commentary that our lives are controlled by cheaters and powerful gangsters. Furthermore, a mountain of books that are wholly profane are published by writers who ought to be put into jails. I would say it is time for a nice little bonfire, and a purge to exterminate garbage.

"If you ask your average man on the street, 'Why do you want to keep living?,' my goodness—most of the time they haven't the slightest. Too many years of toil and struggle. Their souls are infected by venomous blight, and they are unable to function. A nation with honor is broken, and thus the people, in sheer desperation, turn to sermons of fraudulent preachers. Alas, the wretched primordial churches in town—with air that is not sanitary—will offer us nothing substantial, only announcements concerning who died and a devious way to salvation. People continue to pray and to wait for any spectacular blessing so that life will return to the way it was when there was still food on a table. When you could afford a pair of new shoes and a warm winter coat with a liner. Despair and decay have ravaged the land, and die Ordnung is starting to crumble."

Mr. Castillo ordered a schnapps, took a short break, and went on. "The ruling class—we know who they are—fat politicians and pandering puppets. They are the privileged elite who want to deceive us. They are the ones who travel at night in a stately well-guarded cortege, and go with their crooked soothsayers to the important executive meetings. They govern and publish decrees to ensure that all they acquire is stolen. Legally, mind you. And all the while, your typical Fritz will slave like a dog to feed and support a big family. Unfortunately, the hardworking men do not get ahead; instead, they wither and die of the mopes in a gutter. You see, my people are forced to accept what firmly controls them. But who is to say that we cannot reform it.

"Shemokoman, let me assure you. Our state of affairs and affairs of the State have never been so convoluted. But they are going to change, for a fact, very shortly. A brilliant upheaval is coming, and more action is what the human beings desire. Delay is no longer the option. And personally, I look to the stars for much of my good information. Those radiant bodies of light in the sky will show us the way, I am certain. God praise the zodiac.

"Now, as for a timeline . . . The very first stage of reform, I can say, is ready for implementation. It will only require a couple of days to demolish the old regime and establish a new one. The leader will be any man whom we choose to empower with ample charisma. And no nation on earth will ever again even dare to humiliate Deutschland. All of the pain and guilt we endured will be gone forever and ever. We will be strong and healthy and pure, and all that is bad—methodically stricken. Yes, an event will take place in the morning, perhaps tomorrow, in this very town to trigger the start of rebellion. Plenty of blood will attest to the right of a glorious socialist future.

"We will put on the shirts with a cryptic design that people must learn to acknowledge. After which, our men will march into town—Ausführen!—to foment and start agitation. Then, at a place we have yet to determine, the riots begin by people who know it is time for a direful reckoning. Alles vernichten! As courage and hope are finally spreading to all of the downtrodden people, we crush any real opposition now from every strategic position. The timid and meek, of course, will suffer and perish. We may as well call it 'collateral damage,' or perhaps, better yet—'good riddance.' "

It must be conceded that there was a kind of mystique about what that fellow was ardently saying. He was a passionate soul with pretty good sense, in spite of the fact that many would call him a nutcase.

"So what do you have in mind as a plausible pretext?" Shemokoman said. "After all, it has to be something creative."

"Well, a martyr must die and many will mourn," Mr. Castillo replied. "And people with nothing to lose will call for reprisal. For thousands of years the simplest ploy never changes; people are clueless. In any event, I will figure it out in detail. The key to it all is nothing but fine execution. You optimize vital logistics and manage a plan for command and control of your militant forces. And if we should lose and nothing is gained, well—at least for the sake of a righteous endeavor, so be it. At any rate, the world will know very soon about the spirit and valor in Deutschland.

"But now as for you, Shemokoman . . . It doesn't take long for a man like myself to recognize sterling potential. I see that you are a very

talented fellow. So tell me . . . Is there a chance you would care to en-
list in the ranks of my organization? Believe me, you wouldn't be sorry;
and, you would be well taken care of. We are looking for prudent advis-
ers and men with a vision. We need to have people who think on their
feet if getting ahead is the mission. And I will require a keen, loyal staff
to enforce every act of compassion. What do you say? Would you like to
be part of the circle, and—rise to Olympus in glory?"

Nothing was said for a minute or so as the two men stared at each
other and silently pondered. Shemokoman wondered, "The fair history
books will always proclaim that only the *good* is in power. And trial by
simple ordeal on any scale eliminates evil. Precisely who and what you
are, Mr. Castillo . . . well, I am no judge about that. Do what you must
and then we will have the significant answers. A leader in charge of a
state represents the collective will of the people. It is personification;
thus, your legacy always will serve to reflect a tangible national interest. And forasmuch as you cannot admit it, by and large you are driven
by Aryan phantoms."

Then he gave his answer: "No, my good man, I think not. For what
it is worth, my conscience tells me to avoid it. And my decision is final.
I do not care to be part of your hazardous business. But I have to admit,
it's a tempting and fine proposition. The plan in your mind is a brazen
maneuver in need of the delicate balance. Although if that devil we call
the Almighty has any say in the perilous matter, then you are taking
some god-awful chances. However, who knows, you just might pull it
off and be able to celebrate triumph. Mr. Castillo, you have a burning
desire as well as potential, and I have the force of my wits and honest
conviction."

The men continued to parley and finished their meals. Then, as
Shemokoman prepared to leave, he turned to Mr. Castillo and said a
few words: "Well, thanks for the company . . . made my day. I will keep
an eye out on the current events here in your wonderful homeland.
And if I might add—the course that you chart is loaded with danger
and intrigue. A government topples and nothing but carnage and grief
spill into the streets. I hope that some good will come of it all if, in fact,
you really prevail. Only then may we justify sorrow and pain as the cost
of a violent turmoil. The 'best interests' of the people must be obtained
to exonerate death and destruction. Furthermore, far too often the
new government becomes perverse, cruel, and repressive; and nothing

remains except for the need to depose it. Keep that in mind, Kemosabe. Now, good day and I wish you the best."

Shemokoman left the gasthaus and went straight home. As luck would have it, along the way he dropped and busted the Spezi. Forget about making the radler. And now, several days thereafter, unusual thoughts lingered inside his mind. Was the meeting with Mr. Castillo some sort of a strange apparition? No, indeed, it was not; call it a vision or whatever. A man from the past somehow showed up today, intending to alter the future. Mr. Castillo was real as could be, no spirit of megalomania. He was full of life and on his way with wurst and bier to inspire the tormented masses. The public will turn to emotional men when there is a need to get even.

The firebrand, Mr. Castillo, acquired quite the reputation as time went by in the city of München. There was no dearth of opinion about the man who was bucking the system. Some healers even went so far as to say that the man was psychotic. But people did not understand who he was and how he was calling for justice. They seemed to forget about signing a truce, giving up land, and having to suffer intensely. Indeed, they couldn't remember; although most of your countrymen felt it.

As a matter of fact, that man could never be judged by anyone mortal. You see, *he* was Deutschland; *he* was the Federal State. He was the light of a mythical star that people sought after for guidance. They wanted a leader; by god, they sure as hell got one. His rage and guilt, suspicion and fears, weakness and partisan leanings—all passion that welled up inside of the fellow composed a genetic persona. It was a vivid reflection, and the nation did not comprehend it.

The young and the old who tread on the earth must deal with pandemics in culture. They think and believe that they know the whole truth about forces that cause them to function. And words that are heard on the street with sectarian meanings are tailored to move them. Alas, they never take time to impugn and evaluate people who actually say them. After all, that would be a big hassle.

At the start of a day, you gaze at the vane and notice air currents have shifted. And you can do nothing about it except to anticipate canceling meetings. Your fantasy drifts far away into a flawless dimensional quandary as each generation learns to adjust when life and everything else is truly in shambles. Political science, of course, is totally useless.

"This fellow called Mr. Castillo," Shemokoman thought, "he is a man who mustn't be loathed or unceremoniously chided. No, he shouldn't go to the gallows. He is the representation of Many and One who is searching for truth like I have been doing for ages. He seeks to reveal what is hard to behold and topple a bad coalition. And should there be vice inside of his soul, it is only a misunderstanding that we have supposed incorrectly. As a rule, we cannot explain the commendable deeds of another."

Mellow Days

The daily routine. Where would we be without it? Creatures of habit require the logical madness. And there is no reason to think about choice when everyone knows the essentials. Behavior depends upon visceral moods with fully intended comportment. Indeed, nothing but fiction. "To be or not to be" was never a question; it was the answer. So much for a famous quotation suddenly melting. Yes . . . "Melting . . . melting . . . I'm melting . . . Ohh . . ."

His morning began more often than not with a long invigorating run on the trails of Perlacher Forest. It was a beautiful wooded area not far from his home in Giesing. Nothing but physical Nature, so fetching and always untroubled. He knew that the price of good health was firm dedication and painstaking toil. So, he complied.

As hot red blood continued to gush through a strong anatomical system, he ran in the midst of creatures and trees, not causing the slightest disturbance. For it was he, the assiduous racer, the foreign intruder, who now was a guest on top of the Aryan soil. He went over the hills and crossed many bridges, built over purling brooks of crystal clear water.

At the end of each run, he sat on a log at the edge of the forest, where he rested and chatted with native Bavarian people. He freely confessed that he was no flaming insurgent; rather, he was a busy go-getter. So many legions crusading for faith; when, in fact, they are sated with venom. Causes for people are fanciful cares that recurrently should be abandoned.

Shemokoman was constantly swamped with a whole lot of personal business. There were always plenty of chores in need of attention. Like fixing a broken cuckoo clock that hung on the living room wall, or tending a vegetable garden full of tomatoes ripe for the picking, or shopping for food at the main Viktualienmarkt where people were constantly haggling. Such an art, or so they would have us believe. Albeit—in order to live in a prosperous way, we needn't have miserly values.

Once in a while, a thought crossed his mind that demanded cerebral attention. He mused, "I wonder if I could have aunts and uncles or cousins who live here in Deutschland? A long time ago, there was talk in my house about ties to Bavarian breeding. And now every day, I seem to perceive traces of kindred arousing strange feelings inside me. Verily, I need to investigate further."

When he was abroad, Shemokoman rode on the Orient Express to remarkable places every so often. He embarked at the railway station in town each time at the start of the journey. He wanted to see firsthand for himself what life was like for people who didn't have much independence. And it came as no surprise that the strangers whom he saw and met didn't care for liberty or having human rights. They were happy as is and praised the man who gave them their protection. What good is your freedom if safety erodes and another invasion is coming? Man has to be secure and out of danger . . . even if the monarch is a beast.

The longer he stayed in Deutschland, which was almost too much to his liking, the more Shemokoman came to grips with all of the prior confusion. The shackles of distress that agonized him were slowly but surely corroding. By knowing what was right and wrong without undue distortion, his mind was free to concentrate and set him straight about traditional values.

Vadum Francorum

It was the end of a memorable year and now in the holiday season. The faces of people he saw on the street were puffy, magenta, and happy. Yes, everyone had to feel jolly. The city was cold and snow was falling in flakes the size of a biscuit. Shemokoman decided to go up north to Vadum Francorum, to visit some folks and christen the start of a New Year. The latter-day dancer was into an Argentine tango.

After one full day on a busy road competing with other wayfarers, he arrived at the destination. It was your classic Aryan town with old medieval buildings and a maze of cobblestone streets. He booked the very best lodging that was close to the wide river Rhein, and soon he was all settled into the room and planning on what to do next. In short order, he made up his mind to go into town to observe a religious tradition.

As he rode on the trolley for miles and miles through ghettos of sterilization, Shemokoman thought, "No nation on earth will ever surpass Deutschland in the art of divine celebration. It is the best; and god, how they thoroughly love it. This venue is brimming with wholesome delight and loaded with fine decoration. The lighting was carefully placed on the ground to illuminate Gothic cathedrals. And there are red and white candles on all windowsills that glow for the death of a preacher. Wreaths of holly on buildings and doors symbolize biblical legend. And thousands of merchants are making lebkuchen under the red tile rooftops."

Upon his arrival in town, Shemokoman started to roam on the streets. And he pondered, "So now, I will be in the midst of a mob like a clerical man who believes in the holy Messiah. Nativity scenes are displayed everywhere to inspire the faith in a child. Gold, frankincense, and myrrh. Hmm . . . How about unleavened bread for hungry disciples? Something has got to stick to the ribs and be churning inside of the belly. And colorful tinsel is strewn everywhere to adorn the incredible moment. O tall Tanenbaum, you shimmer and glimmer in white, and you are crowned with a sparkling angel. The effect—I admit—is just plain overwhelming; it is enough to sweep away all of my deep melancholy. Verily, I say unto thee that in spite of a subtle distinction regarding the truth, I must acknowledge that the glory of God is the greatest. Perhaps humanity needs it."

A formal dinner was planned for the following day at the home of a friend. Thus, Shemokoman went to dozens of specialty shops, where he obtained an assortment of cheeses, aperitifs, pâtés, small presents, and also sweet fruitcakes. He had to get ready with plenty of gifts to put on the table at mealtime. Yes, a strange connotation, das Gift.

While standing and watching the crowd at the empyreal Christ-Kindl-Markt, he spoke to a casual stranger: "And how are we doing this evening, my friend? It is a sacred occasion; look at the Christians. The believers are having a ball, and the libertine world is perfect. So now, we must smile and gaze at the merry surroundings, give alms to the poor, and pretend that there is no evil."

Shemokoman walked for hours on end as choral music was heard throughout the myriad yuletide concessions. It was a pleasant outing until the weather changed and affected the mood of the people. The temperature dropped to cool off the fun, and snow flurries filled up the pearly sky over Deutschland. So, the ethical comrade got all bundled up in a thick winter coat and wrapped a heavy wool scarf around his neck. He called it a day that would turn into night and took a municipal trolley back to the lodging.

The following evening commenced with the soirée at the estate of a modest patrician. She was a lady of grand reputation, extremely urbane and always in fashion. There were loads of guests who came to her home to have a good meal, to mingle and hear all the gossip. She made wild roast duck and Schwarzwälder ham with all of the usual trimmings. Good gracious! . . . The demons were hungry. And there was simply no way that she could have used even one more ounce of butter to flavor the dishes. However, oh my, but they were so tasty. When everyone finished and seltzer was served, they continued to sit at the table for hours immersed in deep conversation. Mostly, talk about Herod and Pilate. It was the sort of chitchat where nothing at all is remembered.

On Christmas Day morning, another dusting of snow covered a neighborhood more or less woozy. The yards and streets were packed with children at play. Shemokoman looked through a window and admired the frolicsome youngsters. That day was instilled with a message called "hope" for all the respectable people.

"Behold the fine youth that is coming and goes, a wave that is sure to replace us," he thought. "It is a time in life when nothing converts and man is consumed by enchantment. The sounds of the pranks that I hear and recall resemble the glee of a whole congregation that vanished. Perhaps a sure sign will emerge from above to exalt what is made by the Yahweh."

At last, the trip was over. Shemokoman went back to Giesing. And he was told, in no uncertain terms, that it was time to return to his country. But he had no desire to leave right then, and so he destroyed every piece of his personal luggage. It didn't help. Admitting defeat, he complied right away and prepared for the upcoming voyage. Deep down inside, he knew as of late that the unavoidable hour was rapidly coming. Thus, on a cloudy day in early May at the bustling Port of Departure, he boarded a big gray ship with the latter-day dancer and sailed from Bremerhaven back to America.

11

Onus of Bondage

Restoration

Transgressions of trust occur every day with results that are total disaster. A broken promise often entails some bad psychological fallout. Now, for people with standard intentions and simple lifestyles, adjustment to a new status quo is easy, fairly straightforward. The abuse of expected behavior takes place with retribution to follow. Hostilities flare to crest and subside, and before you know it the whole affair has blown over. And thus, the parties move on. On the other hand, the situation is far more complex and heartrending when the stakes are higher than normal. Even a right mighty powerful soul can be ripped into shreds and devoured.

Shemokoman got off of the ship at the busy Port of Arrival. He was home at last in the country that he knew so well and was used to. He stood near a gal that carried a torch, which symbolized victimization. Some people still had no idea of what it honestly stood for. No matter how hard any person may try, the bonds of cold servitude will never be broken completely. Dream as much as you like, but listen to me: people are slaves regardless of what they think or may have been promised. And that is the truth.

After having a bite to eat and leaving the harbor, Shemokoman planned on going straight to Michigan for a reunion. His friends and all the neighbors in Waupakisco Park were anxiously waiting. So he and the latter-day dancer boarded the first available train with all of the personal luggage and departed.

He thought, "How much did everyone change back there? And how will they receive me? The time I spent abroad in Deutschland was not a drop in the bucket. To break the ice, I'll tell them something they may not have heard of. Like . . . their God is never down-and-out, but often suicidal."

The initial impression of what he observed outside was very disturbing. At the Port of Arrival alone, Shemokoman noticed how run-down the area looked. Did people simply give it up and just not care about the native homeland any longer? Or was it always so neglected, and he could not remember? No—it wasn't Deutschland, where everything was cleaner than a whistle.

Fortunately, the farther they traveled away from the Port of Arrival, the better the scenery looked. A clean green countryside emerged, and the Catskills came into view. As he admired the natural beauty constantly passing beside him, the man from Michigan thought about life and how it is clearly divided into phases. So now it was time to break new ground on the next iteration of something.

Day after day as they traveled along, Shemokoman noted the range of perceptible changes. Everything he saw was strange yet somehow, in essence, familiar. The speech, attire, attitudes, music—nothing appeared to be kosher. It made him feel somewhat despondent; Lord have mercy, he just didn't like it. Of course, he was gone for a very long time, but should there be such variation? Alas, those were days that he could not reclaim when he was not at home but had to be elsewhere. And now he knew that pangs of nostalgia were fated to constantly grieve him. From that day forward, Shemokoman always felt deprived and he could not forget it.

"You know, it's funny," he pondered. "Well, not really, but . . . You stay overseas for a couple three years and submit to a great transformation. You bide your time and almost do not know it simply happened. Then you come back to a land where all is the same, and you are the only thing different. It is a stunning, tragic feeling; man oh man, I totally missed it."

The Message

The journey by rail was slated to take about a week, no more. They rode inside of a brand-new coach where everyone spoke in English. Nice. The meals, the service and berthing, and everything else was plainly superior. The trip was mostly uneventful; of course, there has to be a lull before the storm.

And then, it happened. About midway through the fourth day as they approached the Michigan border, a porter called out for Shemokoman because a telegram arrived for him. The fellow was handsomely tipped and the message immediately opened. It contained the following words:

> Shemokoman — (Stop) — Regret to be the bearer of bad
> news — (Stop) — Duane has suddenly taken extremely
> ill — (Stop) — He is currently in a hospital and the healers
> are trying to save him — (Stop) — Unfortunately, they don't
> give him much of a chance — (Stop) — One or two days,
> no more — (Stop) — He always said "When you're dead,
> you're dead" — (Stop) — He'd better hope that he was right.
> — (Stop) — See you soon — (Stop) — A reticent Victim.

The news came as no surprise. Shemokoman knew that from cradle to grave was only a couple of highballs. Just add to the mix that Duane was such a hot number, and yes, a heart submerged in passion will betray a cause to stay among the living. He was a case in point. And there was a day when his body preferred to favor what may have been wicked. Alas, the motives that we think are plain as day far too often have no understanding. A wise savant has yet to prove that judgment can relate to human feelings. And who really knows about those nights that he spent in Calumet City? For sure, not a single goddamned soul with an opinion. What's more, it's none of your beeswax.

Day Before Tomorrow

It isn't that hard to plan for a timely demise, the naysayers tell us. The way to a cold, shallow grave underground requires no strenuous effort. All pros and cons of choices in life are meaningless tripe to the Reaper. We do what we must on account of inclinations and agreements. After feeling the way to the pearly gates, a state of repose awaits us. Sympathy wanes and punishment thrives to make us feel grateful and happy. Thank goodness, the treatment for panic disorder requires no tonic from healers. And still the fools we know on earth are prone to flirt with evil. They simply refuse to avoid it.

As a result of the plight of Duane, Shemokoman was not over-whelmed by anguish. He felt little remorse in light of the bad situation. Although he wistfully pondered the "good old days." . . . They all slipped away so quickly. And now, it was pretty much certain that the expectation of a happy reunion for all intents and purposes had vanished. He explained the sad circumstances to his latter-day dancer, and she was indifferent as well.

But then the woman asked him, "So who exactly was Duane? . . . the long and short of it."

And so, he said to her, "Well, young lady, allow me to tell you. He was a boy with a dream and too many stories for laughter inside of a noggin. How come?! . . . We'll never know. And he was a fellow who wanted perfection in man as if he were perfect himself. Treachery! And he was a warrior who fought every lousy rotten battle for covetous heathens without ever letting them fight for themselves. Duplicity! And he was also a man—the immaculate man—who attempted to cover it up by lounging in hideouts. That is, by squelching the fable. For shame! And now the earth is about to claim one of its own—a knave whose days of going to work, and running 'the shop,' and hunting and fishing, are over. And that is who Duane was."

Ideal Timing

On a hot, muggy late afternoon in June, Shemokoman and the dancer entered his old neighborhood. They arrived at the house with the number 210 on a road that he surely remembered. The smell of fresh toasted corn was still in the air from Postumville. And like so many other places that he observed during the train trip, his town was in need of a prompt revitalization. It was a colorless mix of clutter and ramshackle buildings. A massive community effort was clearly required.

"What happened when I was away during all those years?" he wondered. "It is neglect above and beyond that boggles the mind. And as for the principal reason . . . well, it has to be clowns who couldn't care less about order and sensible standards. People today are lazier than in the past and given to callous indifference."

The white picket fence that enclosed the front yard of the big white house was still in good condition. The home as well was well-maintained: fresh white paint, new roof, new shed, the grass was cut, and all of the hedges were trimmed. At least one household still took pride in how their property looked.

As for the circumstances regarding the ailing man, it was chaotic. After learning the facts and getting the gist of the situation, Shemokoman traveled alone to the local infirmary. For it was there that Duane was now confined to a posh adjustable bed. He was on his back on satin sheets and looking straight up at the ceiling. That room was now a transfer point, a portal into Canaan or perdition. The word "tomorrow" for that man no longer had its meaning. A slow death knell was sounding and discerning folks could hear it. Yes, speak about your justice on sweet Mother Earth. What is the expectation and what do we get in return?! It's complicated.

And now, Duane was thinking, "When I'm dead, I wonder if I'll know it?"

Of course, the patient was all hooked up to an array of the latest contraptions. But nothing helped or really hurt the unresponsive body. For you see, the one celestial Hunter aloft was now moving in for the kill. The fading man was in a jam and violently shaking all over. Forget about the horrors; he was scared to death of croaking. My god, it was no wonder. Roughly forty years of raising hell, and now the show was over.

"But notwithstanding all attending details, I get the sense that something here is different," Shemokoman pondered. "Yes, the defiance of hundreds of ill-fated sons is having its day at the altar. And Duane renounced a curse he had per progeny from many years ago. Praise be to sublimation! . . . And to justice for the children. For sure, it would be nice to have a circle that is broken. Although and in all honesty . . . who knows where he is going if in fact he's heading somewhere?

"He looks for light where it is dark; the soul is in transition as the spirit bids farewell to a body that was racked by holy sisters. Movement happens everywhere, but motion isn't what the man is sensing. He thinks that God will bless his soul if for nothing more than as a part of the tradition. Just one more true Offender at the gates of one Nirvana. My! . . . It is truly mind-bending; and everything he never knew is now so darned apparent."

Then Shemokoman spoke to one of the healers: "I would have to presume that Duane is now drifting and floating away comatosely. His body is weak and calling it quits with decommissioned organs. But in spite of that—what do you think? Can he still hear familiar sounds and words that we are speaking?"

The physician replied, "Well, we know from those who died and then returned to go on living—like Yeshua—that although he cannot feel or move components of the body, this man can make out noises and the voices all around him. You see, hearing is the last to go, unlike the other senses. The physical quantum is gone for good and a specter is taking over. He will die within the hour; I am certain."

"You realize, of course," Shemokoman said, "that here is a fellow who needed the long intermission. Rest and relief, by Jove! . . . He ought to have it. Just look at those wild and desperate eyes; I'm sure he wasn't happy. Desire to perish for all those years was never so sorely neglected. The man is devoid of a lingering care in a life that was truly against him. It's time for him to broach a realm where gratitude and penitence are pointless for a soul that couldn't hack it. And very soon, the searing pain that he could not get rid of will be gone forevermore and then some."

Duplicity

The two men finished talking, and the busy healer went about his business. He made the rounds from room to room to check on other patients. A host of skilled assistants and candy striper nurses were doing everything they could to guarantee good service. As a rule, sick people go to healers and then hope to soon get better. But not this time for someone.

Shemokoman stayed in the room with Duane and thought, "So, you spend sixty-odd years amid civilization trying to carve out a niche. And all you meet are hypocrites and selfish jerks without a shred of virtue. If there's a way to give you hell, without reservation, they'll do it. The explanation is so very simple: human nature at its finest.

"And in the end when you have nothing left and must expire, the traitors with their lackeys come to see and hang around you. They like to make the public think that love is in the air when you are passing. After all, you know they really care because they say so. 'Cool it, bub! . . . Cool it!' With smiles and dull anecdotes, they must convince your family that all you have is need for resignation. And thus, your final wish is: to be a ghost, return to earth, and haunt them."

While standing beside the very last bed that the indisposed man would lie in, Shemokoman said to him, "The night is torrid with treason, my friend, and replete with iniquitous scheming. But not so bad for you, lucky fellow; your timing—of course, was perfect. Five years and nothing, now this . . . What is this? Vanity surfaced again and vengeance recovered. So now, another soul is cursed; and I shall find no solace on the isles with my prophet. Yes, I must walk on roads when it is dark to avoid the recognition. Somehow, because of what I am, my pride could never take it.

"Your life was one parade of scorn, bad feelings, hooch, depression. Without delay, it's time to leave the tree in spite of charlatan-healers. They said your neck isn't broken. Hah! . . . A threat of certain plunder. 'So what!' . . . they always told you. 'Get on with life; forget about Ann Arbor!' I know that you were tortured by the doxy and ashamed of having scratches on the forehead. Thus, you made a place with quiet space and thought that it was over. But now, you're at the trail's end and facing something more again to irk you. You've got to watch it all collapse and visit with Immortals. And once and for all, forget about your mother's dumb approval.

"The body's warm but getting cold; you're tired of glowing for people. Your spirit plunges down into the wide abyss, where every category that relates must duly vanish. And then you go into the great beyond, where shamans who have had it pout and languish. A string of lights of every shape and size, and sort and color, is glittering to gainsay nonexistence that surrounds you. Faster and faster you travel alone, devoid of zoetic sensation, and time's the rogue that you will not put up with. So now, you are where you belong without the endless troubles. You see, reality's the one excuse that man will always have to cling to madness."

Lights Out

Having nothing more to say, Shemokoman stepped away from the fellow. He sat down in a soft blue hospital chair and thought about auld lang syne. What is it about the thought of pleasant days so long ago that causes sadness? If they were good, should they not make us happy? He stayed put right there until the sun went down to keep a vigil. Then it was back to Waupakisco Park to spend the night at the big white house on Jameson Avenue.

The next two days were mostly repetitious, with numerous trips by all concerned to visit the dying man. So much for what the healers know, the high and mighty overlords who fleece us. Too much talk about the use of avant-garde procedures now in health care. Yes, the ultramodern craft; and yes, they love to cut you. It's tough to sit and watch as people kiss their sorry derrières good-bye. And in spite of such despairing circumstances, Magdalena partied round-the-clock and danced each whole night long until the sunrise.

Then on the third day after the start of the whole ordeal, it came to an end. Duane slipped away on the only significant journey just prior to noon. The family tree was by his side when he passed on without a hint of fanfare. And they all felt out of sorts, a little shaken. Although there were no tears, no grieving, no nothing that accompanies those occasions, because it all turned out exactly how the fated man had planned it. A very low-key sort of exit. And why not the devastation? Well, out of spite, he simply didn't want it. And that is the truth.

Of course, some people started in with all their silly observations; always predictable, never amusing. "He's in a better place now," and "Duane can rest in peace," and "His troubles that were nagging him are over, for good."

"My god, the foolish comments!" Shemokoman thought. "Obviously meant to drive me nuts. How do they know where he currently is, or how much trouble he's having? Perhaps the man could use a swig of brew right now to deal with fallen angels, and I'm glad we left the beer inside his coffin. In any event, this much I know for sure—his requiem is clearly in the offing and he's dead."

Shemokoman knew that the last few years for Duane were definitely rough ones. He was racked by physical pain and emotional problems. And just like everyone else in the mix, his life and copious choices were given to fortune. From his earliest days at play on the block until the hour of death, he lived with many spirits who informed him how to function. His not-so-free free will became derailed, and he suffered due to subluxated conscience.

The final thought of a dying man may very well be the plea for sanctification. A dire wish to change the course of when and where he thinks he might be going. Alas . . . Hearken unto my words, all ye Cads of Little Faith and No Submission! A Holy Spirit feels the pain of brokenhearted people, lest ye forget it.

Anna Speaks

The implications of mortality consumed all of Shemokoman's waking hours for the better part of a week. He devoted time to taking care of things like legal business. There were certainly days in that very same home when life was quite a bit different. When people were busy with personal chores and Sticks was on his way to Boy Scout meetings. Burial arrangements were meticulously attended to with everyone helping out as much as possible. And soon the day arrived to take the body to a graveyard. Not too many mourners came to pay their last respects. Perhaps the rainy weather was a factor, or maybe other reasons that we never know about affected turnout.

Anna expeditiously completed her responsibilities concerning the solemn occasion. It was a job that had to get done, and she did it. She always was a marvelous organizer with cryptic notes and reminders all over the place. What's more, she never threw a single thing away and remembered bleak years in the past when almost everyone in America was poverty-stricken. It's hard to change your ways when a pattern has evolved into a habit.

A week passed by in nothing flat after the interment, and another hot summer day in Waupakisco Park was in the making. Shemokoman sat with Anna at her large yellow dining room table in the morning. Oh, how she loved to do that and fritter away the time talking for hours. On that particular day, they spoke about Duane, of course; my goodness, everything happened so fast and now it was over.

After talk of life and death had finally been exhausted, Shemokoman said, "If you don't mind, Anna, I think that now's a real good time to have a special conversation. I'd like to speak with you about some heavy matters. But only if you put up no resistance."

Anna gave approval.

He said, "Most people rarely listen when somebody's talking to them. They only think about themselves, and cutting in, and voicing their opinion. As for me, I like to hear another viewpoint, and I try to understand it. So please—if you will, tell me what you have to say about the ways of women. You cannot lose by telling me the truth, and it also helps to clear a guilty conscience . . . if you have one. In particular, why did you choose Duane to be the man that you would live with?"

The lady was distracted. She almost never talked to anyone about her personal issues. Since the days of her youth, she knew that it was best to be silent to avoid potential trouble. Better that way, when no one knows exactly what you're thinking or you're doing. She stood up and sighed, and went into the kitchen, where she looked out of a window at some children who were playing in the lot. Then, after a while, Anna made a pot of tea and returned to the dining room table.

"All right," she said, "as you please, Shemokoman. I will say a word or two of what I believe is true about the women. And mind you, do not take my insight with a simple grain of salt, as everything I have to say is based on truth and reason. And I know how you feel about sensational perception."

Anna paused for a moment to gather her thoughts, then said, "To begin with, women believe in the ultimate *good* with conviction to righteous devotion. We focus on integrity and try to live for every day and night, avoiding circumstances fraught with evil. Certain things that people do may counterbalance rectitude and are never proper. Yes, propriety, Shemokoman, decorum. Women like drama and fun, a good challenge, flowers and jewelry, gossip, excitement and passion, and whatever else catches our fancy, including men. Indeed, we even care for creepy men. Disgusting, but true. And, we pray to God if we are bad to soothe the soul and supplicate at bedtime. Although I must confess that it is doubtful that he listens. How many times do we have to put up with men who don't keep the commandments? And must women be the only ones who love and always suffer? I say—no. Perhaps the time is finally here to overturn some choices.

"Now, as for men and how they are regarded. Sometimes they're good and treat us right . . . provide a home for which we must be grateful. A family of five, I have no objection to that. Although they are also adept when it comes to a knack for capers to make us deplore them. They can be vile, foolish and cold, cruel and kind at the very same time, and temperamental as well as neurotic. When it comes to trying to figure them out, you have to be patient and savvy. Albeit, a woman can do it."

She sipped her tea and went on: "With hints of betrayal, madness, and play, they share dark secrets on gray afternoons. And we, as if Mesmer himself were duly attending, laugh at a deed and ignore it. 'Pay no further attention, my dear. It is all in the past; why bother . . . simply forget it.' We never confess that it is too hard to renounce the momentum of umbrage. We cannot have that now, can we?! So after thousands of hours of heartache and crying our eyes out, we gaze at the sun and a moon high above to consider what Nature has told us: 'Nay, nay, nay. It is wrong to neglect the paramount Art of Survival.' And thus if something is wrong and doesn't add up, then it's time to change the way of counting.

"So as the limited years are passing by us, one by one the men resign and go to pot so quickly. They were titans, so invincible, who said they couldn't be conquered. And we are left to scrape and scrounge with no one there to help us. And then quite out of the blue, while in a corner that we are backed into, a woman encounters the warrior. It is a chance peremptory meeting; it is a thing that shouldn't have happened. Of course, we know he is there for total destruction. At that time, we say to ourselves, 'I have no regrets; indeed, I love them all so very dearly.' A woman is no apologist, please! Make no mistake about that. A part of the soul that needs to be free must never resort to contrition. From beginning to end we bury the pride and remain indifferent to judgment. Utterly weak and defenseless, no one considers the truth of it all . . . good gracious. History, Shemokoman, history."

Anna took a break and then continued, "Now, regarding matrimony, mi amigo. There is a pretty good reason for vows in a marital contract. Namely, you must fulfill each and every one of them until they're completely exhausted. Then, you can honestly say to yourself, 'A promise was made and I kept it!' And what good is that? . . . Only to border on folly? Yes, vanity wears the ironical smile; and love is a wicked sweet talker. And the mood is a pretty good reason right here for us to call upon laughter. Oh my, what a plausible tale. I've said far too much already.

"You know, Shemokoman. If I should lose my balance now and topple to the floor, I would not forgive my honey. It is always their fault: a way to cast the blame and then incense them. Furthermore, if when I met him that very first time on the tram into the village close to Macon, and fate would have told me the future, well, nothing at all could be different. I would've instantly dashed with no thought about doubt to the arms of a paramour waiting. That devil was plotting to woo me and to invoke a mysterious purpose."

With those final words, she grew quiet.

"For sure," Shemokoman said, "getting married is ticklish business. And, you are right concerning gods who alter and perpetuate appearance. The tale of men and women will always be veiled in pious amusement. What could be better than watching a scene on the stage of a fine lovers' quarrel? Unfortunately, nothing. And the truth is bad for a hesitant man who is born with a delicate conscience. So yes, we must be careful; he may cause the big disaster. Although the stars have been constantly watching and they will punish duplicitous chiselers. In spite of deceit—believe it or not—justice will always prevail. There is no other rendition. So take from the good and leave what is bad, and forget about the junk that only annoys us."

He added, "So now, as for you and I, Anna, we must acknowledge the heavy admission. Namely, that there is only one genuine creed for us to believe in. And, the Tablets of Providence have it."

"Yes, I know," she said. "And it is consoling. Shemokoman, I understand you—unlike the cantankerous others. But oh, how I wish that just one part in my lifetime could have been different. Alas . . . what might've ensued could never occur as a saga that really transpired."

For the rest of the afternoon and all of that evening, Shemokoman and Anna remained at her home. They drank a good deal of black Georgian tea with lemon, ginger, and Yemeni honey, while having a lengthy discussion touching on nothing that shouldn't have mattered. Like how to get hired in Postumville and who was in Jackson again. He also helped to straighten the house and took man's best friend for a walk. Ole Stub was the one in a million. And before he could say Kashpirovsky, it was well past midnight and time to call it a day. He went up the stairs and into the corner bedroom, opened a window to let in cool air, and slept without waking up one single time until morning.

A Date with Catherine

The next day, Shemokoman hooked up with Catherine. She was more than aware that he was in town and anxiously waited to see him. Upon his arrival seven days prior, he sent her a note explaining the somber conditions. She sent her condolences to him and suggested they meet whenever he felt it convenient.

Catherine made a proposal to go out for dinner. So they went to a Slavic restaurant on the south side of town near the old Minges Farm that was close to a curious roadway. You just never know about naming conventions; Nicholas Road was the perfect example.

The restaurant was packed. People were even standing outside and waiting to get in the place. A good indication regarding cuisine; Catherine changed very little. Still the quiet demeanor with poise, and modest, collected, and charming.

After getting a table, taking their seats, and ordering wine from the du jour menu, she inquired, "So, what are you having for dinner?"

Shemokoman replied, "To tell you the truth, the venison steak sounds pretty good to me. Perhaps with a side of pirogi stuffed with potato and cabbage. I also will order Ukrainian borsch with a tulip sniffer of bronze Armenian cognac."

Catherine said that she wasn't too hungry and asked for a pastry with coffee and crème. Then she sighed and remarked, "This has been a tough trip for you. And I am sure the effect of what has occurred has yet to sink in for some of the people. But now it is over, and you can look forward to taking it easy awhile. So tell me, where do you go from here? What are you planning?"

He said, "Well, in a couple of days I need to move on to a place called the Genuine Southwest. I will live in the Lone Star State of Texas, where fearless men who never gave up fought against Crazy Invaders. Courage alone will forever define every tale of heroes and fortune. And when I no longer can stay in that land, heaven only knows what is in store for Shemokoman then. Perhaps I will finally come back to my home to you and my ethical comrades. If only I had a mere touch of control to make it all suddenly happen."

"Hmm . . . ," she replied. "Sounds like another adventure to me; and please, if you have no objection . . . This woman called Magdalena. What is her story?"

The comrade pondered the question; he knew that the answer required a novel. So he would try to condense voluminous chapters into a decent synopsis. "You know, Katya . . . My aspiring latter-day dancer—the sweet Magdalena—is attempting to shine for the world to see, but alas, she is shrouded in darkness. Her world is monochromatically vague, yet still she is probing for color. The problem is that her eyes no longer perceive it because she is cold, sad, and resentful. With nowhere to turn and nothing to do, her life is completely in shambles. Magdalena will always feel good in a crowd where people are prone to neglect her. Waiting, watching, and plotting to brutally hurt any chump she can swing with. She plays with a strain of venom that kills, and still she continues her dancing."

He paused and went on: "There are frequently days when evil appears and would like us to flat out surrender. We must say, 'Move along . . . you ridiculous clod! You don't have what it takes to corrupt me.' However, some people are not so judicious. They promptly give in, cavort and have fun, and then think nothing about it. 'So what?!' they declare. 'Maybe it's naughty, and therefore I happen to like it.' Magdalena is part of that crowd; she is a woman devoid of compunction. You have to be strong and determined; if not, you can expect unpleasant omegas and alphas. People like her will always be angry and hopeless. And that is the truth.

"The dancer is lost in a world of show where charade has replaced mother wit. I tell you her soul is eroding, and her vitality has to be sinking. When the going gets rough, her style reverts to moronic, god-awful deception. She loves to insist on a fraudulent fight to cover up errant behavior. My goodness, she thinks it is clever; the woman is frightened, dejected, and plumpish. And thus, somber days are awaiting the dear Magdalena, who hasn't the will to avoid them. And I am sure she undoubtedly knows it. The rest of her years will be frittered away in the house of a Lady from Dover.

"You see, Catherine. A shiftless Composer in love with himself was close to an Angel of Mercy who pleaded for help to the wonderful prince, who rejected, put down, and abused her. And thus, she was cast into a burning inferno where people must endlessly suffer. It is a scandal of massive proportion, and we can do nothing about it. And dear Magdalena will never consent to assistance that just might revive her. Instead, she prefers to mock and refuse every decent and heartfelt proposal. For the woman I know who dances too much, the honor of man will always be horribly shameful."

As the lady was quietly thinking about the description, Shemokoman mused, "And what do I see that is in it for me? If I were a soothsaying prophet, then the answer could be very simple. However, that isn't the case, and I don't have a blithering clue about the near future. But sooner or later, the woman I know will explode and then call it improvement."

Big Men

The narrative now of Shemokoman turned in another direction. He talked about feminine issues and what women have got to put up with. In particular, he considered interaction between the self-styled Big Men and females, and how the latter are treated so poorly.

"Katya, please listen to me," he said. "Of late, I have noticed many Big Men who are roaming about and searching for souls to defile. They look down from the sky with convertible eyes and spy what is weak and defenseless. And they think that possession of all they can take is righteous because they are holy. They can afford to be happy, and furthermore, they are the scum of the earth.

"They allegedly come from the right side of town where people are wealthy and stingy. They follow the only conspicuous path that leads to their so-called redemption. However, the course that they chart is really the way to incite and to stimulate evil. Big Men, my dear, the biggest— the real big shots . . . always content to watch and to gloat over misery steeped in another. So gracious, so unselfish, and so very wretched. And just look around you, Katya, there is no shortage of what they may covet. The world is lavish, they are unfettered, and we are doomed to confront them. Oh, how they love to despoil the innocent victim. And when they have bitten off too much to chew, the villains abscond into temples to pray for a godsend. How little they know about primitive man and getting it straight to begin with. Enough said. Basta per oggi!"

After dinner, they took a long walk on the moonlit Goguac Prairie, where decades ago a boy from a town in its prime hunted for food with a slingshot. And lo and behold, the God of the Lake told Shemokoman that he was now terribly sorry. It was a cordial rapprochement that helped to bury the hatchet. For her part, Catherine spoke about tireless effort with labor in tragedy theater. As of yet, no one she knew with an angular view was laughing. It was her current vocation, and she had the talent that always impressed a cabal of the casting directors. Describing her latest endeavor—it wasn't more murder and love with betrayal. At long last, they finished the night with a silent accord that people depend on each other.

Comrade Rendezvous

On the following day, all of the ethical comrades got together again for a homecoming celebration. The guest of honor—obviously, Shemokoman. As evening drew near, they went out on the town to carouse and get in on the action. The very first place they decided to go was a bar called One-Eyed Jacks in Postumville. It was your typical dingy smoke-filled taproom loaded with bottles and mirrors. Everything shiny and gleaming to make the customers feel as if they were in some type of an extraterrestrial dreamland.

Shemokoman wasn't too sure about what to expect regarding his comrades. Would they still get along with him? After all, he was gone far away for a number of years and many relationships fail. However, it only required a brief familiarization to realize that nothing had changed in so many ways except for the ages of people.

The Doctor still spoke about medical cures, like how to reduce the painful effect of a bender. And he said he could use a good woman in spite of the fact they don't care to be used. Anastasia was mostly quiet and watchful as always. For her, it was more than enough to have all the ethical comrades together again. Thus, she sat very still for most of the time and treasured the sociable moment. Citizen R. was in very grand style and mixing with legions of students. A lifelong career in education results in a few extra perks. Like . . . he recognized everyone whom he ran into and everyone also knew him. And finally, Major LD and Alabama were nonchalantly soft-pedaling rumors of valor. They both agreed that the scourge of vainglory is not to be found in trenches or in a boneyard.

The group of merrymakers went to various public houses in town. They spent most of their time at a swanky place in Verona, where countless hours were idled away having fun. And it was there that they played game after game on the slickest of shuffleboard tables. They sprinkled the wax on the maple-wood field to make the puck go perfect. Major LD simply could not be defeated. He won every game that he played against dozens of rivals. Yes, he knew about hammers and hangers, and everything else concerning the contest. Some people are natural-born winners, and that is the truth.

They finished the night as morning drew near and everyone made their way homeward. When Shemokoman showed up in Waupakisco Park, all the respectable people were just waking up.

Aftermath

The next morning was cool for a change as the sun watched everyone rise. Now it was time to start packing again for a journey. A trip to the south was about to commence for a man who took pride in the effort. As he assembled the simple belongings, Shemokoman suddenly took very ill. Something was horribly wrong. He was gripped in the throes of a wrenching despair that was caused by atrocious behavior. And nothing was done to prevent it.

He instinctively knew what happened and thought, "Some people insist on tormenting others around them, and there ought to be ways to avoid it. It sure would be nice if the Law of the Jungle was still in effect for the masses. Then I would dish out your justice."

So often we cope with horrific events that occur and profoundly impair us. We just cannot seem to get rid of the pain they occasion. There should be a trick to turn fortune around when all of the odds are against us. Of course, the key to it all is nothing but courage—a powerful god that firmly supports and carries us into the battle. We need to remain ever wary and strong, and also aggressive and prudent. One mustn't give quarter to weakness. And fear is a thief who seeks to intrude and ravages prowess and spirit. Indeed, the mettle of man is how we perform under pressure.

Shemokoman finished all preparations for the upcoming trip. And just before noon on another warm summer day in the Land of Michigan, he arrived at the railway station in Battle Creek with the latter-day dancer. Being fully aware that the future was going to be touchy, well, he was no stranger to that, and the comrade would tackle the issues. Meanwhile, it was time to relax and enjoy a ride in the country. America still had plenty to see and admire.

"It was good to have been here where I belong, regardless," he reflected. "No one can take it away from me despite the intention to do so. A part of the past from the Circle of Time is mine to cherish and have whenever I want it. They'd like to say he flew the coop . . . No way, I'll never do it. Where would humanity be apart from fair serendipitous forces? No two ways about it, simply impoverished."

12

The Genuine Southwest

Lone Star State of Texas

A noisy mob of scrambling people boarded the railroad passenger coach from Platform No. 2. Mind the gap! Every door was secure and the time had arrived to get moving. With a mighty blast from the old steam whistle, the big steel wheels started to screech and slowly go round on the tracks. The big locomotive pulling the cars got up to speed, and soon they were cruising along and making good headway. After several days and nights on the road, the train rolled into a place that was called the Genuine Southwest.

The rosy horizon was dusty and bleak, albeit ungodly exquisite. It was easy to see why this wasn't a place for the timid. Very rugged territory. For miles and miles, and still more miles—there was nothing noteworthy to look at. Only honey mesquite, sagebrush, and tumbleweeds blowing across the ground that was strewn with sun-bleached cattle bones from a roundup. Eventually, they arrived in the Lone Star State of Texas, where long stretches of rolling earth replaced the flat, empty country. They barreled straight through the uncivilized land that was a mecca for so many people. Especially young ones.

After leaving the train at the end of the line, Shemokoman found a place to live in La Enchilada Reál, a smart little town. It was a strangely surreal location, never too dark nor overly light. Just dusky and humid most of the time with sunsets beyond the great mesas. He selected a stepped-level two-story house to inhabit; it was perfectly square and made out of Spanish adobe. The ceilings were high, the walls were thick, and it was fairly good-sized with a courtyard right in the middle.

All in all, the ideal home for people who have to reside in that part of the country. And it didn't take long for him and the dancer to set up a healthy routine. A schedule was needed to regulate life and counter the outbreak of chaos. More of die Ordnung.

The Good Book

Simon the Zealot and Philip were two cowpunchers who also lived in town. They came from the East to be in the West in search of good times and a sweetheart. And La Enchilada Reál was where they hoped to find their coveted spoils. They looked so dashing in brown leather chaps and jingling spurs, with bandanas and ten-gallon hats on top of their heads. The clothing they wore was exceedingly cool on hot summer nights as people they met insisted on calling them dudes.

On certain days when he was free, Shemokoman spent time with both of those fellows. The three of them often went hunting or found a good lake where they could go fishing. Once in a while, a discussion flared up concerning a topic considered taboo. Namely, politics or religion. When that occurred, Shemokoman usually stayed on the sidelines. He saw no point in stating contentious opinions because he didn't want to shake things up with a lecture. Although on occasion, he did make a speech to enlighten the crowd about much of his own understanding.

It came to pass that on a frosty November day at a local tearoom called Thelma's, a conversation commenced about the Good Book. Philip, Simon the Zealot, and Shemokoman were all there at the time, and the former chimed in with his position and feelings: "Well, as for me, I truly believe that the Bible is the result of divine inspiration. After all, you have to admit that the message and story contained therein are perfect. For example, consider the very first chapter: Genesis. Could it really have been any different? I think not."

Then, turning to Shemokoman, Philip said, "And how about you, my illustrious friend. What do you think about Scripture? Or is it your wish to refrain from comments about it?"

There was the air of a definite challenge. Perhaps it was time to give it a go, and the man on the spot started to ponder. At least thirty people were sitting in chairs or leaning against the high papered walls, sipping on tea from the Indies and casually waiting. Of course, they were anxious to hear an emphatic rejoinder.

Shemokoman stared down at the floor, and then he looked up and replied: "My good friends—whom I have known for only a while, a profusion of thought is inside of my mind; and now, I would like to reveal it. I have no desire to bore you to death by trying to say something clever. Instead, I would like to present a few candid ideas and offer a better rendition. It is the only reliable way to ensure that people who listen are happy. Too many sleazy Impostors these days are seeking to dupe or mislead us.

"Now, as for this Bible. It is a legend of lore with a tale that warrants attention. And for many respectable neighbors, we know that it is the very last hope in a world of evil. Indeed, it *is* a very good book, and I have read it hundreds of times from cover to cover. It is a detailed history of kings and queens and certain exceptional beings who were able to talk directly with God, in spite of the fact they were mortal. Outlandish and fairly impressive."

He went on, "But who is to know or can honestly say how much of the book is truth or incredible fiction? Although I am never so foolish as to deplore any collection of thought and ideas that may or may not be authentic. However, I will tell you this much, my diversified friends, and please, do not be alarmed. The splendid Red Sea that is always so blue never parted to grant the escape of Israelites from noble Egyptians, as it is written. And the Walls of Jericho did not come tumbling down as a result of blowing some trumpets—no! Of course, it just didn't happen, as it is written. And *man* wasn't made in the image of God. Rather, we made a God in our image . . . How about that!— It never was written. And hundreds of other abnormal events that are described in the Good Book, as it is written, never took place to sanctify life that is human. And maybe, indeed, there is no other work so cogent, compelling, and brilliant that so amazingly furnishes words to the gullible masses. Alas, in order to have the right answers, you need to be sure you are privy to all the right questions. And that is the name of the game, so do not forget it.

"My friends, I beg to encourage you. Please, find the strength to dispute the equivocal Scripture. Who among us can have any doubt that it will not help in the future? Pray tell . . . I know you desire to praise every word and prove to a God you are holy. But what is the point if we die and discover that earth is the end of the road? I tell you that Nature alone is entirely flawless.

"And now, I will disclose yet another distinct revelation. Namely, this Bible is really the ploy of a secular wizard. Yes! . . . Nobody up in the clouds provided the wherewithal to compose it. It is a book for the meek, created by man, where hope is a ruse and people rely on unique inspirational tales. Like . . . what does the Good Book so cheerfully tell us? Well, get down on your knees, make the sign of a cross, and pray to the Gracious Almighty. After all, it only requires your body and soul; no other donation is needed. I will tell you this much, my friends: That is not what God is about. He is no mystical idol, and he is no star in a spiritual novel, and he does not want to redeem us. And, the *Bible* is not a redoubtable text that describes the omnipotent Father. It is a book with a cover, chapters, pages, and numbers."

The ethical comrade continued, "The clergy whom people regard on the earth exalt every ancient tradition. They tell you a fine after-life will be yours if only you keep the commandments. And that, my friends, is blasphemy . . . of the most contemptible order! Deference to words inscribed on a page—I cannot conceive of a greater debacle. Every day of the year we are told by Men in the Robe to simply accept it. Religion . . . especially good for those who are dying. 'You lousy, pathetic offender. You'd better give us the bloody confession! If not, you are going to hell to be with despicable sinners and Satan.' Until that very last minute, they never let up; they condemn and oppress us. Listen to me, my notorious friends: If you renounce the old way of life and honestly search for a new higher power, then you will soon know the meaning of absolute freedom. You will no longer be bound like a slave to the woe of the pious malarkey. And that is the truth."

After taking a sip of his hot black Georgian tea, Shemokoman said, "I must concede, it's an excellent book that people can read whenever they need it. But please, let's keep it at that. Tastefully penned for desperate souls who often are hurting and cranky. But please, let's keep it at that. You may enjoy and even adore it, revere the Lamb of God, and learn about Joseph from people who tarried in Goshen. But please, let's keep it at that. I cannot conceive of humanity's loss because of esteem for a Bible. If nothing will change, it shouldn't be long and soon we'll be back in the Stone Age.

"My friends, pay attention to me. We live on a globe that is called Mother Earth. It's tilted but doesn't fall over. And we shall grow old and die here as well, like so many devils before us. It is our home with a glorious past and a promising future. And a merciful God we know nothing about is a spirit that must oversee us. I implore you ... harken each day to the voice of your innermost conscience. It is the sound of a God we avow, and it will not ever betray us. Obey her commandments so you can have personal honor. Get plenty of rest, work hard every day, and forget about going to heaven.

"As for the fellow named Yeshua ... He was one hotheaded preacher. And we ought to concede that authenticity favored one heck of a fable. A savior was needed to die on a cross ... and you know the rest of the story. If that man who was slain by a slovenly mob could stand before us right now and speak, his message would stagger the senses. His words would reflect many rational thoughts that we should impress upon neighbors. He would reject all of the evil around us, and he would denounce the stead of his teachings today, and he would revile the very idea of devotion to any such Bible. My friends, we occasionally see a strange thing and deny what good vision has told us. But no matter how odd any notion may seem, we shouldn't reject apperception. And if ever you open your eyes wide enough to overcome form and appearance, then you may behold the light of Eternity's bounty."

Whoa! It was enough to mull over. Shemokoman had nothing more to say. Everyone stared at him and then the hostess served crème brûlée. Nothing wrong with that. And now the clientele required a simple light-hearted diversion. So, they talked about Sir Walter Raleigh and tried to figure out what El Dorado, in truth, could've been. A person, place, or thing—sound familiar? English grammar. There will always be dreamers with stars in their eyes who want to reorder the cosmos. It was a healthy recital intended for lively polemic and humor.

Sun Country Living

That particular winter was cooler than usual in the Genuine Southwest. One might think that being so far south, near the border with Crazy Invaders, it would always be sunny and warm. Not true. In January and February, especially, there was never much snow but the temperature often dipped way below freezing, and a bitter cold wind could prove to be the ultimate nightmare. If that happened, the people stayed inside of their homes and huddled up close to a warm fireplace.

When Shemokoman lived in La Enchilada Reál, he cooked and cleaned, and ate and slept, and didn't see much of a future. He began to think that life couldn't be anything more than days and nights of toil. His stay bestowed new meaning to the expression "the everyday grind." It can get to a point where we question the very nature of human existence. But every now and then, he saw a ray or two of light at the end of the tunnel. Sometimes, we need to look real, real hard to honestly see it.

A tribe of Native American Indians, called Apaches, lived on a big reservation down in Texas. And, in spite of defeat by palefaced men, they remained a nation of proud warriors, women, and children. They cherished the old ancestral lands, and mostly talked among themselves in their own spoken language. And they worshipped the Great Spirit in the sky, who—although gracious and forgiving —never did issue a single commandment. Of course, the People's Interior Ministry in Federal City could've done more to help them out, but didn't.

On one occasion, Shemokoman spent the better part of a day with an Apache brave named Dahkeya, whose clothing was made from deerskin, and he wore a tribal headdress full of big colorful feathers. As it happened, the Indian found many precious stones at a nearby canyon stream—including garnet, silver, and turquoise—that could be used for jewelry and other handicraft items. So he made a present of several gems to his distinguished Michigan blood brother. It was a very nice gesture and promptly acknowledged. The wife of the brave, Chocheta, sat on the ground with her little papoose next to a circular wigwam, banging a tam-tam. As a gift, she gave the friendly visitor a beautiful red dream catcher with all sacred items sewn into the center. So now, he was sure to be lucky. For his part, Shemokoman gave them a weekend pass to a rodeo held at the fairgrounds. Of course, not much could be better than that. And they all agreed there needed to be goodwill among men, and concluded that it would be nice if ever it happened.

Then Dahkeya said, "You know, Shemokoman. My people are often so badly maligned and mocked through no fault of their own. They are marooned on a portion of dear Mother Earth that used to be part of the Great Apache Nation. And at best nowadays, they have to endure a poor miserable life from birth until death. There isn't too much we can do about that, although I will certainly tell you: The day is coming and soon, my friend, when my people shall rise up again. And they will recover all that was brazenly stolen so wrongly from them. Therefore, do not be surprised if we regulate fate with bows and arrows, and rattles and drums, and knives and a buffalo dance, and go on the warpath. It would be great to burn at the stake every gosh-darn white man. Although . . . I look forward to being your friend, honest Injun."

"Well, the feeling is mutual," Shemokoman said, "And I understand about bitter resentment. For thousands of years, this land was yours with nothing to threaten or hurt you. You were the masters of Nature; and, you were the eminent redskins. But then one day, the marauders appeared, pillaged your home, and you were no match for their power. In the end, your people gave up, acknowledged defeat, and accepted a one-sided treaty. Outrageous! And that's about it. The message is clear as a bell. You win some; you lose some."

He paused and went on, "Sometimes, when alone, I think to myself . . . 'Were I a brave from a Native American culture, I would have colored my face—for sure long ago—with oils and paint, and sharpened the tips of my arrows held in a quiver, and convinced my Indian brothers to start a rebellion. It is high time to avenge a filthy injustice. A rose is a rose is a thorn.'"

The men continued to chat for several more hours. The indigenous people got a raw deal concerning their living conditions. They didn't deserve to have to put up with the hardship. They needed a voice in support of the cause to bring about change for improvement. But talk is cheap; it takes wampum to get firewater.

Finally, the powwow broke up and the guest returned to his home.

Bull in the Road

One afternoon, Shemokoman was returning home from a trip to the Rio Grande. He was walking alone in the vast, empty reaches of wilderness in West Texas. There wasn't too much to see out there, only a wavy mirage that rippled up into the sky on the horizon. And now, upon glancing ahead quite a ways, he noticed that something was in the road. At first he couldn't make it out but then as he got closer, he realized that it was a Red Brahman bull.

He finally arrived at the very spot where the animal was standing. He walked up to the beast, stood directly in front of him, and they stared eye-to-eye at each other for more than an hour. Then the affected rapport began to unravel.

"So tell me, my friend," Shemokoman said, "is it your custom to stand in the road like this? . . . Or did you come here on a lark? I am inclined to believe in the latter; however, I'm starting to honestly doubt it. And . . . do you think you can do whatever you please because you are big and imposing? Bulls aren't supposed to be in the road; it's risky as well as illegal. Not to mention the fact that you are blocking the bloody way of my ground transportation."

He looked at the bull for a moment or so as if expecting an answer. "Maybe you're lost, confused, or bummed out. I really don't care for excuses. It just doesn't pay to presume you're a guy who can go it alone as a maverick. What's more, on a day like today, you should be out in a pasture grazing with cows who think you're a dreamboat. I'm sure that your family and friends are growing concerned about your behavior.

"And now, for a nice little secret. I've heard credible rumors—through the grapevine, of course—that the Red Brahman bull can generate speech like a man. Of course, you would never admit it; and I can't say as I honestly blame you. Anyway, on brisk autumn nights when the whistling wind blows in from the chilly northeast and the full moon is dancing in back of gray clouds that are drifting, you and your kind are romping about with plenty of gossip and chatter. And you continue to talk while chewing the grass, as lookouts ensure that no human people are listening. So please, just tell me the truth, my friend. Why are you standing here in the road? You are no paranoid crackpot."

At first the brute was reluctant to talk and silent with slight agitation. But he knew it was time to dance the proverbial jig. So he hung his head low, and then he looked up and proclaimed in a casual manner, "There is much about the Red Brahman bull that you do not know, Shemokoman. For example—you're still in the dark regarding some problems we tolerate during the nighttime. The fact is that most of us have insomnia, with no healers to write a prescription. So if you consider our temperament more closely with that in mind, it will explain a great deal about cattle behavior. Cattle—detestable word! I don't like it. But now you desire to know something else. Namely, why do I stand in the road? Believe me, the answer is simple."

The bull explained, "After my difficult work on the farm, where I slave away endlessly, my aches and pains begin to afflict and upset me. Life is not easy for creatures like me; we often break down, and it is hard to recover. Wearisome days and only brief nights with too little rest are a problem. And how would you like to be born in a barn? I tell you, the stigma is frightening. Plus, branding and slaughterhouse tales we hear are cause for abundant concern."

The big guy adjusted his tie, snapped his tail, and then he went on with a speech: "I went to a rally demanding more hay. The silos are pretty much empty. They told me, 'Get lost . . . Go back to your stall. Your beef isn't fit for attention.' Oh, what a big disappointment! I tell you . . . I get no respect.

"And after a while, something inside of me bellowed: 'Abandon tradition!' I had to discover a far better way of coping with tension and trouble. So I came to this road where I currently stand, to forget about gloom and misfortune. And day by day, I began to improve and feel better. You see, Shemokoman . . . the road is a place that is always in play, with ramblers coming and going. Here in the road, I'm no longer upset about pulling my weight . . . like more than a ton. And—here in the road, I am no longer irked by fencing that serves to restrain me. Out here in the road, I have freedom, and there is little confusion to vex me. So there is your explanation. What do you think? It is the truth."

Shemokoman replied, "Well, I'm beginning to see why the bulls, cows, and doggies would sooner stampede. If I were in your hooves, it wouldn't take much to tick me off . . . get entirely bent out of shape."

"Yes," the creature continued, "freedom, my friend—even the animals need it. And I get a small dose of recognition as well by congenial travelers. People see me and the comments are made; who cares about what they are saying. For sure, it's a pretty good feeling, as they have many good thoughts and a few that do not bear repeating. Indeed, they cannot believe it—a bull in the road; for children, the sight is amusing. Yes, the masses are glad when they see it is I, and they know that a bull is no plaything."

"Hmm . . . ," Shemokoman thought. "So here I encounter a bull in the road who does it to deal with depression. Perhaps there is too much harassment on farms and his liberty needs to be cared for. So why should it be disconcerting to me? It is no great inconvenience, as I can simply pass by and continue my trip through the region. Too many people believe that the earth is only for human consumption."

Then he asked the bull, "But honestly, friend. Do you not think it is risky out here where you are to be passively standing? I don't want to see you get hurt."

The animal smiled and answered, "No problem, Shemokoman. Albeit, I thank you for honest concern. But when have you ever heard of a bull involved in a row on the High Way? Never; it just doesn't happen. So please, my friend—just keep me in mind and all that I candidly mentioned. I do not talk with just any old chap who calls upon me for discussion. Indeed, our conversation was quite the exclusive occurrence. First time that I spoke with a person. However, I've heard about you—a faithful defender of heaven on earth and of anyone blamed for getting too cozy with virtue. You are a man of his word for everyone living in Nature. We must get together again for a nice little parley."

The man from Michigan spoke with the bull for only a few minutes longer. It was a very rare chance to have an encounter with such an amazing creature. Then he politely bade farewell to the fellow and continued on his way.

As he strolled along and pondered the curious meeting, Shemokoman looked overhead at a sight that staggered the senses. A gigantic comet streaked down through the sky, plunged to the earth, and crashed with a booming explosion. It struck the ground exactly where the bull was standing and killed him.

"My god!" he thought. "What a tragical ending. Now he will truly discover his ultimate freedom. Oh well . . . there will be life, and there will be death, and man will never be able to understand either. It is a shame."

Shemokoman arrived back home at La Enchilada Reál late in the evening. No one was there to greet him; the latter-day dancer was doing a two-step. He sat at the dining room table, tired and hungry. So he had a big, thick, juicy medium-rare sirloin steak with a tall glass of milk for his supper. The meal just seemed to be prefect. Then he went to bed and slept until sunrise.

Big Sandy Desert

If you ask anyone who has been in the Lone Star State of Texas what it was like, they tell you with no hesitation: Life can be rough and tough, and you don't stay for long unless you were born and belong there. It is a home for those who want to get more out of life than an armchair. Shemokoman felt the same way. Yeah, it was a great place to visit; although he couldn't remain there forever. So, after only a year, he decided to move to find something more to his liking. Thus, he hit the road again, but this time—Magdalena didn't go with him. Said that she wanted to stay behind and go out every night to be dancing. To work in seedy saloons in town and live on a Double Bar ranch. To be a free spirit, drink champagne flips, listen to ragtime music, and pretend that nobody will blame her. Thank god for small favors, and closure.

It happens a lot that we follow a hunch and press onward without too much thinking. It didn't take long, and another small town called Nueva Roma turned up as his next destination. It was much farther south and more to the west, in a place called the Big Sandy Desert.

"My goodness, I hate to keep moving," Shemokoman thought. "I lack what is steady and normal; I am not stable. My stages of life are like phases of war with nothing but organized chaos. Must habits be weak for the will to be strong? I don't even care about wealth, rejection, or kindness. Once again, it is time to take stock in myself and sense what I need for survival. Otherwise, I risk an appalling fiasco."

Nueva Roma

Nueva Roma was pleasing in many respects to those who lived there. It was always hot, dry, and sunny, from each magnificent crack of dawn until every breathtaking sunset. A cause for dejection while being someplace was never so clearly precluded. There was no need for shoveling snow or donning the heavy down parka. Moreover, historic monuments stood on every street corner to brave fallen heroes who struggled and died for freedom, lest ye forget it.

Shemokoman made arrangements to live on the east side of town in a barrio called Pantano Flats. His home was a big white mansion with towers and turrets, surrounded by arid terrain with plenty of cactus. The neighbors he met were respectable folks, nothing audacious, revolting, or funny about them. Simply your typical run-of-the-mill who couldn't stop doting on jackals. He enjoyed the locale and quickly made friends as always.

In spite of whatever somebody may say, the desert is loaded with things to do. It needn't be lonely and boring, as there is much to see and explore. When time was at hand, Shemokoman went hiking on wilderness trails where he saw mule deer, fox, and coyotes, and also watched big, lanky jackrabbits bouncing across the wide-open spaces. He visited old Hispanic missions, where the believers lived like ascetics. And he went up in the high Catalinas to chill and dine with a friend in Mount Lemmon. He couldn't go wrong by taking a trip on Saturday morning to browse at the local swap meet. All in all, there were no conspicuous drawbacks.

A Walk in the Night

Winter soon passed, it never got cold, and now it was early in spring. Shemokoman often took long walks alone when there was time on his hands. On one particular evening and night, a chance to get out developed. He didn't think twice, got all dressed up, and thought about where best to go. Then, as soon as the sun slid under the rosy horizon, he left his home and went to the beckoning desert.

A gorgeous full moon and twinkling stars overhead were shining so brightly. There wasn't a cloud in the sky anywhere to obscure the heavenly bodies. A very strong wind that was gusting all day had died down and stopped blowing entirely. The southwestern air was thin and serene as echoes from canyons rumbled throughout the terrain.

More specifically, Shemokoman went to a place that was called the Sonoran. He walked for miles and miles, and ventured deep into the splendid, mysterious region. He went up and over the high mountaintops and crossed broad stretches of wasteland where the antelope, badgers, hawks, and scorpions watched him plugging along. It was their home and he knew it. While going up one small hill early on that was full of big red lava boulders, he almost stepped on a diamondback rattlesnake. The serpent was all coiled up, ready to strike and hissing like crazy—extremely upset and rightly so. Shemokoman excused himself and continued on his way.

He passed through a series of eerie ghost towns where the laughter and sobs of spirits who happened to be there were heard very faintly. But the miners who thought about striking it rich were swinging the pickax no longer. And the parson who tried to convert renegades was preaching the gospel no more. And girls who worked in the glitzy theaters had no one to serve at the tables. Nothing but old abandoned buildings that used to be home to some very real souls who also were human. What happened? Where did it all go? Everything now was falling apart on the way to de rigueur nostalgia. Reminiscence, of course, for those we esteem who are under the script on a tombstone.

After a couple of hours of serious hiking, Shemokoman came upon an old run-down saloon alongside the road. It was a wooden two-story building with three or four boarded-up windows. A rusty lone metal shingle was hanging directly above the entrance. It read "Das Wüstenhaus Gila." And then he heard voices inside of the place. Something was certainly cooking.

He thought, "What in the world is going on here? What in god's name are they doing so deep in the desert? Very suspicious."

Shemokoman pushed on a pair of batwing doors and stepped inside for a quick look around. Was anything real or was it a misty illusion? He knew he had wandered a fairly long time, but there was no trace of confusion. The contents of one big rectangular room were not too impressive but startling.

Your typical bar was along the back wall, complete with all of the trappings. Behind it—a short rotund bartender, who had a big dark Dalí mustache, was cleaning and drying the sparkling glasses. Of course, he was in no great hurry. In the middle of the room, there was one large circular table where a group of six men was seated in chairs, laughing and joking, smoking and drinking, and playing a round of straight poker. The gamblers were wearing those large cowboy hats and sporting dark signature glasses. The appearance of each of the rollicking fellows was just like all of the others. They must have come in from a long cattle drive to quench a strong thirst with the hard stuff.

The rest of the place was pretty much empty. Only a couple three busted-up chairs, a pair of antique sideboards, a dusty piano, and a grandfather clock that must've been broken for ages. The walls were enhanced with cameo mirrors and pictures with scenes from an Aryan storybook tale. Rapunzel, no less. The lighting was dim, provided by candles in brass chandeliers on the ceiling.

On account of a need to do something astute, Shemokoman went to the bar and uttered one word, "Whiskey." After getting his shot and facing away from the motley collection of people, he ingested the vile concoction in one single gulp—gasping and choking. And after a second or two had passed by, he looked at the barman straight in the eyes and said to him that it was "smoooth." Then, he turned around and gazed at the gambling cowpokes.

Brush with Crazy Invaders

And now, Shemokoman spoke up and said, "Pardon me, gentlemen. Didn't mean to interrupt your game. But you see . . . I was taking a walk in the Big Sandy Desert when—lo and behold—I stumbled upon this place. And you've got to admit it's a little bit strange that a saloon is here with people and drinks so far from civilization."

The straggly men all smiled and stared at each other. Then they looked at the stranger with understandable curiosity. One of them—the obvious leader—stood up and extended his arm for a friendly handshake. To avoid the semblance of being unfriendly and rude, it was time to break the ice and follow through with a part of tradition.

Shemokoman shook the man's hand and thought, "Obscene. But it is the custom here in this part of the world. As for me when greeting a stranger, I simply prefer to offer a nod or bow from the waist as my gesture. Purely a matter of hygiene."

The other man said in a very firm manner, "Mister, my name is Immanuel Bleu. And I am a Crazy Invader. And these are my ethical brothers, with whom I have ridden on many lonely and wearisome trails. We eat and we drink and sing our songs, and watch out for the back of each other. It is more dangerous to live among men than to live among animal creatures. Our home is in Guadalajara, where our mother is waiting to see us. Dear Mama still works in the fields—on a large banana plantation—and has yet to go more than twenty-five miles away from the home she was born in. And now, who are you?"

"Well, Mr. Bleu," he replied, "how do you do. My name is Shemokoman. And I hail from the Land of Michigan. My Potawatomi friends, who are the Keepers of Fire and Knowledge, inform me by way of smoke signals that the sky and the earth are at odds about sleep, so tonight you will need to be careful when going to bed. I sense that you render goodwill to all men without any spite or derision; it is a blessing. Life is too short for hatred, bushwhacking, and teardrops. So anyway, once again, please, excuse the intrusion."

The outlaw adjusted the brim of his hat while looking askance at his brothers. Then he gazed at the stranger again and said, "No problemo, amigo. It is no big interruption. In fact, it is good now and then to see a new face here in the dark mausoleum. And we are just friendly cowpunchers who needed a drink as well as diversion. But let me digress if I may . . . as there is something you maybe can help with. You see, year after year I look for a break, you know what I mean—frustration regarding employment. But nothin' I do seems to ever pan out, and it's tough to get by in the winter. It's tough. Now when I'm lookin' at you, I see the potential for plenty of good information. So, if it's not any big secret, I'd sure like to know what a man's gotta do to get a small piece of the action. Like, I'm at the end of my rope."

The Crazy Invader was dearly in need of right-minded advice and guidance. Down on his luck in a bottomless rut, somebody needed to straighten him out with a decent suggestion. Shemokoman said, "You know, Immanuel Bleu, the way I see it, you only require a practical dream to believe in. Namely, a job that is fun, constructive, and also rewarding. You need a profession that offers sufficient excitement; and, you have to give up what you currently do and make use of Hispanic potential. Yes, it is time for you to embark on a total one-eighty because only a gambler can ever end up as a winner. Now, you said you can sing—a man of the arts—and that is no trivial talent. So, how about joining the opera? Have you ever thought about that?"

"No," he replied, very muddled. "Can't say as I have."

The ethical comrade continued, "Well, perhaps it is time for you to turn over that very next leaf in your lifetime. The world of high society and those mezzo-sopranos await you. Of course, it will require much dedication and the investment of infinite labor. But I will tell you this much, my friend—you can do it! To sing is an art above all of the rest, to go under the lights and deliver a stellar performance. The night is ablaze and the audience thrills to your music. You are the star up high in the sky, and your voice enamors the people. Surrounded by grace and lovely urbane prima donnas, too many sirens are courting your elegant favor. I can see it all now in the theaters of Guadalajara. You— Immanuel Bleu. Yes, you are the toast of the town."

Life is divine when uncertainty fades whether Satan or God has arranged it. Immanuel Bleu was suddenly filled with emotion. For once in his life, he envisioned a fate that was more than a second-rate hustle down on the border. His eyes were shooting from side to side and blood in his body was boiling. He stood on his feet, raised both of his arms, and declared with a thunderous passion, "Yes . . . by god! Yes, I am sure I can do it!"

And now Shemokoman noted, "Every day we exist, whoever you are, is replete with something of value. Nothing can ever be wasted, just as everything has to be useful. The ultimate goal is to recognize skill; to develop and then to exploit it. People spend far too much time every day trying to change the immutable, reconcile the irreconcilable, and destroy what can never be vanquished. And thus, I say to you here and now, Mr. Bleu: forget about insignificant tripe and focus on what is important. Yes, we may live for ambition and musing; it is not sinful. And we shall die for a purpose as well, don't ever forget it. My friend, you told me a minute ago that you are game for a piece of the action. Well, I believe that we have a solution. All that you want and need is waiting, like now, in trendy playhouses."

Immanuel Bleu was bewildered as he stared at the snappy newcomer. The time had arrived for a man who was going in circles to straighten it up. With so little hope to consider before, a true innovation was needed. How inconceivable: the opera.

He said, "Well, Shemokoman, I sure do appreciate all the advice that you gave me. I shall rejoice tonight and start a new life beginning tomorrow. Every marquee in the CIR—that is, the Crazy Invader Republic—will very soon herald a fabulous triumph. A big, new famous kahuna is coming to town."

The mood in the joint now changed as tension abated. Shemokoman joined in on their gambling card game and had nothing but fun with a bunch of those derelict gauchos. Good and bad hands, fancy shuffling, raises and calls, and a bunch of the wickedest card tricks. In spite of the fact that bandits are often dishonest, all was aboveboard; there was no cheating. How soon we forget about moments of joy that keep us in stitches for hours. Poker, you know—a very enlightening pastime. It teaches man how to be patient and when it is time to cut losses and fold. It teaches man how to best manage the stress when overwhelming odds appear to be mounting. It teaches man how to be gracious no matter if one is the winner or loser. It basically teaches man how to get by in a world that punishes dumbbells. Yes, poker, for sure, a definite character builder. And who ever said it was evil?

It was getting late and time to call it quits, so everyone packed it in and started for home. When Shemokoman stepped outside of the place, he ran into the bartender who was sweeping a dusty veranda. He asked the fellow, "So, how in the world did a place like this acquire the name 'Das Wüstenhaus Gila'? There must be a tale behind it."

The man replied with a chuckle, "You know, it's funny that you should ask, my friend, because it really is one heck of a story. Had to do with a fellow named Mr. Castillo. He visited here awhile back, was drinking cherry schnapps, and—"

"My good sir," Shemokoman cut him short. "You needn't say anything more. Believe me, I can imagine how the whole nine yards went down. And here is a tip of three gold doubloons for your time and hospitality. It is a nice little joint that you operate here; I look forward to coming again."

As he started to go back to civilization, suddenly—as if a mysterious power provoked him—Shemokoman turned around to take one last look at the saloon. But unfortunately, Das Wüstenhaus Gila was gone.

He thought, "Could it be possible that I am dreaming? Time will tell."

Days of Eventual Musing

Besides love, God, and country, there is fishing. A splendid outdoor sport that men get hooked on. And if you want to know why man enjoys it, then all you have to do is feast on walleye. Glory be! Shemokoman went to lakes and streams many a time to try his luck at angling. On one occasion, he wanted to see if a brand-new spinner was as good as he was promised. Unfortunately, he didn't have a lot of bites or land a mess of keepers. Although it just didn't matter. His job was not to use the bait and set the hook, and catch the fish to feed the hungry children. For what it's worth, the days of good providers mostly ended long ago, thanks to progress.

While living far away from home, the refugee from Michigan continued to think about friendship: "To have a true devoted friend requires mind and patience. It is something you must work on and enhance from day to day. It will make you rich when you are poor, dirt poor as poor can be. Epicurus was right: we must never take a friend for granted. Furthermore, just one mistake and all is lost, as someone can't be trusted. 'He said to me . . . I said to him . . . and that was that, forever.' Careless remarks made off-the-cuff will estrange your friend for certain. And even though the years go by, you never do recover.

Then you spend your empty time alone and so downtrodden, sitting by a wishing well reflecting on the blunder. Perhaps I understand why Yeshua taught the people to 'love thy enemy.' "

It was a Sunday morning with lots of time to explore the local surroundings. He hit the road and it didn't take long for a Voice Within to get up to childish mischief. The prankster said: "Hey . . . where are we?" Laughter, endless laughter. Down the street and around the corner, and past the old Hispanic churches. The prankster: "Hey . . . where are we?" Laughter, endless laughter. Moving on . . . through the main shopping district and across the town square. The prankster: "Hey . . . where are we?" Laughter, endless laughter. Up and over the railroad tracks, past a fork in the road, and through the intersection with Ajo Way. The prankster: "Hey . . . where are we?" Laughter, endless laughter. Behind the rows and rows of Hopi shops and other handicraft boutiques. The prankster: "Hey . . . where are we?" Laughter, endless laughter. And hence, the saga continued.

Shemokoman preferred to have his modest expectations. He never owned or wanted much in the way of earthly possessions. It was more than enough for him to pursue the simple pleasures in life that people miss out on. Regardless of what they promised him about a great perspective, he knew the sun would never shine for mankind any brighter.

One More Adieu

Three years rolled by lickety-split for Shemokoman in the Southwest. And the time arrived—it always does—for him to run along. Alas, the tempting locale could never work out as a suitable home in the long run. From the moment he first arrived, he knew it was only a transient venue. The Native American tribes; and, the scorching heat that proved to be never-ending. Hispanic comida, Cinco de Mayo, the absence of all counterculture, and those miles of dry, empty desert; oh well, every single thing was truly perfect. Who knows, perhaps we depend upon quite a bit less than more to be honestly happy.

After saying good-bye to Simon the Zealot, Philip, and all the rest of his friends, he pulled up stakes and promptly left the area. He mused, "At least my life is not what one could say is dull and boring? Albeit, I cannot let a simple stitch upset my ataraxia."

Disposition of the Arrogant Felon

While moving along, Shemokoman thought about law and order—how best to administer justice. Perhaps a legal revision or two in effect would make things better. Out with the old and in with the new, and a promise for something befitting.

He pondered, "It is true, there exist wicked people we know who deliberately wander among us. They have eyes for the night, with ice-cold skin and a knack for causing affliction. They extol what is bad and abhor the good because of innate predilections. Yes, for them a nice little crime delivers the feeling of gratification. It is a wanton disgrace for them to be ecstatically proud of. They enjoy the nefarious deed and believe that there is no harm in trashing the life of another. Just do as you please and break every rule in the book, so what?! . . . Who cares? Perhaps the slovenly creatures are not even human.

"Unfortunately, they have no conscience, no god, no semblance of truth, no nothing except for defiance. They are debauched, comport with dregs, and are loaded with hatred. And yet, they come forth to accuse and condemn, and without any shame, to affirm that 'we are upstanding and righteous. Yes, we the commendable swingers.' Excuse me! What should we do with the scoundrels? And what about law on the books to apply? And how must we firmly enforce it? Of course, we will show them a merciful side, just as they did for the victims. It is time to get tough with some harsh punishment and show them that we are not kidding. An eye for an eye—and nothing could ever be more apropos for a felon."

Part III

*I'm getting tired of hearing the word "forgiveness"
instead of "justice." It is a cop-out. In particular,
the will to power for requital is forsaken.*

13

❦

Where No-Man's Land Is Perfect

East Coast

During a glorious autumn, Shemokoman moved to the East Coast of America and took up residence in Federal City, the national capital. The town was impressive with huge government buildings, museums and theaters, historical places of interest, and millions of servants who did whatever it took to accumulate power. He went there expecting to see for himself what it was like to be among so many people. For sure, it had to be different.

He lived in a two-story brownstone flat on the outskirts of town by the Potomac River. There was nothing to see on the walls in his home except for a coat of beige paint. It is a color that should have been banned long ago because it is neutral and sickening. He had no desire to furnish the place aside from a few of the basics. A couch, the table and chairs, a dresser, and a Southampton four-poster bed. Of course, it would be just another way station that soon he would have to abandon.

His neighbors were Mesopotamian folk who sat on the floor and ate chicken. Born and raised in Babylon, those characters were often apt to get rowdy. They also made unleavened flatbread, brandished new, terrible weapons for better protection, and talked about hand-knotted silk Persian rugs from Kashan. In spite of a keen predilection, everyone sensed that they were indifferent jihadists.

One evening, Shemokoman sat on his balcony ledge and gazed at the courtyard below where children were playing a ball game. A big fellow named Klem joined in on the fun, in spite of the fact that he was ten years older than everyone else. His age and size apparently just didn't matter. And when Klem was able to carry the ball, no one so much as laid a hand on the guy. He scored hundreds of times to prove it, mowing everyone down to the ground who stood in his way to unparalleled triumph. Talk about absolute carnage.

"The fellow I watch," Shemokoman thought, "is clueless regarding the meaning of real competition. He never grew up and out of a need to somehow achieve recognition. Oh well, whatever it takes to be happy, and more power to him."

A phase of adjustment now confronted Shemokoman. He was alone without anyone there as a friend whom he could hang out with. The prospect was gone for an uncomplicated agenda. So what would he do to conform to a new situation? In spite of the fact that volition of choice appeared to be all too authentic, he had to give in without giving up and give everything else to the demons. Why must we sacrifice faith and our pride for only a chance at contentment? It seems like a lot to relinquish when you are forced to be betting the hard way. Although, for sure, he more clearly envisioned a way to ascend to the High Road.

He pondered, "I am beginning to think that man is basically evil. I try to do good, and what do I get in return? The heathens reject and betray me. I show them respect, and all that I feel is regret and a deluge of heartache. No one can fully be trusted. And that is the truth."

Rossiya

Shemokoman used every trick that he could with intent to improve understanding. He didn't lose sight of the Pillars of Strength to which he was tethered and fated. So now with a wish to continue his search and advance even quite a bit further, he decided to travel again overseas to another side of the planet. He sought to observe firsthand for himself what certain people were like and if they might be any different. Accordingly, he arranged for a trip to cross the Ocean and visit a place called Rossiya.

After several months of preparation, he boarded a big gray ship at the Port of Departure. The precise location for where he was bound, the Province of Buryatia, was deep in the eastern part of a great Motherland. He heard many stories and read a great deal about the people who lived there. They were disciples of science and art who made a wide range of major contributions over the years. Yes, the amazing Rossiya; it was a truly formidable country. Although he had to consider the flip side.

Rossiya was big, a treacherous place and most of the time unforgiving, where your slightest mistake was always a threat to survival. At the top of the heap, *His Majesty* pulled every string on the tyrannized people and maintained a political structure that was replete with dreadful conditions. And to ensure that a strong opposition never threatened to make any inroads, the relentless and ruthless Cheka for state security was established. Anyone anytime anywhere was removed if the State didn't care for your program. Welcome! . . . To the Passportnaya Sistema and to the glamorous gulag.

The illegitimate social order was based on fear and coercion. And why was that so? Well, a long time ago, after ages of war, the people themselves gave away absolute power. They calmly proclaimed to a paranoid tsar, "Do what you must to ensure that never—no, never again . . . we will not lose fifty million." And so, a government plan was put into place that even agreed to make purges. Geographical size and climate as well as relations with very bad neighbors were additional reasons to lay out and set up the cruel dictatorial structure. Some people decried what they said was too much oppression, and thus, their voices were silenced forever. And nobody smiled on any occasion, but everyone said they were happy.

Buryatia

On a freezing cold Monday evening during November, Shemokoman arrived in the Buryat Province capital city, Ulan Ude. After the very long journey, he was extremely tired and hungry. So after grabbing a bite to eat and catching a motorized trolley, he made his way to the lodging at the luxurious Baikal Hotel. As he stood in front of the main entranceway and collected his thoughts and impressions, it was obvious that something strange was going on at the socialist venue. All of the people were feeling no pain as they staggered around up and down the streets in a big celebration.

He spoke with a local constable regarding the odd situation. The lawman told him that people in town were observing Revolution Day.

"Of course," Shemokoman thought to himself. "How could I ever forget it? And something else is happening here; namely, social unrest is a part of the much bigger picture. These men and women have every right to go on a spree on occasion; however, the Party has let the party get out of control. It tells me the truth about life in this town and the mood in an outlying region. Desperation with plenty of pain is what they are feeling. The future is bleak, the past was a sham, and today is high time for a shindig. Tasty poison for pleasant sedation; it is a way to attenuate anguish. I doubt that they are all just terribly thirsty. And none of these people will think in the least about thousands of dead fallen heroes; instead, like Mr. J., their only desire is booze in the gullet. It'll take ages to turn it around with perceptible change that will be for the better."

He grabbed his luggage and went up the stairway to enter the big yellow building. He pushed forward on two enormous wooden doors and went in the lodging. After confirming the room reservation, he decided to call it a day. And then as he passed the Grand Entertainment Ballroom, he saw it was packed with a cluster of reveling bodies. Everyone—drinking and dancing as a musician was giving a concert. It was Vertinsky! . . . With a selection of favorite songs. The sound was so loud; my goodness, a terrible racket.

Suddenly, one of the female types grabbed him by the arm and whispered into his ear, "Hey, where do you think you're goin' . . . you stage-door Johnny? Come on inside, and give this poor Siberian lass a little attention."

In response to the pleasing intrusion, Shemokoman replied with the greatest of candor: "Comrade! I wish that I could, but alas, I cannot. The early frigid morning is rapidly coming. So as for tonight, I haven't the time to impress anyone by dancing a tango or fox-trot. You know what I mean. Right?"

Then, having carefully passed the polluted beautiful girl, the visitor knew he would live to regret it. The charm and desire, her class and torrid appearance; and, that lavender gloss and shadow were notably stunning. Good fortune was instantly passing him by as he continued to walk and thought about tactics. But no, there was nothing remaining; and yes, she was certainly something. All was exposed in the blink of an eye, and everything told him that she was an absolute darling. But the potential for ecstasy vanished and his spirit was evermore dampened. And that is some more of your truth about life; it happens in radical places. People connect for a second or two, then barely move on, and wonder about "what could have been" for a lifetime.

On the way to his room in a stairwell, the ethical comrade dropped to his knees and pleaded for weakness or courage. One or the other, as something was better than having to put up with nothing. The woman behind found comfort alone at her table. She bitterly wept for the better part of at least two to three minutes.

Old Woman

In spite of resolve to get much-needed rest, Shemokoman had a hard time falling asleep. So he got up out of bed, put warm clothing on, and went downstairs to hang around in the lobby. There wasn't too much going on anymore; all of the people had left and the place was quiet. Then he stepped out of the fancy hotel for a breath of fresh air in the nighttime.

The streets were empty and silent as well; the festivities finally had ended. He looked up at the sky and thought, "No, nothing is different above in the stellar dominion. The very same moon and stars are there to beguile me. And Nature will always be thrilling, as it is no cheap imitation created by One who needs to be piously worshipped. For heaven's sake! . . . Who cares about more information? Perhaps it is best to be in the dark without any clarification. Perhaps it is best to be out of the loop instead of a jerk in the in-crowd."

Shemokoman reached into one of his pockets and took out a fresh cigarette. He lit it up, and soon he was puffing away. It really delivered the taste, outstanding tobacco. He stood in the crisp winter air and decided to blow a couple of smoke rings. Uh-huh, perfect circles. Then he glanced across the street at the old town square. The Buryats erected a statue right at the front of the great open space. It was the head of a man and—indeed—strangely familiar. The fellow had sharp pointy ears and cold piercing eyes, and he was undoubtedly evil. Great Scott! . . . It was Mephisto.

"Do they not see who they extol?" he thought. "How could the comrades have missed it? Perhaps I will start a petition to have it removed and completely demolished. Although, what good would it do? To them he is some kind of hero. I guess that for now, I've got no other choice than to let the matter slide and simply forget it."

While standing alone outside by his lodging, Shemokoman was approached by a little old woman. It was your quintessential Slavic babushka. Her head was wrapped in a purple silk scarf and she wore hundreds of layers of clothing. Her smooth pinkish face, like the rest of her kind, must have been chiseled from granite. And, of course, she was bright-eyed, chipper, and beaming.

In light of the fellow's appearance, she instantly knew that he wasn't a man of her country. Rather, a foreigner. She walked right up to him, and stopped and stared, mumbled a bit, inspecting the image and features. It put the stranger on the spot; he needed to say something cordial.

"Greetings to you, madam," Shemokoman said. "And how are we doing this evening?"

With an inquisitive air and lack of restraint, the woman continued to scrutinize him. And finally, she said, "I'm fine, couldn't be better. Although my husband passed out in the alley. Pridurok! So, what is your name and where are you from? . . . And why did you come to my town?"

"Well, my name is Shemokoman," he replied. "And I hail from the Land of Michigan in America. I came to your land in peace to observe and learn as much as I can for edification."

She said, "Well, peace or no peace, what does it honestly matter? There's always another war on the way, just waiting for someone to start it. And obviously, this is your very first trip to Ulan Ude because we haven't allowed one single stranger to come here for seventy years. Our town was especially closed to the *running dogs* of capitalism, and that was the way we preferred it. But everything changes with time; you learn to accept it. So how do you like my comrades so far? I'm sure there must already be many lasting impressions."

"Indeed, you live in a wonderful place," he said. "And there will be much for me to remember. I really enjoyed the splendid debauchery here in your town this evening. I am sure that the head over there is pleased as punch at overindulgence."

She snapped back, "Don't get smart with me, buster. You think your country is better than mine, huh? Well, let me tell you a thing or two. Nothing compares to Rossiya; it is the best! For example, regarding myself: I have a nine square meter flat right in the middle of Ulan Ude. My living space—like everyone else—is more than sufficient. I have a garden with dill and cucumbers, potatoes and carrots, turnips and cabbage, and everything needed to always stay healthy and fit. My cat is a Persian from Vladivostok; his name is Kasik Petrovich. And to tell you the truth, we don't give a hoot if the Center is crashing and burning!

"For the last forty years, I worked day and night doing manual labor I'm proud of. Running feeders and screeners with crushers in the People's Garment Factory, Number 138.2, on Botanical Street. My benefits there were incredibly good and all was according to Plan. So what if I didn't save nothing at all; I had a good time and drank vodka. And now, I'm retired with a pension and I have all of my babushka friends. We continue to talk about men—what a shame! One shortage, I truly regret.

"And I have every conceivable privilege that one may expect in this miserable lifetime. Okay, let me give you a sample. My food— borsch, pirogi, pelmeni, black bread and vinaigrette salad, Georgian tea, and, especially—chocolate, straight from the Red Star Plant in Moskva. Can't—beat—that. And as for the medical care, well, I never wait more than two or three days to get an appointment with healers. For as long as I've lived, it was always like that; we have to get used to some things. Regarding my recreation: I take long enjoyable walks in the Great Workers' and Peasants' Park, visit the State Museum, and I may shop in the Gostiniy Dvor', drinking a beer, whenever I want to. Very nice touch. Our churches, shrines, and temples, no doubt—the best anyplace in the world. And, with special permission straight from the leaders who cheat us, I can travel to Petrograd and stroll on the Nevsky. An extravagant town, built on the bones of people who sang when bridges were open at nighttime. Oh, those White Nights! . . ."

The old woman got a little choked up but didn't waver from having her say. "And what do you have in your country? Well, allow me to talk about that. To begin with, nothing but violent thugs and criminal cases. No one can go anywhere these days without being mugged or possibly murdered. Especially in the big cities. And how about high unemployment? Tell me, where do you find a good job? Meanwhile . . . the government grows, the economy slows, and bureaucrats couldn't care less. They feign a concern and laugh at the poverty-stricken. In every last town, billions of homeless people are lying in gutters and sleeping on benches. The way that you treat your comrades, it is an outrage."

She went on, "Illness and death are surging ahead; your health-care system is broken. The cost is too high and only the rich can afford it.

Perhaps a way to effectively deal with the issue of depopulation. We just never know what the Ruling Class may be up to. Now, do we?! Then, of course . . . you have the glamour of Tinseltown; it is the center of greed and corruption. Another new scandal explodes every day with all the despicable details. Although, I've got to admit that some of it frequently gets pretty juicy. But we don't have any of that. No! The State decides what is good and bad, and the public obeys—no objection. And finally, you have religion. It is a holy solution for sinners. Never could stomach that rubbish myself—an obvious fraud to control the masses who haven't the sense to see through it. Sanctimonious people in church who declare that immoral behavior is evil. Goodness, what do they know about values? And what can they say about virtue? I will tell you, nothing. Nothing at all. Not one blasted thing. Hypocrites—every last one of them. Our leaders have shown with reliable proof that God is a scandalous rip-off. There is no Gracious Almighty, and I will hope we are right about that."

Shemokoman glanced at the big sculpted head across the street in the square. Then he said to the woman: "The case you provide is convincing, of course; my country has numerous problems. But you see, it is the cost we endure and accept for freedom. Perhaps it is right or maybe it's wrong; time will decide what may or may not have been better. Furthermore—as for the people who live in Rossiya, in spite of the fact that religion is scorned, they should be counting their blessings. Everything here outside of the holiday bash appears to be normal. Perhaps I can learn a thing or two during my stay in your dreamland. And I am not trying to be funny."

The babushka squinted her eyes and smiled because she was glad that he seemed to be understanding. Then the woman said, "Yes, maybe you can at that. And summing up regarding my tirade, you see, I know what goes on everywhere in the civilized world. I know what I'm talking about. Because every day I read *Pravda*."

With those words, the woman adjusted her socialist clothing, bundled up as best as possible, and walked away to wherever, avoiding the alley. Shemokoman looked in the distance where the silhouette of a tall mountain range pierced the moonlit horizon.

He thought, "Life in my land is not what she thinks, that woman of much propaganda. I wonder if there was ever a day when avoiding the Truth was considered. Probably not. She was content with a myth that didn't annoy or badly confuse her. And now at this time, it plainly appears that she is declining and happy. Whatever it takes: so be it! On the other hand . . . perhaps it is I with too much official conditioning." Then he went back to his room.

Ice Festival

As it turned out, Shemokoman didn't get much sleep. Two or three hours, no more. After waking up the following morning, he drudgingly got to his feet and prepared for the upcoming day. One thing was for sure: he had to be constantly moving. The bitter cold temperature outside could instantly freeze a body to death that didn't have good circulation.

During the first day, he explored the maze of streets in town and observed many hungover comrades. He browsed in stores and dined in popular places. Especially—stolovayas. He wanted to interact with local tradition and anything else that happened to cultivate interest. And then, that very same evening, Shemokoman was treated to an exceptionally pleasant surprise. He went to the Workers' Park of Culture and Leisure, where a big celebration was in full swing. There were amusement-type rides for young and old, concessions with local cuisine, and glittering displays of beautiful sculpture made completely of ice.

When he entered the grounds at the gala event and appeared unlike the others, the townspeople instantly mobbed him. His arrival resembled the second coming of Jesus with superstar status. Young Buryats especially were thrilled by the presence of somebody totally different. Everyone circled around the stranger and asked him loads of questions. A frenzy ensued that lasted for two to three hours.

A night on the town in Ulan Ude was just what the Doctor had ordered. Shemokoman knew that memories worth keeping are made when people can think about the good times spent together. You cannot effect any meaningful mental advantage according to how much we struggle and suffer, and that is the truth. So he looked forward to meeting a person or two and didn't expect any hassle.

Tatiana and sister Natasha served as his very own personal escorts. They remained by his side the whole evening long and provided the intimate friendship. More than anything else, the trips on a fifty-foot ice slide were unbelievably thrilling. While standing together, the three of them slid down the long, slippery slope dozens of times to a heavenly finish. And it was always the same at the bottom: a delightful loss of balance, a spectacular tumble and fall, followed by one magnificent crash into a snowdrift. And regardless of where he decided to look during that fabulous outing, the picture was the same. Unreal.

And then, all at once, everything changed. Shemokoman felt a deep sense of melancholy for much of the rest of his time at the special occasion. He stood and watched as thousands of folks had so much fun it was chilling. How could they all be feeling so good? After all, those men and women didn't have much, and life was hard as hell in their ideological country.

"So what am I honestly missing?" he thought. "And, why is it that I do not live in this place where no one has negative feelings? Something is out of whack, a little bit funny. For me it could be the sort of a home where everything falls into place and people are happy. Alas . . . Greed! . . . The scourge of your average American chump; and, it is the big separator."

Shemokoman finished his festival visit and slowly walked back to the lodging. He thought about all he observed at the park and mused about affluent people. "What good would it do for me to be rich? Indeed, I would rather have nothing. All wealth that I ever acquire is only a burden. The more we have, the more we want, and bandits are trying to steal it. It gets to a point where life is a drag and we travel alone incognito. I have to find solace like everyone here and stick to a modest lifestyle. Perhaps I need to adhere to a more spartan type of existence."

Sibir'

The province of Buryatia was part of a much bigger region called Sibir'. And during the next several weeks, Shemokoman hiked throughout that entire snow-covered area. He followed the trails that went up and over the Sayan Mountains and ventured north into the tundra, where not even one single tree could ever be growing. His wanderings took him from kayaking on the Selenga to the sacred fig in the Buddhist Ivolga Monastery. And he had to admit that all that he saw was something that he should remember. It made him feel noble and worthless.

It came to pass that after a while, he arrived at the deepest fresh-water lake in the world. It was Baikal. So, he chartered a boat and sailed away to a promising fishing location. The time had arrived to angle for socialist keepers. However, he didn't catch much at all that day, not even the small-fries were biting. Wistfully, he thought about days long ago at Bass Lake when his basket was filled up with bluegills.

Due Process

After the fishing event and moving along in a nonchalant way, Shemokoman felt like exploring and walking forever. It's easy to think if we're healthy and strong that nothing else honestly matters. Only additional footsteps.

As fate would have it, he happened upon an angry mob of women who were in a small village called Chuda. They were mad at a man who was married and had a big family because the fellow committed adultery. His wife and their children were standing nearby and watching as the female types insisted on capital punishment. The accused was backed up next to a wall in front of the furious ladies, all of whom were holding big rocks in their hands. Just then, Shemokoman pushed his way through the crowd of skirts and elegant headgear and stood beside the fellow.

"Let she who is without sin cast the first stone!" he declared.

The offender was thereupon pelted to death by a volley of stones so great that one cannot imagine. Then his wife and their children merrily walked away, laughing and thanking the neighbors. Maybe there really is justice in this world after all. For sure, that slimy philanderer would "go, and sin no more."

Bliss in ShokanZem

Shemokoman decided to visit the province of ShokanZem in the far southern parts of Rossiya. It was nothing but wild terrain down there with almost no civilization. He roamed far and wide through a part of the world that clearly was open and endless. Everywhere—lean rolling steppe-countryside with arable, dark black soil where anything man desired to plant could be growing.

Nomads, who lived in thatched huts called yurtas, comprised the indigenous people. And a camel's back afforded the ground transportation. Shemokoman was smitten by love for life in a land where time was at a standstill. He thought, "But there was a day when Batu and his kind were rulers, and never obliging. Brutality reigned together with law and disorder."

After several days and nights of constant travel on the road, Shemokoman came to a village called Staro Selo, his destination. It was your typical sleepy simmering hamlet with log cabins, horses, and wagons. Barefoot straggly kids were chasing chickens, dogs, and each other as cattle and sheep were grazing about on the farmland. Billowy smoke from cinder-block chimneys rose high in the sky of a khanate. The women were doing the laundry and hanging the linen on clotheslines to dry.

When he checked in at the lodging, a hostess greeted the guest with bread and salt per Slavic tradition. The visitor sensed they were glad to finally see him, not always the case. They provided a cozy room for his stay and furnished all staple provisions. And to mark the occasion of his arrival, they built a new dining facility and set up a trail for workouts.

Without a doubt, the most exceptional part of the new location was the incredible landscape. Shemokoman lived at the base of the breathtaking Dzungarian mountain range. Simple words are of such little use in any attempt to describe that vast geographic formation. With spellbinding beauty and grandeur, the regal snow-covered peaks rose up to enhance the heavens above them. And just like gods that we know and esteem, they soared unabashed, yielding to basically nothing.

He pondered, "And to think some people have the nerve to say they've seen it all. Well, they haven't laid eyes on this to thoroughly floor them."

In his room, Shemokoman unpacked his luggage and got everything arranged exactly the way that he wanted. Very discriminating, as usual. Then he ate lunch in the dining hall and conversed with the glory of Nina, a beautiful hostess. She was a cheerful, well-informed woman who had the lightest of light blue eyes. And after the meal, he went outside and took a walk, and thought about all of the people he met so far in Staro Selo.

He mused, "No doubt in my mind—it takes all kinds. And nothing will ever be easy for them, especially kicking the bucket."

Shortly thereafter, he went to bed.

Dire Consternation

The next day, Shemokoman woke up at the crack of dawn. His very first thought was that of a dream he had the night before. Specifically—somewhere far away, he entered and dashed through a pueblo that was full of small, colorful casas. He was chasing a shadow for reasons unknown on navy-blue roads that were narrow. Many high walls surrounded the place and superstitious padres prayed to gods on totem poles. The sons and daughters of local Culinas were yelling at frustrated mothers making tortillas. And he could not escape from all of the madness. Shemokoman tried to make sense of it all, and of course, he was able to do it. But what's the use? . . . Your typical fettered bondservant is normally rattled. He also managed to get a good sleep, and so he was ready to rumble.

Nobody else was up and about as he quietly slipped outside to exercise. A long, slow, easy run; yes, nothing could be any better. After doing some stretching and bending to loosen up, Shemokoman started to jog. Around and around he went on the black cinder track, plugging away. A short while later, he looked at his watch; an hour already elapsed. That was enough; time to wrap it up and do something different.

Just then, a sentry who was on foot patrol approached him and said, "Good morning, sir. And may I ask, How are we doing today?"

He smiled and answered, "Well, I could be better, or I could be worse. It all has to do with perspective. But we shouldn't complain about life in the least, as I can give you eight hundred and seventy-two reasons for my opinion."

The guard understood it completely, and he was grateful. To fully appreciate comfort in life, it helps to know how so many others have suffered.

How Propensities End

It came to pass that after his physical training, Shemokoman went to a nearby bench to rest for a spell. He lit up a fresh cigarette, took a drag, started to cough, and then got a little bit dizzy. And as the insidious soft white vapor entered and jolted his body, his lungs gave voice to a protest: "The time has arrived for you, my friend. You need to quit smoking, and now. All good things must come to an end; you know what we mean, so stop it. Otherwise, you will be pushing up daisies."

The message was loud and clear; he couldn't object. As a matter of fact, Shemokoman was more than willing to do it. He gazed at the mountains far off in the distance and thought, "And I also do it for you, my friends, to honor a noble existence. Unlike myself, you are not fated to perish . . . No—you will be part of the wonderful earth forever. Therefore, your lofty summits have that impeccable trait called immortality. And, as far as I know, only the gods lay claim to such a high office. But the days of my life with a body and soul are numbered and set to expire. Therefore, I need to conform to the will of a hopefully generous Almighty Father. It is a fair request."

With both hands, he crushed the cellophane package and destroyed the contents inside. Then he threw it away; it was the last pack, forever. No more blowing those magical rings to entertain wide-eyed children.

"Habits," he mused, "so easy to break in spite of the scary foreboding. To do the right thing requires a pittance of courage. You think you will die in spite of the fact that now you can go about living. One has to respond to a moral behest and shatter the force of desire. And yet, it's a horrible struggle for so many addicts."

Preoccupation

During the stay at Staro Selo, which lasted exactly a fortnight, there was plenty of talk with stubborn men expressing their expert opinions. For the most part, Shemokoman only listened because he couldn't get a word in edgewise.

"Slavic people are like that," he thought. "They rant and rave, and shred a mere discussion into pieces. It's a way of life for them; and, they do it without even thinking. Oh, how they love to quarrel, and no subject is ever off-limits. They always wage a war of the words, without a single interlude or standards. Unfortunately, nothing is ever resolved because it's more like entertainment, and a vital chronic custom that they use to let the steam off. Yes, a way to cope with tension on account of much oppression. And although they say the talking points are heavy and important, the really sticky issues get no serious attention. For sure, the only reliable way to avoid a knock on the door at night when they are sleeping."

Looking around at the splendid location, Shemokoman thought about spending his time in the slow lane. "One day, I shall live in a spacious white home with columns in front of the dwelling. And, a sunroom for tea and reading my books will be right above the main entrance. The house will have plenty of colorful rooms with high vaulted ceilings to keep the cool air inside during the summer. And hundreds of windows everywhere, to allow the sunlight to enter and brighten my sanctum. Hand-knotted medallions and matching runners will cover the chestnut flooring. Servants and maids shall reside there as well to attend to the housework and chores. Every day, every night—the same routine with nothing to hamper my freedom. I want to enjoy the agreeable life as Nature so rightly intended. And I will stroll by the brook in a flowery glade with seed at Ceresco during the saffron harvest."

Do Svidaniya

A night went away and a day reappeared, cajoling humanity's favor. The morning horizon was hazy and rouge; in essence, it was surreal. Sweet Eos had done it again, a pièce de résistance. Shemokoman finished his trip to Staro Selo and thereupon pronto departed. And while cutting across a great wide plain, he watched a pair of Kazakh children tending haystacks in a horse-drawn wagon.

"It's good they don't know any better," he thought. "I hope that nobody will tell them. And one way or another, a day will arrive when I will come back here to join them."

Soon thereafter, the ethical comrade from Michigan boarded a big gray ship at the Port of Departure. He sailed across the Ocean and returned to America.

14

Presence of Mind on the Wire

Home for a While

The summer soon passed, autumn slipped by, and before he could say Kashpirovsky, winter arrived again. Shemokoman went to the Land of Michigan for a vacation. He needed some downtime and rest to get rid of fatigue and rejuvenate power. And, as always, the yuletide season caused a great wave of inspiration in him. It was a time of the year when, in spite of so many dilemmas, people could count on a breather. Goodwill toward man replaced many cynical notions.

Upon his arrival in Battle Creek, he noticed that members of the Optimist Club were giving out Christmas trees. And a whole lot of people were waiting in line to receive one. It appeared that the staff was short-handed, as only a couple of fellows, Wayne and Garfield, were working. So he decided to help them out and two full days passed by very quickly.

When he was finished with that and while crossing through town in the morning, he ran into a group of volunteers who were ringing bells and collecting assorted donations. Indeed, charity mellows the conscience, and it is superlative kindness. He made up his mind to lend them a hand, and another forty-eight hours flew by in a jiffy.

Shemokoman went to a ballet performance on Christmas Eve day at the main auditorium in town. A Slavic dance troupe from Rossiya staged the extravagant show called *Swan Lake*. It was a sterling production and certainly managed to bring down the house. At the end of the show, he met with a few danseurs and ballerinas from Petrograd. Everyone sipped on a vintage champagne, ate black caviar, and munched on gourmet potatoes. And it was right about then that someone offhandedly noted, "To live in a world devoid of the arts simply could never be worth it."

Then somebody dropped a hint that maybe it would.

The following day, it was mild outside. There wasn't a cloud in the sky. Shemokoman spent most of his time at Anna's home in Waupakisco Park. They sat at her yellow dining room table and talked about current events and respectable people. She was also anxious to hear the details concerning his travel abroad. Black and gray squirrels were in the backyard, digging up nuts they saved during autumn for winter. It's really amazing how they remember exactly where everything's buried. Icicles under the eaves on the roof above the back porch were starting to melt in the sunshine.

Citizen R. was right. Not too much had changed in the old neighborhood; everything looked the same. The old pumphouse was still churning away, and Vince was across the street guarding the sidewalk. Later on that very same evening, they enjoyed an outstanding dinner: roast duck with all of the trimmings. Anna always was a great cook. She especially knew how to prepare the wild cuisine, like pheasant, pat, venison, goose, and rabbit. When nightfall arrived to shroud the sweet earth with darkness that made him feel drowsy, Shemokoman called it a day. He hit the sack and dreamed that he was way up north near Mesick, hunting for big morels deep in the forest.

Breakfast was served in the big white house at exactly half past seven. For as long as it was remembered, the morning meal was ready at that time. No exceptions, force of habit; Anna couldn't change her pattern. Hot black Georgian tea with sweet blueberry tarts, plus a bowl of cabbage soup, would get Shemokoman going. The home was filled with nostalgia from years that passed by everyone too quickly. It was like you still could hear the voice of a young Duane who just returned from hunting up at Kirkland's. And the silver Christmas tree was in the living room, decorated with tinsel and sparkling ornaments, candy canes, chocolate stars and figurines, and the angel at the top.

After he finished up eating, Shemokoman took a walk. As usual, the respectable people spared no effort to celebrate the great Christian holy day. There were bells and wreaths of holly hanging up on all of the doors, and candles on the sills in every window. Christmas lights were wrapped around the trees in many yards and strewn across the houses of the neighbors. They did their best to bring out the holiday spirit. And it worked! . . . Darn near as good as in Deutschland. Any soul with half a heart couldn't help but feel the jubilation. It was a cogent reminder for pagans among us that there is a point to modern religion; namely, effective medication.

He pondered, "And to think that all that I behold one day will be no longer. Science and its theories will replace passé religion. No more celebrations for the masses to get hyped on pure devotion. New beliefs will overtake the hallowed institutions, rejecting what is old and considered out of style. Of course, a man named Santa Claus will have to be forgotten. And people won't remember what it's like to wake up Christmas morning and be merry."

For the better part of the morning, Shemokoman roamed around and chatted with neighbors. Then he went back home and spoke with Anna. He told her that he ran into his comrades and they all made plans to get together in the afternoon. So now, the time arrived for him to roll.

Comrade Reunion

Anastasia lived in a Gothic mansion right on the north edge of town. She used to say that she needed her space, and by golly, now she had it. The decision was made to meet at her home for the upcoming social affair. Everyone showed up at two o'clock sharp and the festive occasion commenced.

The hostess provided dry white wine and aged Armenian cognac for the guests. An assortment of savory goodies, which included imported crackers and cheese, was also put out to snack on. After selecting their drinks and appetizers, everyone went to relax on the patio deck. And even though all of the comrades—except for Shemokoman—lived only a very few miles apart, it was the first time in a long time that they were together again.

Alabama Talks

"So, young man," Anastasia addressed Alabama. "Are you having any luck getting that arm of yours taken care of? Ever since that rotten day when you were in the paddies, I know it gives you trouble. Or is our health-care system too messed up and wounded men don't even get a chance to see a healer?"

"Well, yes, I'm making headway," Alabama said, "but it's not like I expected. You know, it's a hell of a thing—go fight in a war ten thousand miles away because you're conscripted. 'Don't worry at all!' . . . They lie to your face. 'Just go out on patrol and kill the charlies.' I should have retired some deltas instead; my conscience would not have opposed it. And all of a sudden, I look at my arms: the right one was intact, although the left one was in shambles. The next thing I know, I'm told 'Attaboy!' . . . and medals are pinned to my chest. Finally, I come back to this country, only to have a bunch of delinquents call me every name in the book. And for the rest of my life, I end up going from one hospital room into the next. Furthermore, ten years after the fact, it is all pretty clear to me now. There is a reason for rivers of blood and rotting flesh at the site of a battle engagement. Namely, a yacht and a liter of scotch for the Board of Directors.

"They tell me that wisdom develops with age, not to mention—vanity, envy and avarice, conceit, jealousy, cowardice, and perversion. With that in mind, my ethical comrades, I give you the Greedy Warmongers! Dishonest old men who belong in the clink and believe that they are so clever. Leaders with nothing to offer besides what foolish people are after, to wit—vice and corruption. Although, and I have to admit for all of its shortcomings, there is no other country better than here and no other place that is worse. Such is the plight of dichotomous life when prophets are given to thinking. We cling to a myth of freedom for all and pretend that we honestly have it. Oh yes, a nation in total denial."

"Of course, Alabama," Anastasia chimed in, "I think that we know how you feel about war. It had to be hard to go through it. One heck of a bad experience, and thank god it is finally over. So now you are home with a family and friends to brighten each day that betides us. And, there is nothing to threaten you here, save for the Banshees up in Otsego. You know, it always amazes me. They tell us he gave up his life in a war when in fact he really gave nothing. Instead, it was they who took it from him; and for that, they ought to be murdered."

Alabama agreed, "Right on, Anastasia."

Lackadaisical Moments

The afternoon was in full swing for the group of ethical comrades. Citizen R. talked with the Doctor, who just returned from a moose-hunting trip. And lo and behold, the medicine man managed to bag a fine trophy. The head with antlers were splendidly mounted and placed on a wall in his office. In spite of a deep predilection that forced him to follow the path of a healer, the Doctor was really a man who wanted to be outdoors in Nature. What's more, he always enjoyed recounting sensational stories.

As he so mildly put it, "Dead men tell no tales, so I will do it myself in their stead."

In need of fresh air and to stretch out a bit, Major LD went outside for a walk. Alabama and Anastasia elected to join him. There was plenty of ice at the shore of a pond that was located on the estate. Only the center, where ducks and geese were swimming and diving for food, was not frozen over. The three of them strolled at the edge of that body of water and talked about policy matters, namely, warfare. For some strange reason, hammers and sickles were current weapons of choice for present-day villains. And now, there was a movement among your radical lawmakers to confiscate both of the tools and make them illegal. Major LD and Alabama considered the scheme an outrage. So they made plans for the following week to march in a demonstration and voice opposition.

Anastasia noted, "The government types are flipping their lids too quickly. Perhaps an appeal to basic emotion will help everyone in the world to just get along."

After walking and talking for more than an hour, the group started back for the house. Along the way, Anastasia decided to show the men her conservatory. It was a large, glass-enclosed one-story building with beautiful flowers and plants. Smiling and proud of her labor, she posed a question: "So what do you think of my wild ginger, heather, and Florentine lilies?"

Major LD meticulously studied the flora. Then he replied, "You know, I'm not so sure about expert opinion pertaining to plants you are growing. I'm no connoisseur in horticultural matters. Although I must confess that the nomenclature has stirred many amorous notions. It sounds like a dazzling female lineup for any man given to capers."

The hostess smiled. And then Alabama weighed in: "Anastasia, your greenhouse reflects the skill of a gifted savant with incredible talent. The arrangement by classification is totally perfect. You must have had many fine lessons long ago from both of your parents. They obviously taught you all there is to know about having a garden. Then you added your own special touch, and voilà! . . . The final creation. I could stay here for hours and days to simply adore it."

He went on, "A long time ago, I remember walking on Jameson Avenue on my way to the grocery store. Those barbecue chips from Be·Mo; man, they were loaded. And on the other side of Shemokoman's home, your family had many large vegetable gardens neatly arranged behind fences. I always stopped and stared with awe at everything sprouting and growing. It was amazing. And if I was lucky, one of the workers tending the plants tossed me a fresh cucumber, or maybe tomato. Boy, what a treat that was; do I ever miss it. And no, of course, we can't turn back the clock . . . or, possibly, can we?"

The interlocutor paused for a moment, thinking about what he said, and then continued, "Every day we are here is a gift from God, who doesn't take no for an answer. Likewise, forget about yes; that deity isn't concerned about frivolous choices. So we need to remain unassuming; and, we have to be balancing options. Moreover, I am convinced that if we are burdened with doubt and stress nowadays, it is mainly the fault of adults who played in a schoolhouse. Yes, the teachers. Yes, it was they who were guilty as hell! . . . Indeed, the ones we were told to respect. The very same people with opulent homes to which we were never invited. They stood at the head of a class every day and hysterically acted like morons. We had to be still and obey their commands as rage in our bodies consumed us. And there was no other choice in light of required compliance."

"Alabama, you're right," Anastasia said. "And we agree that the truth is like succulent venom. Sweet, although fatally acting in most of the hominoid cases. Furthermore, a long time ago, Shemokoman told me the very same thing as well. The teachers meant well, of course; however, we just didn't get to the basics. The vital essentials were missing, and how did we ever put up with the cretins? And nothing has changed in this day and age; the educational system is plainly defective. Go visit a school and see for yourself. The children are falling further and further behind, and nobody honestly cares, not even the parents."

She continued, "Comrades, it is so nice to think of the years gone by when all that we dreamed about made up a promising future. And as for now, we are still young and forgiving, and that is a major advantage. You know . . . I spoke with a very old woman today. She was a hundred and one; I couldn't believe it. Sharp as a tack, not looking a day over ninety. Probably toxin injections. She parleyed with me as if with a child and asked if I wanted some candy. I couldn't resist and took it.

"'Go play in the sun,' she said to me, 'and be a good girl like always. And tell your mother and father everything anyone says for you to keep totally secret. Also, don't worry about "she told on me"; it is often your duty to tattle. As a result, you will avoid the pain of subconscious repression.'"

Nine Men

When it was finally chow time, one by one the comrades filed into the dining room, where Anastasia served a magnificent dinner. In the holiday tradition, she prepared fine meats and vegetables, dressing and sauces, soups and salad, along with the best condiments. For dessert, there were cakes and pies, crème brûlée, and other delicious confections. Everyone praised the hostess for her effort. They were well aware of her skill in the culinary arts.

At the end of the meal, Citizen R. exclaimed, "Heavens to Murgatroyd! Talk about marvelous food. What a fantastic supper. Nothing could ever top that. But don't tell my wife that I said it."

Everybody agreed with the stated opinion, and R. went on, "Of course, Anastasia, you remember the old saying 'The way to a man's heart is through the stomach.' I do not believe that the timeworn expression has ever been more apropos than today. Men like us have got to eat right to be productive and jolly. Otherwise, a day will arrive when we will be called to account for the lousy nutrition. Too many fools do not understand what it takes to be healthy and function. So, do you concur with my final assessment?"

"My, oh my, Citizen R. For reals, I most certainly do," Anastasia replied. "Why do you think I was married nine times? Each of my husbands murdered the previous one on account of my cooking. Oh, how I do hate and despise it. But I can do nothing about it. I cook and cook and continue to cook each day in my double-line kitchen. Just too many steaks, jealousy, chicken, and bloodshed. Some used a cudgel, others an ax, and the seventh one killed the sixth merely by poisoning one of my biscuits. Poor fellow . . . And simply to think they all just wanted to eat a good meal that I made them. And now, a Man of the Law has even seen fit to restrain my existence. I'm permitted to cook for only my current insignificant other. No exceptions. Do you realize that I, lil' ole me, could be thrown in the slammer tonight for making this dinner? I have to be careful; you must understand. The last thing I need is another constable snooping around and looking for telltale clues."

Anastasia started to weep. It was hard for her to accept the deal with the husbands. A part of her life was causing a deluge of mayhem. Then, Major LD asked her why her man wasn't home at the social occasion. She recovered a bit and replied, "Why, right now he is working, of course. He's a professional boxer deep in the cauldrons at Postumville getting the cereal ready for shipment."

Major LD excused himself and said he'd be back in an hour. As he departed, he whispered to the Doctor, "You know . . . I've got an old friend who is thin as a rail and never been married to boot. I know he will thank me for this one."

The group retired to Anastasia's family room to relax. The walls were covered with typical family pictures and memorabilia. It was apparent by looking around at all of her modest possessions that she was a woman content with next to nothing. Simply no need to obsess with material gain. And in spite of her serial matrimonial intrigue, of which she was never adjudged to be wanton, Anastasia enjoyed the respect of so many people. Like the entire community. The last person she ever thought about was herself.

On Trust

And now, the Doctor broached a topic that started a long conversation. "So, Shemokoman. If it's all right, I would like for us to talk about trust among people. What do you think? Can we trust somebody else? And shall we have faith in the stead of a virtue? Or is trust nothing more than a glimmer of hope to console the incurable dreamer? You see, I'm beginning to favor the skeptic."

Shemokoman knew that a prudent response was expected. He glanced down for a second to think about trust, and then he looked up and replied, "Well, my good Doctor. I must say that although the intent of trust in another is gracious, absolutely not. No, you cannot ever trust people. No time, no place, nobody, no way, no how. Just forget it, a foolish endeavor. By nature, the people we meet and greet are completely corrupt and dishonest. It is a fact; and, we need to conclude it. And like so many other classical virtues, we all aspire to cultivate trust. However, beware! . . . The road is unsafe, the peril is great, and swindlers are dying to gyp you. They do it with joy and a gleam in the eye; my god, what a horrible pity. So sad—however, I speak the inscrutable truth. And how many sleepless nights have I spent because of a misunderstanding. Because the very same people to whom I relinquished all of my trust were sources of horrid betrayal."

He paused and said, "Keep in mind that the minute you give up your trust to somebody else, you are exposed and a target for cranks and purloiners. You instantly have no right to credible doubt or any suspicion. You gave it away, together with pride, the price of astonishing folly. And do you not see that the very same deed must occur in reverse to ensure that collusion is stable? Alas, it just never happens; inveterate knaves are out to finesse you. You cannot depend on conviction or faith to provide any healthy position. Indeed, you will only be shattered. But if you believe that you need to have trust—without it, you surely will perish—then I will give you a fine proposition. You can have trust in humanity's evil.

"And perhaps you may ask—'What about trust in a family?'—to which I will answer directly: Unfortunately, no; a lamentable bad situation. Brothers and sisters, fathers and sons, mothers and virtuous daughters; it just doesn't make any difference. If temptation is great and there is a way—believe me, the rat'll disgrace you. And why is that so? Well, because people can never stop doing you wrong; their vanity always persuades them. And nobody cares if you suffer; it is your problem. You see, the temples of faith for inculpable men will never exist without treason. The world is full of deceivers."

Then Shemokoman asked the Doctor, "So, old pal of mine. May I presume that we're in agreement? And are we of equal opinion?"

"Yes," the Doctor said. "All you say is wise and correct; you speak the gospel truth. Sometimes a pain to swallow."

"Keep in mind, my fellow comrades," Shemokoman went on. "There is no other creature I know of on earth that seeks to manipulate trust. Only the credulous humans, and only to have the advantage. Survival is all that a brute understands; it is not bothered by madness. And now, I should like to investigate trust and take it decidedly further. Let us ask . . . Does trust, indeed, really exist, or is it a ploy contrived by devious chiselers? Well, to begin with . . .

"Let us be very suspicious. For the sake of meticulous rigor, we say that trust may or may not be authentic. What shall we believe? Is there a sensible answer? Well now, allow me to settle what needn't be such a big issue. There is simply no reason to put in long hours of guesswork or vain speculation, as I can tell you with certainty—yes. Trust is a genuine spirit.

"You see, one day after nearly freezing to death while taking supplies up to Skagway and while stoking a smoldering campfire, I met the incredible codger. I was lucky because trust paid me an opportune visit. At that time, I was in dire straits due to my health and a bitter cold winter. So that dependable guy came to my aid and helped me out of a quandary. My word! . . . Pure trust is divine, with a modest persona and awesome charisma like nothing that we can imagine. So what more proof do you need? . . . As my encounter is verification. Definitive. And now, I should like to reveal to you more matters of fact that are knowledge.

"My ethical comrades. . . . There is no common ground for trust, only arresting extremes. It has to be all or nothing, precluding a chance for anything shifty. Trust is all things to your man on the street for all situations wrapped up into one. Protagonist, assailant, prefect, antagonist, educator, warrior, protector, and, a highly predictable forebear. The essence of trust is an august design, but there will be days that are sad and notably brutal. It happens when efforts we spawn are maligned by those who can often delude us. Thus, absolute trust can never be real due to the malice of people. And even though your intent is deserving, a convoluted mind with whom you consort will destroy any trust to believe in. I must confess the demigod has caused despair to me on endless nights that forgot about morning. Therefore, I beseech you. Stay on the good side of trust; it is your duty. Provide the respect and you are assured that trouble and worries will fade like a shadow at nightfall."

Shemokoman took a break. He opened a bottle of dry white wine, the very same vintage a Lancaster farmer once favored. He poured out a nice little hooker and then pressed on. "Thus, in response to the primary question, which is: Can you trust somebody else? Once again, I am telling you no because trust is a languishing virtue. You cannot depend on specific results on account of nefarious villains. Trust is a ruse for people who have an accord that caters to demons. Are you disappointed? Probably not. Most of us know the truth, but we are simply afraid to admit it.

"It is always the same old story. Problems that deal with a value we crave are cause for regrettable heartache. And sensible sensitive feelings are never avoided. To ravage a word that was given as pledge is never considered illicit by too many people. Heathens! They think that desire regardless of truth is fair play in a world of drama. Yes, they are so horribly stricken, and they are brimming with ire to burn you. And as for constraints that temper the soul, where is a cogent reminder?! Nowhere. Instead—distortion and lies, the thrill of a gay escapade and substantial pathetic adventure. It seems like forever the guilty are prancing around us. Although I must tell you this, my ethical comrades. A day will arrive when their sickening ranks will raise the white flag to surrender. Yes, I am sure it will happen. And you must ignore many harrowing cries with pleadings that call for compassion. Allow them to flounder and perish. They, the haughty and vicious Pretenders, deserve every moment of sorrow and vengeance that may be levied upon them.

"So we must be careful with trust, although we needn't be overly skittish, as I am sure there is prudence attending. Perhaps you will seek to obtain even more in the way of a clarification. Namely, 'Does it always have to be like what I'm professing?' Well, the answer depends on what you can really believe in. What should you expect? And do you preclude the potential for something astounding? Of course, anything is possible; but, we must overcome any prospect of hope that may only arise to enslave us. Tell me, is there a saint who is fearless enough to invite absolute depredation? No, I believe he is missing. Thus, for a wish to survive, we have to renounce every rush to the sacred tradition. Verily, trust may be found by legitimate men who do not resort to deception.

"But now, behold! We have a different kind of agreement where trust is excluded completely. It is the finest scheme that one can imagine. No need to respect any terms of accord; instead, we perform an about-face. Who cares for a pledge when people admit that each has no faith in the other. Apprehension and doubt, and dreadful remorse will torment the spirit no longer. You see, trust is an obsolete issue; it is the goat of perpetual joking; it is no longer a bone of contention. Alas—the state of affairs will fail the test of a practical form of alliance. And, the masses will surely reject it. They cannot survive without dependence on daily innate superstition. It is a fraud that they have to acclaim and truly believe in. 'Forever we honor the regal bequest! . . . It is no wretched deceiver. And even though it forsakes the upstanding neighbors among us, who may deny it is worth it? No one. Trust is a crony we seek to empower; and trust—the exemplary scapegoat.' Through no fault of its own, it is a reticent hero.

"Yet, there is one more critical factor. It is a problem that calls for attention. If trust is a natural goal that we seek, then how do we ponder negation? The people are never mistaken. We've got to have trust to invalidate vice or the system devolves into chaos. For the sake of itself, trust is a fetching condition that forestalls any certain preclusion."

The Only Choice

"Thus, you may ask," Shemokoman said, " 'How do we cope with life that is based on a fable?' The best advice I can give anyone is as follows. It will never be easy to deal with the rogue, as trust is a brilliant invention. It is a handy device that people get used to, and we learn to accept every vile degree, like it or not, without question. Unfortunately, trust is a key that opens a door to more than a random debacle. Such is the nature of chance and reliable pretense.

"Meanwhile. . . . As days and nights continue to pass, everyone low will be sinking. They are the ones who taunted the value of critical daily contrition. They are the ones who discredited trust and made fun of your difficult moments. They are the ones who wouldn't give up and exploited a vulnerable conscience. Do you not see what I mean, my ethical comrades? Once and for all, we need to eradicate shame and the foolish compunction. Otherwise, a terrible fate for all of humanity surely awaits us. And all the while, we tread on ground where progenitors sought to exclude the troublesome rubbish. Perhaps, in a way, they may have been fairly successful."

Now, he wrapped it up. "It is a duty and rightly so to forswear any primal presumptions. Concessions of trust in any amount oblige our moral acceptance. And that, my ethical comrades, is a detestable waste of time. Although if you are the sovereign and servant alike, then faith no longer restrains you. Just do as you please, unless, of course, your mood is completely retarded. At which point then, someone is asking for trouble. Thus, you must learn to walk on a serpentine road with courage and strength like a titan as well as with total reliance on nothing. In just such a way, you relegate trust to a status of what is befitting. Who cares about public opinion when your survival is clearly at stake?!"

Mills of Antiquity

Regarding the nature of trust . . . People develop instant awareness of forces that shape and surround them. It is forever the same; indeed, there is no distinction. Now, from one point of view, it seems useless to speak about trust in a literal sense, with—secular motive in man. One cannot foresee any logical purpose in that. Everything—incontrovertible. Forbidden behavior leads to regret that affects anyone who is trying, with allusion to trust in a general way and how it relates to good fortune. On the other hand, is it not so that man leverages trust in pursuit of well-being and virtue? The objective and also a canon of faith that involves some knowledge of reason. Can people not see what is right and wrong?! They have to be honest and careful. They have to select every word with regard so as not to offend the insurgents. And humanity has to forgo what is bad to avoid getting deeper in kimchee. The goal of it all is to hopefully see that mere mortals remain on the uptake.

As the day wore on, the ethical comrades turned to alternative discourse. Shunning contentious affairs, they dwelt upon semi-peripheral matters. Like respect for the dead, who lived for a while with stoic indifference to others. And what does it mean to reject Mr. Right if that would be wrong a priori? And now, far away in the distance in town, one could hear the clamorous ringing of bells inside of a steeple. St. Philip was having a mass with parishioners down on their knees pleading to Yahweh for mercy.

After living so far away for so long, Shemokoman knew that he would return to his home more than every so often. Regarding the big get-together, they ended the fun way late in the night and everyone said their "Good-byes" and went straight home.

Time to Shove Off

More often than not, we cannot put up with a life in a state of abeyance. Our days are depleted by cause and effect, which leads to a variable outcome. The masses thoroughly know it; and, they look at the facts, consider a plan, and berate who is missing in action. And there is no way to break out of the bind; the system extends all the way down to a stratum that plunges no further. So—above all else, stay clear of exotic obsessions; you will get dizzy, collapsing and howling. And pander to pagans and preachers alike when there is no obvious leeway.

Shemokoman stayed in the Land of Michigan roughly another week longer. He spent most of his time with Catherine, and they unwound in the magic of winter. They listened to mandolin music performed by young girls in peasant apparel. And he told her about the strange occurrence that took place in the Big Sandy Desert. For sure, it wasn't a dream; he didn't wake up before going to sleep.

"Why must everything always be so complicated?" he wondered. "It seems that I languish forever. My only intent is to analyze life and bring about mindful awareness. Perhaps I ask for too much. Oh, divine Solitude! I know you are more than a Weilimdorf castle in Deutschland. It is so easy to see why you are the choice of so many."

Town in Decline

Back in his home on the hill above Federal City, Shemokoman sat in a chair and gazed at hysteria spreading beneath him. He didn't feel higher above the big buildings and people, as that is a sentiment fated for brazen Pretenders, remiss and conceited. He was drinking a cup of hot black Georgian tea and thought about Michigan issues.

And he was troubled. "My town, Battle Creek, is engulfed in a mess with life in short order, degrading. Some people have more but many have less, and the constables love a good trouncing. Apathy seems to have ruined their poise, and respect for authority—vanished. Gone are the days of a talk at the fence when neighbors might offer you sugar and cold lemonade. Prosperity replaced by slugs on the dole who tarry about on street corners looking for handouts."

He thought about men in the past who offered so much and also too little. "Of course, the old-timers—they were the champs who defeated the legions of evil. And when they came home the party was already rolling. There were parades in every American town; and who could object to a great celebration for warriors? No one. But it didn't take long for victorious men to completely forget about that which they ought to be doing. They were too busy with personal gain and whooping it up with the buddies. So, the Armies of Wrong and Disaster started to move and go on the offensive. Indeed! . . . What about families and raising a boatload of children? To which, a customer said in a taproom: 'I think it can wait until later.' Such a profusion of weakness; what ever happened to disciplined soldiers?! Every GI who was proud of attire in khakis should have continued to think about where he was marching. Regrettably, the end result is a scandalous mess that has resulted in sadness. Thus, the assault on my home has taken its toll with nobody there to do something constructive about it. Behavior was truly pathetic, and the jovial men of neglect were vile deserters. A serious game has got to have quality players."

Your Number

The sun comes up, you get out of bed and go through a typical morning. Nothing could be more familiar, and everything seems to be normal. You know who you are and sense what you need because of location and knowledge. Reliable rules are there for the obvious reasons. And minor inconsistencies do not bother you.

But then one day after waking up, you feel as though something is different. You go to a window and look at a sky that is pale and so unfamiliar. It should have been dawn just moments ago; so where is the blue you're expecting? What's more, that great yellow star that was christened the Sun doesn't shine on the distant horizon. You gaze at a clock—the hands do not move; perhaps it could use a good winding. You study the room for additional clues, only to think that something is certainly funny. The whole ball of wax is coming apart in spite of the fact that you recently got it together. Huh? . . . Every thing you observe exposes a new deviation. Maybe dependable senses are suddenly failing.

You sit on the edge of your bed and think very hard about basic survival. As time continues to pass you by, many big waves are pounding and crushing your judgment. And now, even the walls you see in the room are expanding and also contracting. It is no trivial quandary;

rather, a jaunt in the center of madness. And what is the reason for trouble? . . . Got to admit that you haven't the faintest. You lie on your back on the floor and stare at the ceiling. Indeed, it is time to concede that "the loyal subalterns of fate have come to collect me."

As you race in a place that is dark and obscure where the light is no longer essential, the body resembles invisible mist as nothing remains for appearance. Your human emotion has withered and waned to stifle a crestfallen spirit minus a feeling . . . or two, or three. And yet, you haven't the will to surrender a soul that was only required for mortals. The Circle of Time has delivered to sever elusive existence forever. And the world departs in a curious way with all of mankind aboard the itinerant vessel.

Eventually, every last one of us will bite the insidious dust and be given the hobnailed boot into the beyond. No ifs, ands, or buts about it. And that is the truth.

Last Battle

It was a gray, dismal wintry afternoon as incredibly huge snowflakes fell, or should we say poured, from the sky and covered the eastern part of the country. Shemokoman got the news. Major LD was gone. He died at the end of a great epic battle, defending the land that he cherished, fighting the Outsiders. According to one who was there, it happened as follows.

The enemy invaded Waupakisco Park on the far western border. They just didn't know when to quit because they were arrogant, pushy, and stupid. And only Major LD was there to protect the homes with all the respectable neighbors. Yes, he was alone and remained to provide the resistance. The man was a veteran warrior whom they could always depend on for certain.

Major LD would fight like the devil until every skirmish was over. He was the ethical comrade who stayed by your side right up to the end if need be. Everyone knew he was born with a tireless passion for violent combat. And just like courageous warriors of yore, he didn't wait for the filthy assailants to sack the park at their leisure. No, no way.

On this occasion, when the enemy host with their shrill battle cries came over the crest of the hill and advanced toward Abingdon Strait, Major LD charged like a lightning bolt into the heart of the rival land army. He slashed and chopped and shattered their ranks, and stripped the ones who laid low of their glistening armor. The fighting with might and main continued for untold staggering hours. Through the dirt and the dust in the heat and the sweat, the harrowing shrieks and screams of the expiring enemy troops could be heard far away by anyone able to listen. The blurry horizon at the Fields of Devonshire was one thick layer of bloody gore with thousands of corpses strewn everywhere as humanity hit a new low point. A long time ago, it was noted by somebody thoughtful that "war is hell." But alas, it is even more chilling.

During the horrible struggle, sheer numbers of enemy troops were not a big factor. Like commanders of old, the major implored his opponent to give him more and more and keep it on coming. And now, surrounded by scores of the savage warmongers, the brave gladiator gave it his final best effort. Screaming, laughing, and mocking their style, the blade of his sword was blazing its way into glory. Suddenly, the invaders became terrified at the valor of such a combatant. So they turned and vamoosed to save their despicable hides. And never again would the likes of those vile offenders be seen anywhere near Waupakisco Park. The enemy truly was conquered.

As he stood all alone at the edge of the big sunken hollow and stared at the grim devastation, tired of asinine warfare, the major dropped down to his knees and everything faded. He felt all confused, like a wandering child who's lost in a forest at nightfall. He looked up at a sky that was falling apart; indeed, it was now unfamiliar. Then he looked down at the flesh that covered his bones and noticed a layer of blood all over the body. His blood. Major LD had suffered a mortal wound to the heart during the heat of the battle.

He cursed the dark shadows of mischievous phantoms that circled and scrambled around him, and he collapsed and lay on his back on the ground of his youth. Oh yes, youth—it came and passed so quickly. Then, in the span of a second or two, he remembered the days that were spent with his ethical comrades. He had no regrets, no sorrow or shame, for he knew that he practiced a Good Life. And finally, with one big gasp of that Michigan air—his last and he certainly knew it, Major LD, son of noble Albert, could not hold on any longer. His dignified head rolled off to one side and he closed up those blue eyes forever. Indeed, a hero passed on to the realm of a Maker.

Again and again, it was recalled in folklore that he was slain by no typical man. The conspiring gods knew it was time to claim one of their own and take him away into heaven. And so it was regarding the life and times of Major LD. He was extolled for selfless conviction and his great patriotic resolve. And all the beholden respectable people for sure would terribly miss him. And that is the truth.

Grief of a Man

After he got the news, Shemokoman just couldn't take it. He completely cracked up, lost track of his mind, smashed everything in sight, and cursed at himself like a madman. Alone in his home, he refused to go out, as he was consumed by remorse and abysmal contrition. He ate nothing at all and drank hundreds of bottles of wine and other rare spirits, especially absinthe. He looked in the mirror at the miserable bum and slandered his very existence. He should not have forsaken the one Waupakisco Park, his only real home on the planet. To hell with a justification, and to hell with the truth and everything else that made him neglect what he shouldn't have. He just wasn't there with the major to fight and die if required for honor.

So, what do you have when you leave it behind for a thrill that is vain and a tale? Alas, a search for the facts and spoils afar is not the illustrious venture. Shemokoman knew why he left Battle Creek; the answer was clear and distressing.

He thought, "To think there are fools who would covet the throes of a curse that befell unto me. How on this earth did I ever allow such an awful fiasco to happen? I wasn't there and nor were the others to help out an ethical comrade who struggled and perished. Yes, Major LD—the defender, the martyr and victor. He was a prince, the trooper, a legend. And I must atone before Nature itself and plead for the grace of forgiveness."

It was a lesson in life and death that Shemokoman would not forget.

15

⌒∞⌒

Five Red Ruby Stars

Moskva

On account of a need to investigate more and because of the pixie in him, Shemokoman decided to visit Rossiya again. He planned to attend a symposium there to explore philosophical theory. The route and destination this time would both be essentially different. First, he would go to the capital city, Moskva, and stay there for a few days. Then he'd be off to a primeval forest called the Pushcha. The trip was scheduled to last for a couple of weeks.

It was a typical springtime morning in March, and the cherry tree blossoms were blooming in Federal City. He stepped out of his brownstone flat to check on the weather. There wasn't a trace of wind or rain; the air was fragrant and balmy. All in all, a perfect day to set out and begin the adventure. Then he went back in his home to do a final inspection. Everything was ready and set to go. And he packed plenty of thick, warm clothing because it would still be cold in Rossiya. So he grabbed his luggage and hit the road one more time for the record.

Upon his arrival at the Port of Departure, Shemokoman boarded a big gray ship that was moored at one of the piers. It didn't take long and soon he was sailing away on yet another trip, crossing the Ocean. While sitting alone in a balcony chair, he thought about lives of ancient explorers: "Nothing but fearless men who constantly faced every tough situation. Who can ever imagine the grief that they were forced to encounter? It was, for sure, a formidable business. They sailed in creaky old vessels of wood, not knowing from minute to minute the chance of disaster. And perhaps they never saw land again after leaving the harbor. Violent storms at sea frequently tore a craft into pieces and sent the men to visit the infamous 'locker.' Fate was in charge and plotted the course, and a casket of rum in the galley was tapped for courage."

After cruising for nearly two weeks and a half, the ship made landfall in a much-fought-over part of the world called Europe. They put into port at a town called Marseille, where Shemokoman disembarked with all his belongings. He was now in a land that used to be great and noted for humanist values. But people he saw the day he arrived were mainly disheveled, and psycho. Especially farmers and bakers. They kept saying "detester" and "tuer."

Shortly thereafter, he boarded a passenger train to continue the journey. And farther along on the rambling road, while going through Deutschland near the Black Forest, the conductor announced a two-hour layover at a small village called Fellbach.

The place was famous for chivalry tales and hills of well-tended vineyards. Shemokoman promptly stepped out of the coach and made his way to a Swabian gasthaus. He polished off eight or nine maßs of bier and a glass of the very best Riesling wine. Then he decided to talk with some of the locals.

It came to pass that he spoke with a man named Johann about losing a much-beloved son. The whole affair took place all on account of a misunderstanding. A foolish one at that. Could it really be so? . . . The face he observed resembled a previous fellow. And how about judging his very own *self*, a chip off the progeny block. Whatever. Then it was back to the train and into the coach; and once again, they traveled along, going east, to the remote destination.

They raced through many old kingdoms, across the Transylvanian Basin, over the hilly terrain of the Eastern Carpathian Mountains, and then into Rossiya. And after two more days of moving along through flat geological places, the trip came to an end at the capital city, Moskva.

It was a quarter past three in the middle of night, and nothing in town was stirring. Shemokoman went to the Hotel Ukraina on the River Moskva across from a government White House. He checked into the place—an excellent choice, in spite of the rumors about the ugly sisters. A tsarina with taste commissioned a marvelous building.

The hotel resembled a medieval palace, stately and very ornate. There were twenty-three stories of liberal space with rooms of every shape and size depending on what was required. Your typical light green socialist color covered the walls and ceilings. And red Oriental runners embellished the floors in all of the hallways. The dimly lit alcoves with sofa and chairs where women preferred to be smoking were there for anyone tired and spent to collect oneself and unwind. And massive marble staircases spiraled from bottom to top throughout the entire building. Meanwhile, the brusque chambermaids who serviced the guests and never showed any emotion either were reading a book approved by the State or grabbing some shut-eye on duty.

So now, it was time to kick back for a while and rest. Shemokoman went to the Bolshevik Café, where he ate a big bowl of borscht with sour cream. He also sampled the fresh caviar, and had a steaming hot cup of black Georgian tea. Then he returned to his room and crashed.

Commie Cloud Nine

The alarm clock sounded at 8:00 a.m. sharp while he was peacefully sleeping. Shemokoman got out of bed to start a new day. Yes, he was a little bit groggy. All of the traveling and difference in time had the effect of disturbing his physical system. He went to a window and looked outside at a town that was swarming with comrades. There was a lot of snow and slush on the streets; they needed to wear big galoshes. He gazed at the oversized walls; indeed, no mistaking the building construction. They were at least three feet thick and mainly designed to keep out the cold. And in spite of the fact that the heat wasn't on, it was still roasting inside of the room. Yes, he was back in Rossiya.

Just then, there was a knock at the door and he opened it up. A hotel clerk was standing alone in the hallway, holding a tray with tortes and rolls, and a glass of fresh orange juice.

"Per your request, sir," he said.

Shemokoman took the tray with the food, tipped the young man, and replied with no obvious accent, "Bol'shoe spasibo." Then he closed the door firmly and had his breakfast.

When he had finished the morning meal, it was time to go outside to see the city. He walked out of his room, locked the door, and gave the key to the lady-dejour. As opposed to normal behavior, this time she gave him a genuine smile. Perhaps she got up on the right side of bed; you never can tell about women.

The ethical comrade went down to the main lobby entrance, and left the building. He sought to explore a land where the culture was old, unjust, and generic. Milk was milk; meat was meat; bread was bread; and every single sign he saw on stores and elsewhere confirmed it.

A Mighty Fortress

Unlike the capital cities in other lands, Moskva was the venue of all that went on in a country. It was the center of politics, economics and business, the arts, education, science, entertainment, social life, industry, sports, religion, and everything else in a civilized nation. It was *the* place to be in majestic Rossiya.

Having strolled on the sidewalks and roadways for quite a long while, Shemokoman arrived at the famous Arbat. It was a part of town where artisans were making and trading their wares, to include: figurines and pottery, jewelry and icons, souvenirs and traditional clothing. Talented painters and scruffy musicians were plying their trades as well. He left the place and continued to walk, passed Saint Basil's Cathedral, and crossed the Beautiful Square. Next, he stopped at a kiosk, obtained kompot, and then walked slowly down to the River Moskva. And it was there that he paused for a moment or two to contemplate striking impressions. It never took long to figure it out, how best to control and handle a foreign connection. He had to blend in, be one of the crowd, and suppose there was nothing to fret over.

Millions of hardworking men and women lived in the heart of Rossiya. It was a place where everyday life was a definite challenge. He thought, "Just look at the faces, gaze into the eyes, and listen to monotone voices. They envision their lot with doubt and foreboding, and never consider resistance. And, they can forget about death; it will do them no good; the State will be waiting wherever in the hereafter to cordially greet them. These people remember the 'yoke' and barbarous horsemen, and tapping the argot on walls in crumbling dungeons. Thus, before they will take that very next step, the ground must invalidate trouble. So when they can finally say 'Davai,' direction was carefully planned on. They do what they must to avoid any real complications; it is a history of woe and sullen conditions. With pain and great sorrow for many long years, there is no hope regarding a future exception."

Shemokoman entered the Kremlin, which, in spite of a public consensus, was the core of a spiritual nation. There were plenty of orthodox churches there and religion was full of believers. You see, as the leaders were pressed to control a great State, they had to maintain law and order. Thus, permission to worship the King of Kings could not be completely dispensed with.

The management process in pinko Rossiya was worthless, though very effective. Every committee and council was issuing orders. There were seldom complaints about anything bad; chaos and crime were mostly unheard of. And, the slightest digression from proper behavior was cause for a trip to the gulag. Plans, plans—just follow the plan; tomatoes are rotting in boxcars.

Senior high-ranking freeloader officials welcomed the visitor. And one hundred grams of only the best were consumed to mark the occasion. Shemokoman noticed the huge Tsar Cannon and carefully studied the weapon. It was a relic of stately proportion that truly symbolized radical power. Then he looked up at the sky, and of course, that fellow was totally awestruck. Five enormous red ruby stars were on top of the towers built into the wall that enclosed the inscrutable complex. And they were spinning around like vanes in the wind of a tempest.

As he stood in the cold, frosty air with churches and history rousing his interest, Shemokoman pondered the thought of impending rebellion: "Can it be true that the great Motherland is unhealthy? Is the pressure of party control, Gosplan, and tyranny steadily mounting? And are the people condemned to put up with blat, a shortage of this and that, and spurious freedom? I feel delicate tremors that rumble the ground as the sign of a country in trouble. Yes, a political change for Rossiya is probably coming."

Ivan the Wonderful

The Cathedral of the Archangel Michael in the Kremlin was one of the oldest churches in Moskva. It had five golden onion-shaped domes, with arches, niches, and gateways made of white limestone. The building itself was a perfect example of Renaissance-style construction. Shemokoman entered a house of God that was full of detestable scoundrels. Dead ones, at that.

It was musty inside, sated with orthodox incense and filled with flickering candlelight. The aura was one of ethereal mystification. Beautiful old iconostasis ran from the floor to the ceiling throughout the structure. He felt as if he had been taken away to somewhere divine by the will of a numinous power. And most importantly, the cathedral contained the burial vault of someone who needed a scolding.

Shemokoman went to the front of the fold and stood by the one and only Ivan the Wonderful. Or, as his friends and family called him—Vanyusha. He stared at the dusty remains of a man who was hated and loved heart and soul by so many comrades.

Then he said, "So, my lord. This is where you ended up—resting in peace in a crypt. Alas, you continue to be a great hero for some, but a villain, in not so good standing, for all of the rest. And now, you must suffer and pay for your deeds; too many to count, I am certain. Do you remember the town of Novgorod? . . . And all of your grim devastation? You had such a good time with cronies who laughed and impaled the men in Kazan. And how about ladies you persecuted way down in the sunny Crimea? And also, the many Livonian children whom you deprived of a mother forever. Maybe by now, you are starting to have second thoughts and getting the picture. Furthermore, the Oprichniki can do nothing for you anymore. Instead, you must wheel and deal with a dreadfully new and perverse set of demons.

"No doubt you recall the day when you asked every priest to perform absolution. Your conscience was starting to suffer, and you did not want to be unforgiven. Of course, they could never . . . but then acquiesced under the threat of a friendly reprisal. Yes, you managed to fully extort a timely acquittal. Albeit, as soon as you left, they called you a tramp and decried your very existence. And oh, by the way, did you notice perhaps? . . . That your omnipotent State—Rossiya—is starting to crumble.

"So if you do not mind, I would sure like to know. How is it that men like yourself are able to rise from the ashes among us? You instigate war to ravage and raze every village with peace-loving people. And then you affirm, 'There was no other choice! . . . I had to ensure and protect the good of a nation. So what if the masses were slain; the will of my God was clearly at stake.' Although you forget about something essential, my lord. Namely, the carnage was your end decision. And there were plenty of times that it could have been stopped; when in fact, you rescinded no order. Rather, you savored the penchant of evil."

The man from Michigan paused and continued, "The wicked are born to contaminate life with a passion for filthy wrongdoing. Just look at their odious faces: always ecstatic when good people suffer. The minute we fold is the moment they want because they're demented and schizo. Young and old, rich and poor, healthy or under the weather. The villains will never be choosy; they have been put on the earth to oppress us. And when it is time to assault and kill, my lord, oh how they enjoy it.

"Now, as for a guy like yourself, the motive to slay everyone who you could was to demonstrate power. You were as sick as a dog but paid no attention to illness. Your plan was to plot, conspire, and scheme to ensure that you rose to the top. It was your only ambition because you had to be king of the mountain. Sound familiar? . . . Of course it does. Then, on account of intense paranoia, you had to destroy everything that was living. So, you killed and killed and continued to kill on account of the lunatic pleasure. It was the sign of a man who is thoroughly ruined, demolished. No family, no friends, no conscience, no nothing; only more blood, you were thirsty. I will tell you this much, my respectable prince: you were no holy archangel. Quite the opposite.

"Vanyusha, please, listen closely to me, and I'll tell you what Destiny said that is not a big secret. Forever, like now, you will burn to a crisp in a crucible teeming with fire. The specifications were of your very own making. Remember? You wanted salvation, to live without end; by Jove, there is justice: you have it. The splendid result for a man like yourself who was proud of revenge and destruction. And you know the unsettling truth by now—that cold embers are really the finish. Too bad about that; you should have been honest and decent. So now, a Yahweh has made up his mind to leave you alone with some hellions. But at least there will be a domain to enslave, although it's not what you expected."

Then, Shemokoman turned around and walked away. He could still hear the sound of mothers in pain who were grieving. One woman deliriously ranted and wailed; a child was frozen to death in her arms. Another was digging a grave for herself because nobody told her she shouldn't. Still another was hunched over pure mutilation of corpses that were piled up high at a gravesite. Perplexed and a little despondent, he had to get out of the gloomy cathedral. Thank god that Ivan the Wonderful was dead.

Without looking back, he thought, "Regarding the evil in man—of course, I know there can be deviations. I have encountered benevolent men in a couple of places. But no, no way, not him, a deplorable tyrant. Ivan could not have been different because he was born the insatiable monster."

After visiting four more orthodox churches there in the socialist compound, Shemokoman went to the Armory Chamber to view the great wealth of Rossiya. As he looked at the wedding gowns and coronation dresses, he started to ponder, "To think that Kathy could fit into this before she was told to wear that one. Preposterous! Maybe it's fake—who knows . . . Perhaps she went on a cabbage soup diet. Without any doubt, the truth is for scatterbrained people. And what is the deal with these carriages? Hmm, around the edge of that axle. Diamonds! I wonder how many; I think I will count them. All right, thirty-eight—and each of the stones must be three carats in size. No wonder the peasants and factory workers prayed for imperial slaughter. The nation was totally out of control, and the tsar was out of his mind. What a relief it had to have been for all the impoverished people when a revolution shattered the Evil Empire."

Man in the River

Shemokoman stayed inside of the Kremlin for only a few minutes more, then left. He passed the Eternal Flame and went to the River Moskva again. As he walked on a path by the slow-moving current, a strange situation developed. Suddenly, he noticed a man in trouble way out in the water; and, he was trying to make it to shore. It was still pretty cold in that part of the world, and large patches of ice were floating around him. And there was nobody else anywhere to be found to assist the unfortunate fellow. Thus, the ethical comrade stood in a clearing of land and shouted out words to encourage the guy. And little by little, the man in distress managed to get near the bank. Then at last, the danger was over completely when he got out of the river and up onto dry, solid ground.

"Holy Moses, you did it!" Shemokoman exclaimed. "A miracle. Most people for sure would have drowned. My friend, I would say that you have to be awfully thankful."

The two men discussed the state of affairs, and what it implied to go under. And eventually—among other things—Shemokoman posed the following question: "So, what is it you do for a living?"

While sitting slumped over, his head in his hands and counting the blessings, the man was quietly resting. Then, in response to the question, he straightened up, gazed out at the river, and stated, "I'm an assassin."

Somewhat bewildered, Shemokoman said, "Well then, what in the heck were you doing out there in the water? I mean, you were headed downstream when someone like you should be going the opposite way. Something is rather peculiar. How did it happen?"

The man was reluctant to speak at first but finally decided to spill a few beans, "Well, you see, I was on my way to visit a friend, Masha the Kleptomaniac, when out of the blue some politicians started to tease and deride me. They even made fun of my gabardine clothing. Imbeciles! Subsequently, a bit of a tiff is putting it mildly, as the row turned into a scuffle. The next thing I know, about four of the goons, well . . . they threw me over the railing of the bridge and into the river. They must've believed it was curtains for me, and I would be sleeping with fishes. Well, we'll see who has the last laugh. Those wisecrackers."

The assassin threw his head back and sighed, and took several deep breaths of cool Russian air. He had to be glad the attempt on his life had been foiled. Then Shemokoman said in a jovial way, "So, what will you do for the rest of the day? Maybe go visit some gangsters?"

The fellow looked at his newfound friend and answered, "Well, first, I've got to go home and get out of these soaking wet clothes. No reason to take a shower, of course; but then I will stop at the banya as a precaution. Boy, do I love getting whacked by pals with a venik, especially birch. And finally, I will go back to work."

While speaking at length with the shady acquaintance, Shemokoman tried his level best to extol a new occupation. A suggestion was made for the man to perform in the opera. After all, plenty of villains sooner or later prove to be darn good at singing. He noted that things would get dicey for an assassin when he'd be older. Other positions offered far more, like medical plans and a pension for when you retire.

The fellow agreed to consider the recommendation, conceding that today was a "wake-up call." Then each of the men bid the other "Fare thee well," and went off in their separate directions.

"Only in Rossiya," Shemokoman thought.

A Close Shave

While crossing through the Patriarch Ponds Park, Shemokoman noticed the Doob Tree Commercial District not far away. So, he went there. Hordes of aggressive vendors were vying to get the attention of patrons. Matryoshka dolls were out on display, and handmade lacquer boxes were going like hotcakes. Spare parts for machines were also high up in demand. And whenever he glanced into small specialty shops and boutiques, it was a real funny story. Inevitably, the saleswomen looked at him as if that fellow were crazy. "How dare he butt in on our female gossiping session!" Thus he excused himself and continued on his way.

Now, it happened that Shemokoman was near the center of town at a busy street corner. He was leaning against one of the socialist buildings to rest and study the people who scurried about. After about five minutes or so, he shoved off to continue the outing. As he did so, suddenly, there was a thundering crash directly behind him, like an explosion. He turned around and shuddered. A huge piece of concrete, which was a part of the building high up, had simply broken away and fell to the sidewalk. And it landed exactly where he was just standing. Shemokoman cringed at the thought of his nearly ill-fated demise on the streets of Moskva in Rossiya.

He concluded, "This country is literally falling apart. The experiment looks to have failed."

Gypsies

It was late in the day and time to return to his lodging. Shemokoman had a long way to go, but he didn't mind because nothing is better than walking. Good for the cardiovascular system. Having managed to cover most of the distance, he arrived at the intersection of two major roads only a block away from where he was staying. So now, he needed to cross the street to be on the other side. And the only way to get there was by way of an underground tunnel. Thus, he descended into the earth and started to go through a dark, narrow passage.

And then quite unexpectedly, about halfway along, he found himself surrounded by a dozen or so small people. They were dressed in soiled old colorful clothes and wore tons of glittery jewelry. And they were not shy but very direct and asked him for valuable items. It was a wandering band of gypsies.

Rather than shun the poor little drifters, Shemokoman reached deep into one of his pockets and pulled out a handful of gemstones. Next, he tossed them into the air above the fun-loving marauders. They gathered the loot and were overwhelmingly grateful. Then they took off.

It was the very first time that he had ever encountered those people. He thought, "I have read many stories about them. And there is legend concerning their exploits. It was nice to finally meet a bunch of the rogues, so full of rascality."

Shemokoman returned to the Hotel Ukraina, and went into the Bolshevik Café. He ordered a cup of hot black Georgian tea along with a slice of sweet kulich bread that was smothered in creamy butter. He sat by himself and watched the respectable comrades who were taking bribes, planning crimes, doing drugs, and dealing in black-market items. He thought, "Tonight, I need to pack my things; tomorrow is going to be busy. It is time to ride on a train going west and continue a marvelous journey. I'll finish the snack, go back to my room, and prepare for the upcoming morning."

In the Pushcha

When a red rooster crowed at the break of day, the man from Michigan sprang out of bed. He started to walk across the room but stopped dead in his tracks. Two things. First of all, where in the world was that rooster? . . . In the middle of sprawling Moskva, no less. Strange.

And second, he looked back at the bed and thought, "I slept so well. My peaceful rest and silent night could not have been very much better. So sound and plenty of dreaming. Indeed . . . Sleep—the Lord of the Virtues. I always take it for granted that I will sleep like a log forever, when in fact, I should be more grateful. For one reason or another, it is a problem for many people. When darkness shrouds the earth at the end of every day, they dread the very thought of going to bed where sleep eludes them."

Shemokoman went downstairs where the hotel staff prepared a buffet breakfast. Despite the fact that he was rather hungry, he didn't have a lot to eat that morning. Too risky, when you have to take a trip. So—bacon and ricochet poached eggs, fried potatoes with onion and mushrooms, and wheat toast with a tall glass of tomato juice managed to do the trick. He also couldn't resist eating a bowl of the sweet shredded carrots. And when he was done, he returned to his room and gathered together all of his personal things. Then, after sitting perfectly still in a chair for a minute per Slavic tradition, he left the hotel.

A conductor who looked at his gold pocket watch issued the last call for boarding. Mind the gap! Then the train rolled out of Moskva right on schedule. The powerful locomotive barreled ahead, piercing through the snow-covered countryside, pulling the passenger cars behind and blowing the loud steam whistle at every crossing. Shemokoman traveled the whole day long; the journey was very relaxing. He stared out the window most of the time and gazed at umpteen miles of socialist farmland. Mainly kolkhozes and sovkhozes. The train made only a couple of stops to service the village people.

Shortly before midnight, Shemokoman arrived at the destination. It was a town called Nova Bandurka, located in a big enchanted forest called the neo-Europa Belovezhskaya Pushcha. Of course, he had never been there before, so all was new and exciting. As he looked around and listened, he couldn't believe what he was hearing. Nothing, not a single thing. It was quintessential silence.

He was lodged in a two-story gray brick building, especially made for him and the other arrivals. All of the standard amenities were there inside of his room. A single bed, the wooden armoire for clothing, a writing desk and chair, and two small nightstands with a Tiffany lamp on top of each one. He unpacked the usual items that would be needed the following morning and then went straight to bed.

Condition the Body

A man could always count on hearing three things in the Pushcha every morning: First, the sound of birds was everywhere, chirping and singing to their hearts' content. Second, dogs were barking constantly.

And they could be real far away because of how sound traveled through the forest. And last, freight trains chugged along in all directions, going to wherever. It was a pleasing medley. Three—the perfect number.

Shemokoman was up and at 'em long before anyone else. It was time to do some exercise to tone and build the body. He slipped into his workout clothing, then went outside and found a place where he could do the training. After stretching out to loosen up, he began to slowly run. And after twenty minutes had elapsed, it was enough. So, he rested.

Next, he did some heavy reps with weights and worked on calisthenics. His heart was beating fast and strong in perfect sinus rhythm. Then he heard a noise that told him someone else was close at hand. A new acquaintance—Andrey—spotted the early bird and came to join him. The men agreed that everyone must stay in shape to show appreciation for a body we are given.

"You know, Andrey," Shemokoman noted, "most people in America prefer to have a sedentary lifestyle. They can barely climb a set of stairs and with each piece of pecan pie grow fatter every day. With that in mind, I think the earth will very soon tip over. What a dreadful prospect that we have to face and deal with. All they do is eat and eat without an intermission. Soon the food will all be gone and we will be in trouble. They never take a single minute from their precious day to do the slightest bit of exercise; and then, of course, all they do is harp about their health-related problems. Yes, we have the basket cases who complain about the issues like a lack of shirts and trousers that are big enough to fit them.

"So tell me . . . How can we respect the clowns who denigrate survival? They betray the heart and blood, the lungs and gut, and every other organ in the body. Meanwhile, they stand and stare right at themselves in broken mirrors for hours and believe they are attractive. Blasphemy, I tell you—a colossal desecration. We need to put them all in special concentration camps where a lack of food and chronic hunger constitute the answer.

"And when at last they twist and bend, and spit up blood, and fire burns inside their bloated bellies—and they suffer every day because they taunted normal fitness, then the body will remind them, 'You idiot! I wasn't held in high regard, and thus I had to struggle. And now, I must rebel because I'm in such poor condition. I simply can't go on to truly function.' And so, out of sheer desperation, the fools will turn to paranormal forces to redeem and finally save them. But alas, it is too late. They made their lousy beds and now it's time for pleasant sleeping. Thus, they perish with resentment and a lot of weight they carried. Although, it could have been notably different, so much better for the slackers. Get off the couch! . . . And move yourself; avert the big disaster. What do you think about that, my friend?"

"Not bad, Shemokoman," Andrey replied. "I understand completely. What you say is prudent judgment, and a man cannot deny it. Of course, you do understand that things are slightly different here in my country. The conditions are never . . . how should I say . . . given to possible druthers. My comrades are forced to be on their feet for most of your average daytime. Running around and doing the radical business. Socialist life is very demanding, and there is frequently little time for physical fitness. We're always on the move without a chance to sit and rest. Thus, I'd have to say that we're in line to get a small exception when it comes to doing workouts. Does it make sense to you?"

Shemokoman responded, "It certainly does, Andrey. Your people here are in the pink without a grueling session at the health club. They have every right to skip a set of twenty repetitions in the morning. I also know your comrades everywhere are fond of Nature, and they take long promenades most every evening. I am sure that in the end they will live much longer, complain far less, and reap what they are sowing in the form of better welfare. It is to their credit, like, the way that they are thinking. So, what do we have on tap for today?"

Andrey took a deep breath of the clean fresh forest air. Exhilarating—yes, without a smidgen of pollution. Then, he answered, "To tell the truth, I don't really know. Most likely, today is reserved for discussion about the Status of Love in the Future. When we go to breakfast, then I will find out for sure."

Philosophy Symposium

Back in his private quarters, Shemokoman changed his clothing and got spruced up a little. Then he stepped outside again and stood on the gabled veranda. For a minute or so, he gazed at the forest and marveled at wonders around him. Next off, he went to the dining facility, where at least twenty people had gathered. He took a seat at one of the tables and ordered some food from the menu. Kasha, fresh black bread with fruit and butter, plus Borjomi water filled the bill that morning.

And when everyone was finished with their breakfast, he excused himself, got up, and departed with Andrey. They walked to the Great Consultation Hall, where the symposium now was in session.

The audience listened to hours of talk as debaters presented their cases. Admissions, agreements, positions, and comments were part of the deep conversation. In the end, they had to conclude that love was a terrible spirit. Yes, a thing that can't be real, but has existence. It was a ruse for vile impostors and a must for incurable dreamers. A way to take advantage of the lonesome and dejected. It was an arrow for the victims, a toy for playful jesters, and it would gradually die in the future. Everyone at the symposium vehemently denounced it.

Shemokoman mused, "It seems to me these people really get it. I think they're on the up and up, enlightened to the max, and have experience. They're sick of love—a dirty trick to play on saps who haven't basic reason to avoid it. If they could throw the switch, get rid of love, I'm sure that every one of them would do it. And all that was concluded here, as of now, is not a disappointment."

Lunchtime arrived and professional cooks provided another great meal. It consisted of hot "ukha" fish soup for starters, followed by grilled sausage with fried potatoes and Olivier salad. There were torts of all sorts for dessert with herbal green tea as the savory chaser. Andrey and Shemokoman finished their fare and walked back to the Great Consultation Hall.

The agenda was full as participants launched straightaway into polemics. A grueling four hours bore witness to many more candid opinions of love. And when at last the working day was finally over, everyone went to their rooms and got ready for dinner. Again, the food was ideally prepared by qualified socialist workers. Bon appétit!

Day after day, the forum continued to probe philosophical matters. From the standpoint of meaningful discourse, it was all a resounding success. The horrible scourge of love that plagued mankind for ages was slated for certain extinction. And nothing at all, in a similar vein, was ever going to replace it. Hallelujah!

Church in Shiva Sloboda

The first weekend at Nova Bandurka coincided with the Christian holiday Easter. Concerning the great resurrection, it is amazing what people believe in. Shemokoman expressed a wish to observe the occasion by going to church as part of the holy tradition. So arrangements were made for him and some others to attend a Saturday midnight service.

As the time approached for their departure, Shemokoman donned a gray woolen suit with a double-breasted vest and paisley tie. Shortly thereafter, the group left Nova Bandurka and traveled on bumpy old country roads to the village of Shiva Sloboda. They arrived in time to hear the invocation as bells were ringing clamorously in a spire.

The service was held in an Orthodox church that was more than five hundred years old. Thousands of candles were burning to honor the King of Kings and furnish light for believers. Numerous paintings of Christian saints together with colorful tapestry covered the cold stone walls. Stained-glass windows depicted important scenes of a biblical nature. And there was only one priest assisted by two clergymen to celebrate the liturgy of the Passion. At the back of the church on a raised wooden tier, the choir was chanting in old Slavonic. "Gospodi Pomiluj" was what they were saying. Over and over, and over and over again, they said the words. If God was listening in, for sure, he had to have gotten the message.

The mass had commenced at the stroke of midnight and lasted for only three hours. About one hundred people attended, mostly elderly ailing comrades. The cathedral didn't have any seats, so everyone was standing up, kneeling down, or resting on the floor. It was an evening of constant hypnotic overintensification.

Shemokoman thought, "This is quite the ordeal between heaven and hell as phantoms are waiting to chide me. At any time now, I expect to see somebody vanish and then reappear. Of course, they worship *that* God from the past; and yet, I have got to admit again . . . charisma! And as for the fellow named Yeshua, he was a real controversial preacher. He heralded vintage ideas at a time when the world required a savior. No doubt he was utterly destitute and a thoroughly tormented man. Yes, a man to promote and firmly defend a righteous type of existence. No wonder they screamed as loud as they could for the likes of a slow crucifixion: 'Make him suffer!' "

"So as for today," he continued to think, "the message of Christ is pretty much mangled and ruined. Too much in the way of contestable creed without any solid foundation. And although I must doubt that all of these people are really fanatical blasphemers, they worship that very same man who said to avoid every swindling idol. But perhaps acceptable levels of glorification may be a good thing. Who knows?! And perhaps a man named Yeshua may have been wrong about some of his teachings. How about that! . . . After all, people do make mistakes."

At last, the service had ended. The congregation was tired and left the cathedral. Outside, the air was cold and calm, and snowflakes fell from a pearly overcast sky. As they settled on branches of aspen and pine, on slanted rooftops and the ground, parishioners made the sign of the cross and stared on high into heaven. And unlike Sunday mornings when the believers hung out in the courtyard after mass, everyone now got all bundled up and went straight home. Within an hour, Shemokoman was back inside of his lodging, cozy and all tuckered out, and falling asleep in his bed.

As he drifted away under the spell of a Sandman, he thought, "Again, they have it all wrong. Christianity didn't conquer evil; but evil has conquered the Christians."

Excursion to Stara Vovorka

When he finally got up after sleeping in the following morning, Shemokoman stepped outdoors to check on the weather. It was mild and clear, not a trace of cloud cover—a promising day to take some kind of excursion. So at breakfast, he asked for advice about where best to go and everyone willingly gave it. Then, as soon as he finished the meal, he promptly got ready and left on a trip.

After an hour or so of steadily walking, Shemokoman came to the town of Stara Vovorka. It seemed like a good place to visit, so he strolled through the busy central square, where people were milling around and chatting with comrades. Next, he went to a marketplace, where shoppers and merchants were haggling. One vendor exclaimed about his Banana potatoes: "They are the best in the world!" And he was right, the ethical comrade noticed it too. The potatoes that grew in Rossiya were sweet and delicious, really unequaled. It was the truth. And most of the handicraft items he saw were charming and rather unique. He acquired a porcelain tea set—ЛФЗ; and a painting of guardian angels. Furthermore, from what he could tell overall, there was adequate local production. Everything needed for daily consumption was there for the general public.

The ethical comrade climbed to the top of a hill with a view of the town below. He sat in the grass and watched for a couple of hours. And for your typical man on the street, that day was exactly like all other Sundays. Business as usual. It appeared that they didn't have any need for religion. Perhaps they were further along than he thought, or they receded and lost it. Everything Christians consider traditionally Easter, well, for them, it just didn't matter. The Powers That Be a long time ago excluded a principal rival. It was another great plan of the State, and the leaders had fully endorsed it.

He pondered, "I do not observe corruption or chaos, or other unseemly behavior. No capital crime, and the overall mood is reserved and pretty much normal. People are walking the family dog and youngsters are running and playing. It appears that there is law and order here in Stara Vovorka. On the other hand, do they really have everything basic for sensible living? How about honor and virtue? . . . Is there a touch of psychology missing? And why is there nobody laughing or crying, expressing emotional feelings? Maybe their hearts and souls are confused, and tired of socialist nonsense. There is a part of mankind that never gives way to suppression. And—no matter how much an imperious State may try to indoctrinate people, it will not manage to ever be rid of the needs of the servile masses. Ideology works, but only so long as the people believe they are happy."

As creatures instilled with a mystical wish, like it or not—man will have need of religion. It is a predisposition, and to abolish the province of God is a substantial miscalculation. In this case, the State had made a terrible choice regarding the stead of believers. It had to return the inviolable right of worship to the demoralized peasants and workers. Inside of their animate physical bodies, the spirits were greatly defiled.

Shemokoman now got up and moved on. He went to the People's Museum and looked at paintings that hung on the walls. Very impressive. There was also sculpture in stone and bronze, and jewelry and other fine art. The mural of Borodino was truly amazing. Such detail, especially the fight for the Bagration flèches. And last but not least, the basket weavers displayed their wares of intricate work and design.

Next, he went to a war memorial deep in the forest Khatyn. Hundreds of villages razed to the ground, a result of methodical evil. It was a place where humanity surely imploded; and, it was a place where Kirill, Pavel, and Sasha terribly suffered. Thousands of comrades were paying respects and mourning with feverish weeping. Your average man anywhere on the earth cannot understand the meaning of grief to those people. It is a state of mind that defies comprehension. The visitors placed pretty flowers on graves and prayed to a number of spirits.

"Would that the bells needn't toll," he thought.

Satisfied with his trip to Stara Vovorka, Shemokoman called it quits. The sun was descending low in the west as he started back to the lodging. Along the way, he met an old man who, though crooked and bent, carried a great heavy load. The fellow was obviously in much pain, although he cheerfully smiled and wasn't about to concede it. And then, for the better part of a very long distance, Shemokoman helped the poor comrade tote the possessions. They talked about hunting and fishing for trout as well as the Law of the Jungle.

When the two men finally arrived at the old-timer's cabin, Shemokoman lent him a hand to straighten things up. And when the fellow offered him pieces of eight as a token of gratitude, he declined and said to the man that "it was nothing." Although he did share a glass of homemade chokecherry wine with the host and his woman. It was a very nice treat, and then he continued to be on his way.

And he mused, "Must I constantly travel so low to the ground in search of a pass to the High Road? And why must the masses go up for success when life is getting them down? Solutions that devastate human potential stand in the way of a purpose. In spite of his physical limitations, the old man figured it out long ago. He doesn't need love, attention, or help, or care about rotten compassion. His spirit is free, and he is at peace in a world rejecting superfluous questions and answers."

Picnic at Lake Gat'

For everyone at the symposium in the Pushcha, the next few days passed by like previous ones. They explored provocative thought and ideas pertaining to amorous notions. They also talked about love for oneself and how it incinerates virtue. Although, to a certain extent, people have got to adore what they are to keep from going berserk.

When one of the staff in charge of the show suggested going somewhere to relax on the weekend, the proposal was roundly accepted. So on the following Saturday afternoon, the entire group went to a grassy meadow at nearby Lake Gat' for a picnic. The spot was surrounded by tall birch trees, and the shoreline was loaded with green lily pads and cattails. It reminded Shemokoman of Bass Lake, and he reflected about the need for a place to call home.

Walking, fishing, and conversation produced a serene atmosphere. Some men played the card game Goat, where no one seemed to care too much for how their luck was running. Still others went to the badminton court to vie in a round of doubles, chasing shuttles. It didn't take long and soon the group had worked up a big appetite.

The professional group of cooks from town prepared a meal to perfection. They grilled shashlik with onions and peppers over glowing coals of hot saksa'ool. They also made fresh fish soup with perch that were caught in the lake just moments before. And when all of the food was ready, someone yelled out "Come and get it!" Truly a feast fit for the tsar.

Following lunch, the men stayed at the lake a few more hours. There was no anger, jealousy, violence, no resent or unseemly behavior. Nothing was putting them out or putting a damper on genuine fun. As dusk approached, they finished an excellent trip and went back to their housing. The lesson was simple: people from all walks of life can get together and have a good time without any fighting. It isn't that hard.

During that very same evening, Shemokoman spoke with a woman named Svetlana who was distraught over personal matters. She explained about numerous family problems and asked for his advice. He noted that her issues were highly complex and required a clever solution. He agreed to carefully listen to her to assess and resolve what he could. She was obviously a woman who struggled with culture and Slavic tradition. And after several hours, a conclusion was finally arrived at. He advised the lady to poison her man and all of the relatives too.

Svetlana was grateful to the man for his time and recommendations, and said that—despite some minor qualms—she most certainly would do it. In appreciation, she gave him a colorful picture book that described every tree in the Pushcha. She also said that her one desire in life was to get the hell out of Rossiya.

And she intimated, "I sure wouldn't mind living in America."

Shemokoman shot back, "Impossible, dear! Socialist girls have got to remain in the homeland. It is their duty. Besides, it's not really as great as what one might expect. Just go to Buryatia; ask the old woman. She knows."

He thanked her for the gift, and then they parted.

Tracks

It came to pass that it was time for Shemokoman to leave the enchanting location. His philosophical business in Nova Bandurka had ended. Thus, on a muggy Saturday morning after exchanging a host of farewells, Andrey took his guest to the local train station, where he boarded Express No. 9. Mind the gap! Shortly thereafter, the big locomotive and all of its passenger coaches were on the way, going east to the capital city.

While looking out the window at the lush green rolling landscape, he pondered, "For hundreds of years that just never end, hatred has wrecked this country. Man destroys his fellow man because of unspeakable evil. Entire families and quaint villages—wiped out and forgotten forever. The blood is spilled as privates and the sergeants follow orders. To tell the truth, it gets to be a twisted sort of pastime. Killing, that is; the power to obliterate the masses. You learn to live without a soul and disregard for conscience. Yes, the comrades who have lived right here especially had it rough. And of course, humanity will never change because it isn't able."

It drizzled outside for an hour or so and then it turned into a downpour. The shifting skies were so alive and glittered with big sheets of crystal raindrops. But eventually, the storm tapered off and stopped, the clouds went away, and the color of the heavens up above resembled sapphire. From what he could tell, the winter had passed in Rossiya; and, they could look forward to springtime.

"Good for them," he thought. "God knows that they deserve it."

It was late into the evening when the train pulled into Moskva right on time. Shemokoman hailed transportation and soon arrived at the Hotel Ukraina. He had a bite to eat at the Bolshevik Café, then went up a big marble staircase to his room and got settled in. Another trip was almost over, and he was glad that everything so far came off like clockwork.

Although he mused, "It seems that all I ever do of late is travel like a rambler. Sometimes I wake up in the night and can't remember where

I'm even staying. The feeling that I sense is mild shock and rather frightening. I need to take it easy, simmer down, and never opt to push the panic button."

The Beating

After several hours of lying in bed under mountains of covers, Shemokoman just couldn't fall asleep. Perhaps a second wind, or perhaps some trepidation. Who knows? So he went downstairs and spent some time drinking tea and reading trashy tabloids. It's true!—a cow jumped over the moon.

A short while later, because it was warm and too stuffy inside of the place, he stepped outside into the cold fresh evening air. And while leaning up against the concrete building and watching mainly absolutely nothing, he witnessed a terrible crime. Two men viciously attacked another fellow in a neighboring courtyard. God only knows the reason why; the assault was more than gruesome. Blood everywhere.

Having finished roughing up the victim, the assailants fled away into the darkness. The comrade who was beaten up lay lifeless on the ground. Luckily, several good Samaritans immediately came to help him.

"Man alive," Shemokoman thought, "speak of god-awful behavior. The villains act like animals where violence is normal. Instinctively—they stalk, attack, and pulverize whomever for uncommonly small accolades, I am sure. And then they laud the deed as something to be proud of. It is quite the crude endeavor in the sorry underworld of corruption. Untouchable scions of fire and brimstone."

Shemokoman went back to his room and slept the rest of the night without even waking. The next morning, he took another choo-choo train that went to the Port of Departure. Then he boarded a big gray ship and sailed across the Ocean back to America. Upon arrival at the destination, he collected all his things and traveled straight to Federal City.

When he reached his home, the place was dark and crickets started chirping. At least one living organism that night was glad to see him. And people can say whatever they like about making a trip to wherever, but the anonymous sage was right: "There's no place like home." To believe otherwise is certain proof that someone's precious heart and soul are missing.

16

Bane of Detachment

Population

Many a day, Shemokoman sat in a chair outside of his home and thought about living. There was still so much that needed a good explanation. Like, why does humanity slaughter itself, and what is the purpose of beauty? My god! . . . He detested pollution and the people who peddled perversion. Moreover, why was he always alone in the quest to clear up a mass of confusion? So simple: the others do not want to hear it. No fear of the truth is safer than faith, but guarantees critical reckoning.

His world was total seclusion right in the middle of millions of people. But there were no walls to restrain him. No Constantine wire or jail cell grilles to close up and lock on the inmate. Forget about tiers, and no center hall, as guards on duty in towers were peacefully sleeping. He was free to come and go as he pleased inside of the fictional cooler. No way to get out; a piece of cake to get inside.

One evening, Shemokoman watched as a phalanx of bodies was moments away from injustice. A group of protesters was marching uptown, and a meeting was on the agenda. The dissidents knew that violence has to be used when rhetoric fails. And war is the way to obtain what we want when someone has lost the advantage. Although did anyone notice the world was visibly shrinking? Everyone closer together and the space in a chamber decreasing. The Circle of Time was contracting as the impossible dream was expanding. It is no cinch to get lost when you're going to hell with Lucifer crowing and drooling.

He recalled his very first trip alone to the national capital region. It was a long time ago and sort of a messy debacle. He got totally lost and could not find his way during the season of summer. Whoever designed the roads in that town must've had rocks in their head. It was a classic result of liberal men who counted on more than their fingers. Talk about lunatic systems. All he remembered was how it was hot, and he could do nothing about it. Only suffer and melt. And just when he was about to keel over and perish due to exhaustion, he deciphered the code and made a redeeming departure.

Appearance of Evil Inside

Now, it happened one day that Destiny started to mess with Shemokoman's fitness again. He was living alone and the demons who preyed on the body knew that they could hurt him. Skullduggery. It's really too bad that spirits look forward to having such fun with our welfare. Otherwise, we'd all probably live for a good while longer.

On a cool Sunday morning in springtime, he went to a market in town to pick up provisions. On the way back, he suffered from symptoms, in essence, that tore him to pieces. He got dizzy and vision was blurry; the body was weak, and he had trouble with breathing. His chest was shaking, and rising and falling with wild, sporadic convulsions. In spite of desire to shake it, alas, he could do nothing to stop it. There was sharp pain in the arms, his back, and the legs; his heart was racing and pounding as if to explode right out of the body. Thus, he was caught unawares and defenseless, with no one around to witness a horrible scandal.

After about thirty minutes or so, the problem got better and then went away completely. Shemokoman had contracted a brand-new affliction. It was the sort of abnormal condition that he knew could imperil survival. Intuitively, we know when an illness has got to be seriously taken. He slowly walked home and hoped it would be just a totally random occurrence. And that was a perfect example of wishful thinking.

It can happen so fast, in the bat of an eye. You pass through a gate that instantly closes behind you. There is no turning back, so don't even try as you enter the realm of charade and mysterious umbras. Yet one more difficult round for the heavy contender. Your time has arrived to deal with a deadly disorder. A problem for those who must brazenly, stubbornly fight it. Such was the case that day, unlike many others.

His hardship—most likely, the standard result of travail he had to put up with. You simply don't burden the body that way with far too much toil and hassle. And now, at least once every two or three weeks, the evil inside would be causing the terrible trouble. In public he acted like nothing was wrong, so many creative excuses. Albeit, he knew that somehow in the end the problem he faced would have a solution.

The Politician

Spring went away and summer arrived in the American East. Shemokoman went to the Ocean, where he sat on the beach and swam in the cool, salty water. And then, while sunning himself and sipping on cold lemonade, he received a telegram from a one Mr. N. It read:

> Greetings, Old Chap — (Stop) — Please, meet me in the
> lobby near the Main Breakfast Parlor Room of the Hotel Bête
> Noire at Dupont Circle in town at 5:30 am on Wednesday —
> (Stop) — Thank you — (Stop) — V/R, N

The request was from a good fellow whom Shemokoman could depend on. So, he decided to go.

It came to pass that on the day of the prearranged meeting, he rose out of bed quite early and prepared for the upcoming business. After a breakfast of biscuits and honey with hot black Georgian tea as the chaser, he left his home, caught a trolley, and rode into Federal City.

A magnificent dawn was breaking when he arrived at the fancy hotel. People had flooded the streets everywhere, going to work and doing their personal errands. He entered the place through the main entranceway and looked around at all of the chic furnishings. Yes, it was a swanky joint all right, everything vintage and polished. Plush davenports, provincial wing chairs, antique vases, and brass wall sconces, plus plenty of gold candelabra. He sat down on a bench and waited to meet his acquaintance.

Shortly thereafter, Mr. N. arrived through a side corridor. They greeted each other and spoke for a while, and then went into the Main Breakfast Parlor room to check on the scheduled proceedings. A few moments later, directly across from where they were standing, an entourage of about twenty men and women came into the room. The ethnicity was unmistakable; they were all Slavic. A very tall man with scars on his face stood out in the group of esteemed dignitaries. Well, how about that . . . It was Lokmat Vissarionovich Zhigulovskiy, at your service.

Shemokoman knew quite a bit about the big guy. He was a soldier turned politician who lived in Rossiya. During the previous months, he mounted a massive campaign with solid support to run for president in his country. However, last-minute scheming forced him to abandon the effort in favor of a secret alliance with front-running candidate Zhadny. Then, after the honest election where Zhadny got all of the popular vote, Lokmat was appointed to head up the scrupulous Cheka.

It didn't take long amid rising civil unrest for a disillusioned Zhigulovskiy to want to do something about it. He desired more power by way of benevolent turmoil. Id est, revolution. He truly believed that the leaders were selling him out and betraying the State with her comrades. There was far too much corruption; and, the *running dogs* of the West as well were plotting with socialist traitors.

The army was fully behind Lokmat, and for sure he may have succeeded. However, the Inner Circle exposed him, and the coup he desired was thwarted. He was given his walking papers and then went quietly back to Tula, his hometown, to think things over. And now, he was here in America with the wife—an extremely gracious lady—and a horde of his favorite henchmen.

Following introductions, the entire group sat down at a large dining table, where everyone ordered breakfast. Shemokoman requested Tyrolean Gruyère cheese with rye crackers, salmon, and ricochet poached eggs on wheat toast with tomato juice. Nothing too heavy or rich.

Then, amid a barrage of small talk, he asked the aspiring leader, "So, Lokmat Vissarionovich. It is my understanding that you decided, putting it mildly, to pass on the national scene for now. I guess you could say, lay low and steer clear of theatrics. Perhaps you can build a political base by working in regional government in the near future?"

Zhigulovskiy replied, "Yes, you are right, my respectable comrade. For me, it is time for a break. So when I go back to Rossiya, I plan to chill in my quiet hometown, where I was born and grew up in the country. I need to spend time with my dipsomaniac chums and swig samogon before lunchtime. Eye-openers strengthen the body, and only a man who is thirsty should drink them. Next, I will go to Siberian land, where the troikas glide over the tundra. There, I should easily win governorship of the large Ozhivlashka Province. It is a region with plenty of wealth because of the gold and silver, iron and copper, and the aluminum far underground for foil in kitchens. People all over the world are greatly in need of mineral resources. Then, after living and working five years in the sticks, I will be ready to seize the final position. Führer! Whoops . . . I mean, president, of Rossiya."

"And what will you do about people who put up resistance?" Shemokoman asked. "And what about villains who'll want to move in and take what you have as the leader? Devious men will be fighting with you for the right to experience power. What about handling them? After all, you're dealing with punks in the big league."

Lokmat replied, "Of course, like anywhere else, there will be issues. Although I am sure we can easily manage the problems. The people are standing behind me because they know I am loyal and trusted. Without any doubt, they will faithfully do what I tell them to do, without fail. If not, they take a vacation out to the gulag where they are punished.

"You see, the situation for us is like this. On the one hand, we have the extreme Left. The radicals. Nothing but filth and slime that I will crush at the very beginning. They never serve any practical purpose. All they do is complain and complain; the world should be like a fable. And when there is nothing to grumble about, they tell you that something is fishy. Trouble causers—all of them, and frequently violent too. They can best serve my tyrannical State in a hard-labor camp in the east, or rotting in prisons. And I will give them a Garden of Eden, by god! . . . And freedom to go to the love-in. Oh yes, I will certainly do it.

"And then we have got the far Right. Fascist swine! . . . And in a way, no significant difference from those on the Left. Wild and foolish with jingo ideas—they want to go back, further back, further back—and live before time was created. I tell you, they're totally crazy; they would debilitate much of the country. The Right advocates a grand megalomaniac social order at the expense of your hardworking comrade. Clearly, they want to destroy us; and clearly, I have to defeat them. Therefore, I will smoke out their ranks and haul them away to a slammer to be with the Liberals. And for the aeons to come in Rossiya, there will not be any want of employment."

Lokmat sipped on aged Armenian cognac in a tulip glass and continued, "And then in between, we have everything else. A gaggle of lazy avengers. A wayward mélange that will need psychological guidance. They are a threat to the power of leaders who rule with desire for law and order. You see, they attempt on the sly to convince and convert every coward and skeptical thinker. Although they don't even have a position. Morons. However, of course, we will always have people without an opinion; and maybe I cut them a break so long as they simply don't cause a disturbance."

Silence hung over the room. And, Shemokoman thought about meanings of words and how best to interpret and parse them.

The man continued to speak: "You know, it is really quite simple. Conservatives feel that there is a difference between what is right and wrong. And immutable laws require the charge of enduring committed conviction. They do what they will on account of they must and anything else is forbidden. People should live according to rules of the conscience; it is the moral intention of Nature. Although I sense rampant abuse by conservative men who've attained astronomical power. The challenge is how to control the insufferable jerks."

"On the other hand," he went on, "liberals believe that there is no such thing as right or wrong. Just do as you please, whatever, in life; no one has power to judge you. For ladies and men with a liberal mind, there cannot be true universals. Behavior should be the result of a wish depending on personal feelings. If chaos ensues, well, that is a shame; excessive oppression most likely had to have caused it. And if there is any advice that they thoroughly hate, it is when they are told to go out and work for a living. Such brutality! . . . The inhumanity! The challenge is how to contain the intransigent kooks."

"Very interesting, comrade," Shemokoman chimed in. "And tell me, Lokmat, regarding your personal safety. Do you have ample protection? After all, a man in your position has to be wary of treacherous rivals. There is far too much crime in this day and age in Rossiya."

The fellow chuckled. "Why, of course I do, Shemokoman. My security force consists of only the very best cold-blooded henchmen. And I will tell you something else, my friend . . . You are wise to bring up the subject. A man such as myself needs to constantly think about safety. Every place that I go any time of the day potentially harbors a gangster. Especially cagey assassins who are good swimmers."

"Well, have you ever thought about changing your current profession?" Shemokoman asked. "For example—with your baritone voice, you could be singing in opera. Or maybe a big apparatchik in Kansk, or in Saint Petersburg dishing out orders?"

The charismatic big guy replied, "No, my friend, not really. And honestly, I couldn't do it. You see, my comrades who live in Rossiya are counting on me to inspire and lead them. Public service is my way of life, and I need to make a big difference. Anything else would amount to a willful desertion. And I could never have that on my conscience."

And now, Shemokoman thought, "For sure, the greatest fantasy of all for politicians. That is, to think that the citizens in their country must like them. Has he not heard? The masses from Vladivostok to Smolensk can't stand them. The people hate their guts and would like to strangle them. All that they do is to rip someone off and break every meaningless promise. But then again, who knows? Perhaps this man—Lokmat—is different and honest."

After everyone had finished their breakfast, Shemokoman discussed the possibility of working in Rossiya for Zhigulovskiy. However, something just didn't seem kosher. Choosing sides is a tricky affair and always has big implications. So he politely declined the invitation.

The ambitious politician stayed in America two more days. And when all was said and done, he and his suite returned to the cold Motherland. As planned, he traveled to Tula, where he spent ample time on the block with all of his friends. Then it was off to Ozhivlashka Province, where he was elected and served as the governor. A very prestigious position of socialist power. For more than a year, he ruled over the land and acquired respect of the people. But before long—in view of the upcoming star that he was with unusual high aspirations—someone took sinister notice.

It came to pass that Shemokoman woke up one morning and read sad news in the local gazette. The headline was as follows: "General Lokmat Vissarionovich Zhigulovskiy Perishes in Mysterious Accident in Siberian Wasteland."

The ethical comrade wasn't surprised. Somewhat touched, it is true; after all, he worked with the fellow. But he knew when the stakes are as high as they were, the potential for loss is much greater. And for people who think they can live on the edge, it only takes once—the innocuous miscalculation, and you are a certified goner.

Friendship

Catherine Hesse traveled to Federal City every so often to see her friend. And on each occasion when she left, Shemokoman followed her parting wave until she was clean out of sight. Talk about scathing privation, although many people have got to go through it. And she went back to a land that was mostly surrounded by water and shaped like a mitten.

At those moments, he thought to himself, "I've racked up too many years in Federal City. It is time to get out of this rat race."

And then one day, Shemokoman started to think about friendship again. He mused, "If the intent of a man is to feel good in life, then friendship is clearly required. After all, regular people depend on it for support and to make them feel happy. Who can refute the position? We are societal sociable creatures. And it frequently takes many hard long years to develop the faith one needs to have in another.

"So how do we make a true friend? Viz., what is the standard prescription? Mainly, a wise understanding of people, determination, and keen mother wit. Honesty, mutual respect, and fidelity must combine to be the essential foundation. It doesn't happen overnight; it is a lengthy process. And to prevent complications, we have to avoid pretenders and carefully search for a decent acquaintance. Moreover, we needn't be overly scrupulous regarding the mien of a prospect. Simplicity rules; just go with the flow and you will be fine in the end. Also, no silver doubloons, no ducats of gold will help in the quest for a friend. Quite the opposite. Wealth is a curse in that sort of endeavor; a genuine friend is never for sale."

Shemokoman made a steaming hot cup of black Georgian tea and continued to ponder: "It is easy to recognize people without any friends. They are dishonest, repulsive, hateful, self-centered, and prone to be out of their tree. They frequently wander about in dark alleyways from loser to creepy panhandler, and live in a ghetto with tramps who used to be higher in fancy places. They laugh at jokes and anecdotes that aren't in the least bit funny, and they haven't the need to prove one single thing to anyone whom they run into. All they can do is to barely get by where audacity spoils contentment."

It was getting late and he now fell asleep in a chair for several hours. He had a few dreams about villains who were corrupt but thought it was normal. Alas, there is no shortage of counterintuitive life to slightly annoy us. It is too bad that we cannot control it; nobody wants to expose a repression. And when he woke up, he just didn't bother to think about friendship at all.

Praskovya

Every so often, Shemokoman still managed to visit Rossiya. He enjoyed the culture, cuisine, the levity, and a mentality he could relate to—phylogenetic and bourgeois. The red caviar on fresh black bread with sweet cream butter provided temptation that he was unable to part with. Very satisfying, as they say.

On one occasion, he was in Novosibirsk and met a woman named Praskovya. She could not have looked any finer. The somber demeanor, elitist remarks, and shy disposition were such a benign combination. She was as sharp as a tack and ready to quarrel. Of course, she was wearing that lavender gloss per the latest fashion of all the young ladies.

Shemokoman spoke for a while with her and she started to talk without stopping. On and on and on like nobody's business. In a country where freedom of speech was disparaged, he was a little bit puzzled. She was the noted exception; and, she wasn't about to shut up. Time and again for the rest of his trip, he rendezvoused with Praskovya. They went to the Philharmonia to listen to classical concerts and shopped for socialist clothing in the GUM, dined in trendy cafés, and took long, slow promenades till late in the evening.

In due course, Shemokoman went back to America. And it didn't take long for Praskovya to arrange for a trip to see him. Who would have guessed that a Young Pioneer would manage to cleverly do it? But she did, and with a clandestine agenda. Unfortunately, there would be days up ahead for her that were stormy and cold, when she would outright betray her very own conscience. It is amazing what people can do to alleviate guilt and placate desire. Almost anything. And at the end of the day, the seeker of truth found himself in his brownstone flat together with one more companion. The Moirai struck again.

Hope for the Best

What a depressing perspective. To constantly have one's health on the mind and there is no way to resolve it. Well aware that a good constitution recently suffered a major disaster, Shemokoman struggled constantly with the persistent new adversary. And much of the time, there was copious pain just waiting to hurt him at sunrise. He frequently went to healers who gave him various potions and tonics, and said, "It's probably all in your head. Just go home and try to forget it."

He had to consider the adverse effect of a new pathological status on close interaction with people. In particular, he thought about Praskovya: "This woman does not really know who I am. I met her when I was defective. I am not what I was or what I should be in the future. I am not me. And what does my darling Praskovya perceive? . . . For sure, the ghost of a comrade. Shemokoman doesn't exist anymore in spite of the form and appearance. Rather, my body is sick and perhaps will never recover. Although, what if my wretched disorder in fact goes away? . . . Or it is cured and I promptly recover? I still have my strength and may live many years without any other affliction. Indeed . . . 'What if . . . what if and what if?' Two words that I have to get used to."

The tempestuous part of his life never reversed or even subsided. To deal with it all, he had to put up with some awkward and difficult moments. He learned to submit to much more of the same with troubling days that did not allow for concession. When unconditional war has been waged, you can only dig in and attempt to tenaciously fight it.

The Exclusion

Some people we know are accustomed to getting their way all of the time. Praskovya was part of that crowd. If she made up her mind, it was written in stone and no one or nothing could change it. It was her way to alleviate pain from everything lousy that happened during a lifetime. The woman was no soft touch; or, at least, she didn't believe it. Now, for those who fit into that type of a mold, life will be constant defiance. They're always determined to stand their own ground and connive for whatever they covet. Although, perseverance can last for only so long until languor will ravage the conscience.

It happened on one mild day in the fall that Praskovya was walking to market alone on a primrose path through a forest. Suddenly, a dazzling golden chariot that was drawn by two black stallions came out of the blue and stopped right in front of the woman. Two gods—Avarice and Generosity stood tall in the cab, having decided to pay the lady a visit. It was well known that these two immortals always traveled together, serving the needs of each other. He was so fond of collecting the goods, and she couldn't stop with the giving.

When Avarice saw Praskovya and noticed the treasure she quietly carried, he started to gloat and immediately told her, in no uncertain terms, "If you do not mind, I'll take it right now. Just give it to me or else. I'm not in the mood to play games with an obstinate woman."

Generosity watched with stoic indifference and said nothing at all regarding the imminent plunder. After all, she knew that when it was her turn, he would be there to support her. So now, Praskovya was fully aware of her plight; and, it was useless to challenge their power. With nothing to do and nowhere to turn, the lady was thoroughly shattered. She was no match for the fair, formidable gods who confronted her. Every trick in the book that she always employed would do her no good at the moment. She had to give in, turning over the goods, and forget about trying to fight it. Thus, she relinquished a treasure.

For the longest time, the victim stood frozen, forlorn in the throes of dejection. She honestly didn't give something away; Avarice took it from her. And glaring with sterile pretension, the thief admired his novel possession. Then he declared, "And no! A thousand times no, beloved Praskovya! Forgiveness is out of the question for you."

Then the pair of gods took off.

Eventually, Praskovya dragged herself home. She was in shock and total denial. The forces of evil or justice, who knows, were wicked and viciously thorough. She lay down on her bed, not moving at all for days, which seemed like forever. Healers tried to help her, of course—completely to no avail. She stared into space and chided the stars with wild, delirious ravings. And then at times, she softly inquired, "Why did it happen to me? . . . More pain. Why must I evermore suffer?"

From the day of the hapless purloining, Praskovya was never the same. She didn't say much, and her behavior was totally different—mostly detached, cross, and resentful. It was the terrible wake of traumatization. But now she needed somebody to blame for such a horrendous ordeal. Every particular crime that occurs requires a cold perpetrator. Thus, it would always be his fault. Furthermore, it would take many years to create and restore the loss of a fine stolen treasure. However, in one way or another, the woman would do it.

Fate is too often regarded by man as such a deplorable swindler. To get a fair shake is something we cannot depend on. And nothing will ever decidedly change; get on with your life and enjoy it. The trees, a moon, the salt of the earth, and even more news about warfare—it is a grievous mistake to deny that everything here is perfection. And come what may, the Yahweh has got to enforce immutable order. Just ask Praskovya—she knows.

We speak of the will, but what is the will? A wish to invite devastation? Nothing will ever be sacred, just as nothing can really be evil. And there is only a will that is will to itself in lieu of a big revelation.

Private domains float away in the wind like seed of a dandelion flower. They never adjust to wishes of men who can barely make do until passing. Yes, everything follows a pattern; like it or not, we are bound by convention. And people compete in a world embellished by trustworthy senses with reason. Of course, we have to respect the innate understanding, as it is the only connection with plausible meaning. A touch of this, a dash of that, and poof!! . . . Divine inspiration. Just like a god; but something is wrong . . . Of course, we are blessed without any actual power. Alas, for us to exist in a relative way, we are precluded from handling everyday matters. Rather, something above or maybe below, or in those places we never can go, will manage them for us.

Nippon-koku

Shemokoman knew it was time to journey abroad for more exploration. So, as another winter was coming his way, he decided to go to Nippon-koku in the Orient. After packing the usual items, he left his home in Federal City and went to the Port of Departure, where he boarded another big gray ship and prepared for distant adventure.

The captain and crew, and the passengers, sailed across the Ocean blue. There was nothing to see at sea every day except for the wavy green water. They made one brief stop along the way at some tropical isles to obtain a store of fresh macadamia nuts and pineapple fruit for people to snack on.

Two weeks later, the ship arrived at the port of Yokohama-cho in a country composed of thousands of green smoking islands. After getting his luggage and leaving the vessel, Shemokoman hailed a rickshaw for transportation to lodging at the luxurious Ichiban Tower. The accommodations were more than outstanding, and now it was late in the evening. He had a quick bite to eat at the Yum Yum Café, and then it was off to his room to catch up on much-needed sleep.

The next morning, Shemokoman rolled out of bed quite early as always. It was nice to be rested and ready to get the ball rolling. He noticed a very big window that spanned across the west wall of the room. It was covered with red brocade draperies and a sheer liner next to the glass. Curious, he opened the curtains from left to right, unprepared for a sight that would greatly affect him.

To begin with, he looked down at the populous town below with exorbitant human congestion. The streets were alive with droves of industrious people. Mostly afoot or riding on bikes, they darted around and conducted their personal business. Markets of every imaginable type were loaded with shoppers and merchants. And when he glanced up to gaze far off in the distance, that fellow could not believe what he was now seeing. It was Mount Fuji! And my goodness, it was astounding. With a perfectly snow-covered summit on top, the mountain itself took up the whole horizon. What a sensational treat for anyone at any age to delight in. For such a long time, he could not turn away from a view that enamored the senses. The locals said that it was a god, and he was inclined to believe them.

His trip was arranged to last for a week and several excursions were slated. He had to get out, to walk and observe, to see unusual places and mix with the people. On the first day, Shemokoman hit the streets early. He went to the Chūō commercial district, browsed for a couple of hours, and acquired a few souvenirchiks. Like—folding fans, iromuji kimonos, and chopsticks. And every encounter with someone he met was precisely the ticket he needed. The people were clean, polite, and full of discussion. And when the chance presented itself, he was especially fond of the bowing.

"At least I don't have to shake anyone's hand," he thought. "A formality rather disgusting. Why should I want to touch somebody else when meeting your typical stranger? It is obscene and frankly outrageous;

it is a custom that must be abolished. Now, on the other hand, the bow . . . So graceful and thoroughly civil."

Purification

During the afternoon, Shemokoman went to a place where people paid homage to Shinto immortals. He considered it wise wherever he was to render respect to deities of all denominations. Like the pagan gods: Amaterasu and Izanagi. And so, he stood squarely among a unique collection of beautiful sanctified buildings.

The Grand Shinto Shrine in "low town" was one of the oldest religious sanctums in the world. It was built hundreds of years ago by pious people to honor their spirits. An exquisite square symmetrical temple served as the heart of the complex. For many years, Shemokoman wanted to go there to see for himself what it was like, and now he had finally made it.

A priest and priestess in long white robes were standing together and talking about ecclesiastical matters. He approached the pair and inquired, "Excuse me please, Your Excellency . . . madam. If I may, I would like to speak with you for a minute or so. My name is Shemokoman, and I traveled afar from my native Land of Michigan to visit your marvelous country. I have patiently waited for many long years to come right here and see this remarkable compound."

He continued, "I studied your people, the culture, religion, and also nibbled on sushi. Finally, I concluded that I had to visit your place for mainly two principal reasons. First, there was a day, and a sad one at that, when warriors from our two great nations did battle against one another. Millions of countrymen died fighting for pride and ostensible freedom. No one was right, nobody was wrong; war is a plague that serves the rich and degraded. I have long felt the need to come here and pray for men who perished in that detestable struggle. Secondly, I know about your Purification Ceremony and specifically what it entails. And I was wondering . . . Is there any possibility that I can take part in such a ritual today?"

"Of course, Shemokoman!" the priest replied. "It is a pleasure to finally meet you. Many moons ago, we were informed by way of smoke signals that you were alive and slated to stay in this world. And we have plenty of time right now, I believe, to indulge your solemn request. So let us commence and seek absolution with the immaculate Kami."

Shemokoman bowed and responded, "Hai! Hai!"

The Holy Ones led their guest to a large cistern of water, a portion of which they sprinkled on him and over themselves as well. Then they turned toward the temple and bowed to the gods to acknowledge the start of the service. The spirits were pleased and a bright yellow sun came out from behind a cloud directly above them. Next, the priest recited several prayers that were accompanied by mysterious hand gestures. Shemokoman took the occasion in stride and felt the effect of devotion.

And now, they walked up a small set of stairs to the entrance of the temple and stepped inside. Food was prepared and offered up for atonement. More prayers soon followed and chanting commenced, which continued for quite a long while. The priest recited the Norito Verses on behalf of the priestess and the guest, asking the gods for peace and good cheer in all the days of their lives.

At the conclusion of supplication, sakaki branches—another oblation—were placed on a table in front of divine figurines. And after bowing three times and clapping their hands, then bowing once more per tradition, a period of silence followed. Finally, the offerings were taken away by the gods, and everyone went back outside, where they bowed one last time to the temple. The ceremony was over, having lasted for roughly an hour.

Without a doubt, the purification rite was very refreshing. Shemokoman thanked the high priest and priestess for their time and hospitality. He also met shamans and kagura dancers who said they were happy to see him. And after making a pledge to return someday, the visitor departed.

Asian Persuasion

For the rest of the day, the ethical comrade explored the countryside of Nippon-koku. First, he saw the Imperial Palace and walked in the miniature gardens. They didn't resemble anything back in his country; there was something unreal and very aesthetic about them. The grounds were laid out according to how a Creator remodeled perspective with everything little, but giving impressions of volume with bigger dimensions. The native terrain was posh and fragrant, and made the human observer feel strangely transported. Furthermore, the temple he saw on the palace grounds had to be grand and amazing. After all, it was the home of the emperor, a ruler of sanctified peerage.

Next, he toured the great Kamakura Daibutsu Buddha to glean what he could for insight. Shemokoman slipped inside of the giant bronze statue, where he hoped to undergo a big revelation. But nothing unusual happened. It was one more spiritual buildup and another discouraging letdown.

"Hmm . . . ," he thought, "so what does it mean to have an epiphany? I've yet to experience a single occurrence of any such manifestation. Probably nonsense. And why does this guy always sit on the ground with legs that are crossed, meditating? I guess he is very enlightened. So does he expect the sublime panegyric? . . . And am I supposed to respect him?"

Shemokoman went to the Straits of Nemuro to look at volcanoes on islands. A mild, balmy breeze was blowing so nicely—and then, suddenly, he dropped down to the ground on his knees that buckled completely. The paroxysmal assailant was back with one more vicious attack to stifle well-being. For sure, it was going to be stressful.

His vision was failing and pain radiated throughout every part of the body. He barely could breathe in a regular way and desperately gasped for air. The heart was aching, and stopping and starting without any natural rhythm. He had to survive to improve what he could, even though he was certainly fading. Panic attacked to frazzle his poise and the process of positive thinking. He lay down on his back on the soft cool earth and gazed at the wide-open sky. Perhaps, just one of the countless again, or maybe the final performance.

The demons inside him were having their fun like so many times in the past. And he thought, "Why do I feel like the *Son* convicted by Pilate? It must be a crime to be honest, so they feel right about giving me torture. It is a hideous way to intentionally make me acknowledge my mortal existence. I cannot control or stop it for even an instant. Indeed, I am no wise overman; instead, I give you the real underdog. He is the one we should cheer for, and he is the one you must die for. My only request—allow me to live for fifty more years in this body. I still have a temple of faith to erect for disciples and cynical jokers."

Fortunately, the horrible symptoms slowly abated and finally ended. By pushing through alternate periods of walking and rest, Shemokoman managed to weather a tough situation. So now, it was time to enjoy a well-deserved breather, although he knew the disorder would surely return with more of the same to afflict him. It was just a matter of time; alas, his portion of fate was explicit.

Sayonara

At the end of the day, Shemokoman returned to the Ichiban Tower. Aside from the final few hours, it was a pretty good week, all things considered. He continued to stay in Nippon-koku for two more days to see what he could and converse with the courteous people. Then he sailed across the Ocean on yet another enormous gray ship back to his country.

The National Capital

A predisposition of people who live in small towns and outlying regions will always be the attraction to big metropolitan places. Most notably capital cities. Privilege and power with foolhardy hope are much of the source of enchantment. They want to be part of a crowded morass and think there is safety in numbers. What could be better than lost in a maze of byways and building construction where the public equates you to nothing? It is a dream for people who want to have more and believe that they truly have earned it. Alas, you cannot demolish a myth that serves so many so well who are senseless.

There was a day not that long ago when Rome was the perfect example. To be a citizen of that great empire was something that someone might honestly die for. It was the ultimate status. So is there nothing to lose and something to gain by leaving those rustic surroundings? How was a man really meant to exist to make sure that he truly is happy? All that we crave as opposed to our needs should wisely be given its due, because to make a mistake about where we should live is a blunder we cannot afford. Scrounging for remnants of pleasure in pain in a city can be disconcerting. Although, to be fair, a fortified camp is a solid defensive position. The Great Khan was right.

Most people in Federal City were fully absorbed by a government system. It gave them enough satisfaction just to be part of community business. They did precisely what they were told to do without a delay and reluctance, and cheered at the great coliseum like mad on Sundays. So much pride and a true-blue sense of belonging as they enjoyed every day and never considered the latent debut of a downside. The future was vague; the past—a blank; and the present was here for the hedons. Talk about rationalization; never the hint of opposing positions. Someone created the "straight and narrow" to justify healthy deception.

Amazingly, unlike in other great civilizations, anyone anywhere who wished to live in Federal City confronted no legal obstruction. The gates were always wide open for people who wanted to enter and stay there. No wonder it wouldn't take long until the town was completely in ruins. There needed to be a way to evaluate migrants.

Shemokoman thought, "Only the best for political slime who live without any purpose. Every thing a reprobate could ever want and they needn't be rich to afford it. Although if wealth is a problem, then put on a mask, devise a plan, and steal what you want in the daytime. The rich already have far too much, and besides, they'll never miss it. The capital streets are full of young men who enjoy nothing more than a hustle."

"But no, by god!" he said to himself. "Never for me, I cannot. There is no advantage to living here, or anywhere else in the world. My time has arrived and the odyssey soon will be over. Like the Oracle said—'I should travel afar' . . . to collect and exploit information. I observed what I should and learned what I could, and now it is time to make plans to return to my home. Potawatomi braves, my ethical comrades, and madcaps are waiting to greet me."

Siegfried Inherits a Fortune

One afternoon in the dog days of summer, Shemokoman took a stroll through the center of town. As of late, he was spending way too much time in his flat and starting to be too reclusive. We need to get out every once in a while; you don't want to lose it completely.

After leaving his place and walking for roughly an hour, he wound up at a Deutsche café called the Augustiner Keller. Having been there a lot in the past, Shemokoman knew all the names of the servants. He went in the front door, past the kitchen and cooks, down a short flight of stairs, and into the main dining area, where he said "Grüß Gott" to the dapper Herr Ober—Matthias. Then he noticed and joined a group of some friends, namely—Heidi, Siegfried, Gretchen, and Karl. A sprightly young gal by the name of Pauline came to their table for orders. He asked for the Zwiebelrostbraten with gemischte salad and a radler as well for the drink.

"Guten Tag, ladies and gentlemen," he greeted the foursome. They all turned around and looked to the rear, expecting to see different people. "And how are we doing today?"

Siegfried replied, "Well, my life could be better or it could be worse. My feelings are just about frazzled."

"And why is that, pray tell?" Shemokoman asked.

Somewhat choked up, Siegfried replied, "Well, you see . . . my old uncle George, who was fit as an ox, just passed away, of course, euphemistically speaking. He was a hundred and five but didn't look one single day over eighty or ninety. Ate a lot of yogurt. Praise the Lord! And there was a day—I remember it well—when that fellow was happy and busy. He was never pretentious, selfish, or grim; one hell of a family relation. We buried him two days ago."

"My condolences. Please, go on," Shemokoman said.

Siegfried continued, "Well, he was simply at home, said he didn't feel well, and then he lay down on the couch for a nap. And that was all she wrote. The man passed away in his sleep—thank god; the way that I wouldn't mind going. So now he is gone; no major surprise. There is no getting around it. A person may die in so many strange ways to reveal about how they were living."

"Right you are," Shemokoman noted. "So tell me, what else are you thinking?"

"You see, old chap," Siegfried went on, "this is where it gets tricky. I was the sole surviving heir because there is nobody else in the family alive anymore. So he bequeathed a respectable fortune to me, and still I just cannot believe it. Gold and silver, and diamonds and rubies; now I'm terrifically rich. And thus, so many dear friends whom I do not recall are asking for trivial favors. How pathetic. I need to be wise and take care of my wealth, and try to protect and preserve it."

"And here is to you, mythological friend, heroic bold slayer of dragons!" exclaimed Karl—as he proposed a toast to honor the newly affluent Siegfried. Everyone clinked their glasses together and polished off a strong little hooker of bourbon. Kentucky is more than a coal miner's dream and a place that is famous for horses.

Shortly thereafter, Shemokoman said, "You know, Siegfried, I was just thinking. Now that you are a man of means, you cannot take kindly to folly. A benevolent plan for generous deeds has got to be part of your future. After all, what is the point in having so much if not to responsibly use it? In and of itself, a great deal of wealth can be a formidable burden."

Siegfried smiled and said, "It has to be nice to be constantly right, and your comment was not an exception. I need to adjust to a new status quo and think about what I am doing. Some people tell me that now I have plenty of power. So I have to be conscientious wherever I use it. And power is freedom to do as you please with little to check the behavior. Therefore, I need to ensure that nothing I do will ever be rendered as evil . . . That is a must. And wealth is also a stepping-stone, leading to new and unusual vistas. My distance away from the physical world has got to remain within reason. The Achaeans would never forgive me should I do something impulsive and witless. And I will give plenty of loot to the needy, that is, the poverty-stricken and people who dismally suffer. Boy oh boy, it is enough to consider."

Idolatry

"Well put, Siegfried," Shemokoman said. "Indeed, you are wise for your years. And let me say a few words about something else that is closely related. Namely, the implications of sudden prosperity and how it can alter persona. Restrain it, enhance or redeem it, and sometimes greatly profane it. The main thing I would suggest is that you continue to be your *self* and remain the good fellow you are. Remember the days when freedom for you was a game of tag in the barnyard. Oh, by the way, you're 'it.'

"Of course, it's all a matter of what to expect, what we reject, and what to forget that is trifling. Yes, my friends, the epicurean trend is always in style. And modern culture is laden with vice for people who think the End of the World is coming. You see, one of the villains is ripping us off; I refer to an old adversary. A devil who never goes down for the count and never gives up in a struggle. A genuine fiend who knows how to pillage the soul of a virtuous man. My friends, I am talking about Idolatry.

"In my sporadically prudent opinion, I think we advanced to a point of uncivilization where the hominoids, to whom we are closely related, have no intention of spending life as—and if I may use the reflexive—themselves. Instead, they desire to be a man or a god to whom they accord their full undivided devotion. They want to be their idol.

"Identification, whatever it is and wherever we are, must always remain on the person. If a stranger appears and says, 'Who are you?,' you say to him: 'It is me, and don't you forget it.' You and I must earn respect by staying far away from deplorable idols. They love to intrigue and defile their prey; a crying shame, they couldn't care less about honor.

"So who is to blame and what is the cause and how could something so terrible ever have happened? At this point, I need to add a word or two about those dizzy teachers. For it was they who avoided hearing us out and going the extra mile to help and support us. And it was they who allowed the bullies to push us around without being punished. And it was they who played favorites with popular pets in order to be in good standing. Moreover, they told us that we could be Almighty God by taking their final exams. Lies, lies, despicable lies! No one can be a Jehovah. A Bible, as well, gave warning about the appearance of 'strange gods before us,' lest ye forget it. Of course in the end, it is a fait accompli; and proselytes beg for redemption as they belatedly castigate evil.

"My friends, it is time to get personal here. I need to make an admission. Even our brothers and sisters, sons and daughters, mothers and fathers are smitten by idols. Yes, they are asunder and scooting away further and further into a nominal kingdom. Like much of the crowd, they chased a dream and a cunning play-actor seduced them. Idolatry—at your service. Blasphemy, I tell you!... An effort to sabotage Nature itself, plus all she affords to the masses. Nothing can ever be better than men as they are without any extras."

Heidi remarked, "Shemokoman, I understand you. This demon—Idolatry ... yet one more threat on the wing to our very survival. So how do we deal with the scoundrel?"

"Well, at present, my friend," he said, "we are in peril because of the horrible villain. It is the lowest of low-life stalkers and a clever conniving wallflower. Like so many other degenerate creeps, Idolatry seeks to recruit and completely control us. And it will always desire to deeply infect the kindred we strive to empower. Id est, our youth. To say the least, a rather detestable monster.

"While biding its time and corrupting the souls it obtains by way of entrapment, Idolatry doesn't relent after getting new victims. Without hesitation, it corners a mark and soon they are into its clutches. And yes, it will even take vegans; and no, it will never rebuke you. So what does Idolatry promise? Well, we will shine like a sun for utopian eyes, and walk on the water without ever sinking to bottom, and glisten atop snowy mountains on the redoubtable summits of glory. Nothing but stars in the eyes with total elation. Of course, we will not even care about going to dinner. Ultimately, it will steal away pride and self-respect, and leave us to rot in a gutter. It jeers at the thought of compunction; and—believe me, I am not joking.

"But let me respond to your question. Specifically, what can we do to defeat it? My friends, we must act like responsible men and plunge straightaway into combat. We need to ensure that it is thoroughly vanquished. My point of view is the only solution; and, we cannot wait for the sleazy behemoth to trash us. The battlefield lies anyplace there is life, where Idolatry prowls for its quarry. And people at risk must learn to exist without any thought of the shyster. Once and for all, we need to get rid of a scourge that threatens the future. Also, we have to reform the people it hurt and tell them the truth about worship. Just let us hope that they really believe us."

Siegfried chimed in, "Indeed, you are very well-spoken, Shemokoman. And you implore in a way that demands nothing less than agreement. It is a cogent position. By the way . . . was there a fellow you met on a train to whom we are slightly beholden?"

Shemokoman smiled and answered, "Yes, there most certainly was. And how do you know about him, my friend? You must have been doing some research. Be that as it may . . . now, I need to propose a toast."

He held up his glass and went on, "To a very brave man who came to this country two hundred years ago on a four-masted sailing vessel called the *Barque Comet*. He dared to cross over the turbulent main that was defiant and savagely raging. He must have been fearless, as bold as they come, far better than people today. And he was no scandalous idol, for sure; he was no abject pariah; rather, he is the one to admire. As a matter of fact, he put his pajamas under the pillow each morning. To Gottlob Friedrich!"

The party of five stayed together during that evening. Convivial talk to comfort the soul flowed in back channels between them. And a prim ordinary was out of this world, plain luscious. A band of merry musicians played Swabian folk songs, while ambrosial candles inside the café were casting their light and warmth on satisfied patrons. It will always take fire wherever we are to ignite inner power that drives us. It is how we manage to shine as well as regale the shadows that tease us.

Eventually, the entire group left the Augustiner Keller and went to a few other taphouses. And when the day was finally over, Shemokoman was content. There was no reason to lodge a complaint as he plied a sensational format. He slowly walked home and pondered the reason why so many men and women are prone to be racy. Just go to your work, take care of the kids, and anything goes because you have toiled and earned it. It is a lousy position, and tragedy comes to the insolent heathens.

Then the comrade thought of the Infinite Spirit: "I could never be God, no way. I couldn't serve as the Gracious Almighty. And constantly roam throughout heaven where people are dead but insist they're alive. In paradise, no less. Where sinners would always be praying to me and asking to have my forgiveness. I would damn every one of those smug infidels! . . . And hell would be soon overcrowded. To be in a place where my only son would be crucified, die, and be buried. It's not a magnificent prospect; I would finagle to rescue and save him. And what if a culprit who didn't belong managed to slip through the pearly gates? What if I made a mistake as God, who has to be totally perfect? Verily, my personal wish is to be what I am and let somebody else take charge of existence. It is more than enough to be only a man without a phenomenal purpose."

17

Above the Retractable Slope

Ready to Snap

For people of age and it needn't be much, it's hard to collect the laurels they thought were forthcoming. You get to a point that is later in life and suddenly everything changes. Instead of belief, your only concern pertains to a blanket reversal of ethical questions. And although you may wish for the right to explain, that day is by far long gone. Now you are the hapless defendant nobody is judging. So much for a chance to get even; you may forget about moral polemics. You held out for respect but now understand it is you who must quietly give it. And the crowded menagerie that we call our home is too apathetic for pity. Why so? After all, what about those golden years? Perhaps it was all misconception.

With little or no advanced warning, you are committed to slow degradation. And a Yahweh handles the method of public accounting. More debits and credits and also the mental deceivers. All the while, you strive to extol the past in a way that delimits authentic perception. The "good old days" most likely were part of a spell that was cast upon greenhorns. In spite of despair, you must never invoke the wrath of delusional musing. A far better choice is to encourage devotion to forces of Nature. And speak to a Lord whom we mustn't deny and proclaim without consciously lying . . . "I just couldn't help it." Your patience, of course, will have to submit, and you will descend quite a ways before ever rising.

Go back to the day when a dose of pious persuasion was very important. When the disciples you knew in Waupakisco Park were still in the mood for religion. Amen. Although what they lauded was wrong, and little was right, and depravity just didn't matter. You see, the tricks of the trade were fine insofar as they knew how to shrewdly apply them. And the stead of Omnipotent Power was really a secretive intimate matter as well as a handy excuse to simply avoid the tradition on Sunday. Yes, nothing but personal preference; it was the finest example of treason.

They put up a church right square in the middle of where we were playing the ball game. "Cool it, bub! . . . Cool it!" The neighbors were told that somebody hoped a chapel would bring them together. Alas, whenever you passed by that spiritual place, the carpers were constantly asking, "So, where are the holy believers?" No one appeared to be praying to God, who was counting on better attendance. It was a big disappointment. But maybe, in fact, the building was used for some other kind of a purpose, like sleeping it off in the morning or for the meetings to formulate purges. The joyous acclaim that was coming their way, regardless of how they obtained it, well—we shouldn't expect any pat on the back when nothing was done to deserve it.

Survival is prime; composure—a must. Integrity has to comply as is and wander all over in limbo. Meanwhile, you have to be strong for the good of the next generation. So tell every brother you see on the way that now you are ready to join a crusade in search of the fabulous grail, whatever it is. Such an illustrious calling, although the cynics will say it's appalling. And when you conclude there is no other choice, then enter the swirling tempest. Believe it or not, you will emerge as a titan. Such is the lore and delirium of many corpulent cereal heroes.

Shemokoman sat in a hard wooden chair with his legs propped up on a hassock. He thought, "Are there some telling conclusions I see that emerge from prevailing chaos? All devastation that fell to my lot should not have occurred, but it happened. When all that we know about life is a blast, it is hard to imagine cohesion. So much for another perspective; oh, I do wish sometimes that my sense perception could be what is called paranormal. But then I would never be human; and, there could be nothing substantial that I would covet and ardently fight for. In any event, I was given two eyes and other supplies to investigate Nature around me. And I am really not sure up to now if anything's better."

"I manage to think like the devil," he mused, "in order to clear up confusion. And sooner or later, I cannot give in to give up what a drifter has garnered. There will be nothing to help any man who was lax when he should have been working. Yes, my friend—our world is old cosmological light that radiates out of a spectrum. And light is the source of creation, and it is truly what has to define us. But then in the end, the darkness appears to offer a deal for something of paramount value. It may be the first in a wholesale trade; or who knows? ... A final transaction. But don't even think of attempting to flip any old paradoxical credos. All heed is a sham and you cannot go back to Milton."

Insanity

It was your typical overcast autumn day in Federal City. Black ravens were swarming up high in the sky with a fine demonstration of teamwork. Politicians and minions were swinging the vote as the government kept getting larger. Soon it would burst and all the debris would cover the rest of the planet. Shemokoman lounged at a favorite Venetian cantina with friends outside on the patio under a table umbrella.

They spoke about current events and why the news always had to be breaking. A simple result of scaremongers who were then running the media business. It was a methodical devious way to invite and retain undivided attention. And now, one of the men at the table noticed a scruffy old fellow who acted quite strangely. He was out in the street and talked to himself while doing a series of cartwheels. Then he hopped up on the seat of a high unicycle and pedaled both backward and forward. For sure, he was one of the ill-fated few who coped with a mild derangement. And what was the reason for that? Well, perhaps he was born with a preconscious-mania problem.

Then somebody casually noted, "That rascal belongs in a nuthouse, certainly not among regular people."

After a moment or so, Shemokoman said, "You know, gentlemen. Perhaps I need to say a few words regarding those people who seem to be off of their rockers. And I should note right away that all I profess must always be carefully rendered. It gets personal, you know. So let us weigh in on this awful affliction and attempt to add something of value. To begin with ... What are the signs and symptoms? And what does it mean to be crazy?"

He went on, "Well, insanity starts where good reason departs and everything normal gets flaky. The mind is at odds with a healthy depiction of Nature, and behavior that is right or wrong avoids any semblance of order. And even though sense perception delivers the truth to a working receptor, a man is not able to think like he should, as judgment goes out of commission. There is no longer secure recognition; everything now is a slight misconception. The understanding is surely impaired by forces that alter impression.

"Up is down, and in is out, and nobody cares about nothing. A lunatic carries a sign that reads 'The sky is lopsided and falling.' At least, that is the way that it frequently seems to those who are smitten by madness. The mentally ill are sick in the head: deranged, delirious comrades, pushing the buttons and pulling mechanical levers. Strange thoughts overlap, the spirit is gone, and wisdom is fully derailed. Coherence in life no longer depends on a colorful dream they were having. The world is dark in spite of the fact that a sun will be shining forever. They are castaways who stop and stare at you and me because the sight and sound of us intrigues them. People go loco for reasons, you know; it just doesn't randomly happen. The case depends on how the rift occurred on account of a breakdown.

"So on it goes, and how do you feel? . . . Disturbingly, sanity reeling. The intellect melts into pearly clouds above the alluvial landscape. So much for the old aspiration because, without consent, the *self* gives way to behavior with little awareness. Depression, aggression, delusion, and vile addictions . . . plus paranoia. There is no end to fancy medical labels. And then, quite unexpectedly, they take you to the treatment institution with padded cells to keep you out of danger. You! . . . By god, the one and only martyr of mental remission. And how they love to implement emotive persecution to watch you try to fight incarceration as you wither like the orange lotus flower. And they say that you are sick!

"Now, what comes to pass when someone snaps and sanity forsakes them? Well, perhaps a recollection from a bygone day that turned into a complex. Or maybe altercations with a parent who proved to be too much to cope with. Or perhaps a chronic problem that he or she could tolerate no longer. Or perchance the loneliness of every boring Sunday when we tarried on an empty street feeling down and out in nasty weather. People lose their minds when they are sick with no control, and tired of the archetypal canons. You see, it's not a toggle switch that goes off and on according to our fancy. A cause for such an illness is perplexing; even though an answer does exist. The trick is how to find it.

"Also, we must pay heed to multitudes of colleagues and the neighbors. The ones you knew for many moons without an obvious problem. They smiled and mingled with everyone else, but there was just something about them. So now they live in Bellevue, where they sit and stare at talking points and wait for orange capsules that will calm them. And was there a real deviation? Maybe behavior considered neurotic? With open minds, they freaked us out when nothing should've caused them agitation. Too many years of nirvana apparently caused one hell of a nightmare. They . . . the esteemed functionaries; and they . . . the cantankerous handlers. Degenerate souls who preferred to recall when malice and mischief were lovely. But lo and behold, their sanity waned and fell into medical confines."

Shemokoman couldn't resist, ordered cannoli, and then continued, "What good is life when all that you observe needs realignment? When all that you behold isn't what you want to see; rather, it is bizarre, askew and wry, and so unpleasant. When every sound you listen to isn't what you want to hear? When all that you recall isn't what you want to bring to mind, remember? Perhaps it is how they view the world when the time arrives to ditch their senses. When nothing is left to exalt or degrade, and everything borders on chaos. Turmoil in and delirium out; demented conceptions are brewing. So much for the logical rational man as they tell you he needs intervention.

"In years gone by on several occasions, I had the chance to meet with many patients in mental asylums. And although the birds were clearly mad, I understood at once that they were not so incoherent. Yes—very well-informed, and they could argue like debaters. Knew everything on all accounts; remaining deferential and respectful. Maybe what we have is just a version of the gulag in our country. And for want of better lingo to define them, the healers like to say that they are 'funny' . . . at the farm. But perhaps the joke is on us, my friends, as they are the only ones laughing.

"Furthermore, allow me to inform you that . . . the psychos who were dissed and counted out have ponied up to watch the pageant. Yes, they're locked away and waiting, and could not care less about their pseudo freedom. For them, it isn't bondage—rather, like a playpen, as they spend their time so blithe and still in chains berating sacrificial bubbles. For it is a place where the spirits can dance and nobody ruffles the inmate. Reality has many notable perks, but insanity rules without any. Yes, the madhouse is full of divisible men who need therapeutic assistance. They do not see what is stable and real but agree to let demons exploit them. What's more, it is no easy task to give up the ship and chuck everything that is normal because, I will tell you, my trustworthy friends, that to go batty requires courage. Just try it, you'll see what I mean."

He finished up, "If a man is disposed to habitual doubt with suspicion that begs iteration, he is probably stuck in the Circle of Time and damaged beyond recognition. Again and again, the action repeats; it just never ends to his liking. In view of a loop that will not terminate, we think that he really is crazy. Although, who is to say what is right or wrong; it just might be it is we who need calibration. And who is to say about different results? Good Lord! . . . he has finally got one. In order to sensibly figure it out, you need to go off of the deep end. Enough said. Basta per oggi."

Everyone there understood him. Although the gist of the spiel was mind-boggling. Some men at the table were anxious to voice and defend a divergent opinion. So there was talk and additional talk about the whole range of abnormal behavior. Finally, all the discussion came to an end and Shemokoman went home.

Along the way, he thought about health-care facilities where men of prestige with plenty of clout never bother to find real solutions. Instead, they are good at amusing themselves and raking in sizable fortunes. They never regard what Asclepius said about plans to improve a profession. For them, the practice of medical work is more than a wanton obsession; it is their prison.

Australia

Shemokoman heard of a faraway place that promised more cognitive insight. So he decided to take a trip overseas to the so-called Land Down Under. It was time to venture afar once again to explore on a fact-finding junket. To clear up confusion, look for the truth, and experience life in the fullest. He still wasn't tired of searching for knowledge and wisdom. Thus, he intended to go to Australia.

The trip required a detailed plan to avoid any possible hitches. He made the arrangements and soon the agenda was ready. The day to shove off then finally arrived, a summer Sunday morning. He left his home on the hill near Federal City and traveled for several days to the Port of Departure. Then he boarded another big gray ship with all of his personal luggage. The vessel was soon underway, crossing the Ocean.

A captain and crew provided safe passage to the remote destination. All seafaring accommodations could not have been better, namely: spacious berthing, a superior mess with outstanding cuisine, and facilities for recreation. Elderly folks and youngsters alike played shuffleboard on the main deck. And after several days en route, they crossed the Great Barrier Reef and approached a warm, hazy continent.

The ship pulled into the harbor at night and dropped a big iron anchor. Shemokoman grabbed his belongings, hailed transportation, and traveled to lodging in a town called Rockhampton. So now, he stood on the opposite side of the earth where all was reversed, to include the time and seasons. In spite of the fact it was winter down there, the weather was pleasant and balmy. After settling in, he went to a local diner that was called the Purple Roo and had dinner with some of the blokes.

Because he managed to rest and sleep during most of the maritime voyage, after having his fill of Australian food—like emu and boomerang berries—Shemokoman wasn't too tired. He left the place and started to walk by a river called the Fitzroy that flowed through the center of town. The cobblestone streets were quiet and dark as he ambled along beside the moonlit water. Not long thereafter, he ran into a mate who gave him advice.

The fellow said, "You have to be very alert and careful here in my native Rockhampton. There are plenty of cranky saltwater crocs lurking about and waiting to eat you alive. People I knew who used to live here took too many nocturnal walks and ended up missing. And please, believe what I say, old chap, 'cause it is the absolute truth."

After heeding the serious warning, Shemokoman resumed his walk in the night.

Eventually, he returned to the room at his lodging. After hitting the sack and falling asleep, he dreamed that he was back in Waupakisco Park, playing hide-and-seek in the lot with all of his friends. "Five-ten-fifteen-twenty . . . Ready or not, here I come!" And who is to say we can never go back to a place and time in the past? You have to figure it out . . . exactly "how" . . . and desire to do it. If it is conceivable, it is achievable.

Sangeet

The night went away and morning arrived. Shemokoman woke up and got out of bed. He felt rested and ready for action and the adrenaline flowed in his body. But he took his time as there was no rush, freshened up, and dressed himself in the latest backcountry attire. Yevgeny could not have looked better strolling on Nevsky. Then, after breakfast, he went into town.

There was hardly a soul on the streets anywhere, only the shopkeepers minding their storefronts. Most of them now were sweeping away the debris from pedestrian sidewalks. His favorite bright yellow sun in the sky was shining through bottle and palm trees, while strong monsoonal trade winds were blowing robustly for sailing ships that were out on the Ocean.

He thought, "What a thoroughly wonderful day for a mate who is not in emotional doldrums. I am on top of the world—or maybe the bottom—and nothing is rotten in Denmark."

As he wandered along and took in the local surroundings, Shemokoman heard the unmistakable sound of a sitar off in the distance. It was too good to be true, and it was the music intended for gods. The lengthy notes and fine raga chords were a type of pacification that offered a way to go higher. So he computed direction as best as he could and set off on a course that would lead him straight to the source.

Not long thereafter, he caught sight of a man who sat on the ground and was playing a teakwood sitar. Shemokoman approached the musician and, for a while, just stood there and listened. The talented fellow was good on the ax and he mesmerized people who heard him.

When the music was over, the maestro stood up and introduced himself: "Good morning, everyone. My name is Sangeet, and I hope you enjoyed the selection. It was an original piece; I wrote it myself while camping on Assateague Island. Love those wild ponies, but don't ever feed them."

Shemokoman spoke up. "Yeah, mon! Bravo! A perfect example of musical art with panache to win over skeptics. And I do not know of a better device on this earth than the sitar to inspire my feelings. It delivers a message to those who honestly need it."

Then Sangeet inquired, "And who, may I ask, are you, my friend? Are you an Angel of Mercy?"

"No," Shemokoman said. "Can't say as I am."

Sangeet asked, "Well then, are you a Prophet of Doom?"

"No, not me, no way," Shemokoman answered.

Sangeet went on, "Or perhaps, you are the Man of the House, a dodger, a lowly outcast?"

"No, I am not," Shemokoman said. "Do you give up?"

And thus the musician conceded, "Yes, I do. So tell me . . . Who in the heck are you?"

He replied, "I am Shemokoman. And I hail from the one and only Land of Michigan, where no one is king and the Potawatomi chiefs don't gamble with sharpers. And now regarding you, sir. From whence comest thou?"

"Well," Sangeet replied, "I was born in the west, grew up in the east, and now I reside in the south. And I will die in the north if I have any say-so about it. I learned to play the sitar in the Hindu Kush wearing a turban, baggy pants, and very long shirt. And it was in those self-same mountains that I studied the works of Krishna and Upanishadi as well. I have to confess that it didn't take long with exposure to Eastern culture that my fate was indelibly sealed. Like the Great Beyond where Eternity reigns, I hope the scores I write will last forever. So what brings you to this land, Shemokoman? Perhaps the fascination of going Down Under? Or could it possibly be that you have another intention?"

He answered, "Well, to tell you the truth, I'm here to explore and see what I can, and make a few friends in the process. I have many free days to roam far and wide in your country, where I will plunder the masses for knowledge. The world is teeming with raw observational data that is just waiting for someone to gather. It is my very first visit here; and I must admit, the impression is one of enchantment."

The conversation ended shortly afterward. Then Sangeet provided more entertainment. Shemokoman listened, and gradually now a very large crowd gathered around the performer. For almost one more solid hour, celestial music filled the air and the hearts of starry-eyed people. And when it was over, the audience cried, "Encore! . . . Encore! . . . Encore!" Of course, Sangeet could not refuse, and there was a grand finale.

At the conclusion of the concert, Shemokoman asked his new acquaintance, "So, how long are you going to stay here in Rockhampton?"

Sangeet replied, "Well, at least for one more week. Then I have to go south to put on a show that I promised for liberal students at the Temple of Infinite Power. What a marvelous place and recently built; I hope that my musical fest will bring down the house. A Tasmanian devil I met on the road agreed to warm up the crowd with plenty of screeching."

"Sounds good," Shemokoman said. "Thus, I will come here each day of the week until you depart. I need to drop out, fire up, and tune in, as my friend Jerry T. from the block used to advise me. But now I have got to be going."

So, they bowed to each other and parted. And for the rest of the afternoon, the ethical comrade traipsed around town and sampled a full range of bitters. They were thirst-quenching and tasty, and the locale was becoming unsteady. He also arranged for a trip on the following day that would take him to see some rough real estate deep in the province of Queensland.

Crocodile Stewed

The outing commenced at six o'clock sharp in the a.m. Shemokoman left town, going north, and followed the Wallaby Trail. There was nothing to see for miles and miles other than brown swampy earth as well as the open areas of red rock. Off in the distance, a few small mountains appeared here and there to break up a level horizon. The bleak panorama was pretty much what he expected.

After a while, he stumbled upon a rough-looking sort of homestead. He passed through an old wooden gate and spotted an elderly fellow who was digging the ground, chopping up wood, and mending a broken fence.

The two men approached each other and exchanged introductory pleasantries. The old-timer said he was Matthew, an appellation we cannot object to. And he was surprised to see Shemokoman so far out of town in the boondocks. Thus, Matthew asked the stranger what he was up to.

And he explained, "Actually, I'm here in your land for just a few days to see and learn what I can for edification. I want to observe your way of life and watch and talk with the people. In this day and age, we have to be sharp if we really desire to cut it. I've constantly heard so many good things about your exceptional country. Mainly, that there is plenty of opportunity for the ambitious entrepreneurs. And also, people I know who are singing the blues threaten to pack up and move here."

"Well," Matthew replied, "I'm glad you decided to come to my place to visit the humble surroundings. It is not very often that people drop by on account of the rural seclusion. So it's nice to have company once in a while to break up the tedious humdrum. Now, just look over there at the edge of the pond with a couple of shoals in the middle."

Shemokoman gazed where the man was pointing and said, "Sorry, my friend, but I don't see anything special."

Then the host more precisely suggested where the visitor needed to look. And soon the enormous creature came into focus. Shemokoman said, "Okay, now I see. My god, what a croc. So big and close, scary and eerily silent. To top things off, it appears to me he is grinning. And the beautiful part is how he can blend into Nature. There is almost no way for your average person to spot him."

Matthew said, "And that is the point of it all, short and sweet. In order to see what is plainly the truth, you need to be carefully looking. You cannot be wearing the blinders; and, you have to be keen and perceptive. In no time flat, that primordial beast can eat a whole human like nothing. One single mistake, and you will not live to regret it. This is no place for a guy and his gal to go on the afternoon picnic."

It was plain to see that Matthew welcomed having a mate to converse with. He gave his guest the nickel tour around the farm and provided a thorough description. He was currently building hundreds of metal enclosures for wild dingoes, koalas, and serpents. And shortly thereafter, when both of the men had grown a bit hungry, they had an unusual snack that consisted of native cuisine. Crocodile stew. It was a savory treat bursting with flavor, chewy and tangy. Then they both went back outside and roamed around the place.

A couple more hours of trudging through soft, boggy marshland passed by for Shemokoman. Then he told the fellow that he needed to go back to town. He expressed appreciation for the reception and departed. Matthew, along with his farm and the wildlife creatures, were left to enjoy many glorious days and years that surely would follow.

Rockhampton

During the rest of his trip overseas, Shemokoman settled into a daily routine. He got up at sunrise each morning, had breakfast at the Purple Roo, and then went into town. First off, he sat on a wrought-iron bench in a park and read through the local gazette. After that, he'd wander through dozens of specialty shops where every merchant and client were making a deal. They could not have cared less about value as such; they were obsessed with the bargaining process. And last but not least, he met with Sangeet during the afternoon hours and listened to more of the heavenly sitar music. That in itself was totally worth it. It was an excellent way to relax and forget about issues that plagued him.

One day toward the end of his visit, he decided to venture away from the coast as far as possible into the mainland. It was time for him to explore and go into the Outback. Shemokoman wanted to observe firsthand the reason for all the commotion. It was supposed to be such a great escapade, and he expected a thrill every minute. Although a funny thing happened. The farther along that he traveled into the barren unsettled terrain, the more he began to regret it.

Eventually, he stopped on a desolate stretch of road and imploringly asked of himself, "Where in the hell am I going? Nothing out here is exciting. No sign of people or anything else, only a genuine wasteland. How enticing, yet how depressing. It is time to cut my losses and go back to where I just came from."

So he turned around and started to make his way back to civilization. But somehow Shemokoman got slightly lost, passed by the town of Rockhampton, and wound up at the shore of the Coral Sea in the coastal village Yeppoon. While standing at the water's edge, he saw the Keppel Islands off in the distance. Another breathtaking sight. Unfortunately, he felt that old sharp melancholy of loneliness again, as it was one more place that before too long he would be leaving. And most likely—never come back.

He thought, "I think the pace in this here town is something I could handle. The speed of light is way too fast for them, and they don't like it. I would spend each day and every night with folks who aren't afraid to ask the younger generation: What is justice? Alas, I must pitch in and help them out during the yuletide season at the Optimist Club in Michigan. Maybe in another life if, in fact, I have one."

Poverty

On the last day of his trip to Australia, Shemokoman went into town as usual. The streets were uncommonly quiet, no one seemed to be working, and the marketplace was empty. Of course, there was a reason; it was a public holiday. Namely, a king and queen who hated God and also detested each other were celebrating sixty years of marriage.

Sangeet and Shemokoman talked up a storm for the better part of the morning and long afternoon. The former started off, "To tell you the truth, there is nothing I despise more than poverty. Day in day out, I see it all around me. Even right here in a prosperous town, too many people are stricken. Their clothes are tattered and torn, they have no decent food at mealtime, the living conditions are awful, and they cannot afford even a small glass of wine. And chances to better their station in life have never been so unrealistic. My friend . . . like you, I've traveled the world over and visited many places. My tired eyes and other senses at no time are not about to trick me. They tell me the truth about men on earth, and it is so very depressing. The wealthy goons pretend they care as they joke about more destitution. Indeed, it is a sad day for humanity when so many must do with so little."

"You're right, of course," Shemokoman said. "The extent of the problem—disgraceful. It never abates, and there is no sign of improvement. In the hills and towns, the central plains, and deep inside of a forest, the shameful condition is growing. One need look no further than on the streets of Federal City, where, from dawn until dusk, they pilfer bread despite the hurricane season. You'd think a country as rich as ours could help the paupers out. But no. The needy are mocked and chided by cynical people who angrily clamor—'I am fed up with the sight of these crummy panhandlers.' Ratfinks . . . every last one of them.

"Unfortunately, we have to leave the poor alone, don't interfere, and let them fend for themselves. That way, they do not sense the degradation, and they keep their self-respect. I tried in the past to lend them a hand; a tough proposition, indeed. It doesn't work; they brush you off and reject it. And regarding those generous people whom you so graciously mention and care for, they promise a big contribution—three cheers!—with smiles of love and betrayal. Their nature is to jeer and laugh at bums who live in sewers. Yes, beware of devious charitable men who were purveyors of greed in the past. So now, they've had their fill of overindulgence, and it's time for noble deeds to cleanse a conscience. Right."

"No doubt, we know," Sangeet declared, "that there never will be a solution. Too many people with too much to lose and the Uppity Class isn't stupid. They must ensure by cracking whips that nothing ever changes in the future. But we can help by walking down the streets and dark alleyways in order to distribute alms to vagrants. By giving out some food and even steins of booze for whatever ails them, we do as much as anyone who tries to make a difference. And it's a funny thing, Shemokoman: they haven't the need for any god, but marvel at the mercy from wherever. Oh, what a terrible plight, with us for ages. Perhaps it could all disappear straightaway with the help of a magic wand. Alas, the people who run the degenerate show preclude any type of advantage. They simply do not care about despicable dilemmas."

Shemokoman chimed in, "Sangeet, the words you choose to break it down could not be better. I'm glad that we both speak the English language. And here is another thought that I believe is directly related. If only the sages of days gone by would have spent as much time on man as they did on religion, then the world would be a whole lot different today. They paid so much attention to God that people were nearly forgotten. I guess that they just couldn't help it; yes, the sinners who longed for redemption. And what is the point of devotion for various cultures? Well, it is good for the rich and bad for the poor, the canons of sanctification. Subservient rags have got to believe that a much better world is coming; God praise! What could be finer for desperate souls than legitimate misinformation? It is the way to alert any god in the main that man is a floundering creature. Divinity thrives and the poor continue to take one hell of a pounding.

"The royal curators would urge you to pray for a guy who is down on his luck as if the Holy Lord responds to human pleadings. The God I know does not distribute grace to poor trespassers; and, the God I know does not have much to do with our salvation. Without a doubt, he's a neutral party; and, he even knows in detail what we're thinking. Rather impressive. And people in need should never believe in the chance of a miracle happening, as they will do better by placing a bet on the shoo-in. But oh, what a harrowing way to consider admission of what is mistaken. The indigents always have little to gain, but they are not sycophants, fawning."

Sangeet piped up, "Still, I have got to believe there is goodness out there someplace in the swirling cosmos. Every so often, I close my eyes and incontrovertibly see it."

"And right you are about that, Sangeet," Shemokoman said to the artist. "Many fine people have got what it takes to achieve the cachet of perfection. Thus, I will come full circle again to finish my part of a heavy discussion. We must aspire to lead a Good Life; it is no mystical secret. There are so many ways to expire on earth, but only one way to be living. And people who figure it out do not require a chattering healer. There is no need for a parable laden with fraud to completely mislead us. We have to be guided by only one voice, which is called the infallible conscience."

They finished their talk and called it a day. Shemokoman had supper in town, where he sampled the prawns on a barbie with sweet potatoes. Very delicious. After that, he took another nice, slow walk along the Fitzroy River where he thought about human privation. "They cry in the night in bed when asleep because of chagrin and repute to weep in the daytime. But at least impoverished people who mourn have someone to fancy at sunrise. Hmm . . . allow me to give him a name. Perhaps, they praise Osiris or Ea, or maybe . . . better yet—a kindly Yahweh."

Allegory of the Thin Man

It was almost time to go back to America. Thus, Shemokoman spent the evening and night packing up things in his room. At breakfast the following morning, he talked with a corpulent merchant from Venice who was known far and wide as the Thin Man. The acquaintance professed to be modest and clean, a typical average fellow.

The Thin Man was munching on hot johnnycakes, eggs, and prosciutto, and wheat bread with coffee and cream. He let on with bombast about all of his personal business. Mainly, he spoke about ravaging women and men, and duping the credulous patsies. And just when the both of them finished their meals, that reprobate made a proposal.

He said, "You know, my ethical comrade. I sense that your turbulent life is comprised of contention and copious hardship. And those unpredictable years are fast disappearing. How would you like to go sit on the beach inside a palatial cabana, and bask in the sun with all that you want and carouse like there is no tomorrow?"

"Sounds like a plan," Shemokoman said. "What do you want in return?"

The fellow replied, "Just give me your soul and then you may have whatever the body desires."

Shemokoman looked at the Prince of Darkness and thought about carnal seduction. "No thank you, my man," he said, "as I have heard about you and the bad propositions you offer. Save your iniquitous pitch for somebody else . . . like, perhaps a deviant man on the street who is willing to trade everything in the book for worldly pleasure. Moreover, the day of demise for you is certainly looming above the horizon. Yes, the piper will surely come calling; and nothing at all you say or do will affect one hell of a downfall. And that is the truth, as well as the fact that I know there will be a tomorrow."

The demon stood up, turned sideways, and in a puff of white smoke instantly vanished into thin air. Some villains just don't want to hear it. Shemokoman thought, "The saga of man is a tale of pain on account of recurrent temptation. One would think that humanity finally would know how to deal with a treacherous devil. How much will it take until smoldering bones can provoke a response that is needed? The time has arrived as never before to confront what is wrong and replace it. But I'm not going to hold my breath."

Full Steam Ahead

The hour arrived for Shemokoman to board a big gray ship at the Port of Departure. He would not have objected to staying a brief while longer. The indigenous people, the climate, and even some mild corruption were very appealing. It was nice for a change to go to a tavern with a sign at the entrance that read "Smokers Welcome." After the last call announcement, all passengers went to their berthing stations aboard the great seafaring vessel. And then in short order, the ship was sailing on its way to America.

The fresh salty air of a cool ocean breeze can put you to sleep in a heartbeat. Shemokoman leaned back in a chaise recliner deck chair, closed his eyes, and dozed off into heavenly slumber. It was nice to relax so effortlessly without any trouble to bother him. And now, his subconscious mind was starting to wander, moving from one train of thought on to another.

A crackling campfire was blazing away in the woods not far from Bass Lake. Next. Radiant smiles on innocent faces of Hopi braves lit up the night in the north Catalinas. Next. He took a long trip with Duane to fish on the ice at Pine Lake one wintry morning. A man can be free for a moment or two if he yields to the power of dreamland.

Suddenly, Shemokoman woke up because he was smacked on the knee by a bouncing beach ball of a child standing beside him. After looking around, he saw without doubt that no one was watching the youngster. Perhaps he was lost or abandoned. The situation was quickly resolved with the help of a shipboard attendant. A mother insisted that she had an eye on the child without interruption. To Shemokoman, it appeared to be just the opposite; namely, the woman was clearly neglectful. Then again, some men are accused of being so overprotective. Impossible!

He reflected, "Certain women should not be allowed to pursue reproduction. It is no God-given birthright, and they are often not fit for the duty. They haven't a clue regarding support and care of a child in Nature. It is more than a frivolous game that you play when the psyche desires amusement. And I have observed that when the going gets rough, they even resort to desertion. They tell us to give them a little more 'space' while drinking martinis with riffraff."

The return trip took longer than expected because a colossal typhoon impeded the progress. The ship's captain and crew employed the gamut of awesome maneuvers to navigate safely through and away from the danger. And when the peril had passed, the sailors demanded a ration of fortified bumbo. It's hard to get rid of tradition when scullions, who ought to be ten fathoms deep in the blue, have you over a barrel.

Five weeks after leaving the Land Down Under, the journey across the Ocean was finally over. Shemokoman was back in his native country. He traveled by train for a couple of days and made it to Federal City. He went up the hill and through the front door; that refugee was sorely in need of some downtime. It was good to be home, no doubt about that, but now he knew something was cooking. A single glance in every room confirmed a sneaking suspicion. Praskovya was gone, along with a lot of his personal valued possessions. There are no bad women, there are no good women, there are only women.

One cannot have doubt that traumatic events will precipitate hefty reactions. Almost nothing can ever affect the plan of a lady who's bound and determined. Thoughts about life now pervaded his mind to make him feel not so astounded. Shemokoman knew that a new status quo was in store so he had to accept it. You see, the woman he met in Moskva was fully beguiled by prominent preachers. Although it was she . . . indeed! . . . who made the important decision. Firm and decisively final. It was a perfect example of subterfuge and socialist courage in females. The sun went down more slowly than ever that mild and troublesome evening. It allowed just slightly more light to come into a room for a jaded disciple.

18

Bloodline

Are We There Yet?

Step by silent step, Shemokoman knew he was walking. He looked down at the ground that was under his feet and mused about soaring with eagles. Then he glanced up at the sky way over his head and thought about digging to China. In spite of a glitch to make sense of it all, there was a point in the process.

He thought, "She said it was love. Yes, let it be love! Love is the great panacea. But when the going got rough, the love in her heart turned out to be so inconvenient. It never fails."

Starting from scratch, you give it your best with or without evolution. It isn't enough to back out of the crowd and insist you're a freewheeling maverick. Truly a major mistake. Of course, exalted is fine, but we mustn't abolish the good of preceding tradition. To see and to know about primitive truth is all that one ever needs to really be happy. Furthermore, it would be wrong for someone to be transcendental; and it can be right to deprecate stylish thinking.

Every object we sense that remodels the mind must manifest stable appearance. Otherwise, nothing we know can ever be real and something can never be certain. A spoon will always be only a spoon until anyone proves it is different. And light we collect can only be light; it is the way to explain the impossible milieu. And man will detect the reflection he wants and dispense with extraneous content. Of course, it is tough to regard what essentially *is*; impressions by and large are meant to elude us. Moreover, there is no need to have discouraging knowledge; and, it is not bad to avoid the big disappointment. Albeit, can anything worthless be useless? There is a point in compiling nonsense and putting your cards on the table.

Clean Bill

Concerning those people who suffer, let us consider a sample. If one is deserving and justice is part of the picture, a day will arrive to convince us that serendipitous forces are working. Shortly after his return from Australia, Shemokoman fully recovered from his medically harmful condition. The problems he had in the body and mind just went away and no longer continued to hurt him. He needed a fix regardless of how and where it eventually happened. Destiny threw in a towel of damask; she had to give up on the fellow.

A horrible blow to health in man is caused by evil intrusion. And the only way to reverse it is by way of relentless persistence. One must never lose faith in a cure for disorders that often beset us because it is all that we really have to pin any hopes on. Shemokoman never asked "Why?"; . . . and he didn't pretend to be special. And, he didn't expect the mercy of God to heal up an ailing body.

Pragmatic Clarification

Experience teaches us plenty in life, but what do we know to begin with? Undoubtedly, nothing of any significant value. So please, forget about forms and strange allegories as well as everything anyone says about our previous knowledge; it is a colossal deception. To learn what we must and use what we have, we need to go out and survive in the animal kingdom. Then and only then, we will be ready for enemy action.

A quest for the truth in matters that count is certainly much to one's credit. For plenty of years, Shemokoman constantly searched for good information. He traveled wherever he needed to go to locate and finally get it. And time and again, there couldn't be doubt that he had made a quantum improvement. He never gave up and didn't give in; but giving was what he was best at.

He thought, "As for all of the heathens I notice around me . . . They pursue every deed in a manner to please the *self* with so little thinking. Human behavior is largely defective because the intent is never at issue. Have they not heard it is vile and wrong to abuse someone else in the process? So—devise a good plan, do not be afraid, and do what is right for a play in the court of injustice. And then we can see how much the tramp gets away with."

It was time to recall the ambrosial scent, to admire the goldenrod flower and other myriad natural wonders. Here, we allude to a wanton occasion that happened. In back of the school in the whispering wind where no one was fond of compassion, the delight of a random familiar event despoiled two souls that enjoyed it. Of course, go ahead and take what you see, in spite of the bad consequences. Although, be advised, you may very soon chide the discretion of such a decision. They couldn't renounce a duplicitous gleam that compelled them ahead to more outrage. No wonder the challenge of stemming the tide is more than a futile endeavor.

And thus, for a while, they cherish the day when a crime was no more than a pastime. However, just feast your eyes on additional truth and what is forthcoming for cretins. "Cool it, bub! . . . Cool it!" For they will have aeons, in fact a forever, to ponder the fences they scaled. And fate will ensure that they never replace the dear reminiscence with something to make them forget it. Whatever they were, believe that they are, or presume they will be in the future is nothing like what they amount to. It appears that a dull repertory has suddenly vanished, and a cauldron of searing perdition awaits to delight them.

Shemokoman tackled the constant barrage of anomalous personal issues. With a chain mail glove, a big metal shield, and Circassian saber for combat, he frequently stood at the edge of a plain and prepared for additional warfare. Whenever we notice that something's amiss and danger imperils survival, we have to get up and do what is right if you care about breathing tomorrow. By god, we have got to be fearless. Life is a gift for only the brave and impassionate, nobody else. Time and again, he threw down the gauntlet to call out the foe he confronted. And when the fighting was over at last, he knew where he stood because he was the only one standing.

It came to pass that he pondered felicity, and thought, "At the end of the day, when the sun went down and the moon slowly rambled above them, they went to the woods and commingled with ravishing Nature. As they ran from the brook and danced through a glade, and sang a sweet song, and whirled about in the orchard under the starlight, they were happy and pure, and nothing was wrong in creation. The earth was a mythical kingdom and they refused to condemn or neglect it. You see, there was plenty to do for a primitive man, so splendid when knowledge was missing. When people knew nothing, euphoria flowed, and everything was in abundance. Alas, we carelessly let it all wither away—replaced by silly ideas of fraudulent prophets.

"Although we may still entertain the chance to recover a primal unsullied potential. I suggest that you go far away to the brink and contemplate life without any major distraction. For it is there you will notice a previous day with a foregoing intimate feeling. Do not hesitate to accept it; the days of yore were not a mixed blessing; they were the essence of perfect contentment. Learn to recall and enjoy what we were a long time ago at the start of the very beginning."

Imperative Standards

While he sat in a chair drinking tea on the hill by his flat in Federal City, Shemokoman dreamed of a day when he would return to Michigan. He thought, "How can somebody not miss it? . . . Human behavior defies comprehension. They have a wish to be selfish and lonesome. Why are there so many zombies among us?"

In some ways, it seemed that little had changed in spite of so many years that slowly passed by. He rose up from the seat and paced to and fro in the tall green grass that was growing. He was still in a yard enclosed by a fence, reflecting on various matters. Then he stopped for a moment and thought, "Now and forever as never before, it burns with a secular mantra. Nihilism—in one country. People despise the very idea of shaping a decent tomorrow. Instead, today is their choice and they want to suppress whatever is moral and truthful. A future replete with contemptible men is all they expect in the long run. The masses are lawless and angry as hell, and proclaim to the smiling hostess: 'Give us the blueberry cheesecake, dear! . . . And fill up the tumblers with cognac. Good for digestion, you know.' They have not heard that the body and soul will decay in collinear fashion. And, the crest of a wave called 'blatant neglect' is bound to come slamming into them."

He needed to be near the people he knew and live in a home beside neighbors. He remembered the crick at the base of the hill that was loaded with tadpoles in springtime. Yes, the one that led over to Speeds; and, the one frozen over in winter. Shemokoman wanted to sit in the shade in the lot under the elm tree. He needed to go for a walk in the woods and be with the animal creatures. And it was always so nice when the Oracle wanted to probe metaphysical issues. Of course, he thought about Catherine, who was the lady whom he had respect for.

And now, a time and a place were recalled where a fellow put on a performance. "A scene from a tale with boys and girls on skates to engender nostalgia. I do not know why, but my time by the sea is a part of the finite adventure. I cannot deny or ever dispute it; indeed, the truth is a baffling quandary. For I was there at the bay on the ice long ago at the very cold Harlingen coastline. Spinning in circles, falling in snow, and chasing a ghost who promised me glee and nirvana. It was a tangible side of my faceted life where fortune is never at issue. And, the day is completely forgotten; albeit, the memories are sundry and vivid. Meanwhile, crude libertines have got to be brutally slaughtered!"

He pondered, "There is a time when they brazenly feel that life itself is at their disposal. And, they really can climb to the top of a hill and make such a very big difference. Alas, it is only mistaken ambition; too much pretension, so little awareness. With nothing but dreams and a noble intent, they embark on the difficult journey. But it doesn't take long, and Nature reacts at the attempt to reform the enduring. They try to subdue a formidable world that crushes their spirit instead. So, tell me if you shouldn't mind, my friend. Who is the runaway slave and who is the master? And, who has the absolute power? And what do they honestly hope to achieve as men with so little to offer? I will tell you this much, my respectable brothers and sisters, and hearken unto the voice of someone who's been there. We live and we die with a quiet 'hurrah,' and your legacy vanishes with you. But our presence on earth—a mere wisp of it all—can never be fully extinguished. Something remains. And that is the truth."

As Shemokoman looked at humanity's lair, an anomaly altered sensation. For a moment or two, divergence was gone between earth and the heaven above it. He didn't observe any separate places; it was like everything blended together. There was no apparent distinction; so, what could he in fact have been seeing? Well, he saw nothing at all in your typical way as the elements rippled around him. There was no explicit perception; rather, a sort of miraculous vision where all he beheld that is really was, no two ways about it, for certain. Shemokoman saw the truth, and it was a lot of hard work but worth it. And that is precisely how it can be to enlighten an ethical comrade.

The sun was now gradually sinking below the divide of a crimson horizon. The moon came out and soon the sky was a tapestry brimming with starlight. It arrived from afar over millions of years and formed a glowing facade of unparalleled beauty. How was it that so many people entirely missed it? Maybe they simply forgot to look up because they were too busy working. Or perhaps they were coveting valuable goods or beating the children to death and decided to skip it. Never does anything happen on earth if Nature itself by design doesn't approve it. Go figure.

"No, nothing can ever be different," he thought. "It is a privilege we tender for living. And only a man who is heavy or light can talk about breaking the system. That is, if he is partial to pay dirt, and, if he is holy and lucky. I need to get plenty of sleep tonight and be up just prior to daybreak so I can proclaim to the people: 'Look! Everyone . . . look! The sun is coming up! The happy-go-lucky is rising! Get out of your houses now so that you can see it.' "